Praise for *Lily of the Field:*

"One of the unsung (at least until now) heroes of the genre, as good as Le Carré."—*Chicago Tribune*

"Lawton has always pushed the boundaries of the series crime novel, edging ever closer to broad-canvas historical fiction, but this time he has leaped the fence altogether. Like Dennis Lehane in *The Given Day*, Lawton introduces multiple characters and stories in a sweeping tale that comes together at a particular historical moment, but unlike Lehane, he does all that without abandoning his series hero or the continuity established in the previous volumes. . . . A truly multitextured tale."
—*Booklist* (starred review)

"Few novelists have given me more pleasure in recent years than John Lawton. . . . Lawton writes with such style, intelligence, irreverence, political sophistication, and keen understanding of the strengths, weaknesses, and glorious eccentricities of his fellow Brits."
—Patrick Anderson, *The Washington Post*

"With each book John Lawton pushes the thriller's boundaries outwards. Now, in *A Lily of the Field*, a thriller that's also a first-class novel, he's extended even his range. Those of us who thought we knew all there was to know about the period between the start of the Second World War and the dropping of The Bomb find, thanks to Lawton's immaculate research, that we didn't."
—Ariana Franklin, author of *Mistress of the Art of Death*

"A fascinating story that incorporates accident, murder, mass murder, and espionage, which evokes the best of John Le Carré. . . . It's the work of a writer at the peak of his powers."
—Margaret Cannon, *The Globe and Mail*

"His books about Inspector Frederick Troy, a London homicide detective in the era around WWII, are consistently rewarding blends of historical espionage and police procedural."   —*The Seattle Times*

"A complex and compelling mystery that will not be forgotten quickly. Highly recommended."
—*Library Journal*

"Lawton deftly lays out Europe as it changed, with all of its intimate costs exposed."
—Clea Simon, *The Boston Phoenix*

"Readers will enjoy this profound tale that takes the audience from the beginning of the Nazi aggression into the beginning of the Cold War."
—*The Midwest Book Review*

"John Lawton finds himself in the same boat as the late Patrick O'Brian—a sublimely elegant historical novelist as addictive as crack but overlooked by too many readers for too long. Like O'Brian, he inhabits his periods' twentieth-century tipping points witnessed by the rich and richly ambivalent sleuth Troy—with an ownership that leaves most history-bothering authors looking like day-trippers." —*The Daily Telegraph*

"Lawton writes with authority. His characters convince, and so does their world. Admirable, ambitious, and haunting, this is the sort of thriller that defies categorization. I look forward with enthusiasm to the next one."
—*The Spectator*

"John Lawton's books contain such a wealth of period detail, character description, and background information that they are lifted out of any category. Every word is enriched by the author's sophistication and irreverent intelligence, by his meticulous research and his wit."
—*Literary Review*

"Lawton's Troy books are less detective stories or intelligence thrillers than novels that include both murders and spies—novels as much about how people and societies grow and change as about the complex messes that Troy finds himself tidying up for his adopted country."
—*The Independent*

"Lawton handles the chronology with exemplary ease and intelligence."
—*The Guardian*

"Top-notch police/espionage . . . Such a grand tapestry with so much vibrant color and form that the book belongs on the shelf squarely between John Le Carré and Alan Furst, embracing both the stunned pain of England and the dark desperation of the rest of Europe during and immediately after the war. . . . There are enough layers, and enough beautifully wrought satisfactions, that this book goes onto my "desert island" list: a book I'd be willing to read multiple times."
—Beth Kanell, *Kingdom Books*

A LILY OF THE FIELD

A LILY OF THE FIELD

John Lawton

Grove Press
New York

Printed in the United States of America
Published simultaneously in Canada

ISBN-13: 978-0-8021-4546-8

Grove Press
an imprint of Grove/Atlantic, Inc.
841 Broadway
New York, NY 10003

Distributed by Publishers Group West

www.groveatlantic.com

11 12 13 14   10 9 8 7 6 5 4 3 2

for
Allan Little

A LILY OF THE FIELD

Prologue

London: March, or even February, 1948
A Park

It had not been the hardest winter. That had been the previous winter
—the deluge that was 1947. London like an iceberg, the Home Coun-
ties one vast undulating eiderdown of white, snowbound villages in
Derbyshire dug out by German POWs many miles and years from home
—a bizarre reminder that we had "won the war." War. Winter. He had
thought he might not live through either. He had. The English, who
could talk the smallest of small talk about weather, had deemed 1948 to
be "not bad" or, if feeling loquacious, "nowt to write home about."
But now, as the earth cracked with the first green tips of spring, the bold
budding of crocus and daffodil that seemed to bring grey-toothed smiles
to the grey faces of the downtrodden victors of the World War among
whom he lived, he found no joy in it. It had come too late to save him.
This winter would not kill him. The last would. And all the others that
preceded it.

He took a silver hip flask from his inside pocket and downed a little
Armagnac.

"André, I cannot do this anymore."

Skolnik had been pretending to read the *Post,* billowing pages spread
out in front of him screening his face from the drifting gaze of passersby.
He stopped, turned his head to look directly at Viktor.

"What?"

"I have to stop now."

The newspaper was folded for maximum rustle. It conveyed the
emotions André pretended long ago to have disowned in favor of calm,
unrufflable detachment.

"Viktor. You cannot just stop. You cannot simply quit. What was it
you think you joined all those years ago? A gentleman's club? As though

you can turn in your membership when brandy and billiards begin to bore you?"

Viktor took another sip of Armagnac, then passed the flask to André.

"Nineteen eighteen," he said softly as Skolnik helped himself to a hefty swig. "Nineteen eighteen."

"What?'

"Nineteen eighteen—that's when I joined. Were you even born then?"

"Not that it matters, but I was at school."

The flask was handed back, the paper slapped down between them.

"You cannot stop just because it suits you to stop."

Viktor sighed a soft, whispery, "Really," of exasperation. "Why can I not stop?"

"Because the Communist Party of the Soviet Union simply doesn't work that way."

I

Audacity

f

I would love to be like the lilies of the field.
Someone who managed to read this age correctly
would surely have learned just this:
to be like a lily of the field.
ETTY HILLESUM, *diary entry for* SEPTEMBER 22, 1943
(*died Auschwitz* NOVEMBER 30, 1943), Etty: A Diary (published 1981)

§ I

Vienna: February 9, 1934

The war began as a whisper—a creeping sussurus that she came to hear in every corner of her childhood—by the time it finally banged on the door and rattled the windows it had come to seem like nature itself. It had always been there, whispered, hinted, spoken, bawled. It was the inevitable, it was the way things were—like winter or spring.

There was a whisper of war. Even at ten years old Méret could hear it. Her father had come home from the theatre a year ago, slapped the paper down on the dining table, and in his rant against "this buffoon Hitler" had forgotten to kiss her. He always kissed her when he came home from work. The first thing he did, even before he kissed his wife. It coincided with Méret's getting home from school. Her father was the Herr Direktor of the Artemis Theatre. He would take a couple of hours off midafternoon, before the box office opened for the evening performance, take tea with his wife and daughter in his apartment, return to the theatre and not be home again until hours after Méret had been put to bed.

"How can they let themselves be so deceived? How can Germans be so stupid? It couldn't happen here. If he'd stayed in Austria we'd have seen through him. Imagine it—a corporal from Linz hijacking an entire country? It couldn't happen here!"

Now he brought her the consequences of the Nazis seizing power. One year on, and some of those collared in the first roundups, in the wake of the burning of the Reichstag, were being set free. Mostly they were left-wing, intellectual, or both, and the Nazis either regarded a spell in Oranienburg as intellectual rehabilitation or they expected them to leave. Many did leave. Vienna, where most of Austria's quarter of a million Jews lived, was swelling with an influx of German Jews, German leftwingers, and German intellectuals.

7

"Darling girl, if I mention the name Viktor Rosen do you know of whom I speak?"

Of course she did. Viktor Rosen might not be the most famous pianist in the German speaking world, but he was close to it.

"He is living in Vienna now. In Berggasse. Close to Professor Freud. He called in at the theatre today. I had the opportunity of a chat with him. He is taking on pupils."

Imre paused to watch his daughter's reaction.

She set down her teacup and with the gravitas that only a preadolescent can muster when talking to an exasperating adult, replied, "Papa, Herr Rosen is a pianist."

"The cello is his second instrument. Just as the piano is yours."

Now she could see what he was saying. She concealed her joy—it came naturally to her.

"And," said her father, "he has agreed to take you on for both instruments."

She wished she could hug him, she wished she could sing her joy. Her father scooped her up and saved her from expressions of love and gratitude that would have been clumsy and embarrassing. He hugged her and spun her around and set her back on the carpet in the middle of the room a little dizzy from the ride. He smiled his pleasure; her mother, gently tearful, wept hers. Méret would repay his joy. Of course she would. She would play for him. Music said it all. She'd never had much need of words. Music was her code.

§2

Vienna: February 11, 1934

Punctuality was her vice. She was early for everything. She had begged her father not to usher her in to her first meeting with Rosen. Instead he had seen her to the door in Berggasse and reluctantly left her to it. She had reassured him—Vienna was home, she had lived here all her life, and Herr Rosen lived but three streets away. What could befall her standing in the street?

Imre had checked his pocket watch, noted that, as ever, she had got him where they needed to be with time in hand, kissed her on her half-turned cheek, walked to the corner, turned for one last look, and left.

Méret sat on a bench, her three-quarter-size cello by Bausch of Leipzig next to her, immaculate in its battered black case, wrapped up in winter black herself—black coat, black hat, black gloves—against the February cold. She was slightly smaller than the cello.

An old man emerged from Number 19, white beard against a black collar, the glowing tip of a cigar, plumes of pungent smoke wafting over her as he passed her way. A slight wincing, a contraction of the skin around one eye, as though his jaw ached or some such.

"Good morning, young lady."

Méret all but whispered her response. Professor Freud scared her. She had met him many times. At the Artemis Theatre where her father worked, at her home, where Sigmund and Martha Freud were numbered among her father's guests—and she knew he had treated her cousin Elsa—"difficult cousin Elsa," as her mother referred to her—but treated for what she did not know, no more than she knew what it was that might be difficult about Elsa. Professor Freud was some kind of doctor. The scary kind.

One minute before her wristwatch told her she was due, she pulled on the bell. The woodland child tapping at the door of the gingerbread house. A maid, skinny and pinch-faced, white upon black, told her to come in. The woman hardly looked at her, as though children were beneath notice. Up a wide staircase, dusty and hollow sounding, to the apartment on the first floor. Into a huge room looking out onto the Berggasse through floor-to-ceiling windows that seemed impossibly high.

"Herr Professor will be with you shortly."

And with that the door closed behind her and she found herself alone in the room.

It was a room much like the parlour in her grandmother's apartment. Dark-panelled walls that simply cried out for Empire furniture—for weight and substance and toe-stubbing ugliness, for curtains that cascaded in thick folds like water held in some perpetual slow motion. Once, this room had been like her grandmother's, she could tell—marks on the boards where some heavy piece had stood for years, horizontal lines of dust along the

9

walls where pictures had hung as long—full of the overstuffed, grandiose furniture of the last century. This room had been stripped. Acres of empty shelving, a chandelier missing half its bulbs. Now the only objects were two small armchairs, sat upon the bare, carpetless boards like perching sparrows, dwarfed by the emptiness surrounding, facing each other—and two musical instruments. A full-size concert grand piano bearing the words "Bechstein, Berlin" on its upturned lid—and a cello, propped on a stand.

She was peering into the cello through the f-holes, curious as to the maker, when she heard footsteps upon the boards behind her.

"It is a Goffriler, from the eighteenth century. Far, far older than my piano."

Méret straightened up to her full four feet ten, and found herself looking at a tall, elegant, well-dressed man of indeterminate age—older than her father, perhaps, but then how old was her father? Younger than her grandfather, greying hair, lots of fine lines about the eyes, and nicotine on the fingers of his right hand—the hand he now held out, and down, to her.

"Good afternoon, young lady. Viktor Rosen at your service. Musician."

She shook the hand.

"Méret Voytek. Schoolgirl . . . and musician."

This brought a smile to his face. Teeth also stained with nicotine.

"You were curious about the cello?"

"I'm sorry. Mama tells me I should not be nosy."

"Curiosity is not nosiness, my dear. Take a peek. Do you know Latin?"

She nodded.

"There is a large, if fading, label. And while the light is too dim for my old eyes I doubt it will be for yours."

She bent again, peered into an f-hole. It was like looking into a treasure chest. A flaking paper of history . . . a pirate's map.

Mattio Goffriller
Fece
in Venezia
~
Anno 1707

She hadn't heard of this man. She would have known the name of Stradivari, and perhaps one or two others. Perhaps all the best cello makers were once Italian, just as the English had once made the best pianos. Her cello was German.

"May I see?"

Professor Rosen was gesturing towards her cello case, palm open, not touching without permission. Méret shrugged her coat off onto the back of a chair and took the cello from its case. It was beautiful, not scarred or marked in any way and next to the Goffriler it looked cheap and modern.

Rosen peered at the instrument much as she had peered at his.

"Bausch? Am I right?"

She nodded, somewhat surprised.

"I started on a Bausch," he said. "Shall we hear the little fellow sing?"

She had chosen the piece herself. Four minutes from the first movement of Kodály's Cello Sonata op. 8, written almost twenty years ago, in the depth of the war.

She played it faithfully but not well, she thought. She lacked feeling, but then the piece itself lacked feeling. Or the feeling was one she could not relate to—perhaps the music was of its time, of war and misery, things of which she knew nothing.

Herr Rosen could hear this.

He said. "You don't like the piece, do you? Why pick a piece you don't like?"

What she did and didn't like was contingent upon what she knew. Her father took her to concerts, she had heard many Mozart piano concertos, all of Schubert's string quartets, and most of Mahler's symphonies—she adored the adagio from the unfinished Tenth and his orchestration of *Death and the Maiden*. Papa had once taken her to a Schoenberg concert but it had not spoken to her. Papa admitted that it had been years before it spoke to him, or to anyone he knew, and that at the premiere of Schoenberg's first Chamber Symphony—contrapuntal chaos as one critic dubbed it—he had watched Mahler stand alone amid the boos and hisses, clapping until the hall emptied.

"My grandfather bought me the score," she said.

"Your Hungarian grandfather? Herr Voytek?"

"Yes."

"So, simple patriotism, perhaps? A Hungarian grandfather buys you the score of Hungary's leading composer?"

Méret had nothing to say to this. Was patriotism simple? She had no idea. There were so many countries in her family history about which to feel remotely patriotic.

"Laudable," said Rosen, "but patriotism is never enough."

"And . . ." she hesitated, not wishing to invoke another response she would not understand. "And there is so little written for solo cello. So much is with piano accompaniment. Papa plays the piano, but Papa is hardly ever at home in the evenings."

"Quite so . . . the theatre."

"Yes. The theatre."

"Then we must find . . . no, I must arrange music for you. I shall be as fast and as cavalier as Liszt was with Bach. Now tell me, who do you really like?"

In truth she did not dislike Kodály. His *Háry János* spoke to her as a fairy tale might. The music made her want to laugh and dance, although she did little of either.

"Schubert," she said, and meant it. "And Mozart and Scarlatti and Bach and Fauré and Debussy and—"

"Stop, stop," said Rosen. But he was smiling as he said it.

"And what of Johann Strauss? Is he not synonymous with Vienna? Is he not part and parcel with Klimt and Schnitzler?"

She'd never heard of Klimt or Schnitzler. She thought *synonymous* might mean "the same as" and took her chance.

"That would simply be patriotic," she said. "Besides, one can have too much of a good thing."

Rosen was laughing now, happily hoist with his own petard. He rose from his chair, touched her gently on the shoulder, took his cigarettes from his jacket pocket, tapped one against the silver case, lit up, and stood, still smiling, almost giggling through the first puffs of smoke, looking out of the window onto the Berggasse.

When he returned, stubbing out the cigarette with a muttered "filthy habit," he said, "How right you are, young lady. One cannot waltz through life. The waltz is . . . a pleasant diversion . . . let us save it for a celebration. Now, is there anything you would like to ask me?"

"Yes," she said. "I am to tell Papa when I get home whether or not I am your pupil."

"Child, could you not read my face, the pleasure I took in your playing of a miserable work? Indeed, you are my pupil. I have never heard anyone of your age play so well."

"And . . ."

"And?"

If she understood what he had said about the waltz aright, he had given her her cue.

"Papa says we live in interesting times."

Rosen looked a little baffled, but nodded and agreed.

"But Papa doesn't mean interesting, he means bad."

Rosen thought for a moment.

"And your question is?"

"Papa says the Germans locked you up. Is that true?"

"Yes," said Rosen. "Not for long, but they imprisoned me near Berlin, in a camp called Oranienburg."

"Was it . . . awful?"

"Yes. It was awful, but it could have been worse. The Nazis weren't trying to kill us, they were trying to scare us."

"Why?"

"Why what? Why were they trying to scare us or why did they lock us up?"

She had meant both and said so softly, wondering if she had not already overstepped the mark. But Rosen sighed and stretched and seemed far more sad than annoyed.

"They locked up many artists and intellectuals. We were all people who did not share their politics or who had no politics at all—although I find that hard to believe whenever I hear it uttered, and in the long run 'I have no politics' is a cardboard shield that won't stop a single bullet—and the hope was that we would be frightened into conforming or leaving. As you can see, I chose the latter."

"Why Vienna? Why not London or Paris?"

"It's easier to say why not Vienna than why Vienna? Music flows through the city deeper than the Danube. The opera houses thrill to Wagner every evening, and every afternoon the cafés relax to a thé dansant.

Haydn, Schubert, and Mozart all lived and worked here . . . Beethoven even played piano in a café on Himmelpfortgasse . . . to this day Franz Lehár sits at his piano and composes fripperies with a songbird perched upon his shoulder and, who knows, perhaps whispering the melody in his ear? What do you suppose the bird is? A linnet? A nightingale?"

One hand seemed to pluck the linnet from his shoulder, to cup and hold it at his ear—then the palm opened and released the invisible bird to the air.

He was playing with her. She realized that. Grown-ups who had little knowledge of children, grown-ups without children of their own, often played more than her parents, and hence overplayed. The mixture of playful gestures and complex words did not win her. She had no idea what a frippery was and Lehár was just a name to her.

"And if music were not enough," he went on, strung out on the washing line of his own words, "it is a city of ideas, of Freud and Herzl and Wittgenstein. Did you know the Emperor Marcus Aurelius died here?"

Of all those names the only one she knew was Professor Freud's.

"No," she replied, "I did not. But I know Professor Freud. He lives in the next apartment block."

"Ah, . . . I have not yet had the honour."

"I could introduce you."

Rosen smiled at the precocity of this, and her brain found time to catch up with her tongue.

"I mean . . . Papa could."

"Of course. Papa."

"Papa says . . ."

She felt the sentence dribble away to nothing.

"Papa says?"

"Papa says that you left everything behind when you fled Germany."

Rosen gazed around the room, his right hand sweeping in an encompassing gesture, encouraging her to look where he looked.

"Well, not everything. The cello came with me, the piano followed a day later. And while these bookcases look to me as though they have stood here empty since Franz Josef was a boy, my books will arrive from Berlin any day now to fill them. And behind my cartloads of books, there will be German Jews by the thousand, some lucky enough to take it all with them, some who will most certainly, as you put it, leave everything behind."

"Papa says it could not happen here. But he says it in the same tone of voice with which he says 'let Papa kiss it better.'"

She could tell Professor Rosen was weighing up what he might say next. He was holding in the balance her urgent questions and her tender age.

"Your father is a kind and clever man. Without him I might be stranded at the border, or searching fruitlessly for an apartment. But . . ."

He let the word hang, just as though he had his foot upon the sustain pedal. A prolonged "but" dying away in the vast emptiness of the room, only to be caught at its faintest.

"But . . . you hear the music in your father's voice aright. He cannot kiss it better. This is beyond repair. It could happen here. It *will* happen here."

"Will you tell me? Will you tell when you think 'it' will happen here?"

"If I have foresight enough to know, I will tell anyone who will listen, but first of all I shall tell you. I will leave before it happens here. And if I leave, you will be the first to know."

"And should I leave? Should Mama and Papa leave?"

"It's not for me to say. It is for your father to decide. And, of course, you're not Jewish."

"Does that make a difference?"

"In a year or two or five who knows? Right now it is all the difference in the world. But we are forgetting something vital as we redraw the map of Europe."

"We are?"

"The piano. You have prepared a piece for the piano?"

"Yes. But I have another question."

"Ask, child."

"Whatever happens when I play the piano, I am still your pupil? You said I was your pupil."

"And so you are."

"Whatever happens?"

"Whatever happens."

She played what Papa called her party piece, as she had played it at family gatherings since the age of five. It had been played by hundreds, perhaps thousands, of children over a century and more—hammered out in dissonance and delight for parental pleasure.

A Beethoven bagatelle in A minor: *Für Elise.*
But she played it to perfection, and brought a smile to Rosen's lips.

§3

Vienna: February 12, 1934

At the end of the street, the red and cream trams turned around and the conductor would emerge with a long, hooked pole and reverse the steel arm that skated along the overhead wires to pick up the current. It was a common sight to see trams stand idle awhile, two crews chatting and smoking as their routes and shifts met a five-minute overlap. There was even a glass and iron hut with a dull copper roof and a belching, coal-burning stove to accommodate them on winter mornings such as this.

But these trams had been idle too long, and when the conductor locked the doors and took his leather bag of small change and walked off to the hut, a word was whispered down the long queue that in its present context baffled her.

"Strike."

On the tabula of the mind she tried to write the word. *Streik? Streich?* In fairy tales, the ones her father had read to her when she was very small, giants and ogres were felled by a *streich*—often tripped up by cunning, giggling boys and girls. It was close to meaning a prank. But who was playing a prank on whom?

It was close to meaningless.

"Strike."

Suddenly, her mother was behind her, a hand upon her shoulder, saying, "You must come home, now."

"But . . . but . . . school. It is Monday. A school day."

The hand slipped from shoulder to upper arm, gripping her firmly and pulling her out of the queue.

"Don't argue. We are going home. Today you must study at home."

Her mother took her by the hand and walked her back the way she had come.

"But I have art today. I can't possibly miss art!"

"You shall miss everything until all this is over. Do you hear me? You must not go out of the house until all this is over."

"Until all what is over?"

In the afternoon. As the light of day faded. In her room. She paused in practicing her scales at the sound of raised voices—a misnomer, only her mother's voice was ever raised.

"Why must you get involved? It's got nothing to do with us!"

She could not hear her father's reply. Only a tone of voice she knew well . . . the reasonable, placatory, futile, gentle music of a gentle man.

And then her mother once more.

"For Christ's sake, Imre, are you trying to get us all killed?"

Her father did not come home between opening up the theatre and the night's performance. Méret and her mother ate in near silence. Méret not daring to ask any questions, her mother mouthing only platitudes about Méret's studies, telling her she was bright enough to miss a few days at school. Besides, nobody else would be going to school, either, so what was lost?

At night she heard noises in the street. Not close by but not distant.

In the morning, her father came into her bedroom, hugged her and told her she was a lucky girl who'd been given another day off school.

On the second night she heard gunfire, not pistols or rifles but big guns, cannons, echoing across the city from the workingmen's apartments in Karlmarxhof.

Her bedroom door opened quietly. She closed her eyes and pretended to be asleep, smelt the dark scent of cologne and tobacco that seemed always to wrap itself around her father, inviting her to bury her face in his clothes, and then heard him whisper, "It's alright. She's sleeping."

In the morning the barber called. It was her father's treat to have the barber call on him, rather than he on the barber, two or three times a week. When she was smaller she had thought it fun to let Herr Knobloch daub her face with foam from the brush and pretend to shave her. But blade never touched flesh—the gleaming edge of his cutthroat razor lay folded in a stainless steel bowl—only the back of a plastic comb shaved the white blobs from her top lip and hairless chin.

Today, her father stretched out in the chair he kept at his desk in the study, the razor gliding gently, bloodlessly across his cheeks, exchanging wisdom with Herr Knobloch.

"I mean," Knobloch was saying, "it can't happen here, but all the same . . . you can't help worrying . . . I mean . . . where's it all going to end? A bloke doesn't feel safe in his own home. What with Heimwehr bully boys and those Nazis taking their orders from Germany . . . I ask you, are we part of Germany now?"

Most days Imre could make Knobloch laugh—gently pricking at the bubbles of his workingman's pride and his workingman's half-hearted mix of opportunism and socialism. Today he didn't even try.

"Not yet," he said simply.

"Not yet? You mean . . . ?"

"Yes. One day. And perhaps soon."

"What? Greater Germany? I'm not German. You're not German. I ask you, Herr Direktor, what is Germany? Brown shirts, boiled cabbage, and jackboots. What is Vienna? A good cup of coffee and a fag. That's Vienna. Caffs and barber shops . . . and . . ."

"Theatres," Imre concluded for him.

"Yeah. Sorry. O'course. Theatres too. Not that I ever been in one."

"You should. We serve a good cup of coffee and we sell fags."

Now Knobloch laughed. Now Knobloch noticed Méret.

"Hello, young lady."

Her muttered reply was scarcely audible. She loved to watch the morning ritual of her father's shave. It was better than any parade, as good as any film at the cinema. Because her father was the star, relaxed and trusting and pampered—waited on cheek and jowl. And the touch of magic as his face was revealed, strip by strip, the peeling away of layers, a gentle flaying, as the razor skimmed across his skin. She knew the strokes of the razor by heart. Knobloch never varied. He had mapped the face so well, knew which flick of the blade would catch what bristle. She loved to watch. She hated to speak. Knobloch was so friendly it was . . . scary.

"Remember when I used to shave you?"

Now he leaned down and dabbed a single fleck of foam onto her top lip. Now he grinned, now he laughed.

Her father was standing. Smiling.

"Knobloch, Knobloch. You will get us all shot."

Just before her father wiped her lip clean, she caught sight of herself in the mirror. The old joker had given her a Hitler toothbrush moustache. Even her father thought it was funny.

§4

Méret perceived the politics of her time and place in the only way a child can. In pieces. A jigsaw she would never be able to arrange into a whole. Her father made efforts to explain to her what had happened, but her mother stopped him with, "The girl is only ten, Imre." Just as she had said at all the punctuation points of Méret's life—"only seven," "only eight," "only nine." She wondered if one day her mother might mention her age without the prefacing "only." When she was twenty-one would she be "only twenty-one"?

What she knew was what she saw—sandbags set out at street corners to shield machine-gun emplacements—slogans painted onto brick walls— young men in uniform, some in black trousers, some in brown shirts, some, oddly, in white socks—emblematic of she knew not what. What she knew was what she heard: cries in the street, whispers in the cafés, the occasional explosion, the less occasional sound of gunfire, the rumble of an armoured car across the cobblestones; arguments between her parents that were hushed the moment they could see that she was listening.

It was an unassembled pattern of fragments, and as such she perceived her native land aright. Austria was an unassembled pattern of fragments.

Two weeks later, at her sixth visit to Rosen's apartment, she arrived to find the floor littered with packing cases and books, and Rosen sitting in the middle, not, as was his habit, in a neat two-piece black suit, but in braces and shirtsleeves, the cuffs rolled back, blowing the dust off a book.

"We will begin a little late today," he said. "I have to clear a way through or you'll never find a spot to put down your cello. Indeed, I cannot get to the piano. The complete works of Count Tolstoy have become an obstacle course."

She had never seen so many books. When she was very small it had seemed to her that her father possessed all the books in the world. They lined all four sides of his study—under the window, over the window—and reached right up to the ceiling. Then, one afternoon, he had taken her to call on Professor Freud and she realized that her father possessed most of the books in the world but that Professor Freud possessed more. Herr Rosen had almost as many as Freud and she wasn't counting the volumes of sheet music.

Stacking up the Russians on the shelves she noticed the title of one very fat book, in faded gold along its spine: *Memoirs of a Revolutionist* by Prince Peter Kropotkin.

"May I ask," she said, "what is a revolutionist?"

"One who makes a revolution. Or are you no wiser with that definition?"

"It is something that revolves. Like a wheel?"

"In a sense. It is a change in the order of society. In that sense it revolves and another group finds itself at the top. As though a wheel of people had been spun. In France a hundred and fifty years ago, the poor took over, killed the rich, and made all the changes they could . . . from fixing the price of bread to changing the names of the months in the calendar."

"How odd. Why would they do that?"

"I've never really understood it myself. But it has a romantic feel to it. And, of course, a descriptive quality. November means nothing. It isn't even the ninth month. *Brumaire* . . . now that really says something about the autumn, doesn't it?"

"Foggy?"

"Yes, foggy."

"And where would we be now on the poor people's calendar?"

Rosen had to think about this.

"I can't be certain. It's a long time since I studied history . . . but tell me, what was the day like as you walked here?"

"It was windy."

"Then I think we would be in *Ventôse*. The windy month."

She had finished sorting the Kropotkins as they spoke and was well into the Tolstoys.

"My father will not tell me what happened."

Rosen looked baffled.

"What happened when?"

"In the middle of the month. In the days after I first came here. Was that a revolution?"

"Well, my dear, I am not your father, and with all respect to your father . . . if I had children I would answer their questions."

"It is Mama," she said. "It always is. If she gets her way I'll never know what happens. I'll never know where babies come from and I'll end up believing the nonsense the other girls tell me at school."

Rosen grinned. She thought he might even have swallowed laughter.

"I won't answer the latter. That really *is* a matter for your mother. But I am happy to talk politics to you. No, it was not a revolution. If anything it was a counterrevolution. The powers that be trying to nip the activities and the workers in the bud with a surprise attack. The result? The workers struck, they refused to go to work, no trains, no trams . . . and the powers that be attacked them again. This time not with rifle butts but with Howitzers."

"Cannons?"

"Yes, cannons. You must have heard them. The police and the army fired upon the workers' flats."

"Were the poor people killed?"

"Yes. I think many were killed. But I have heard figures bandied about from dozens to hundreds. Only one thing is certain."

"What is that?"

"That many more have been locked up. The camp at Wöllersdorf must be bulging at the seams. But then there are so many factions one could lock up . . . the fascists, the socialists, the social democrats, the communists, the patriots—who in reality are Nazis. In a country of six million there may well be six million factions."

He could see now that he had lost her.

She wiped the spine of a Tolstoy and read out, "*The Kreutzer Sonata.* It is a book of music?"

"No, my dear. It is a book about music, a novel about the power of music to affect us. Have you not heard of Beethoven's *Kreutzer Sonata*?"

She shook her head. Now that Tolstoy was shelved, the way through to the piano and his cello was clear. He crossed the floor, set the Goffriler

21

between his legs, tilted the neck slightly to the left, and with the bow in his right hand struck up the intense, dramatic opening of the *adagio sostenuto,* the first movement of the *Kreutzer Sonata.*

He stopped at the moment the piano should cut in.

"You like?" he said simply.

Like? She felt blasted, as though the notes had pierced her flesh and entered her blood.

She just nodded.

"I have only two hands," he said. "Unpack your cello. I will find the score and we shall learn the piece. No exercises today, no scales, we shall play the music of the gods."

§5

When, four months later, the chancellor of Austria, Engelbert Dollfuss—a man so short he was known as Millimetternich—was assassinated in a failed Nazi coup, it was Rosen, not her father, who explained things to her.

He had no idea how much she understood. For all that she asked questions, the child seemed to have so few reactions. She nodded as she always did, accepting silently what he said.

Then they went back to Beethoven.

§6

April 1936

She was twelve now and had grown surprisingly quickly. Rosen insisted on measuring her. She was baffled, but compliant. She slipped off her shoes, stood on the end of the tape. He put his hand flat on the top of her head, compressing the thick waves of black hair, and told her she was a fraction over one metre fifty-five.

"Why?"

"I just wanted to be certain. You are such a slender girl, you have a knack of looking smaller than you are. I wanted to be certain you were big enough."

"Big enough for what?"

Rosen gestured, an open palm and extended arm, across the room to where his Goffriler cello stood poised upon its metal mount.

"You're joking."

"My dear girl, I know I make a lot of jokes. It is a weakness and often lands me in hot water. But not this time, or did you really think you could perform in public on your child's cello?"

"I'm performing in public? Do you think I'm ready?"

"I think with a bit of practice we might both be ready."

She sat, wrapped around the cello, fingertips touching the patina of centuries, feeling the muted orange glow of the wood all but seep into her hands.

She drew the bow across the strings, back and forth, hearing the upper register like a bird trilling in the treetops, the low like the rumble of an approaching train in a tunnel.

She was grinning at Rosen now. Brimful of pleasure. Revelling in the tones of a perfect instrument.

"It fits," he said simply.

"You didn't have to measure me for this," she replied.

"Perhaps not. But it was fun."

"And we are performing where exactly?"

§7

May 1936

Imre Voytek was immensely proud of his theatre on Josefstadt. The Artemis had been begun in the year of the Secession movement, 1898, in the modern style, the *Jugendstil,* favoured by the architect Otto Wagner, with flourishes and filigree by Kolo Moser. The money soon ran out. The interior boasted a frieze that was considered daringly decadent in its depiction of the goddess after whom the theatre was named, that might or might not be the work of Gustav Klimt. No one was quite sure. The Secessionists had been approached, a frieze commissioned, and in the autumn of 1899 a short, silent, beardy bloke wearing a smock the size of a bell tent had shown up and spent three days roughing out a design, fresco-style, onto the still damp plaster above the bar. He might have been Klimt. He might not. No one had dared break the silence to ask. On the fourth day, the day the money ran out, it was unfinished and the artist conspicuously as absent as the funding. It was still unfinished when Klimt died in 1918. It was still unfinished when Imre took over the theatre some ten years later. But Imre's first act was to engage a "disciple" of Klimt's to finish it "in the style of" Klimt.

He was delighted with the outcome and remarked to his partner, Phillipe Julius, that it was "better than the real thing."

"How so?"

"Look at the use of red and the deep blues. Klimt would have just plastered gold leaf everywhere."

"Indeed. It was his trademark. I can hardly think red and blue better."

"Better? OK, cheaper. It's a damn sight cheaper! Do you know how much gold leaf costs?"

"Imre, do we really weigh up art as though it were merely double entry bookkeeping?"

Méret had never paid much attention to the frieze. Breasts did not interest her. She had been fascinated at first sight by Moser's exterior façade, a row of columns each ornamented in the *Art Nouveau* style with

24

swirls and loops and feathers. She thought of it as being like a row of peacocks viewed from the back. Half a dozen strutting, fanning peacocks. Much to his wife's annoyance, Imre had adopted this image and every so often would say something like "Just off to the peacock's bum," only to be sanctioned with a po-faced "Imre! *Pas devant l'enfant!*"

The acoustics inside the theatre had been acknowledged from the opening night as being exceptional, and within a matter of weeks the theatre had become a venue for music as well as drama. Two nights a month it would play host to small orchestras or quartets and trios of chamber music.

When Rosen asked for a night in May, Imre leapt at the chance. A Viktor Rosen recital would guarantee a full house. When Rosen said he would be dueting with his daughter, Imre said, "Viktor. Are you sure? The girl is only twelve."

"Of course, I'm sure. She is the most talented musician I have ever met at any age."

It was a challenging programme—they would play their much-rehearsed *Kreutzer Sonata* and César Franck's Sonata in B major. The Franck Rosen had chosen for the contrast. It was a gentler, more lyrical piece than the Beethoven—but still energetic, passionate. Each lasted more than half an hour. Imre worried about the strain on his daughter and he tried as delicately as he could to raise the matter with Rosen.

"She's tougher than you think," Rosen replied. "And so determined. But . . . I shall open each half with some Chopin—or with whatever is at my fingertips on the night and we will take an interval of at least twenty minutes. She will be fine."

Imre knew better than to raise the issue with his daughter, she would only turn her hardest face upon him and say something firm, uncompromising, and humourless.

To Imre she looked so small as she stepped onto the stage. Rosen's arm extended an introduction—but he said nothing. It occurred to Imre that in offering no such fluff as "a talented young lady" or "a tender age," Rosen was treating his daughter like an adult. She walked on in a plain black dress, precise and unfussy, took her seat, embraced her cello with her right arm, swiftly tuned up, and, the bow in her left hand poised above the strings, nodded once to Rosen and struck up the notes.

An hour and a half later the audience was on its feet. Vienna had a new mistress, and a proud father stood at the back of the stalls wiping away tears of joy.

In the bar, closer to midnight, under the breasts of Artemis, Rosen was on his third Armagnac and Imre had finished half a bottle of claret and was in a mood to be joyously drunk and finish the rest.

"You know, I meant what I said. The girl is a rare talent."

"I know," said Imre, feeling he might weep again. "I'd have to be deaf not to know."

"The *direktor* of the Symphony Orchestra was in the house tonight. He wants her for his youth orchestra. Can I take it you would have no objection?"

"Of course not."

"It would mean changing schools in a few years."

"Why is that?"

"Because at sixteen she would be eligible for the Konservatorium."

"Viktor, it hasn't been called that since I was a boy. It's the Imperial Academy of Music or some such guff . . . quite possibly the only bit of empire we have left."

"It's a dilemma."

"Is it?"

"Imre, Méret is a child of silence and passion. If it were not for the feeling she expresses through her cello one might almost say she was a cold child."

"Almost, but not quite. But her mother . . . well she gets it from her mother."

"I have no children. I cannot advise you on her upbringing. But I would ask you to ask yourself. Might she not be better off in a normal school, where she will socialize with normal children rather than an elite of the gifted?"

"Surely you would want her to go to the academy?"

"Of course . . . but I speak as a tutor not a father."

"Then she must go. I know exactly what you mean. I've seen it myself a thousand times. There is a detachment that is disturbing. It may be it is necessary for her dedication, but it is disturbing nonetheless . . . it makes me sad sometimes. But I can give her what she needs. I know I can.

She is loved. She will come to no harm. She is loved. That's her name after all."

"Sorry, Imre. I don't follow you there."

"Méret. It means 'the beloved.'"

"In what language?"

"Egyptian I think. Or perhaps Greek. I've never studied either. I hit the buffers at Latin."

§8

November 1937

Since 1926, Imre had worked side by side with Phillipe Julius. A man as Viennese as he was himself, but with origins as mixed as his own. The Voyteks had come west a generation ago from Hungary. The Julius family had travelled east from France at about the same time. Central Europe was less a fixed point in geography—more a flying carpet.

They were very different men and made a close and practical partnership. Imre could run a business, any business, on the back of an envelope sitting in a café or bar and delegating to all and sundry. Julius brooded, alternating between prolonged periods of isolated contemplation and the manipulation of crowds of actors into cast and play. As managing director and artistic director they were perfectly matched and were nicknamed Castor and Pollux in the small world of Viennese theatre.

They had made their mark with Strindberg's *The Ghost Sonata,* and brought Vienna to its feet with a modern-dress version of *As You Like It.* "What will the twins do next?" was a common question in the columns of Vienna's newspapers and magazines.

It was the question Imre put to Julius as they sat in the Café Landtmann late in November of 1937.

Julius took a surprisingly long time to answer. For a minute or two Imre continued to scribble on his envelopes and to push them around the table until an order arose. Seeing Julius's hand pick up and cradle his cup of thick Brauner coffee, Imre looked up.

"Phillipe? I asked—"

"I heard you, Imre."

"And?"

"Imre. I have to go now."

"After lunch, then."

"I mean I have to leave Vienna. Leave Austria."

"Leave Vienna?"

"Before the bastards get here. You've said often enough yourself the Nazis mean to have us."

Imre sat back amazed. He could and should have anticipated this. But he hadn't.

"Then perhaps we should all leave?"

"Why? You're not Jewish. I'm not sure I'd go myself if I weren't. Vienna is home. I've known no other home. But I am Jewish. I've not set foot in a synagogue in forty years—and if I wanted third-rate theatre I'd visit one of our rivals rather than a synagogue—but that won't save me. You . . . no, you stay . . . someone has to keep an eye on Artemis after all. Besides, apart from hating Nazis, do you really have any politics? I've always thought 'live and let live' summed up your politics rather neatly."

"Live and let live?!?"

"Forget I said it. Just keep your mouth shut about Nazis and you'll survive. There'll be a war. Possibly a short one. The English Royal Navy will sink their ships. The French will kick the shit out of their army at the Maginot Line. Then I'll come back. We'll pick up where we left off."

"So what do we do next?"

"I've been working on a new translation of the *Oresteia*. I'll leave you the text and a few notes . . . and I'll see you . . ."

"Quite. When?"

"Oh . . . about 1940 I should think."

§9

When Imre told his daughter about Julius leaving, she was silent—when was she not?—and eventually said, simply, "1940," and "Unimaginable."

"I suppose it must seem that way to anyone of your age. I might just as well have said 2000. Now that really is unimaginable."

The following day, the first day of December—a Wednesday—Méret called on Rosen just after dusk for her after-school tuition, feeling she was the harbinger of news. She had grown accustomed to Rosen feeding her pieces of history, paring it off from chaos to give her manageable, digestible chunks. Now she had something to offer in return—the morsel that was Phillipe Julius leaving for Paris. She felt it was a mirror, her news reflecting the life of Rosen himself.

The big room was bare. Stripped back to what it had been the first time she saw it. The books, the all-but-endless collected editions of Europe's masters—Goethe, Schiller, Tolstoy, Gogol, Dostoevsky, Balzac, Dickens—that she had sorted and shelved with him were gone. The rugs were rolled up and tied, the Bechstein was bound and wrapped in a carapace of heavy felt and standing on edge with its three legs pointing at her like a slaughtered rhinoceros.

Only the two chairs remained. The two chairs and the cello.

"How long have you known?"

It was the most adult statement she had ever uttered, powerful in its elisions of expression and its complexities of assumption and meaning.

He stood before her, elegant in his simple two-piece black suit—she had come to think of it as his uniform—hands clasped in front of him, paused on the brink of difficulty.

"I decided on Sunday."

"I was here on Sunday. We always meet on Sundays."

"I decided after you left."

"And you did what? Just called the removal men on Monday morning and had them load up four years of your life."

"I think from your tone, my dear, you mean four years of yours. I have moved before. I have packed and run before. The act is well within my grasp. It revives no old pain, so I cope with the new one entirely."

"New pain?"

"Parting is such sweet sorrow."

She had not the emotional vocabulary to work it out and utter it, but it seemed to her that this must be what lovers leaving felt like. And that that was what he meant. And that was absurd. He was . . . what was he? Fifty? And she was thirteen going on fourteen.

It was a spell crying out to be broken. Rosen unclasped his hands and did what he always did, took out his silver cigarette case, tapped a cigarette against the side of it, lit up, turned his head, and blew the first whiffs of smoke away.

"Play for me," he said.

"One last time?"

"Why should it be the last? And don't answer that. Just play."

"What shall I play?"

"You've been practicing a piece in private."

"How did you know?"

"Just play for me, Méret."

She wrapped herself around the cello, felt again the sensation she always felt, of music and the lifeblood of time seeping into her flesh, and struck up the piece she had rehearsed as a surprise for him—Bach's Cello Suite no. 3, the sixth movement. *Gigue.*

"Shadows and light," Rosen said when she had finished.

"Yes," she replied, for that was what it was.

§ 10

She arrived home in a taxi cab. It was the only way to manage. Rosen had paid the cabbie in advance, and the noise she made staggering up the stairs with her newfound burden alerted her father, who came down to the first landing and, in the half light that the single overhead bulb cast on them, said, "What on earth have you got there?"

"A cello, Papa. A 1707 Mattio Goffriler cello."

§11

"Did he say where he was going?"

"To London."

"Good God, why London? Why not Paris or Amsterdam? What does London have to offer? The madman Thomas Beecham. Beecham waving his baton in the pouring rain for a nation of philistines in wet wool and false teeth!"

"Papa, I didn't ask why London, but Viktor told me all the same. He thinks Paris will fall. He thinks Amsterdam will fall."

"Amsterdam? But Holland is neutral."

Imre thought a moment about the stupidity of what he had just said—Julius would have laughed him into blushes for that—and added, "I suppose Viktor has seen what the Nazis can do. He told me everything about his flight from Germany."

"Me, too."

"And the cello? He just gave you the cello?"

"Yes. He called it 'portable property,' but he didn't explain what that meant."

"I think he meant the cello was valuable. Is it worth much?"

"A fortune, Papa. It is worth a fortune."

"Bloody hell!"

And from the kitchen her mother's voice, "Imre! *Pas devant!*"

§12

Being, as Viktor had promised her, "the first to know," she never doubted. The Germans were coming. But in never doubting she never imagined. "The Germans are coming" remained a phrase and conjured no reality. The reality was not that the Germans were coming but that Rosen was gone.

On March 14, 1938, the Germans took Vienna without a shot being fired. Hitler's cavalcade rolled into the city to a rapturous reception.

Méret thought she would be kept home as she had been during the workers' strike and in the dangerous days following the death of Dollfuss, but her father had talked her mother around.

"She's growing up. This is the world in which she will have to live. God knows, I wish it weren't, but this is the world in which she will have to live . . . or change it."

So she was allowed out, not to change the world but to mingle with the thousands, the hundreds of thousands, who crowded into the Heldenplatz to see forty staff cars roll up to the Hofburg, to have their cheers drowned out by a Luftwaffe fly pass, to hear the Führer address his Ostmark from a balcony of the old Hapsburg palace.

"I know that the old eastern capital of the German *Reich* will do justice to its new tasks just as she once solved and mastered the old ones."

But she was more interested in the new patriots than in Hitler. Vienna had, throughout her childhood, been a city of paramilitaries—of young men strutting around in riding britches, or lots of leather belts with straps and buckles, or shirts in odd colours, sporting arcane insignia. Something in the Viennese that loved a uniform as much as a waltz—the Heimwehr, the Jewish Youth Bund, the Schutzbund, the Patriotic Youth Movement, the Loyal League of Left-handed Lutheran Housepainters— every so often one or other of them got banned, which fanned the flames of membership wonderfully by reducing the uniform to a badge worn secretly behind the lapel, as discreet as Mae West's cleavage, as gratifying as a mason's handshake. Now the brownshirts were openly on the streets, and those without brown shirts sported striking red brassards— a black swastika on a white circle. A waltz, a good cup of coffee, an Apfelstrudel, a uniform, and a speech from a bored dictator. What more could Vienna ask?

She drifted off. Enough is enough and the mob would go on cheering long after Hitler had showed his contempt and vanished from the balcony. Turning from the Heldenpaltz to head north toward home, she passed a face she thought she knew, arm raised, head up, cheering till he was hoarse.

She stared at the arm bearing the brassard until he noticed her.

"Hello, young lady."

"Hello, Herr Knobloch."

It was her father's barber. The man who had daubed her with a tooth-brush Hitler moustache. The same lackadaisical socialist who had never wanted to be German and had been stunned when told by her father that they all would be one day soon. Now that one day had arrived.

Knobloch lowered his arm and clapped a palm across the swastika, not so much concealing it as reassuring himself that it was still there and that that was what the girl was staring at.

He turned and the two walked up the street side by side.

"I know what you're thinking," he said.

"Do you, Herr Knobloch?"

"But it's easy. Dead easy. If you can't beat 'em, join 'em.'"

"What happened to 'it can't happen here'?"

"It *has* happened. Just as your dad said it would."

"Tell me, Herr Knobloch, do you think my father will want his beard shaved by a Nazi?"

"I'm not a Nazi."

"Then what are you?"

"I'm a survivor."

"And this is what you do to survive?"

"What? Just putting on me armband and giving a few cheers so the neighbours can see? That's nothin', that's nothin' to what we might end up doing. I know your dad's the clever one, but I'll make a prediction now. I don't know, you don't know, and your dad don't know what any of us will have to do to survive."

They walked on a few streets in silence. The sound of cheering faded into the background, and they came to a parting of their ways.

Knobloch pulled off his brassard and stuffed it into a jacket pocket.

"Tell your dad I'll be round in the mornin' at the usual time. Nazi or no Nazi, I'll bet he still wants his shave."

He smiled. He was not an unpleasant man. A simple man, she thought, a bit of a wag. But she could not tell if his pretense that things might now go on as normal was meant to reassure her or just himself.

"I'll tell him," she said.

§ 13

Méret had been in the Vienna Youth Orchestra since June 1936—a matter of weeks after her professional debut with Rosen—and had found herself the youngest member. In the best of circumstances she did not make friends easily. To make friends at all was on the fringe of her nature, but she had found herself adopted, rescued from her own silence, by three musicians in the youth orchestra—Magda Ewald (trombone), two years older; Roberto Cacciato (clarinet), a year older; and Inge Reiter (viola), also two years older. Magda was Austrian through and through, Roberto was the son of Italian immigrants, Inge was as Viennese as Magda—but Jewish.

Inge was not a practicing Jew and could not name a single member of her family who was. Asked when the family had secularized, her father Jakob "Jack" Reiter would usually reply, "When did the ark crash on Ararat? It must have been the day after that."

Jack Reiter was an acquaintance of her father's. Perhaps a friend, perhaps not. He ran a cinema just around the corner from the Artemis Theatre. Imre had treated its opening with some contempt. Working with Shakespeare and Schiller, he had no need of Mary Pickford or Douglas Fairbanks. And certainly no need of the competition. But when Reiter gave over evenings to the new German cinema, to the work of Fritz Lang or F.W. Murnau, Imre softened, all but conceded that the cinema might be art. Méret had been to the cinema many times with her father, had been terrified by *Nosferatu,* dazzled by *Metropolis,* awed by the prescience of Dietrich and Nazimova. Was there another earthly creature as ugly as Max Schreck? Was there another earthly creature as beautiful as Marlene Dietrich? Was there another earthly creature as graceful as Alla Nazimova?

When their daughters became friends, Imre's enthusiasm all but burst. Ever the conciliator, peacemaker, fixer, he suggested that they had the makings of a string quartet. Neither girl showed much interest in this, but Jack Reiter quashed the idea with a plain statement of the times.

"Imre, I doubt you will have so much as a moment's difficulty recruiting the two violinists, and we have no shortage of venues, but do you really think anyone but you will want their children associating professionally with Jews?"

The idea had died on Jack's lips and in her father's heart. Méret never thought about it again.

In the days after the fall of Austria, Méret continued to wander the city—her father's "change the world" diminishing in her mind with every day that passed. It seemed to her that Vienna was now one vast and endless parade. Every organization that could teach men to march in step did so. She viewed what Vienna was enduring, what it was becoming, what it had so half-heartedly willed into being, with a glassy detachment. It was something seen reflected in a shop window.

There were Jews on their hands and knees scrubbing graffiti from the paving stones in the street—there was talk of rabbis being forced to clean public lavatories armed only with toothbrushes. And soon Jews were excluded entirely from public life, from the civil service, from the universities . . . from the press.

Passing the Reiters's home, a few streets from her own, she found Inge sitting outside the apartment building. A large hand-painted sign next to her read: "Apartment sale. Everything must go. Bargains for all."

"What's going on?"

"Isn't it obvious? We're selling up."

"Why?"

"My father has lost his job."

"Why?"

"He's a Jew in what the Nazis say is a vital arm of communications."

"What on earth does that mean?"

"Only that he shows newsreels in the cinema. That makes him part of communications. The Nazis are getting rid of all the Jews in newspapers and radio. By this stretch of logic, that now includes my father. He won't be paid at the end of the month, and perhaps not for months to come, so we must sell to live."

"Everything?"

"God knows. Our neighbours have turned into crows and we are just carrion. They offer us pennies for things my father worked hard to buy and he accepts."

35

A fat old woman wrapped in black emerged with a handful of cutlery, cackling out loud about the low price she had paid, loudly proclaiming that she had got the better of a Jew. She shuffled on down the street without even noticing Inge or Méret.

Méret stepped into the hallway, heard the bumping hubbub from the rooms above, climbed the stairs to the sitting room where a sad, pale Herr Reiter sat taking change in an old tobacco tin, listening with none of his daughter's anger or impatience as people he had known a lifetime argued over coppers and robbed him blind.

Passing the bathroom on her way to Inge's room, she saw Frau Reiter sitting on the linen basket, red-faced and angry. Seeing Méret watching she kicked the door to. In Inge's bedroom all her books and toys were laid on the desk. Childhood spread out like a deck of cards. Among them was a black-faced doll, canvas body stuffed with cotton rags, its head a shiny orb of porcelain with painted curls and red lips. Years ago, Méret's father had bought her a china-head doll with painted flaxen curls and blue eyes. The head was cracked now, the blue paint of the eyes flaking. Inge had taken better care of hers. Méret had always wanted a second china doll—some girlish daydream that the dolls would talk to one another when she wasn't there, and if she came home early and crept in she might catch them, out of their box and talking, like characters in a Hans Christian Andersen tale. It was a fantasy of an eight- or nine-year-old, which she found surprisingly alive at fourteen.

She picked up the doll, slipped quietly past the bathroom door, wove her way among the jostling arses of fat old women to Jack Reiter with his open tobacco tin. She dropped a *zwei groschen* coin into the tin. Reiter scarcely looked at her. She ran down the stairs, banged into another of the fat old women and spun round to find herself on the pavement facing Inge, clutching the black-faced doll.

"How could you?" Inge said. "How could you?"

They never spoke again.

She held the doll tightly all the way home.

If she had her way they'd never part.

Was there another earthly creature as low as Méret Voytek?

§14

A week after the Anschluss the youth orchestra assembled for its nine a.m. Monday morning rehearsal.

There were three notable absences: Doktor Judt, the conductor; Inge Reiter, viola . . . and all the other Jewish musicians.

In Doktor Judt's place stood another *doktor*—Doktor Sauerwald, who introduced himself as the Reich commissar for the city of Vienna. In turn, he introduced their new conductor, Professor Kaiserman. They all knew Kaiserman; he'd stood in for Judt on numerous occasions and taught piano at the Konservatorium where many of the musicians were studying. He wasn't Judt, who wooed them, coaxed them, badgered them, berated them—all with a twinkle in his eye—but he would do. They would get on with Kaiserman.

"You will not miss the Jews," Sauerwald said to no response.

"Vienna is a resourceful city, a city of talent—your new conductor will fill these empty seats with good Aryan musicians."

It was obvious why they'd sacked Judt—the man was far too liberal to be tolerated by the Nazis in a position of influence over youth. It was less obvious where they'd find "good Aryan musicians"—the absence of the Jews put their numbers down by more than a third.

"From this moment on you are all enrolled in the Hitler Youth; from this moment on you are musicians of the Third Reich!"

From this moment on they were a part orchestra. Dressing them in brown wouldn't make them whole.

Sauerwald gave Kaiserman the stage and left. Kaiserman endeared himself to his young musicians at once by saying, "It's all right. You won't have to wear the uniforms except when the party needs an orchestra."

This broke the silence. Everyone talked at once. Méret found herself wondering why or when the Nazi party would ever have need of an orchestra.

Kaiserman took several minutes to regain control—but with both arms in the air and the palms of his hands horizontal, dipping, patting the air with a gentle motion, he conducted the remnants of his orchestra back to silence. He pointed at a boy who played second violin. The boy stood up.

"Herr Professor, where will we find these musicians?"

"I don't know."

"Where will we find musicians as good as Lasky or Beidermann or Kaitz or Blumenfeld?"

"I don't know that, either."

By mid-April they were up to strength again, without being up to par. The newcomers were treated by their fellow musicians as second-raters until they could prove otherwise. And by the end of April the uniforms of the Hitler Youth and the Bund Deutscher Mädel, in which Méret found herself idly enlisted, had been issued. It created another division to add to that between first- and second-rate—those who wore the uniform unasked, those who wore it only when asked, and the bold few who would not wear it when asked.

Among the latter was Roberto Cacciato. A club foot—one leg an inch shorter than the other, and a thick sole added to his left boot—made him, he argued, unfit for and hence exempt from any military service. Why therefore should he wear a uniform of any kind? He wore instead the unofficial uniform of the proletariat—the navy pea jacket and the round cap with a small peak. A modest if unsubtle statement that in any other organization in the Reich would have cost him a beating.

The first time she was asked, Méret donned the uniform. She could be happy in a white blouse and a black skirt. Only the jacket rankled. The usual SA baby-shit brown with the usual red, white, and black swastika on the arm. Taking her seat among the cellists she caught sight of Roberto, defiantly working-class blue. He winked at her. He read her mind it seemed. This was her Knobloch moment. He knew it, she knew it. This was what she did to survive.

§15

At home she practiced what Viktor Rosen had taught her on an 1859 Bösendorfer upright. A piano made in Vienna—a piano forever associated with Vienna. This particular specimen was well-travelled. Her great-grandfather had had it shipped new to Budapest, her grandfather had brought it back with him when he settled in Vienna some thirty years later, and her father had had it lugged around the city from apartment to apartment as his fortunes improved.

"One more move and we might have room for a grand," he would say every so often, although not lately.

Méret reminded him early on that Bösendorfer made the largest grand piano in the world, with ninety-seven keys.

"Oh, we'll knock down a wall or something. We'll do without a bathroom and piddle in the street with the urchins."

"Papa!"

He wouldn't dare say anything so rude except when her mother was out.

She was out now. Méret was at the piano, running through scales. Her father was wandering around, slitting open his mail from the third post of the day with a paper knife, often as not discarding the letter and keeping the envelope.

Her mother came in. Groceries in a small wicker basket, followed by the maid—more groceries in a large wicker basket.

Her father was halfway through a sentence—"My dear, did you remember . . ."—when he noticed the red, white, and black swastika brassard on her arm and on the maid's.

"Have you taken leave of your senses!?!"

Her mother's hand wrapped around the swastika, much the same gesture Knobloch had used, but she was trying to conceal it, protect it.

"Have you gone mad, woman?"

"Imre, you don't understand. We cannot go down the street—"

He tore it off in a swift movement, lunged for the maid but she fled to the kitchen, screaming, and slammed the door.

Then her mother squared off to her father and slapped his face. And he slapped her back, so hard she stood rigid for a moment scarcely believing he had done this. Then the tears welled in her eyes, the red imprint of his hand spread out across her cheek, and a trickle of blood crept down from one nostril.

Imre went to the theatre for the night's performance and did not come back. He had a large couch in his office. By one in the morning, having listened for the sound of his return, Méret concluded he was using the couch to sleep on.

§16

She called on her father at the theatre on her way home from school the following day. She had not the words to say what she wished to say. She simply knew that she wanted to say something rather than go home to a continuation of last night's mood. Even if she said nothing her father would fill the silence—he always did—and she would listen. Perhaps they would even go home together.

She found him in the lobby, sitting alone at a table, the customary scattering of envelopes and papers, scribbles and doodles spread out in front of him, watching sadly as two workmen perched on trestles behind the bar whitewashed the goddess Artemis—golden breasts and red hair still very visible beneath the first thin coat.

She came up next to him quietly. Put a hand on his shoulder. He knew her touch and did not look up.

"Would they paint over a Titian?" he said. "The blue behind her head is surely the same colour as the sky in *Diana and Callisto*? Doesn't the Diana of the *Death of Actaeon* sit on a cloak of the same red on which our Artemis sprawls? Thank God I never had the money to buy a Picasso or we'd be watching that go under the whitewash, too."

The workmen shuffled their buttocks along to the end of their plank to begin a second coat of whitewash. Titian, Picasso. It was all the same to a five-inch brush and a roller. Imre stood up and put on his jacket.

"That's one of many things not to like about Nazis. We live in a world of infinite colours and they see everything in black and white."

"No, Papa. Brown and white."

Méret so rarely made jokes. It took her father a few seconds to realize she had actually said something funny. And then he laughed so loudly, the men on their plank turned to see what he was laughing at.

With his left hand he wiped his eyes and with his right handed her a letter from the office of the Reich commissar, Doktor Sauerwald.

"Here's another laugh for you. The buggers have sent me a list of plays I may not permit to be performed."

Méret glanced down the page.

"*A Midsummer Night's Dream?*"

"Oh, quite," said her father. "Definitely subversive. A cast of unruly working men and mischievous fairies. Trade unionists and anarchists."

"*A Doll's House?*"

"A woman's place is in the home? *Kinder, kirche, küche?* Don't look for logic. There isn't any. You mark my words it'll be music next. You'll find yourself stuck with an approved list of suitably Germanic composers."

Later that week, when Professor Kaiserman read out the approved list she was relieved to find that Bach, Haydn, and Mozart were on it. Stravinsky, Schoenberg, and Mahler were not.

The decadents and the Jews.

§ 17

On February 14, 1940, Méret turned sixteen and entered the Imperial Academy of Music—still known to all musicians as the Konservatorium.

She had never auditioned for anything before. The youth orchestra had taken her on the strength of her first recital with Viktor.

She emerged from the audition having been politely told she was accepted. She found the reserve, the lack of response in the selection panel, disturbing.

"They'd never applaud a student," Magda Ewald (trombone) told her. "It simply wouldn't do. But I can tell you now old Hoffmann was almost in tears and Professor Magnes had to sit on her hands to stop herself clapping. You're not just 'in,' Méret, you're 'it.'"

"It?"

"Oh, don't be so dense . . . don't make me fish around for a metaphor . . . you're Viktor Rosen's protégée . . . that should be 'it' enough. Were they ever going to turn down Viktor Rosen's protégée?"

"Do you really think they remember Viktor?"

Magda didn't answer. It was a stupid question.

The unstupid question, the only question that mattered, occurred unuttered to both of them.

Where is Viktor Rosen now?

§18

June 1940
Heaven's Gate Internment Camp
Port Erin, Isle of Man

It felt like going on holiday. His suitcase packed for a summer week by a lake in Hungary with his parents. It wasn't a holiday. It was one prison to another. As prisons went Szabo had liked Heaven's Gate. It had been home for six months. Ever since the British declared him an enemy alien and stuck him on a train to Liverpool last November. Hungary hadn't joined the Axis. It would, inevitably—under Hitler's wing Hungary had seized its slice of Czechoslovakia, had swallowed the Subcarpathian Rus whole after but a single day of independence. It hadn't joined yet, but it would. He had had the misfortune to be born in Vienna—capital of the Austro-Hungarian Empire, that other "sick man of Europe"—an empire that had dissolved itself before the last war had even finished, when he was just a boy. Many of his fellow prisoners were Viennese. He had family in Vienna—great aunts, aunts, uncles, and cousins—and had visited it many times in his childhood. "Viennese" was not a badge he would wear with any pride—it was an inappropriate label not worth the effort it took to shrug it off.

Once, a guard had asked, "Hungries, Austrians, Krauts. Wossa difference, then?"

He had replied in Magyar, a language few Englishmen had ever heard and which resembled no other language in Europe.

"Wossat mean then? That ain't no German."

"It means—Hungary is a large, faraway country of which you know fuck all."

He had liked Heaven's Gate. He had not gone hungry, no one had hit him, no one had even shouted at him. He had found time to practice his flute. He had found time to study, although not the texts or materials he needed to study, so study had perhaps become merely reading. Not the same thing by any stretch. He had arrived utterly ignorant of the work of Dornford Yates and P.G. Wodehouse and was leaving thinking of them as an important insight into the lives and mores of his captors —the English.

Arthur Kornfeld—the real Viennese—came in and threw himself down on the cot that Szabo had just stripped back to mattress and pillow.

"I know where you're going."

"How many cigarettes did that cost you?"

"None. I just asked Jenkins. Far too decent even to think of hinting at a bribe."

"Decency? It will be the death of men like Lieutenant Jenkins."

Kornfeld bounced up again like a jack-in-the-box.

"Karel, do you have no curiosity about your own fate? I tell you I know and you launch a debate on the English character!"

"Australia," Szabo said simply. "It's bound to be Australia."

"Well, you're wrong. You've got the wrong pink bit. All the others are going to Australia. You're going to Canada. A ferry back to Liverpool, then a ship to Canada."

Szabo unhooked his overcoat from the back of the door and draped it across his suitcase. All his actions saying "ready" and frustrating Kornfeld.

"I'm sure they have their reasons," he said almost casually.

"I'd be more inclined to say they have a plan."

43

"Plan? No, Arthur. If they had a plan they would never have locked us up. We were far more use to them in universities and laboratories than we ever were here. Do you think they even know what a nuclear physicist does? Do you think they've even heard of Schrödinger or Dirac?"

"Depends on who you mean by *they*. The home secretary? The prime minister? Probably not. Jenkins, our immediate captor—he only knows because we've told him, and he's logged it in what passes loosely for his mind because it might come in handy for filling in a crossword puzzle some day. But somewhere out there somebody knows and pretty soon they'll realize who we are . . . what we are . . . what we have . . . what we know. Think of them as children. Think of Europe as the drawing room and England as the kindergarten of Europe. They are innocents. They actually boast of not having been invaded since 1066. When in fact all that means is that they have lived outside of the mainstream of Europe. They are innocents."

"Innocents or blunderers. And can we trust either to win this war?"

"Trust me. They have a plan."

Szabo looked out of the window. A charabanc was parked on the tarmacadam that had been the rounders court when Heaven's Gate had been a girls' school. He surely did not have long now.

"Why do people say 'trust me'? Simply to ask for something or state something implies trust, as trust is the basis of such intercourse. But to emphasize trust implies distrust. Invokes distrust. Saying 'trust me' has the opposite effect. It begets distrust. Saying 'trust me' means you cannot trust me. As certainly as, 'I will still respect you in the morning,' means that I most certainly will not."

"You know, Karel, I do hope you find good company on the ship. A week with no one to listen to your aphorisms will drive you insane."

Down on the tarmac, Lieutenant Jenkins had appeared with a clipboard, wearing his uniform, as Kornfeld had once so pithily put it, "thrown on like a couple of potato sacks." He was gazing around in his habitual lackadaisical way in the hope that someone would turn up without him having to go and look for them. He didn't need to scratch his head; metaphorically, Jenkins was always scratching his head. And even at this distance Szabo could hear the soft sighs of bafflement and exasperation. The clipboard surely held a list of names. And his name was surely on that list. He would not keep Jenkins waiting. The thought that the fate of Europe lay in the hands of Englishmen like Rowly Jenkins and Bertie Wooster was an awful prospect.

§19

There was no quiet interlude. Only a day after the interned had departed for Douglas, Liverpool, and the waiting boats for Canada or Australia, a new lot arrived. Tired, baffled, scared.

As ever, Max Drax staged a welcome, effusive and insistent in the same airy breath of Old World charm.

They dragged one of the dining tables into the hall—a desk for Kornfeld to set his papers on. Not that Kornfeld gave a damn, but Drax was adamant that in the absence of anything resembling proper records on the part of the British, they should keep their own.

"Once, we were a tribe," he had said, speaking as a Jew.

"Once, we were a nation," he had said speaking as a German.

"Now we are a family."

And it had fallen to Kornfeld, neither Jew nor German but willing to accept the broad strokes of Drax's brush, to keep the documents of the family album up to date. It had also fallen to him to keep them dry.

Oskar Siebert, an exiled Viennese policeman who had been there longer than any of them—hard, after all, to convince anyone that you might be the one Viennese cop not actually in the Nazi party—had his share of the table taken up with a row of teacups and the largest teapot in the history of catering, and was relishing a trick he had learnt from the endless battalions of English women, who poured tea at every opportunity, of lining up the cups and pouring a continuous stream of tea. Alas, it was not a lesson he had learnt well.

Suddenly, he heard a ghost speak.

The dying words of Goethe.

45

"Mehr licht!"

But it was only old Drax asking someone to throw the light switch as the first of the newcomers came in from the breaking storm.

A huge man, six foot two or more, in a crumpled Savile Row suit that showed its class through every crease, seemed to be leading a motley of twenty or so.

Drax addressed him, as he did every arrival until experience taught otherwise, in German.

The big man replied in flawless English that he was, "fine with English," and Kornfeld readily deduced that this was yet another long-term resident, doubtless convinced of his own Englishness, caught in the net of a foreign birth and contradictory truths. They were getting more common. And they always led. Some with a belligerent resentment, others with a calm affability that told everyone—Wops, kikes, and Krauts —that it was all "cricket" and everything would be alright "by close of play." He'd come to think of it as the modus operandi of men like Lieutenant Jenkins. And this man was one of those.

"I'm Rod Troy," he said. "Of Hampstead."

Drax intervened, introduced Kornfeld, explained the purpose of keeping records, and asked, gently, insistently, if he would not mind stating for said records his origins.

Troy was not offended in the slightest.

He called out across Drax to Kornfeld, "I'm Rodyon Troy, from Vienna. I think you'll find quite a few of us are."

Now Drax was shaking his hand, a joyous two-handed grip, and Kornfeld found himself facing the other kind of English foreigner—the belligerent. Short, surly, saturnine.

"Abel Jakobson. Danzig. Now, where's me bleedin' tea?"

Siebert pushed a cup in his direction, glanced at Kornfeld, eyes rolling momentarily, sarcastically, to heaven.

"Right here, Danzig. Hot and wet as they say in your part of London."

"What part o' London might that be?"

"Oh . . ." Siebert feigned thinking. "Whitechapel or Stepney. Not far off the Mile End Road I shouldn't wonder."

"You're a smartarse, ain't yer?"

"I should say I am."

"An' a copper, too, if I ain't mistaken?"

"Touché, Herr Stepney. Touché."

Kornfeld moved on to the only part of this process that remotely interested him. The assembly of his string quartet. They had lost their second violin when Anton Bruch had departed on the same train as Szabo.

"Do you by any chance play the violin?"

But Abel Jakobson did not.

Nor did the skinny man with the big ears who stood next in line. "Josef Hummel, Vienna. I play nothing."

A gentle man with a troubled face, followed by another belligerent. A man as well dressed as Troy, almost rippling with wealth and dignity, but with little of his patience.

There was something vaguely familiar about his face. No . . . not vaguely, something precisely familiar . . . the only thing eluding him was the name.

"Viktor Rosen. Berlin. I play the piano and I play it better with sugar in my tea."

§20

Szabo spent a week under canvas in the Liverpool borough of Huyton. It appeared to be some sort of housing project, commandeered by the military, crudely fenced off with barbed wire and stuffed full of wogs. As the interned entered, the council workmen had left. The neat, semidetached houses had walls and roofs but neither doors nor windows. The English packed their captives in half a dozen to a room.

A near silent, oh-so-polite lance corporal—stopping short of calling him "sir"—showed Szabo to what might one day become the back lawn or, the English being English, the potato and cabbage patch of this unfinished house, and pointed at a small green tent.

"Is that it?" Szabo said.

"'Ouses is full. 'Slutely chocca."

"Supposing it rains?"

47

A voice behind them chipped in, "Then I'll bring you an umbrella."

A lieutenant of he knew not what regiment. A carbon copy of Rowly Jenkins—good grief, did they make them on a production line like Ford cars?—scruffy, déshabillé, simply oozing that familiar mixture of class and incompetence. The scientist in Szabo hated it. The flautist warmed to it at once. It would be as well to get to know him. Who knew how long he'd have to live in a tent.

"Karel Szabo," he held out his hand and had no truck with the past tense. "I teach physics at Cambridge."

The officer shook.

"Rupert Feather. I read history at Cambridge. But don't ask me anything about it. Can't remember a damn thing. Even been known to get the date of the Battle of Hastings muddled up."

"Muddled up with what?"

Feather hooted with laughter.

The lance corporal didn't even smile and Szabo readily deduced that England was always at war. Not necessarily with Germany but with itself.

Two nights later it rained. Dripped through the ancient canvas and down the back of his neck.

Entirely to Szabo's surprise, about half an hour before dusk, Feather showed up with an umbrella.

"You know," he said, "you're one of the lucky ones."

"How so?"

"Tent to yourself when other buggers are crammed into rooms like sardines into tins."

"I'll try to remember that."

At the end of the week, the lance corporal led half a dozen Tommies around the camp, yelling, "Bound for South Australia"—banging on walls and shaking on tent poles.

Szabo had had enough of tents, enough of England. He stood with his suitcase packed hoping to be steered off to a ship, any ship, regardless of what Kornfeld had told him about Canada. What did it matter? Canada? Australia? The pink bits on the map.

But Lieutenant Feather pulled him out of the line with, "Not you, old son. You're one of the lucky ones."

"You keep telling me that. I find it hard to believe."

"Canada for you."

"When?"

"Dunno. And if I did I couldn't tell you."

"Then let me go to Australia. It is warm. It is dry."

"Sorry. No can do."

But the next morning he called in person, bending double under the tent flap.

"It's today. You're off."

"Don't tell me," said Szabo. "I'm one of the lucky ones."

§21

The SS *Harlech* sailed for Canada on July 3, 1940. Two thousand prisoners and, it seemed, almost as many crew and guards, steaming westward in the shadow of a Royal Navy destroyer.

They had cleared the coast of Donegal. An army captain in charge of their guards addressed as many as could fit into the main dining room of the ship.

He was nervous, not in the "oh crikey" diffident manner that hid anything real that men of his class wanted hidden, but shot through with something Szabo perceived as akin to shock.

"I have news."

He looked down at the small piece of paper in his right hand. Looked up again. Szabo could almost swear there were tears forming in the corners of his eyes.

"I have really quite awful news. The *Dorset Castle,* which sailed from Liverpool for Australia yesterday, with, as I'm sure you all know, many detainees . . ."

For God's sake man, just spit it out.

"With . . . er, many detainees on board . . . er . . . was torpedoed in the North Atlantic and went down . . . with, er . . . considerable loss of life . . ."

Whatever he had to say next was swamped in the uproar that followed, so he filled his lungs, voice breaking along with his heart and yelled, "As many as half are thought to have drowned."

Through the hubbub, through the torrent of grief, Szabo heard his "I am sorry, I am so sorry." And he knew the truth of the platitudes uttered by men like Rowly Jenkins and Rupert Feather. He was indeed one of the lucky ones.

That night, lucky once more in that he had a bottom bunk, Szabo listened as two men on top conversed across the foot-wide aisle that separated their bunks.

"Linsky. For sure Linsky was one."

"He was. And both the Meyer brothers."

"Spiegelmann, and that little fellow we met in the barracks in Suffolk."

"Zuckermann. His name was Zuckermann."

"*Ja*. Nathan Zuckermann."

"*Und* . . . Gottlieb."

"Big Gottlieb or little Gottlieb?"

"The little one, Amos Gottlieb."

"Was not big Gottlieb his brother?"

"I think not. And . . . Berkovich, Halevi, Feinstein . . ."

"No. Not Feinstein. I saw him as we boarded today."

"Posner, Grossmann . . ."

It was the Jewish *Book of the Dead*. As they recited more and more names it became to Szabo like an abstract, vocal music, an opera in a language one had never learnt. A lullaby. And the Singers and the Shlombergs, the Gombergs and the Goldmanns, the Rubins and the Rosenblooms lulled him into sleep.

§22

Ontario resembled Finland. Szabo had never been to Finland but he had been fascinated by maps since he was a boy. Finland was a land of lakes. Ontario was a land of lakes. He just hadn't known it.

They had disembarked in Quebec, been robbed of anything worth stealing by the guards, and stuck on a train to Nipigon on the shores of Lake Superior, halfway to Winnipeg.

Szabo heard one detainee ask where they were and heard the guard reply, "India." And the look on the detainee's face showed not a hint of incredulity.

They moaned the loss of their possessions. Szabo had lost nothing. Anything of value had been stripped from him within forty-eight hours of his arrest back in November. He'd learnt to do without a wristwatch, and on the Isle of Man had learnt to tell the time just by looking at the sky. Robbed of his fountain pen he had made do with pencils. No one had ever thought fit to steal pencils from him.

Once on board the train each man received a cardboard box.

The man sat opposite Szabo—one of those who had endlessly recited the list of the dead, and whose name, he had learnt, was Fettermann, shook his box. It rattled.

"Perhaps the Canadians have seen fit to return my grandfather's pocket watch, and the silver bands with which I used to hold up my shirtsleeves."

But it was food—food in generous amounts. Cheese, fruit, onions, sardines, bread—a tin mug and a knife-fork-and-spoon combination that clipped together over a central rivet to form an object that Man Ray or Marcel Duchamp might have labeled and exhibited as "*trouvé.*"

"What," said Fettermann, "is this? A foon? Or a snife?"

"Enough," said his friend, "for each to slit his throat. Welcome to the New World."

"Ah, a final train ride to death, but at least the cutlery shall match."

Later, nightfall. Bunk beds lowered on chains, clean sheets, hot water from a stove. It was, he knew, better by far than the conditions back in Liverpool.

Fettermann looked at him, smiling as he rinsed his face, knowing, too, that he was better off, sighing with the pleasure of it all.

"Welcome to the New World," Szabo said.

"At last he speaks!"

Almost three days later they arrived at Nipigon. A mining camp swathed in barbed wire . . . devoid of beds, blankets, furniture. Bleak in summer, unimaginable in winter.

"Welcome to the New World," Fettermann rippled with irony.

But he was wrong. Only days later, truckloads of tables and chairs arrived. Beds, blankets, towels . . . and food by the box load. More food than Szabo had seen since the last time he ate at high table in his Cambridge college. Canada might not roast you a swan, but it would slay you the fatted calf.

Sitting down to a lunch of steak on white bread, oozing butter, with fried tomatoes, pickled gherkins, and mustard, Szabo felt certain Fetterman would repeat the by now habitual cliché.

Instead, he said, "One cannot help but wonder what the catch is."

Suspicious by nature or distrustful by experience, it was weeks before they came to accept that there was no catch. The only catch was to be in Canada itself. To be imprisoned in Canada. To be imprisoned in Canada and to partake of its abundance from behind barbed wire.

Fetterman found a new catchphrase. Every box he opened was greeted with the words, "O, Canada."

Bees buzzed in cigarette trees, over lemonade springs while hens laid soft-boiled eggs and a bluebird sang on the big rock-candy mountain.

O, Canada.

No lake of gin, no whisky flowing down the mountainside, but the inventive among them soon built a still and made a tolerable vodka from potatoes—while the enterprising among them reopened the mine's metalwork shop and turned out iron crosses and swastikas to sell to their gullible captors, who, after all, assumed that they were all Nazis anyway.

O, Canada.

§23

There was a uniform that nobody wore. A silly, flat hat, a grey jacket with a red circle seared into the back like a target, blue trousers with vivid red stripes along the seams. There seemed to be a shortage of matching clown shoes in the larger sizes.

Come September, the shortening days and plummeting temperatures at last reassured them all that it was indeed Canada and not India, and

Szabo took to wearing the jacket under his overcoat. At the beginning of October a young lieutenant—all long, skinny limbs and Adam's apple, the North American variation on Jenkins and Feather—came around to tell him to don the full uniform as he was wanted on the outside.

"Why?"

"I don't get told things like that. Somebody in town wants to see you, and it's regulations that you wear the uniform when you leave camp. Makes it easier to spot you if you run."

"Run? There's three foot of snow out there."

"Okay. Makes it easier to spot you when you slide ass over tit. Who cares? Just put the damn thing on and I'll drive you downtown."

Downtown was a six-mile drive to what the Canadians referred to as the nearest city and what Szabo would scarcely have graced with the term "village."

In the lobby of the Statler, a three-storey, wooden Victorian hotel, every casement rattling in the wind, another young man was waiting. Well-dressed, well-groomed. A very different body type. No Jenkins, no Feather. A man bursting at the seams of his expensive suit with hard-earned muscle. A player of contact sports, all shoulders and knuckles, warming his hands over a potbellied stove the size of an elephant's arse. The hands paused in midair like a boastful fisherman. Then one extended to shake his, fingers fat as bratwurst.

"Ron Katzenbach. What can I get you? A year inside, I bet you could kill for a drink."

"Not quite," said Szabo. "But after homemade vodka, a drop of real bourbon wouldn't come amiss."

The lieutenant perked up at this, and then perked down again as Katzenbach said, "Lieutenant, would you give us the room?"

The lieutenant looked around. They were the only people there.

"I get it," he said, getting it far too slowly. "Spook stuff."

"How elegantly you put it. Just give us half an hour."

He summoned a waiter, ordered bourbon on the rocks for the two of them.

"I hear you play the flute?"

It was a question, Szabo thought. The polite passing of the time of day until the waiter had done and departed. And it wasn't a question. Whoever this man was he'd read the file, and some more.

"They find you a flute to play?"

"They found me a ukulele," Szabo said.

"So, what did you do?"

"I learnt to play the ukulele," Szabo said flatly.

Katzenbach laughed loudly at this, his hands ferreting around in his pockets as though he had lost something, to produce a small black notebook such as a court reporter might use.

"You like Canada?"

Were they still chatting or had the turning of pages in the notebook brought them to the rub?

"One barbed-wire fence is much the same as another. I've seen next to nothing of Canada."

"Me, neither."

Szabo could not tell an American accent from a Canadian. But then again, who can?

Katzenbach went on, "In fact, this is my first time. Instead of seeing the sights I get to see a one-horse town in . . . where are we . . . Alberta?"

"You're not even close. We're still in Ontario. You can travel for *days* and still be in Ontario. Now, tell me. What does Uncle Sam want with me?"

The notebook lay flat in front of Katzenbach. They were definitely not chatting anymore.

"In 1937, you applied for a United States visa?"

"Did I? Thirty-six, thirty-seven. I really can't remember."

"It was January 1937."

"I'm sure you're right."

"You wanted to emigrate?"

"I had emigrated. I left Hungary in the summer of '29. In January '37, I was in London."

"You didn't like England?"

"I liked England very much. I simply needed a job and at that time I was having difficulty finding one. I filled out the forms. Handed them in at your embassy, and before I heard anything, King's College, Cambridge, offered me a fellowship. I didn't pursue the application. I don't recall that I ever heard from your people. The forms no doubt ended up in a wastepaper basket in Grosvenor Square."

Another pretence of patting down his own pockets and Katzenbach unfolded three pages of typed paper with handwritten entries and set them out on the table between them.

It was like seeing history turn full circle, the bread cast upon the waters. Almost moving.

"May I?"

"Sure."

The ink of his signature had turned brown with age and four years seemed to him like another lifetime.

He looked at his address—the boarding house in Primrose Hill where he had lived for the best part of a year—at the cramped handwriting as he had run out of space to summarize his career and credentials.

Katzenbach said, "I bet we did reply. Be damn rude not to. But if we didn't, let me apologize now and say, formally, that we are inclined to grant your request."

Szabo was grateful. He doubted it showed in his face. He was also slightly baffled, and rather thought that did. Sooner or later they'd want him—Kornfeld had been right about that—it was just that he'd resigned himself to it being later.

"I didn't pack my ukulele," he said.

Katzenbach smiled at this.

"It won't be today. It can't be today. You'll go back to the camp. I'll get some temporary accommodation set up, and then . . ."

A big hand with its fat fingers in the air, the sentence wafted away.

"And then you'll send for me?"

"No. Then I'll come and get you."

"To go where? Washington? New York?"

"Not so fast. It'll be Toronto. Then in the new year maybe we cross the border. It all depends."

"On what?"

"Oh, Dr. Szabo, you know I can't answer that."

§24

The young lieutenant chatted amiably all the way back, to monosyllabic answers from Szabo.

Over dinner—more inch-thick steak and a small hill of buttered spuds—Fettermann asked, "What was all that about? Do you suddenly have brothel privileges in town?"

Szabo could not resist the moment; one first, one last throwaway indiscretion.

"I shall be leaving you soon."

"For why?"

"Uncle Sam is building an atomic bomb."

Fetterman chewed on his beef. For all that he was skin and bone, he was an accomplished trencherman and never let his words get in the way of his grub.

"Before I was arrested (munch munch), before we met, I was a (munch munch) jeweller. For all I understood (munch munch), you just told me the moon is made of Wiener schnitzel. (Munch munch munch). Atomic, shmatomic. I should know?"

But that was the pleasure. The only people he could ever tell were those to whom it would be meaningless.

"Gideon, if it turns out that the moon is made of Wiener schnitzel, I shall be sure to bring you back a slice."

"Good. Beef is all very well. But you can have too much of a good thing."

Fetterman began to sing to the tune of an old Strauss waltz, "He's going to the moon, the moon, the moon. He's going to the moon."

And Szabo knew that old Fetterman would remember nothing of this.

§25

London: October 1940

Arthur Kornfeld and Viktor Rosen travelled up to London on the same train. Bureaucracy had messed them about. Granted their freedom, they had left the Isle of Man on the same boat as the two Stepney tailors—the belligerent Abel Jakobson, who preferred his anglicized Billy Jacks, and mild-mannered, big-eared Viennese refugee, Josef Hummel—but an identity check as they docked at Liverpool had split them up and Jacks and Hummel found themselves on an earlier train, Kornfeld and Rosen on a later.

"They might have waited," Kornfeld said.

"Why so bitter about it? We have just spent more than three months incarcerated with them. I in the same room as Jacks. You can count yourself lucky you didn't share with him. An opinion on everything. They probably no more want to chat to us on a four-hour train journey than I to them."

"I had thought better of it Viktor. I had thought better of us all. I had come to think of us as family."

He was not the only one.

Rod Troy met them at Euston. RAF blue and wings pinned to his chest. He'd been free since August.

"I just saw Joe and Billy, not more than an hour ago. I knew if I hung on I'd catch the two of you sooner or later. I can't hang about. I've a couple of questions and then I must dash. Are you okay for rooms?"

"Of course," Rosen replied. "I still have my apartment in Chelsea. It's been mothballed while I was at His Majesty's Pleasure. Arthur will spend a day with me before he goes down to Cambridge."

"Fine. Make that two days. I'm in town on RAF business but I've a forty-eight-hour pass starting tomorrow. Due back at base on Saturday evening. I've Saturday lunch arranged. You two, me, Billy, Joe—a reunion."

"But," said Rosen, "we have scarcely parted."

"You might have . . . I haven't clapped eyes on you blokes for two months. I want to hear Arthur and Joe dispense wisdom, I want to hear you play the piano, I want to hear Billy grumble about something . . . and I want you all to meet my little brother."

"Rod," Kornfeld said, "I really must get back to Cambridge. I'm sorry. I would love to—"

Rod clapped him on the shoulder.

"Another time, Arthur. There'll be plenty of other times. We'll make it into a regular reunion."

After he'd gone, in a taxi heading south to Chelsea, neither spoke until they had reached the bottom of Gower Street. Then Rosen said, "I didn't know he had a brother."

"Then Viktor, dare I say, you did not listen to the man. Rod is one to take the burden of the world upon his shoulders, and none more burdensome than this brother that peppers his conversation."

"Really? Can't say I noticed. Black sheep of the family I suppose?"

"*Au contraire*. Would you believe the boy is a Scotland Yard detective? Sergeant Troy?"

§26

"The boy" was an apt description. Sergeant Troy was clearly stamped from the same mould as Rod, but in miniature. Rod was six foot two or more, Rosen doubted the brother made five foot six—but he was dark in the way Rod was dark, with thick black hair, obsidian eyes, and a touch of the Slav about him that marked him out as being not-quite-an-Englishman. He looked about eighteen. He looked far too pretty to be termed handsome yet. He looked like the star of all those awful British B feature films that had been one of their inflicted entertainments on the Isle of Man: James Mason. He looked as though Rod had just dragged him up from sleep. And he was peppered with tiny scabs as though he had just survived an encounter with . . . with what? The answer was embarrassingly obvious, the man had been in an air raid. A reminder that "the boy" was, indeed, a serving police officer. Best not to ask.

He introduced himself—"Viktor Rosen. I play ze joanna"—to squeals of laughter from Hummel and a roaring guffaw from Rod and Billy Jacks, all too easily amused by his grasp of patois.

Somewhere in the cross-talk that followed, he heard young Troy say, "I heard you play in Berlin in 1929. You were playing Schumann."

And before Rosen could acknowledge this with the customary pleasantry, Rod had them all at the table—the refugees, his brother, his mother—and he talked no more to the younger Troy until the meal was over and host and guests affably pissed.

Rod's mother, Lady Troy, asked if he would play for her. Rosen had been expecting this and at idle moments had quietly worked out what he would play. He had a recollection of Rod telling him months ago that his mother had studied with Debussy.

She showed him into a room of powdery red walls, heavy red curtains, deeply upholstered red furniture—and a full Steinway grand piano. The rest traipsed in behind him, still pissed and giggly, but the first thing any pianist learns is how to shut an audience up with a look.

He played *Estampes,* music so liquid it all but puddled at his feet: *Pagodes, La Soirée dans Grenade, Jardins sous la pluie.* When he had finished, in the hiatus when he knew he had finished but his audience wasn't quite sure, he looked at Sergeant Troy and was almost certain he had fallen asleep. But his eyes opened, his hands met, and he led a soft round of applause.

An old man who had not been in the room when he first sat down came up and shook his hand.

"Alex Troy, paterfamilias. So glad I arrived home in time."

And he was gone before Rosen could say more.

Young Troy struggled to his feet.

"Are you okay?" Rosen asked.

"Bit of a bang on the head. Occupational hazard."

"You get hit often?"

"I suppose I do. But in this case it was a Luftwaffe high explosive. Brought the building down on my head and, in the matter of one small piece of masonry, I mean that literally."

He stumbled, Rosen caught him and sat him on the piano stool. He looked around for assistance but they were alone in the room now.

"I'll be fine," Troy said. "As I was saying, occupational hazard."

He shook himself, suddenly snapping into alertness.

Rosen probed gently.

"Your brother tells me you are no mean pianist yourself?"

"He flatters me. I was keen before I joined the force, but from then until this summer I lived without a piano in the house. I bought myself a Bösendorfer in June."

"And now you play again?"

"It was . . . an optimistic move. I play but . . ."

"Play for me now."

"Honestly, I couldn't."

"Please. In Berlin I had pupils, in Vienna I had pupils. Since I got to England there have been none. It was always a pleasure and a stimulus to me to work with pupils. I had a girl cellist who could move a stone statue to tears."

"Okay," said Troy. "But I warn you, London brick does not weep at the sound of my fingers on ivory."

He played Rosen a couple of minutes from the middle section of Ravel's *Gaspard de la nuit,* based on poems by some bloke whose name he'd forgotten—the only bit that was not punctuated by staccato, bone-tingling percussives. It was a bit wet, a bit Frenchy, a bit dreamy—but if Rosen liked *Estampes* he might well like this. And it had a good left hand. Troy liked a good left hand. He was left-handed. Ravel had even written a full-length concerto, left hand only, for some bloke, whose name he'd forgotten, who'd lost his right arm in the last war.

"You have talent," Rosen said when he had finished.

What else can one say to that but "thank you"?

"You practice every day?"

"No," said Troy. "I'm lazy that way."

"Then try to be less lazy some other way. Give a good talent a sporting chance. And come to me for lessons."

"Okay," said Troy. "I will."

But he didn't.

§27

Toronto: November 1940

Six weeks after their first meeting, Ron Katzenbach drove out to the camp and collected Szabo. He installed him in what the English would have called "digs." A room in a private home on Albany Street, a block south of Bloor, with a Scottish landlady who was dusting flour from hand to apron as she greeted him.

Leaving, Katzenbach said, "Get out and about. See something of the town. Just check in with the cops every Thursday morning."

"And if I make a run for it?"

"I can't think why you'd want to . . . But Mrs. Macleod will shoot you. Don't let cookies and clean sheets take you in. She works for Uncle Sam as surely as I do."

Szabo didn't doubt it.

He lodged with Mrs. Macleod for three months, ate everything she put in front of him, listened to her pining for the old country, and wondered where she hid her pistol.

On the coldest of winter nights—Toronto locked into a merciless iron snowball—she would serve him haggis and a nip. Haggis turned out not to be so baffling as the word suggested and with its minced offal boiled in a sheep's stomach it resembled in taste and sheer portability the *kokoretsi* he had been accustomed to in Hungary. A delicacy of both comfort and convenience. A nip turned out to be three fingers of scotch in a tumbler —and as he tuned out to Mrs. Macleod's Highland musings, he wondered if he would be a refugee forever, always thinking of food before anything else, and whether the life of the mind would ever be restored to its rightful place ahead of the life of the belly. He was warm and well fed, but his mind was numb.

O, Canada.

Towards the end of February, Katzenbach showed up again. Another of Uncle Sam's nephews in tow. An utterly different kind of nephew.

This one seemed scarcely to fill his suit. A lean, bright-eyed young man, about Szabo's own age, with a cold, bony handshake.

"Dr. Szabo, I'm Ed Donnelly."

Szabo gripped the hand a moment too long, and Donnelly responded by leaning in toward him as though anticipating a shared confidence.

"Are we building an atomic bomb, Mr. Donnelly?"

Szabo let go. Donnelly drew back sharply but he was smiling as he opened his briefcase and slid papers out onto Mrs. Macleod's burnished dining table.

"You'll have to forgive me, Dr. Szabo, but I must answer a question with a question. Is Germany building an atomic bomb?"

Katzenbach stepped in.

"Why don't we all sit down?"

It bought the two of them a heartbeat and more.

"I haven't been in Germany in a long time," Szabo said.

"But you lived there? You worked there?"

"Yes, for almost four years. But I left when Hitler came to power in 1933."

"At the same time as Edward Teller and Leo Szilard?"

The mention of names was resonant. Another piece of the picture spun through space and time and fell into place. He'd worked with both in Berlin. He couldn't abide Teller. Almost exactly the same age as himself, quite possibly a genius, but prone to infighting and rivalry—a limping little toad as Szabo had quickly come to think of him. Szilard was ten years older, a friend and a mentor. The physicist's physicist.

"Yes," he said. "On the same day; in fact, the same train as Leo Szilard."

"But . . . you're not Jewish."

"I don't think one has to be Jewish to recognize the threat. Leo and I saw eye to eye on that. Germany was hell bent on dominating Europe. It was time to leave. I could not go home, after what I'd seen in my youth . . . Budapest switching from empire to soviet to fascist in a matter of weeks, and so little to tell the one from the other. I spent six months in Vienna. I never thought Austria would be much of an obstacle to Nazism, but it took those six months for me to realize they'd probably collaborate with it. Then, two years in Paris . . . on to England . . . a story you surely know by now."

"Dominate Europe?"

"Yes."

"So . . . is Germany building an atomic bomb?"

He wasn't sure where Teller was now, but Szilard had been at Columbia University, in New York, since 1938. This, whatever it was, was Leo's doing.

"Why don't you ask Leo?"

"I did. He said to ask you."

It finally broke the ice. Szabo smiled, Donnelly laughed, and the infection spread. Katzenbach laughed without quite knowing what he was laughing at.

"Yes, Mr. Donnelly. Germany is building an atomic bomb. Most Western countries have the know-how, as you might put it . . . and Hitler loves his toys . . . they've had access to ample supplies of radium since they took the Sudentenland and they banned the export of uranium a while back. I think that's all the evidence you need . . . but . . . ."

"But?"

"It won't work."

"How come?"

"A lack of talent . . . perhaps a lack of will."

"Really? From here it looks like they have both, in spades."

"They have Heisenberg. They could have had Teller, Szilard, and a dozen others, but Teller and Szilard are here."

"And so are you."

"And so am I. Somewhat reluctantly."

"So . . . why won't it work?"

"When I say *will* I might better say *resources,* or perhaps *focus.* There might be an incompatibility of aims. Perhaps winning the war is incompatible with the chosen goal."

"Which is?"

"To kill the Jews."

"And killing Jews is what . . . a kind of false focus . . . a drain on resources?"

"Both of those and more. It is a factory of death when they should be building a factory of . . . of atoms."

"Factory of death. That's a metaphor, right? You don't actually think they're industrializing the killing of Jews?"

63

"I say again. I left Germany in 1933. At that time the Nazis seemed to think that physics itself was some form of Jewish black magic. I don't know what they're up to. I simply know of what they are capable."

Donnelly mused on this a moment, turning a rubber-tipped pencil end over end on the tabletop.

"That's really politics. So, tell me straight. Tell me as a scientist. Why won't it work?"

"Heisenberg's ideas will prevail in Germany. He is wedded to the use of tritium. They will obtain this from deuterium reactions. But the ratio of tritium to deuterium is very low. Germany will waste time and money trying to produce large quantities of heavy water, as a neutron moderator and, hence, a source of small quantities of tritium. I cannot say it will be useless to them. But it is the long way 'round. And we should not concern ourselves with it. Building heavy water reactors would be an . . . an indulgence. An indulgence the Germans have not even begun— they seem to be relying on a conquered Norway to supply their heavy water. The bomb that will work most readily is uranium-235 triggered by more uranium-235. That, too, is scarce and needs to be isolated from uranium-238 at a ratio of greater than one hundred to one. There are several ways we could do this—chemical diffusion, electromagnetic separation, and at a pinch, thermal diffusion. None of them easy. But if we start now . . . and when we need neutron moderation, the process can be moderated by pure graphite or at least as pure as we can make it— that's free from boron. We can get around to the tritium later. Right now we need about six or seven kilos of pure uranium isotope. And I'm sorry to have lectured you."

"Six or seven kilos? That's a lot less than many of your colleagues are saying."

"A little more than fourteen pounds, in two unequal portions, brought together with sufficient impact."

"You mean just slam the two together? Hit one chunk of uranium with another chunk?"

Donnelly gently punched the fist of his right hand into the open palm of his left, like a baseball catcher with a mitt.

"If you like," Szabo said.

"As Old World as an ironclad firing a cannonball."

"Not quite, but a pleasing simile."

Donnelly spread the papers out in a fan in front of him. Szabo recognized the familiar buff covers, the hand-cut octavo paper with its tactile ragged edges. His last paper at Cambridge, mailed off that day in 1939 when he was interned—and there were even a couple he'd written for *Die Naturwissenschaften* and *Zeitschrift für Physik* when he was scarcely out of his teens.

"I read a couple of your papers."

Of course he had; for all his diffidence this man was a pro. Not a practicing physicist, but a keen observer.

"The paper on heavy water seems almost personal, as though you had it in for Heisenberg?"

The truth would be such a long answer, so Szabo shrugged the question off with a white lie.

"Not so, I hardly know the man."

"And the paper on uranium-235 and particle collision is impressive but somewhat inconclusive."

"Inconclusive?"

"I thought you . . . kinda pulled your punches at the end."

"By which you mean I did not assert what I did not know to be true."

"Stick your neck out, Dr. Szabo. You're among friends here. And besides, Ron doesn't understand a damn thing, do you, Ron?"

Ron was mid lighting up a cigarette and froze with the flame on his lighter hovering at the end of his Camel.

"Understand? Hell, I wasn't even listening."

Szabo said, slowly, almost pedantically, "The absorption of additional neutrons by uranium-235, under particle bombardment, will lead us into unknown areas. You might say that that's what physics does. Neutron absorption has been an accepted notion since Enrico Fermi first proved radiative capture about five years ago. It's the key to the next unknown. At the time I was writing, the product of such experiments as Fermi's tended to be regarded as isotopes of uranium or mistaken for lighter elements, and the possibility of a chain reaction was something even Leo Szilard, its earliest proponent, referred to as 'moonshine.' Until January 1939, no one was certain that nuclear fission was possible—the term itself did not exist. I was trying to state, perhaps too cautiously for clarity, my conviction that there were—or would be—distinct transuranic elements, products of fission, and to point out where this was leading. I was not the first to suggest this and I gather while I've been interned—after all, the people censoring my mail tend not to censor what they cannot understand—that there has been proof, a new element: atomic number 93, named neptunium, discovered only last year. But it's unstable. The beta decay is very rapid—the half-life not much more than two days. I was theorizing something much more dramatic. Something of enormous power—with the potential for fission in a sustained chain reaction. And if I'm right . . . in a sense, it'll take us back to the creation. Moonshine or not, there'll be something new under the sun."

"Such as?"

Szabo was reluctant to cross every *T* and dot every *I* but did.

"Another new element, with properties unseen in nature. Beyond uranium. Something man has synthesized. Something highly radioactive. Not an isotope of any known element. A new addition to the periodic table."

"And highly fissile?"

"That, too."

"More so than uranium-235?"

"Yes."

"A bigger bang for your buck?"

"The buck is yours, not mine, Mr. Donnelly, but yes, a much bigger bang."

"I thought that was what you meant."

Donnelly stood, swept Szabo's published papers back into his briefcase.

"It was a pleasure meeting you, doctor. Ron will be making arrangements to move you to New York shortly."

The bony handshake once more. This time it was Donnelly who held on a moment too long and said, sotto voce, "You were right, by the way."

He was halfway out of the door before Szabo could say, "You mean they've found it? The new element?"

Donnelly turned, tugging on the brim of his hat.

"Yep."

"If it's not a secret . . . who?"

"It *is* a secret, but it was Glenn Seaborg at Berkeley."

It was a silly question, a trivial question of no importance to science, but he had to ask, "What did Seaborg call it?"

"He hasn't yet. You care to take a crack at it?"

"That would be presumptuous."

"Nah . . . if the British hadn't locked you up . . . who knows, it coulda been you."

Indeed it could. And he doubted anyone would name an element seaborgium.

"After uranium and neptunium, plutonium would seem rather obvious."

"Until we run out of planets? Plutonium. I'll pass it on."

§28

Katzenbach put him on a train to New York.

"You'll be met at Penn station."

"How will I know them?"

"They'll know you."

As the train pulled away, Szabo stood in the window. Katzenbach cupped his hands and yelled, "All that genius and you name the fucking thing after Mickey Mouse's dog!"

So, he had been listening after all.

§29

New York: January 1941

It had been an uncomfortable ten-hour journey across New York state to turn sharply down the Hudson Valley. He could picture it better. October or November, at leaf fall or spring. Niagara had been a distant roar and a miasmic spray. January had rendered most of Upstate New

York, the river plain between the Catskills and the Adirondacks, featureless. And the evening mist had turned the Hudson Valley into a grey blur. He could see himself taking the trip for pleasure one day, if only to compensate for there having been none this time.

Penn Station was wonderful. British railway stations tended to have all the divine madness of Piranesi hammered out in steel and meandering off into nowhere, labyrinths of footbridges and walkways in the sky, as chaotic as their cities. This was neoclassic steel, an intricate, ordered latticework supporting arches, domes, and vaults—the old forms of masonry freely interpreted by the seemingly fragile elements of what had so recently been a new technology. It was like watching time bend. The railway passenger in him moved forward; the scientist in him looked up in awe, turned upon his heels and walked backwards bumping into people unapologetically—until one them didn't move grudgingly out of his way and dynamic physics's corniest law came into play . . . the old immoveable object.

He had been expecting Leo Szilard.

This wasn't Leo Szilard.

For one thing she was too tall, for another too beautiful, and for a third she was she.

"Hello, Karel. It's been an age, hasn't it?"

She kissed him lightly on one cheek, even as he was wrestling her name from the depths of consciousness.

Zette Borg. The low-temperature physicist from his days in Cambridge. Zette Borg—known by all the men as the Ice Queen, but less for her specialization than for her nature. Americans would not be so coy—he'd bet they called her a ball breaker.

"Zette. How good of you to meet me."

Of course Leo would recruit her. It made sense. The low-temperature people, once you got them off their obsession with absolute zero, knew as much about particle behaviour as anyone.

It had been an age. He struggled to remember when. Many, most, of his colleagues had gathered around him when he had been told he would be interned in 1939. Had she been one of those?

"Leo's rather tied up this evening. He'll join us later if he can. If not . . . *a domani.*"

68

She slipped one arm through his and steered him firmly through the waiting room to the cab ramp.

"Forty-fourth and Broadway," she told the driver.

She settled back. Szabo could not settle. Everything was a question. He could ask a thousand questions if she let him.

"Is that where we work? Or where we live?"

"Neither. I've a table for two booked at Sardi's. I figured the first thing you'd want is a decent meal."

Figured. How very American. *Meal* . . . how very . . . how very refugee . . . the life of the belly.

O, Canada.

O, America.

O, Manhattan.

§30

He'd seen nothing like Sardi's since his last visit to Vienna. If London had anything like this—a crowded room decked with the detritus of showbiz, buzzing with the bustle of Broadway—he hadn't found it—or, more precisely, no one had bothered to show it to him. His English colleagues took him to their clubs and professional bodies the Athenaeum or the Royal Society, and on one bizarre occasion the Swedenborg Society—rather than restaurants. There was one London club devoted to the theatre— the Garrick—but he'd never been there and he doubted very much whether it had photographs of Greta Garbo and Myrna Loy on the walls or whether it served cannelloni.

Sardi's was alive. He'd been in London clubs where he could swear none but the waiters were. And he remembered a novel by Dorothy somebody or other—there'd been a copy in the makeshift library in the Ontario camp—in which a London club member dies in his leather armchair, clutching his scotch and soda and his copy of *The Times*, and no one notices for two days.

"Stop grinning and order!"

He snapped to to find himself holding a Sardi's menu and being gently berated by the most beautiful woman he'd ever seen.

"Anyway, what's so funny?" she added.

"The English," he replied.

She looked around and said a little too loudly, "Well, I bet there are none of the buggers in here tonight. And I never found them funny for a moment."

By the main course she was ready to talk shop. She never used the words *nuclear, fission,* or *bomb,* but it occurred to Szabo that they could probably discuss the assassination of J. Edgar Hoover and not be overheard in the hubbub.

"Leo is trying to gather the Oxbridge team around him. He wants Rudolf Peierls—who somehow managed to escape internment. And he wants Hermann Bondi, who didn't. They came for Hermann about six months after they came for you. The silly sods. Just when I thought that sort of nonsense had stopped, they had another push and rounded up every Italian chef in London and the finest minds in Cambridge. By June, you couldn't put tomato sauce on your neutrinos for love or money."

It hadn't been a team. Too disparate for that. It was perhaps an invisible web of ideas, of exchange. She was being, dare he think it, sentimental. He doubted she ever felt that way about an individual.

"Hermann is here," he said.

"Here? Where?"

"I meant in Canada. I don't know where. We didn't get sent to the same camp. But he was on the boat coming over."

"Then I'm sure Leo will find him. Meanwhile, Peierls is back in England—probably determining the atomic weight of boiled cabbage or some such rot—when he should be with us."

"The last I heard, and admittedly I am out of touch, Peierls was designing a cyclotron. Hardly boiled cabbage"

"Don't be obtuse. You know what I mean. The English wouldn't let him work on radar because it was vital war work and he was German. As a matter of fact, he has citizenship now, and he's working on thermal diffusion, but I rather think that's only because they haven't a clue that this, too, might be vital war work. The English can be such idiots."

Szabo could not disagree with this, but Zette had a hatred of England that could not be shared or emulated by someone not born and brought up there.

§31

She had an apartment on West Seventy-third, just off Central Park, in the looming shadow of the Dakota building.

When Szabo asked where he might be staying, she took him home with her.

The fuck was passionate and heartless. She took him with a loud desperation. He was a machine—the rod to her cleft. After eighteen months and more of enforced celibacy he found it in him not to mind being ravished by beauty. His own desperation much the quieter.

§32

In the morning, she sat opposite him at the tiny kitchen table. A crimson terrycloth dressing gown up to her cheekbones, her hair lost in a high white spiral turban of towel. The most beautiful barber's pole in the world.

In all the camps he had been in there had been men whose sense of deprivation would express itself verbally after only a matter of hours. Interned for weeks, months even, one had to learn to turn off to the sexual fantasists for whom life without women was no life at all or else the welter of sexual imagery—so often begun as testament to virtue and beauty, and so soon descended to "what I wouldn't do to her if I got half a chance"—would bore and appal the most polite of listeners. Zette

71

Borg, devoid of all makeup, damp and staring into her coffee, was the stuff of wankers' dreams. What wouldn't the priapic internee do to her given the half chance? Probably what he had just done.

The smell of coffee, better by far than anything that had passed by that name in Canada or England, drew him out of his reverie.

"Do you know if Leo has made any arrangements for me to live or work?"

She looked up. He could almost swear she was smiling.

"Work? Well you're on the staff of Columbia University. In fact, I think you'll find at the end of the month that you've been on the payroll since the first of the month. American universities are generous. The equivalent of £1250 a year and you won't have to teach a thing. We none of us do. We pursue our livelihood in theories. Live? Usually they'd book you into the Taft hotel in Times Square. There's a Taft in every city. A bit like Woolworths or the Home and Colonial. It seems that when he wasn't busy being president, Mr. Taft opened hotels wherever he went. The one in Times Square is particularly bad. In fact it's a knocking shop."

"Knocking shop?"

"English slang for a brothel. It's *not* a brothel, of course. It's the sort of hotel to which you'd take a woman to whom you were not married. I rescued you from that."

"And now?"

"You might as well stay here."

Such diffidence. As though she might simply shrug and say "so what" if he opted for the knocking shop.

"I mean, it's not over till it's over, is it?"

She took her coffee and vanished once more into the bathroom.

Szabo wondered about the imprecision of "it."

§33

Leo Szilard chose to live in a hotel. Hotels supplied him with something that struck at the heart of the refugee sensibility—room service.

For tea, he chose the nearest thing he could find to a patisserie in the vicinity of Zette's apartment—on Columbus Avenue between Seventy-first and Seventy-second streets.

"They have this überphrase—" he told Szabo.

"Überphrase?"

"A catchall. It is *diner*. It can mean several things. At one extreme ham and eggs . . . 'sunnyside up' I understand—it's logical, graphic—'over easy' baffles me . . . at the other extreme *diner* might mean cake and tea. Never presume what *diner* means until you see their menu. That, and don't cross against the lights are all you need to know about life in New York."

"Really?"

"Oh, I was forgetting their coffee. I think it violates one of the laws of physics. One cannot see through real coffee down to the trademark on the bottom of the cup. It ought not to be possible, any more than one can see through the Large Magellanic Cloud. Yet the Americans have done this. After years of patient experiment they have made coffee so thin one can see through it. Who knows what America might yet achieve? With our help they might bend light or fuse hydrogen atoms."

"But we're here for tea. Why am I suddenly apprehensive about a pot of tea?"

"Don't be. I have trained them to make tea. Pot to the kettle—"

"—Not kettle to the pot? Leo, you're beginning to sound almost English. The very people from whom you just rescued me. Isn't it time you told me why?"

It was typical of Leo to move effortlessly between the flippant and the serious.

"Eighteen months ago, I went to see Einstein and the two of us composed a letter to President Roosevelt urging the development of a United States atomic project. We were quite clear about our belief that the Germans were doing the same. It was months before we received any reply, and while the reply was positive, we still have next to no funding. Hence the convenience of Columbia University. At Einstein's request, you and Zette are on salary until I *do* have funding. Meanwhile, I have raised money . . . privately . . ."

"Privately?"

"Begged, borrowed, scrounged . . . the last word fits best—that is what I have become, a scrounger . . . scrounging to begin industrial production of graphite and uranium."

"Then you've raised a fortune."

"Shall I say *modest* production. I intend to build a reactor."

Szabo thought better of pressing Leo too far on this. He could not conceive of the building of a nuclear reactor as a modest enterprise.

"What's my role?"

"Help Fermi build the reactor. It will take a while before we can do anything off the drawing board. Meanwhile, you have an office . . ."

"I've seen it. It's empty. I don't have a drawing board. A desk, a chair. Not so much as a speck of dust or a paper clip."

"I love empty. Empty is beautiful. The beauty of empty is you get to fill it. We may be short of money, but we are rich in talent. We already have an ad hoc coalition of minds. Arthur Compton at Chicago, Enrico Fermi and Isidor Rabi here at Columbia, Hans Bethe at Cornell, Eugene Wigner at Princeton. All us meddling foreigners. And of course we have Teller. I couldn't keep Teller out of this if I tried."

"And long-term?"

"Long-term? Long-term we need uranium in quantity. I hear rumours of huge stockpiles of uranium oxide out on Staten Island, but that's Staten Island for you. It's very existence is a rumour. I've never met anyone who's been there. It may be mythical. And, of course, we need plutonium, too."

"They called it plutonium?"

"I'm not sure they had any choice. At least fifty different people suggested it. And who would ever call an element seaborgium? So . . . while you build us a graphite reactor, others will go down the parallel routes. Build more cyclotrons, plants for chemical diffusion, perhaps a heavy-water reactor to make plutonium-239."

It was almost the last thing he expected. A heavy-water reactor. The very thing he had deemed a waste of time in the extraction of deuterium was now the bottle that held the genie of plutonium.

"You know, Leo, I recall the English had a phrase to describe what you are doing. They call it belt and braces."

"Oh? What does it mean?"

"It means a man in deep fear of his trousers falling down."

§34

In the June of 1942, Magda Ewald (trombone) vanished. Méret did not ask what had become of her. No one did. She was replaced in the Vienna Youth Orchestra by a skinny boy who looked as though he did not have the lungs to play brass, and played nowhere near as well as Magda.

§35

Chicago: December 2, 1942

It was twenty feet high, twenty five feet across, and looked for all the world like a giant doorknob. They called it a pile—and they had built it by piling up layers of dead graphite in alternate layers with graphite carrying a uranium load. It was nicknamed the egg-boiling experiment, but its formal name was Nuclear Reactor CP-1.

Despairing of ever getting his pile completed by commercial firms, Enrico Fermi had taken over a squash court under the stand at Stagg football field, University of Chicago, and assembled two teams of scientists to build the pile themselves. The bomb beneath the bleachers, Szabo called it. No one bothered to tell the University of Chicago.

Szabo thought he would freeze in the big, unheated squash court, but the sheer effort of lifting hundreds of thousands of pounds of blocks into place offset any cold. It was like a game he had played in childhood, when his father had challenged him to build a sphere with the multi-coloured wooden blocks in his toy box. And when he succeeded they had all the fun of knocking it down and building it all over again. What he would never get used to was the dirt. Graphite dust on every surface, turning the floor into a skating rink, and everyone in the room into a nigger minstrel, black of face and white of teeth.

They were still filthy when the observers arrived, thirty to forty people crowding the balcony of the squash court to watch the test. Outside it was even colder than inside. Leo Szilard arrived bundled up in his Astrakhan overcoat and homburg and gloves and galoshes. He could have been at home in Budapest, wandering in from a winter stroll down some forgotten boulevard in some forgotten decade of a forgotten empire. Once inside he didn't take any of it off.

Around noon, a safety device cut in prematurely and shut the reactor down far short of critical. Most men would have sworn, Fermi just said, "I'm hungry, let's get lunch."

They trekked outside across snow so cold it shone blue and creaked like a wooden ship when they set foot on it. The Americans had just introduced petrol rationing. Leo said, "The day they ration cake I surrender to Hitler."

It was gone quarter to four before the reactor approached critical again. The last cadmium rod limiting the reaction was slowly removed at 3:48. The uranium went into spontaneous fission and began a chain reaction that Fermi shut down after four and a half minutes. They had generated half a watt of power.

Szabo had known what to expect of the pile. It wouldn't buzz or hum; it wouldn't melt down. He had no expectations of his colleagues. He had wondered if they'd cheer—after all they'd been present at the world's first chain reaction—but the mood was quiet. There had been no whizzes and bangs, just the mechanical recording of data on a roll.

Fellow Hungarian Eugene Wigner would not let the moment fizzle out, and with a straw-bound bottle of Chianti seduced the Italian in Fermi away from the scientist long enough to splash wine into paper cups. There was no toast. They all looked at Fermi in silence. Then someone said, "Enrico, this is history. You must sign the bottle." And he did.

Twenty minutes later, only Szabo, Fermi, and Leo were left on the balcony. Someone had taken the piece of history home with them.

Leo's mood had changed, but then Szabo had always known it would. "Enrico, this will go down as a black day in the history of mankind." Fermi said nothing.

Nor did Szabo.

§36

Vienna: February 14, 1944

It was her birthday.

Her twentieth.

A hurry-home day.

She had no idea what her father had planned. Before the war he had surprised her. Something unimagined, something extravagant. These days he surprised her in more modest ways, but still surprised her.

She boarded a tram at dusk, just outside the Konservatorium. There was snow on the streets. Not enough to stop a tram—little or nothing could do that—but it left the interior dank and moist, the floorboards running with water, the passengers glistening, the windows blurry with condensation.

Two stops on, a man took the empty seat next to her. It was gloomy, no lamps lit for Allied bombers to see from above, and she only realized it was Roberto Cacciato when he spoke to her.

She had been in a daydream, mentally rehearsing her part in a Mozart symphony. Her right hand twitching at the neck of an invisible cello.

"What have I missed?" he said.

It jerked her back to the moment.

"Oh . . . the Prague. You missed the Prague symphony. In fact, I think you've missed every rehearsal we've had for it."

"Doesn't matter. Not much for a clarinet to do in it. Besides, I know the part backwards."

"Why don't you come?"

He tapped the brown paper parcel he was holding.

"There are other things one must do."

She was about to ask him what he meant when the tram braked suddenly. She wiped at the condensation on the window next to her. There were soldiers running in the street, then the front door of the tram opened and an SS Hauptsturmführer stepped onto the platform.

She turned to look at Roberto, but as the front door had opened so had the rear and he had leapt through it to the street and run off.

As he rounded the back of the tram, running as fast as a man with a club foot can, three soldiers out in the square shouldered their carbines almost idly, and without a word of warning, shot him in the back.

He fell face down on the thin sheet of snow, a spreading red stain over his heart on the back of his blue jacket, his hat cartwheeling off to spin to a standstill twenty paces away.

One of the soldiers turned the body over with his boot, then gestured with a thumbs-down to the other two.

She turned her head away. Every head in the tram was facing forward, every head practicing what she had not, and what every Viennese had learned since the fickle day they had cheered Hitler into the Heldenplatz—see no evil. This was how Vienna survived.

Only one face looked back at her. The SS Hauptsturmführer. He picked up the brown paper parcel next to her.

"Yours?" he said simply.

Hear no evil.

"No. N . . . n . . . no."

Speak no evil.

"It was . . ."

"His? The boy's? Fine, you come along with me, young lady."

With one hand he hefted the parcel, with the other he took her by the arm—firmly enough to let her know that if she squirmed or tried to break his grip he would hurt her.

They took her in an open car with a flapping canvas roof to a police station in Marokkanergasse, south of the city centre near the Belvedere gardens.

Sitting alone in a cell she thought it could not be long before her father came to collect her—explanations, apologies, bribes, although one had to be very careful how one bribed a German. But her father never came. In the morning a guard awoke her at first light and, feeling stiff, cold, and sleepless, she was hustled into a police van and driven off again.

Through the grille that separated her from the driver she could see that they were crossing the entire city centre to reach the northern side. For a while she thought that they might simply be taking her home. A good ticking off and returned to the bosom of her family. But the van turned right towards the Danube Canal and pulled up at the Rossauer Lände Prison, a monstrosity in red and dirty cream brick not half a kilometre from her parents' apartment.

She knew Rossauer Lände. It was where the Jews had been held in the early days of the war, prior to being relocated in the east. There had been much talk of the new towns in the eastern Reich, there had been endless radio broadcasts at school—lectures by Hitler himself—on the matter of *Lebensraum*. Plenty of people had told her that the Jews would be better off in the east. There was talk of a new town just for Jews, Osswichim, or Auswiczin, or some such Polish word. But mostly there was little talk of the Jews and no one ever seemed to hear from them. Another motto the Viennese had learnt in the eagerness of their lazy embrace of national socialism was "out of sight, out of mind"—and among the new tasks the Führer had set them that day in the Heldenplatz, the most daunting, and the least mentioned, was "what to do with the Jews?": "The Jewish Problem," as it was so neatly called, as though it were no more than a matter of faulty plumbing or a blocked drain.

Alone in a cell once more she could hear nothing but the sound of doors banging down distant corridors and of water dripping. There were no human noises, no voices, no footsteps. And then it dawned on her. The prison was empty, and it was empty because Vienna had no more Jews. Once, at the end of the decade, there had been close to a quarter of a million. Now there were none.

§37

The following morning she awoke, stiffer than the day before, and feeling decidedly grubby. An almost irresistible urge to scratch.

Still her father did not come.

Around ten in the morning a guard came and led her into an office overlooking the Danube Canal.

One desk, two chairs. Rows of empty shelving. It was as though they'd opened up and ripped off the dust covers just for her.

Leaning against the desk was the Hauptsturmführer who had arrested her. Roberto's brown paper parcel was on the desk, one corner torn open.

The Hauptsturmführer swung the shutters to cut the glare of the eastern light and motioned to her to sit.

"You're a mystery, aren't you?"

"I'm sorry, sir?"

He sat down behind the desk. He was almost relaxed, the top two buttons of his tunic undone. Oak leaves and flashes of lightning.

"Yesterday and the day before we smashed a resistance cell."

"I had nothing to do with that."

"But you knew the boy we shot. The boy on the tram. You were sitting with him."

"Yes. I knew him. Roberto—"

"—Cacciato. Clarinet player with the Vienna Youth Orchestra. And you are?"

"I'm the principal cellist."

"I meant your name."

"Voytek, sir. Méret Voytek."

"Voytek? That's not an Austrian name. You aren't Jewish?"

"If I were Jewish, sir, I would be obliged to wear a yellow star."

"Indeed. So what are you?"

"My grandfather was Hungarian. He came here in the days of the empire."

He was shaking his head now—unbelieving.

"It's not a Hungarian name, either. You aren't Jewish?"

"No, sir. The name is Polish. My grandfather used to tell me that his grandfather was Polish in the time of Napoleon. One emperor came west, another emperor came east, and Poles fled south. My grandfather said Hungary could make nothing of the surname, so his grandfather's Christian name became our surname. I have always been a Voytek. I have never been Jewish. It is a Christian name."

"It seems you have half Europe flowing in your veins. A true child of

80

the ancien régime. So, Fraulein Voytek. How did you know Roberto Cacciato?"

"From the orchestra, and he was the year above me at the Konservatorium."

"Why were you on the tram together?"

"I was on my way home after rehearsal. Two or three stops after I got on Roberto just appeared next to me."

"You were not travelling together?"

"No, sir."

"You weren't a member of his cell?"

"No, sir, ask them. They will surely tell you."

"No can do. We smashed them to pieces I'm afraid. You're the sole survivor."

It was shocking and strange. He was almost sighing at the stupidity of his own men and she was the sole survivor of something to which she'd never belonged. She wanted to ask how many young men and women had been killed but didn't dare.

"And I suppose you know nothing about this?"

He tore more of the wrapping away from the parcel and spread a couple of dozen flyers out in front of her in a fan.

There was a red hammer and sickle, a black mailed fist, and in blue the slogan "Resist or Die."

"Crude and colourful," he said. "And remarkably accurate."

"Please, sir, I have never seen them before. They were left on the seat next to me. Was not the parcel unopened when you found it?"

He said nothing to this, walked over to the window, peeked through the shutters, rummaged in his pockets for his cigarette case, and lit up. Precisely the kind of time-wasting gesture Viktor Rosen used to indulge in.

She twisted in the chair to address him directly.

"Please, sir, you know I am innocent."

He walked back behind the desk, puffing on his cigarette. Footsteps echoing in the empty room. Ruminative, weighing up her life over a few flakes of tobacco.

"Yes. I know that," he said at last. "But it doesn't make a scrap of difference."

"It must."

He shook his head, chin up, exhaling a plume of smoke.

"No, no, no, young lady. You are forgetting the rule of possession."

"Possession?"

"We have you. That is all that matters. We have you."

"You could let me go. Think of it as . . . as throwing back a sprat."

He smiled at the image she had presented him.

"The Third Reich doesn't throw back a sprat. If we did we might one day face an army of sprats."

§38

It was late afternoon before he sent for her again.

His uniform was buttoned now. He was wearing a field-grey great-coat. His cap with its death's head crest sat on the desk where Roberto's parcel had been. He was reading from a brown cardboard file—a spread eagle clutching a swastika in its claws stamped on the cover in red—but the sense of imminent departure was all around him.

They were in transit.

The two of them.

"This will interest you."

He looked up at her. His voice soft and friendly as though sharing a confidence with her.

"To know what informants say about them would surely fascinate anyone? A bit like reading your sister's diary. For example . . . overheard in your local baker's . . . 'Herr Voytek is nothing more than a dreamer . . . a woolly headed man of woolly headed politics' . . . and in the butcher's . . . 'Eva Voytek is a hard-faced bitch . . . a cryptofascist without the guts to come out of her closet.' Does this sound accurate to you?"

Was this what the Nazis had done? Turned every marketplace gossip into an informant? Every street-corner layabout into a secret agent? A world in which everyone spied on everyone else?

"None of it . . . none of it mentions me."

"Fair enough . . ."

He flipped over a page.

"Listen to this. 'That child of theirs . . . a po-faced girl who'll grow up to be a po-faced woman. Talk about a stick up the arse.' Not a phrase I've ever heard before, but I think its meaning is obvious. Do you have a stick up your arse?"

Méret said nothing.

He slapped the file down.

"No, I wouldn't answer that one, either. These people are pathetic. The butcher, the baker, the candlestick maker. They'd all rat you out for a threepenny bit. Let's go."

§39

It was almost dusk. He drove her to the Nordbahnhof himself, without escort. The only sign that she was under arrest was the unbuttoned flap on the holster that held his Luger.

Inside the station an engine was backing a line of boxcars, all with Italian markings, down the track to be coupled to an ancient Imperial Austrian State Railways third-class corridor passenger carriage. A broken boxcar with a shattered axle lay on its side where the Germans had tipped it. She could only think that they'd raided a museum to find its replacement.

Down the platform a hundred odd people cowered behind a cordon of soldiers with fixed bayonets—in the dimness of the blacked-out railway station at dusk the yellow stars on their coats seemed almost luminous.

"Get on before the Italians. They've been thirty-two hours in cattle wagons from Florence, Lucca, Pisa . . . God knows where . . . they're tired, hungry, and frightened and they'll still fight you for an arseworth of space on a bench with no cushions and no upholstery."

Half a dozen carpenters appeared with planks and nails and began to board up the windows. She got on to the train, stood in the corridor, looking back at the Hauptsturmführer as he was looking back at her.

He looked to his left at the crowd of Jews, casually pressed the stud shut on the flap of his holster.

As he turned to leave she said loudly, "Where am I going?"

He turned back, took half a dozen paces closer to her.

Not raising his voice to the level of hers, but audible in the noise of the station, still the friendly tone, still sharing a confidence, "Auschwitz."

Was this the Osswichim, or Auswiczin she'd heard about?

"The town of the Jews? But I am not Jewish!"

"Then you might well survive."

"My father," she said. "My father . . ."

But the carpenters had reached her window. He could not hear her for the banging of hammers, and a few seconds later all she could see through the gap in the boards was his back in the field-grey greatcoat moving away from her.

§40

The Italians crammed in, four and five to a side, children sitting in the aisle between, and the corridors packed.

Next to her a wizened old woman wept continuously. Opposite her a well-dressed man in a black overcoat with a beaver collar, a homburg hat, and pince-nez that perched upon his nose as though glued there. A shiny leather briefcase between his knees—a yellow star sewn to his chest—but then they all wore yellow stars. Within ten minutes of the train pulling away, east towards Czechoslovakia, the rapid Italian chatter slowed and then stopped as though they had exhausted their capacity for talk.

Only the sound of weeping and groaning. The children sat hunched, arms around their knees, silent as if baffled.

She was amazed at how much they carried. One woman appeared to have stripped her bed and bundled it up with a knot. Another had her worldly possessions in a long-handled copper jam pan that sat on her lap. A man in the corner seemed to have lifted the portraits of everyone in his family off the sitting room wall and sat with them bound up in string and clutched to his chest. Somewhere out of sight someone else had carried on a concertina and every so often would play for ten or fifteen minutes—the gaiety of his tunes at odds with their dirgelike progress east.

The man opposite eventually introduced himself in slow, emphatic Italian she assumed he reserved for talking to foreigners.

"Eli Cresca. *Bibliotecario di Lucca*."

Méret's Italian was good. She replied with name and occupation, and asked why he had a knife, fork, and spoon sticking out of the breast pocket of his overcoat.

"Lest I forget," he said. "I am told there are shortages of such things in the new cities of the east. They may have no knives and forks. And if they do, well, mine are silver and saleable. Portable property as such. And they may have librarians already. It might be a while before I could start to earn my living. Who knows, I might be lucky."

The word was startling. *Lucky*. What could any of this have to do with luck?

"Things could improve," Cresca added. "I mean. Last night we were in a cattle truck. A bucket of water to drink from and a barrel to pee in."

"A barrel?"

"Yes. In the middle of the truck for all to use."

"For all to see? Men as well as women?"

"Yes. It was unavoidable. Today, I have a seat and the use of a lavatory that, whilst it may be just a hole onto the tracks below, is behind a door."

This was unbelievable. They had done that—in public—in front of one another?

"Who knows," he said, "what tomorrow may bring."

§41

They had sat all night and most of the next day in a siding in marshland, mist swirling off in the pale sunlight, settling again as dusk approached. Through a gap in the boards she could see that they were on the edge of a town or perhaps a factory complex—whatever it was, the Germans were guarding it with barbed wire, floodlights, and machine-gun posts. The night sky had glowed red and three tall chimneys blew flames into darkness some twenty feet high as though releasing an explosion. And when day had broken a grey haze covered everything and blotted out the sky.

Late in the afternoon the train lurched into motion, through gates, past barbed wire, into the factory.

Somewhere, a band was playing. A ludicrous accompaniment to the confusion into which they had been plunged. A strident, vigorous Hungarian march, Liszt's *Rákóczi*—it was the sort of thing you played to a youth group as they marched off to summer camp.

The clash of steel on steel as the train stopped.

A babble of voices. Screams from somewhere up the line.

"*Raus! Raus!*"

"*Funf zu funf!*"

And still no one moved.

Then the boards on the windows were ripped off as though a hurricane had struck, and rifles smashed the glass.

"*Raus! Raus!*"

"*Funf zu funf!*"

They leapt to the ground, one by one, not five by five.

Up the line, the boxcar doors had opened and the living and the dead fell to the ground in dozens, ghostly creatures in blue-and-white striped pyjamas swarming over them like flies upon a corpse.

An SS Sturmmann turned his attention to the group she had travelled with.

"Drop everything. Line up in fives. In fives! Five by five!"

The woman with the bedding dropped her parcel. The woman with

86

the cooking pan clung on and had it knocked from her hands by a rifle butt.

"You'll get it all back later. Line up. Jews to the left, everyone else to the right."

This caused more confusion. Some went left, some went right, some stayed rooted to the spot, some dropped their possessions, some held on. They were like skittles struck by a wooden ball. Méret, thinking she was in all probability the only non-Jew there, wondered, *To the right of what?*

After the static night and a day in the siding everything was suddenly in motion. Right and left meant too little. Space and direction were inadequate. What counted was that that which had been still was now in motion, shifting like sand beneath her feet.

She followed Cresca. He had been a lifeline for almost two days in a cold, dark, smelly railway carriage. A kindly old man who had shared his food with her and tried to share his optimism. Now, in the reduced world, in the shifting world into which they had just descended, he was all she knew.

The pyjama creatures moved among them, crouched and cowed, whispering, as though they might walk through walls with the merest effort.

"Leave it all. Do as they say. Leave it all. It cannot help you now. It shall not help you now."

An SS Sturmbannführer picked his way among the personal possessions of the Italians, kicking them aside—an elephant in the sitting room, the hooligan at the dining table.

He directed Cresca to the left with a flick of his thumb. Cresca was still clutching his briefcase, his knife, fork, and spoon still stuck out of the top pocket of his overcoat. Telling him to drop the case only made him clutch it more tightly until a rifle butt knocked it from his hand and another knocked him to the ground. The cutlery shot from his pocket onto the trampled slush that covered the earth. With blood streaming into his eyes Signor Cresca at last had vision and seemed to know that where he was going he would have no need of cutlery. He picked up the three pieces of silverware and held them out to Méret. She bent to take them from him but as two soldiers hoisted him up at the armpits to drag him away he dropped them all. She put her fingers into the black snow to retrieve this last gift, and as she did so, a shining black boot placed itself upon her knuckles. She looked up to see the Sturmbannführer smiling at her and as he smiled the pressure from his foot increased.

"You have no yellow star? Why are you mixed in with all this Jew-shit? One would almost think you wished to die."

The boot pressed the hand into the ground, the cutlery digging into her flesh. Just when she thought her knuckles would crack a voice said, "Really, Bruno, if you break her fingers we shall never know how well she plays."

A second Sturmbannführer had appeared at the side of the first, one hand upon the arm in gentle restraint, and behind him, lurking, almost cowering, not daring to meet her eyes, was a scrawny figure in a dirty pleated skirt and a lavender-coloured headscarf. Magda Ewald—once a trombonist of the Vienna Youth Orchestra. Méret had not seen her in years.

"It seems she's a cellist, and the orchestra of the *Frauen-konzentrationslager* has need of a cellist."

With this the first Sturmbannführer lost interest.

"Take the cunt, leave the cutlery.," was all he said.

§42

It was about two hours later. She had lost Magda and clung to one thought—that she might find her again.

Time and geography had dissolved. She had marched—at least that was what the Germans had told them to do: *"Links, links, schnell, schnell!"* It had been more of a ragged, slow footed shuffle—from the ramp, across a muddy crust of trampled snow, through a gate in the barbed wire into a world of barbed wire. Single-storey blockhouses, laid to a grid—row upon row like a motionless machine in bricks and mortar. All the fit young women: none of them too elderly, none of them too young, none of them infirm.

Now she stood naked in the snow, dripping wet from a cold shower, robbed of her clothes, blue with cold, her entire body a moonscape of goose pimples, a smear of blood on her thighs from her broken hymen. The rape of the rubber glove. One of a dozen naked, bloodied women.

The tattoo on her left arm was stinging. She scratched at it and looked down. A five figure number ending 757 . . .

A female guard swathed in an SS greatcoat, feet snug in sheepskin-lined boots, yelled that they should move into the next hut—"*All'interno! All'interno! Hinein! Hinein!*"—and when Méret obediently moved with the others the guard rapped her across the belly with her stick.

"Not you."

She would not watch as the rest of the women were herded in with kicks and slaps and blows from truncheons, and turned away. There was Magda, less than six feet from her. Stock still, feet planted firmly in the snow, hands clasped in front of her. She reminded Méret of a nun. She was pitifully thin, although her eyes seemed to be shining.

"I know what you're feeling," she said.

"You do?"

"You're feeling that you will die now. But you can no longer trust your feelings. You may very well die, but not today. You may very well live, but who knows for how long? You may survive. I have."

"How . . . how . . . long have you . . . ?"

"Since the summer of 1942. Or did you think I'd taken an extended holiday? Now, follow me."

The ice cut her feet, a snail trail pink in the snow as she walked be-hind Magda, between the first and second blocks to a third one behind.

"You will not believe this, at least not right now, but you are lucky. Since last summer they have killed only Jews on arrival. Doesn't mean they won't find a reason to kill you at any point, but right now the master race is too busy exterminating Jews to bother much about us."

"Exterminating?"

"By the thousand, by the hundred thousand—by now it could be millions."

They had reached the hut. Magda threw the door wide and motioned Méret inside.

"All those people who arrived when I did—the Italians?"

There was a pile of clothes dumped on a table. They were not clean clothes. Nor were they her own clothes. There was a pile of shoes on the floor.

"Pick what fits. Find a skirt, a blouse, and a headscarf. Whatever you can find to wear on top of that and keep out the cold. You don't have to wear stripes and they won't shave your head, that's your first privilege —and this is a world of privilege and denial—it makes humanity much easier to control—but if I were you I'd keep it short and always wear a headscarf. You'll be less likely to get lice."

"Privileged. Why privileged?"

"What size shoes? I'll try and find two in the same style."

"Thirty-six. And you're not answering a single question."

Magda knelt on the floor sifting through the shoes. Méret pulled on a pair of cream-coloured cotton knickers with a sense of disgust readily overcome by the greater sense of cold and naked.

"Oh, I can answer any question you like and save you the fun of finding out for yourself. The Italians? They are dead by now. Men with pliers are pulling out their gold teeth as we speak. In a matter of hours their bodies will be ashes. When the ashes are cold, men with rakes will sift them for any gold they might have missed. And in the spring, in two or three months women less privileged than us will scatter those ashes on the ground as fertilizer for corn. And next autumn we shall eat the bread of the dead.

"Meanwhile, the better quality clothes in which they arrived will be shipped west for the benefit of Aryan Hausfraus in Germany. The tat will be reserved for us. So much depends on when they were taken. We have had people arrive straight from the opera, straight from weddings—what are the Germans to do with all those top hats? How many curtains can one make out of a bridal dress? And once, an entire hockey team, seized at half time. It's probably why you and I have pleated skirts and matching blouses to wear on days when we need to look like a marching band. Somewhere there will be piles—no mountains, mountains of things the Germans do not quite know what to do with—all those suitcases, all those pairs of spectacles to dispose of. At least the false teeth are incinerated with their owners. Burned up with the dead.

"Privilege? Well, it saved your life today. You were dealing with one of the biggest bastards in the camp when I spotted you. Jew or no Jew he'd have wasted a bullet on you if you'd gone on provoking him. But Schönbeck was at hand, and when I told him who you were he grabbed you for the *Frauenkonzentrationslager orkestra*. You're our new cellist. I do hope you like Strauss waltzes. We play them every Sunday at the behest of the commandant. And, as you'll have heard, we play tangos almost daily. We have turned the dance of love into the march of the dead."

It was too much. Her body began to shake beyond control. Wet tears upon her cheeks, wet blood upon her thighs. All she wished was that Magda would take her in her arms.

She didn't.

She fished around among the topcoats—found a green woollen jacket in a small size and threw it to Méret to catch. Her arms dangled at her side, useless appendages. The jacket bounced off her breasts and fell to the floor. The tide of disgust rose in her throat.

"Magda, whose clothes are these?"

"Why take ye thought for raiment?"

It was a line from the bible. Something from the New Testament. It was the predicate to something often quoted. Méret could not remember what.

Magda continued to sort through the pile of cast-offs, not looking at her, muttering to herself almost savagely, hissing, ironic curse rather than the words of Christ, "Wherefore, if God so clothe the grass of the field, which today is, and tomorrow is cast into the oven, shall he not much more clothe you?"

"Magda, please! Whose clothes are these?"

"O ye of little faith."

Méret had never heard those five words sound so sneeringly abused, so stripped of meaning.

She bent to pick up the jacket. Magda reached into her pocket and tossed a needle and thread, bound around a small piece of cardboard, down onto it.

"You'll need those."

Rummaging now in the other pocket of her skirt.

"And this."

Méret watched it float down, eddying like an autumn leaf to land on the jacket. A scrap of cotton, a scarlet triangle.

"Sew it on. It means you're a political prisoner."
She who had no politics.
O ye of little faith.

§43

Magda led her outside once more, across a desert of churned snow mingling with yellow clay, and into another blockhouse. It was heated by a potbellied stove and for the first time since she stepped out of the Konservatorium to catch the tram a lifetime ago, she felt warmth around her.

It was a big room, almost split in two by a raised brick platform running down the centre like the spine of some long-dead reptile, surrounded by musical intruments. And along the walls, rising up to the roof beams, bunk upon bunk upon bunk.

"More privilege. In Block Twelve you get your own bunk. The rest of them are packed into concrete tiers like sticks of french bread in a baker's oven. Five, six . . . a dozen to a platform. An experiment in sharing vermin. Here you will never have to wake up next to a corpse. And, of course, our room is always heated. It helps to keep the piano in tune. That it stops us from freezing is no doubt a coincidence."

She stopped in front of a tier of bunks.

"The top one is free."

"Magda. Why do you talk to me as if I had offended you?"

Whatever answer Magda might have made was drowned out by the return of the ladies' orchestra—thirty or forty women, some of them even younger than she was herself—all dressed as ragbag as she was herself —some with long hair tucked under scarves, others shaved back to stubble, red triangles and yellow stars. A dozen nationalities—French, German, Dutch, Belgian, Polish—a flurry of names she would struggle to remember until she had learned to associate name to face to instrument. Once she had the instrument fixed, everything else would fall into place.

§44

In the darkness, the blockhouse chatter subsided into fits of sleep and Magda slipped into the bunk beside her, enfolded her in her arms, and whispered in her ear.

"We can live through this. I don't mean that we can be spared the arbitrariness of killing. They will kill for a whim. But we can survive if we know the rules.

"Guard your bowl and spoon or you'll never get to eat. Never put them down outside the block.

"Eat slowly, it fills the stomach better that way, but never, ever save anything for later. It will be stolen.

"Avoid anyone with a black or green triangle. Prostitutes and murderers.

"Never give food away.

"Never share food.

"Never speak to a guard unless spoken to.

"And never go to the assistance of anyone in trouble or their fate will be yours, too."

§45

The musicians were spared *Appell*. Through the window of the blockhouse Méret could see row upon row of ragged women in prison stripes. It was dawn and they had already been standing for hours. It was torture —torture by cold, torture by endurance, and torture by boredom. She had been familiar with the latter all her life. It was the first demonstration of power in the life a child. The ability of those with power to waste your time, to insult your intelligence with boredom and futility.

Magda appeared next to her.

"I have to play now. We all have to play now. We play them out to work and we play them back again."

"And me?"

"Not today. Another privilege. Just wait here."

A few minutes later a dissonant *Arbeitsmarsch* was struck up somewhere outside.

At the end of the blockhouse a wooden partition carved two rooms out of the barracks. One for the *blockowa,* one for the orchestra conductor. A door opened. A woman in her mid-thirties emerged. Tall, lots of dark-brown hair swept back. It was a familiar figure from her youth, one of the best-known musicians in Vienna—Alma Rosé, daughter of Arnold Rosé, leader of the Vienna Philharmonic, and a niece of Gustav Mahler. She had led the *Wiener Walzermädeln,* a small orchestra renowned for the saccharine musical clichés for which Vienna was famous. In the mid-thirties it had pleased her father to take her to see the *Wiener Walzermädeln* two or three times. They put on a "show." They wore billowing ball gowns that trailed along the floor. They played the kind of music that set his foot tapping, waltzed away his worries, and whisked him back to the turn of the century as surely as a bottle and a half of red wine. It was the kind of music Viktor Rosen abhorred. Too much of a good thing.

"You are our new cellist."

It wasn't a question. Méret said nothing. Alma swept an errant lock of hair back over her right ear—a gesture that took Méret back to a thé dansant that had bored her silly seven or eight years ago. She could see Alma Rosé in her ball gown, she could feel her father's hand enfolding hers.

"Do you know who I am?"

"Yes. I knew you at once. I heard the name Alma last night many times. I did not think it could be you because no one told me it was and because I heard a rumour in Vienna that you had escaped to London."

"I had. My mistake was I came back. Come, follow me."

Inside the *kapo*'s room, Alma had set a cello on a stand. It was cheaply made. In so far as any musical instrument can be mass-produced, it was mass-produced. A bullet had entered at the front, just high of the left f-hole, and exited not in a hole but in a two-foot-long split at the back.

"Do you think you can cope with it?"

Méret sat, quickly tuned up, and played a minute or so of Debussy's cello sonata.

"It's awful. There is a bad vibration along the split—if I were to demand volume of the instrument it would sound more like an orange box than a cello, but the neck is fine. It is not twisted. It seems to stay in tune."

"Good. It's all we have. When I saw you make your debut with Viktor Rosen in 1936, you played a beautiful instrument. What was it?"

"A Mattio Goffriler. 1707."

"When I went into hiding in Holland I left behind a Guadagnini violin dating from 1757."

It seemed they had exchanged sympathies, a common experience in the loss of an instrument that did nothing to take the crispness out of their meeting. It wasn't an audition—that much was clear—it merely felt like an audition. They were cast in their respective roles. The individuals in them had not touched. They, too, were lost.

"You can copy parts, I take it?"

"Yes. Of course."

"I need something large, something loud, something German. We are orchestrating Beethoven's Fifth. They seem to want it. Imagine, not enough violins, not enough percussion, no violas at all, one trombone, two flutes, three guitars, five mandolins, a piano, two accordions, and they ask for Beethoven. Thank God they didn't ask for the Ninth or half a dozen of us would be masquerading as a choir. Could you copy out the parts?"

"Of course. Do we have music paper?"

§46

Her first task was to make music paper. There was ample white paper, and her first adjustment to the mentality of a prisoner was in wondering how Alma had obtained white paper. Patiently she ruled on the staves and took a childish pleasure in drawing in the clefs. The swirl of the treble clef had delighted her since before she learnt to read. In drawing it she was inscribing the key to another world. Her second adjustment to the mentality of a prisoner was to realize that anyone could copy music and that in leaving her alone at the long table in the rehearsal room, while everyone else played marches and tangos in the freezing snow, Alma had given the new girl a break.

Whenever the orchestra stopped, the sound of the camp burst through—bad as the orchestra was, the camp's real sound was a cacophony of whistles and bells, gunfire and screams, dogs barking, men shouting, boots banging, trains hooting. There was never a moment of silence.

She had looked out of the window. A maze of barbed wire. Tall chimneys belching black smoke, the grey, greasy haze low in the sky. Men and women resembling stick insects, beaten into line—into fives, always into fives, the German number for everything—beaten into marching, a rippling wave of dirty blue and white stripes.

As she watched, not fifty yards from the window a woman slipped and fell. The guards kicked her until she rose again, and when she fell again and made no further move to rise, they set the dogs on her.

She turned away, inscribed a treble clef and accepted the invitation to that other world.

She had no idea how long she had managed to lose herself. Music, which all her life had enabled her to blot out anything, like a glass wall, was now a sieve, and she could not control what slipped through. The orchestra was still playing, and beneath the wrong notes of a badly played tango she could still hear the noise of the camp.

A sheet of loosened snow fell past the window. Over her head she could hear the bumps of heavy-footed workmen, scraping away, patching the roof. She quickly filtered the sound out of her mind. Knowing what the noise meant made all the difference.

She had lost herself for several more minutes reading the score of a lively dance by the Argentine composer Alberto Ginastera when she heard a tapping at the window behind her on the far side of the room, leaking in through her sieve.

An arm ending in a lightly clenched fist was hanging down, poised to tap again. She opened the window and looked up. A man's face, a blue and white striped cap clinging on precariously, was looking down at her.

"*Parlez-vous francais? Parla italiano? Sprechen Sie Deutsch?*" he asked without pausing to let her choose.

"All of those," she replied. "But I'm Austrian. From Vienna."

"Ah. I am French. Georges Pasdeloup. Citizen of Paris. Communist. Prisoner. Roofer . . . *et . . . Résistance!*"

She knew she should say something, rattle off her identity. She knew why he'd turned his into a list—it defied the numbers they had tattooed on their left arms—but she couldn't do it. She felt an idiot staring back at him with nothing to say for herself.

He seemed not to mind. The fist that had been hanging down opened. In the palm were three dried and dusty apricots.

"*Prenez! Prenez,* before the bastards see me."

She snatched them from him.

"Where did you get them?"

"Canada, *mam'selle.* The land of plenty. All good things come from Canada."

She was about to thank him when he whispered, "*boche,*" pulled himself back onto the roof, and clumped off to position himself and his bucket of tar over one of the many damp stains on the ceiling.

In the prisons in Vienna she had been fed only bread and water. On the train she would have starved but for Signor Cresca sharing his focaccia and salami, and since she arrived in camp she had eaten what everyone else had—a vegetable soup in which one might search for the vegetable and a hard, grey bread served with a sickly, rancid margarine. Despite everything she had said about sharing, Magda had given her half a sausage without telling how she came by it, saying "you'll be better when your stomach contracts and you learn to live on nothing." She knew now she should save half the apricots for Magda. She ate half and set the rest aside.

Ten minutes later she ate those, too.

That night she asked Magda what Canada meant.

"It's the *Effektenkammer,* the dumping shed where everything that the Germans steal from the dead ends up. All those clothes you and I picked from yesterday came from there. Your own clothes were too good. They're back in Germany by now and whoever owned what you're wearing is dust."

She thought of the dust that had coated the apricots she wasn't going to mention, and how she had thought, and dismissed the thought, that they looked as though they had sat for several days at the bottom of someone's coat pocket.

§47

She was still copying music two days later and the Frenchman was once again working on the roof. She heard the tap at the window and looked over to see his head pop down and pop up again almost as quickly. She turned to see what he had seen: the door opening and the Sturmbannführer who had rescued her on the ramp coming in, flakes of fresh snow gleaming on his greatcoat and cap. He took off both. Knocked them free of snow, scarcely glancing at her.

She clasped her hands in front of her the way Magda habitually did. It spoke piety. Or if not piety, obedience. It told the right lie. He noticed.

He looked from her to the cello propped on its stand.

"Does it play?"

"It does, sir."

"Then prove me right."

It was a momentary déjà vu. He was older and far superior in rank to the Hauptsturmführer who had put her on the train, but his manner was almost identically lackadaisical. As though all this was nothing much to do with him—just a job like any other—and that he'd been happier and more purposeful in some university or other before the war, teaching theology or art history, and if he stuck you on a train to Auschwitz or put a gun to your head it was all a bit of a bore and he might just as well have signed up for a folk song society as the National Socialist Workers' Party.

She cradled the cello and played him the Kodaly she had first played for Viktor Rosen the day they had met. It was miserable, and she felt he deserved misery.

When she had finished he said, "You cannot be happy with the tone, surely?"

Happy—now there was a word devoid of all meaning in the present context.

She told him what she had told Alma Rosé. "At home I had a far finer cello, a Mattio Goffriler."

"And where is it now?"

"I suppose it might well be where I left it. In my parents' apartment."

"And you are from where? Vienna?"

"Yes sir, Vienna."

"And your name?"

"Méret Voytek."

She dearly wanted him to ask why she was where she was—a chance to explain herself and the mistake they had made. But she knew she could not plead and had to be asked.

He didn't ask. He stood up and slipped his arms through the sleeves of his greatcoat.

"I am Sturmbannführer Graf Galen Furst von Schönbeck. Be ready at seven on Friday evening, wear your uniform, and this time play something German."

§48

The next day at first light was her first time with the band that played to the slaves. They assembled where the men's and women's camps met, within yards of the ramp at which the transports arrived, on a banked mound of earth, seated on stools.

They saw the men out to work or die with a foxtrot and paused before the first exodus of women. It was fully light now, the floodlights were off, and a transport that had discharged its human cargo in the middle of the night was still parked at the ramp, all its doors open, a mess of abandoned property scattered in the mud and snow.

From where she was sitting Méret could see the remains of tinned and bottled food, items of clothing, hats and capes, walking sticks and crutches, pans and bowls and cutlery—all the expectant junk of survival that she'd seen on the train with the Italians—and, half buried in the sludge, the shiny head of a china doll like the one she used to have.

She left her seat.

Magda called out to her in a stage whisper, "Méret. Sit down. For God's sake, sit down."

It was only a few feet away, she might reach it and retrieve it before anyone spotted her.

"Méret!"

And as she reached down for the doll she saw that it was not a doll but a baby, its head glazed with frost, its body all but trampled into the ground.

Magda got up and dragged her back.

An SS guard approached but turned away as soon as he saw them seated again. Then the women began to pour towards the gate and the band struck up a waltz from *The Merry Widow*.

Méret sat holding the bow against the strings, wanting the glass wall to descend and cut her off, but it did not. And no act of will on her part invoked it. All she had was the sieve, and the world was leeching through.

"Méret, play something. For God's sake, play anything!"

She hit a badly fingered note. The band was so off-key it scarcely mattered—but she now knew the answer to the question she had silently posed to herself the day the Nazis had taken over the youth orchestra. "Why or when would the Nazi party ever have need of an orchestra?"

This was why.

This was when.

§49

She donned the navy-blue pleated skirt, the white blouse, and the lavender-coloured headscarf that was the uniform of the *Frauen-konzentrationslager Orkestra*. The bullet-damaged cello stood next to her, a matching bullet hole in the case. She waited for von Schönbeck.

"You are clean? You have washed?"

"Yes, sir."

"The commandant's wife is peculiarly sensitive to smells. To body odour. You must always wash."

He led her out of the main gate. Free air smelt no different from prison air. Both were grease in the mouth and nose. She wondered that Frau Commandant could smell the live stinking flesh above the dead stinking flesh.

They followed a track that led towards the smoking chimneys of the crematorium. She had seen the porters of the dead—the *leichenkomando*—pushing handcarts piled with bodies along this track. Then they veered off through a garden gate and a hedge, across a rose garden, its twisted stems stark in the bareness of winter, a crown of thorns waiting to be furled, and in the back door of a large villa—grey pebbled walls and high leaded windows, like something to be seen on a suburban road a few miles from the city centre. A house kept spotless by a do-nothing wife and two maids, from which a husband commuted into town each day.

They had set out a wooden stool for her in the drawing room. She removed her shoes in the kitchen and sat barefoot, head down, waiting for the appearance of her audience. It was the reverse of every concert she had ever given, and when the audience entered it was she who stood. When they sat, she sat.

Then nothing.

Frau Commandant seemed disinclined to look at her. A girl of ten or so seemed restless and fidgety. The commandant looked not at her but at von Schönbeck.

She took in the room. It was almost a parody of life—the life she had left behind less than two weeks ago. It was like no home she had ever lived in—a sideboard displaying Dresden and Meissen china, modern German furniture in light colours without wear or tear, so different from the lived-in chic shabbiness and hand-me-downs of her parents' apartment with its litter of papers and books and sheet music—but it was a home. It was home to the po-faced woman and the restless girl. In the shadow of death this was, she realized, "normal." One could shut out death almost like drawing the curtains on a winter's night.

Von Schönbeck whispered, "What will you play?"

And she whispered back, "The third suite for cello by Johann Sebastian Bach, in the key of C."

Von Schönbeck announced the piece, took his seat on the sofa next to the child, and nodded at her.

She played the prelude with her head down. A minute or so into the allemande, as the piece became more lively, she dared to look up. Each dancing swing of the bow gave her the excuse to raise her head. Frau Commandant was looking at her own hands, the child still fidgeted, but Herr Commandant was concentrating intensely, as one would less on a piece of music than on a discursive argument. A look he maintained until the last notes of the gigue that ended the suite—as though not being moved, he had striven to be moved.

She had not expected good manners, or any manners, but when she had finished the commandant said thank you to her and clapped von Schönbeck on the shoulder, saying, "*Gut, gut.*"

Walking back, she said, "May I ask a question, sir?"

Von Schönbeck nodded.

"Why did I play for the commandant?"

A long intake of breath. She knew at once that he had understood the question.

"He likes to like music. I do not mean by that that he does like music. He knows nothing about music. He likes the idea of music. It goes with his idea of himself, his position and his status. It is a problem."

"A problem, sir?"

"A problem for us—not for you—for us in the party. We need men like the commandant. But we cannot make them cultured. The uniform confers power. It does not confer taste. But it is our problem, and not one to be addressed in a time of war. Your problem is simple—to learn how to please him without making him look or feel ignorant."

An unwise maxim along the lines of a silk purse and sow's ear sprang to mind. She kept it to herself.

"Do you know the rest of the Bach suites?"

"Yes, sir."

"By heart?"

"Of course."

"Then you'll have no problem keeping him happy."

They walked on, captor and captive, strolling like old friends under a sky seared red with burning flesh, a sweet, cloying smell in their nostrils.

Von Schönbeck did not speak again until they reached the door to the music block.

"You were very good, by the way. But your cello sounded like a plywood tea chest."

§50

Two months had passed. It was April, a warm April, and the snow had thawed rapidly. The sun shone, warm breezes blew. Occasionally there were April showers and the roof of the music block began to leak once more.

The orchestra had just returned from playing out the morning work detail. The roofers were at work, patching up with felt and tar.

When Pasdeloup tapped at the window, it was Magda who heard him first. She opened the window, three or four of the women pressing up behind her to see what he wanted or, better still, what he had.

"Where is the pretty Viennese?"

"Lots of us are from Vienna. I'm from Vienna. Am I not pretty?"

This set them giggling. Pasdeloup stuck to his guns.

"The cellist," he said simply.

"Méret, Méret, your boyfriend's calling."

She moved up to the window. Either he was hanging on by his toes or someone was holding him, for he had both arms extended, fists out like a teasing father asking a child to choose.

He opened both hands and gave her apples—not dried, just blotched and wrinkled, apples from last year's harvest. Then his hands dove into his pockets and he produced two more.

"Tomorrow," he said, "as the men march out, whatever you are playing, work in a few bars of the *Marseillaise*. The bastards will never notice but all the French boys will."

"Of course. It will be our—"

"*Boche!*" he cried and vanished upward like a genie, back onto the roof. All heads turned to the door.

An SS guard had entered and behind him two men in stripes lugged in a packing case about five feet high and two across. Stencilled on the front were a series of numbers and a dozen or more words, but all Méret could see were two :

VOYTEK
AUSCHWITZ-BIRKENAU

The guard took an iron jemmy, prised off the front, and left without a word.

They never received packages. And a package this size was unheard of. They approached like children, curiosity mingling with the sense of danger, silently daring each other to look.

Méret yanked at the loose panel. It clattered to the floor. Inside was her cello case, and inside the cello case was her Mattio Goffriler cello.

Things moved so fast. She was at the centre of a storm as hands plucked the case from its packing and the cello from its case.

"My God," a voice was saying, "it's the most beautiful thing I've ever seen."

She did not see who thrust them into her hand. Four sheets of paper, bound together with a staple, headed:

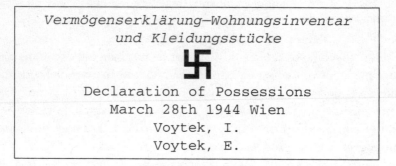

```
Vermögenserklärung—Wohnungsinventar
       und Kleidungsstücke
                卐
      Declaration of Possessions
        March 28th 1944 Wien
            Voytek, I.
            Voytek, E.
```

And there followed a list of everything her parents had ever owned, the entire contents of the apartment in Vienna, room by room, ending in the one she had occupied.

```
Dolls, 2: China head.
1 black. 1 white.
Cello, 1: Italian.
```

And she realized the Germans had killed her parents to obtain her cello.

§51

Summer 1944

In Oak Ridge, Tennessee, they built a city for the atom bomb. The locals called it "Dogpatch." They built another pile, factories the size of apartment blocks, cyclotrons to enrich docile uranium to fissile uranium-235, and they built an outdoor dance floor.

Szabo was a physicist in the hands of engineers, in the hands of the United States Army. It was the Chinese box, every layer revealed another. Except that the peeling away of layers revealed nothing beyond the fact that they existed. No one in any layer was supposed to know what anyone in any other layer was doing. No one was supposed to know the ultimate purpose of the experiment. How many knew they were building a bomb? If they knew, did they comprehend that this was a bomb like no other?

He designed the pile, observed the metamorphosis of the elements, and on occasion, on warm summer nights when the girls who pulled the levers and pushed the buttons that made the thingamajig in a process they none of them understood, turned up to work with flowery cotton dresses tucked under their overalls and baskets of fruit and bread and beer, he would look long into the deep, deep, darkening blue Tennessee sky, awed by nature even as he twisted it, shattered it, and rewrote it, and take to the dance floor.

He had never met a physicist who did not have two left feet. He wasn't bad by that standard, but he had neither the coordination nor the nerve to jitterbug. He waited till the evening mellowed, until the young men had retreated to the edge to drink and laugh, tired and sweaty after lifting women off the floor and over their heads for fifteen minutes of un-European frenzy.

He found himself embraced by a pretty young blonde, strawberry patterns on her dress, bright red lipstick offering permanent temptation, a hint of moisture on her forehead, nut-brown eyes that looked once into his and then buried themselves in his shoulder as the two of them performed a slow shuffle on the boards, the mute smooch of the trumpet competing with the pressure of her hips to tell him it had been far too long since he had had a woman.

It was, not that he had noticed, a ladies' excuse-me.

At the tap on her shoulder, the strawberry-girl looked up, over his shoulder, into the face of the competition, smiled at Szabo and said, "Some other time, prof. Looks like you're in demand tonight." He turned to accept the embrace of Zette Borg.

It had been months. Perhaps more than a year.

The soft cotton of the working girl's dress replaced by the slippery sheen of a silk blouse—the girl's natural, erotic scent suddenly drenched by something French and expensive and oh-so-prewar that masked Zette Borg.

The band was playing "Night and Day," they were under the stars, there was something resembling yearning burning inside of him, and she said, "Leo sent me. Is there somewhere we can talk?"

Szabo had a single man's accommodation. Tarpaper roof and walls as thin as tissue paper, so they drove out onto the highway, passed two motels, and checked into the third as Mr. and Mrs. Parker.

"There was something wrong with Smith?" he asked as she kicked off her shoes and fell back on the bed.

"No. Parker is who you are now. Brown envelope in my handbag."

He fished it out.

An Arizona driving license with a number but no name, and a British passport in the name of Charles Parker.

"I'm not sure I understand."

"The army is a great place for paranoia. Anyone at our level who works at Los Alamos has to have an alias. Even any visitor at the scientific level. Would you believe Niels Bohr is known as Nick Baker? That accent and they give him the name of a cheap American gumshoe."

"And I, with my accent, I am Charles Parker?"

"I don't suppose you can play the saxophone, can you?"

"I don't understand that, either."

"No matter. You're Charlie Parker and, alas, I am Betty Bourke from the moment we leave here. Could be worse. I could be Ella Fitzgerald and then no one would believe either of us. Try checking into a motel under those names."

"Leo is sending me to Los Alamos?"

"Leo is sending both of us. He won't or can't go himself. He's fallen out with the army. You know Leo, you can imagine how he reacts to the military mind. So Leo is sending, Robert Oppenheimer is summoning. Ideally, Oppy would like Leo in person but that's not going to happen."

"So, I follow the trail."

"Eh?"

"I sent the first shipment of plutonium nitrate to Los Alamos only ten days ago."

"Well, as long as we don't have to carry the stuff with us."

Afterwards, each avoiding the damp patch on the sheets, half-asleep, half-awake, half-thinking, half-dreaming, he half-thought half-dreamt not of Zette, the English, Jewish, Cambridge-and-Sorbonne educated, cynical sophisticate but of the girl in the strawberry dress with the down-home Dogpatch accent of whom he knew nothing.

"In what concentration?"

So she wasn't asleep after all. And she was no more thinking of him than he was of her.

"I'm sorry?"

"Plutonium nitrate. In what concentration?"

"I couldn't say without notes, but low."

"Have you considered that you might achieve a higher concentration at lower temperatures?"

"How low?"

"Minus 80. Minus 100. Whatever it takes."

Ah, they were back on her territory now. The pursuit of absolute zero.

"I can't create temperatures that low. I don't have the apparatus."

"When we get to Los Alamos, I'll build it for you."

"Will it work?"

"Maybe. Maybe not."

§ 52

The army would not let them, or any other member of Robert Oppenheimer's team, fly. The train ride took them in a dogleg, from Memphis to Chicago, from Chicago to Lamy, a one-horse town just south of Santa Fe, New Mexico.

A uniformed Wac corporal met them at the rail station, saluted, blushed slightly when neither of them returned the salute.

"Sorry, sir, ma'am. Force of habit. If it moves, salute it."

Inside the gates at Los Alamos, a young lieutenant greeted them with a by-the-numbers lecture on security, secrecy, careless talk, fraternization.

Zette looked at the landscape, stared at the mountains. Ignored him.

"Ma'am?"

"Spare me the lecture, I'm not in your army."

"Ma'am, it's very important that you understand the rules."

"Fuck you, Sunny Jim. I'm not some private you can kick around, I'm the talent. Without me this bomb won't get built."

"Gadget, ma'am, we call it a gadget."

"Okay. Without me this gadget won't get built!"

"And you, sir, you do understand?"

Szabo had politely feigned attention. It cost him nothing.

"Yes, lieutenant. I know the rules. One prison is much like another."

The lieutenant muttered, "Jesus," and walked off.

"Did you have to be quite so rude?" Szabo said.

"I answer to Robert Oppenheimer, not the United States Army. And do you really think it's a prison? Oppy has fought battles with the bastards to give us freedom of movement and freedom of speech. Lecture or no lecture, rules or no rules, we're not trapped here."

He looked around. Mountains, desert, barbed wire. You could no more run from here than you could run from Alcatraz.

"In Germany I narrowly escaped Oranienburg. Plenty of people—friends, colleagues—did not. In England I was locked up in Bury St Edmunds, a place I do not know the name of but somewhere near Manchester, the Isle of Man, another place I cannot identify but somewhere near Liverpool, and in Canada somewhere out on the Great Lakes. Their common characteristic was barbed wire. I appreciate what you say. On an intellectual level. But on the emotional level . . . once I'm behind barbed wire . . . it's just another camp."

She slipped an arm through his. He could almost swear there was affection in her smile.

"You know, Charlie Parker, that's the most intimate thing you've ever told me."

"We don't do intimacy, Betty Bourke. We do sex."

§53

Auschwitz: November 1944

When the Russians got within striking range for their planes, the lights went out. For the first time in nine months Méret saw darkness.

One morning early in November she awoke and vomited. When she could lift her head she made out Magda in the half-light, hanging over the side of her bunk, pale and sweaty with a trickle of vomit on her chin.

"You, too?" she said.

The door burst open, SS banged in, women leapt to their feet and stood at attention.

"*Aufstehen!* Get dressed and muster outside. All of you. *Macht euch fertig!* Get ready to leave! *Schnell! Schnell! Raus!*"

Driving them out of the door and into the cold of morning, an SS Unterscharführer turned back, saw Méret and Magda struggling into their clothes—Magda doubled over, one arm flailing to find a sleeve in her cardigan.

He cupped Méret's chin in one hand and lifted her face.

"Can you walk?"

"I . . . I . . . can. I can."

"No, you can't."

He let her head fall, called out to his men, "Not these two. Leave them behind."

She heard Magda mutter, "This is it. The final fucking selection. Too ill to travel. It's the gas for us."

The Unterscharführer said, "*Krankenbau!*"

Infirmary.

She fell back on the bottom bunk.

Half an hour passed. A train pulled away from the ramp.

The ever-present buzz of Auschwitz, the life inside the machine, dropped to a murmur. The clatter of boots, the screams of women died away—even the bells and whistles seemed lessened. For the first time in nine months Méret heard something like silence.

An hour passed. An infirmary orderly in stripes appeared.

Méret slipped off the bed to the floor.

The room was a mess, clothes abandoned, sheet music scattered, instruments overturned, a double bass knocked from its stand and looking slaughtered.

He hoisted her to her feet, an arm around her shoulders. Braced himself when she buckled at the knees.

"*Krankenbau,*" he said gently.

§54

Auschwitz: January 18, 1945

For weeks now Méret and Magda had played only for each other. Every childhood piece they could think of, transposed for cello and trombone. They sounded like a musical interpretation of Laurel and Hardy.

Meanwhile, Block 12 filled up again. Women grateful for the warmth of the stove.

One morning in mid-January a boom like the gates of hell opening up ripped through the air, a cloud of dust swept past the window, and Magda came running in, wide-eyed and breathless.

"What was the bang?"

"The crém . . . they blew up the crematoria."

"Blew them up? I don't—"

"The lot. Boom!" Both hands in the air, fingers and thumbs pointing upward.

"Boom and they were gone—crems, gas chambers, the lot. They want to kill us now, they'll have to shoot us."

"Mind you," she added. "They might just do that anyway."

As dusk came they began to notice specks of red light around the compound and a change in the air—the smell of burning flesh overlain now with the smell of burning paper—grey flakes of it floating down like confetti.

"They're burning the evidence," said Magda.

"Aren't we evidence?" said Méret.

§55

That night no food was served.

One a.m. Darkness.

"*Raus! Raus!*"

"*Funf zu funf!*"

They lined up in the snow. Smoldering bonfires dotting the darkness with pinpoints of light. A blizzard stirring up around their heads. Grey paper confetti mingling with flakes of snow.

The Germans tried to count them one more time and gave up. Five by five became anything by anything. This was no *Appell* for the sake of it. The sense of urgency was almost palpable. A whisper, woman to woman.

"The Russians are coming, the Russians are coming."

And Magda whispered back to her, "Not soon enough they're not."

They passed under the arch, the motto high above them, *Arbeit Macht Frei*. Just another German lie.

Fifty yards on, an open staff car stopped them.

Von Schönbeck, got out, wrapped against the winter in his jackboots and his field-grey greatcoat with its fur collar. He walked straight up to Méret. She was wearing every scrap of clothing she could find, her head swathed in a piece of torn blanket. She was surprised he knew her.

He took off his greatcoat and held it out to her.

She did not move.

"Take it."

She did not move.

"Take it!"

"Méret, for Christ's sake. Take it before he shoots us," Magda said.

"Take it," von Schönbeck said once more, "You might well survive."

She took it from him without a word. She put her arms in the sleeves, buttoned it, turned up the collar, felt the fur on the back of her neck, looked down at her feet to see the coat trailing in the snow, looked up at von Schönbeck but he had gone.

§56

They were almost at the rear of the column. That the men had marched ahead of them was obvious. Bodies at the side of the road; bodies across the road leaving no option for the women but to walk on corpses.

Méret tried to count the intervals. It seemed the Germans stopped them every hour for a few minutes rest. Some fell asleep in the snow at once, and any who did not rise at the shout of "*Raus!*" were shot where they lay. Anyone who lingered or faltered was shot where they stood.

Just before dawn they were steered off the road and into an abandoned barn.

Méret had dry, grey camp bread. Magda produced half a dozen cooked sausages from her coat pocket.

"You'll never know who I fucked to get these," she said. "Just eat. Remember what the bastard said—you might well survive."

As they marched through the next day it was Magda who began to falter. Méret matched her pace until they were in the last dozen in line. Only stragglers and guards behind.

Another night in a barn—or was it the same night? She was beginning to lose count of days and had long since lost count of hours.

Another day on the road—or was it the same day? They were last now, everyone behind them had been shot. Just one guard to bring up the rear.

Magda could hardly walk at all. Méret propped her up and their pace slowed to nothing more than a slug crawl through the snow. The guard walked blindly past them.

For a moment she thought they were free, that, scarcely less numb than they were themselves, he had turned off to his task and failed to notice them.

Magda sank.

"Leave me."

"*Sssh*. He has forgotten us."

And as she spoke the guard turned back, trudged towards them, unslung his rifle, pointed it at Magda, and said, "*Auf, auf—weitermachen.*"

"No. Shoot me. Shoot me, you crazy bastard!"

For a minute or more he kept his rifle trained on Magda. Méret watched the barrel waving unsteadily, saw his grip slacken.

Then he slung it over his shoulder again, muttered, "What's the fucking point?" and walked off the road and into the woods towards a tumbledown shed.

For several minutes Méret could hear nothing. The silence of landscape under snow, the like of which she had never heard before. A world without music. She had learnt to tell how cold it was from the sound snow made underfoot. The sound was music, the note rising with the fall in temperature as the crust got firmer. And if you didn't move you made no music.

Auschwitz was remote now, no smell of burning flesh, no film of grease at the back of the throat. Vienna remoter still. No music. She could not recall a day without music. Silence was . . . unheard. They were alone, painted onto a fairy-tale landscape, at one with a mute, near-translucent nature—two children, Kay and Gerda, waiting/not waiting for the appearance of the Snow Queen on her silver sleigh. Silent upon a plain in Poland.

Méret recognized this for what it was—the onset of madness, a madness she had held at arm's length, at bow's length, for the best/worst part of a year.

Magda broke the spell.

"Why . . . why aren't we dead?"

Méret put an arm under Magda, lifted her to her feet.

"He's *Wehrmacht*. He's not SS. Maybe he just doesn't care anymore."

And they followed the soldier's footsteps in the snow.

Inside the hut, half the roof had collapsed and he was gathering wood and straw from the debris to light a fire. Méret scooped a clear space on the ground and the soldier turned out his pockets for scraps of paper and a box of matches. Between them they fuelled the fire well into the night. Their eyes never meeting.

When he was ready to sleep, the soldier slipped his arms from the sleeves of his greatcoat and sat inside it like a wigwam, head down below the collar, snoring. Méret copied him, buttoned von Schönbeck's greatcoat around herself and Magda—she a human blanket for Magda, Magda a human blanket for her—and slept.

She awoke alone. No German soldier. No Magda.

It was light.

She heard feet on snow.

Magda put her head in the door.

"He's gone," she said. "He was gone before I woke up."

And as she spoke Méret heard a diesel engine and watched Magda turn in the doorway and vanish.

"Magda? Magda?"

Then feet, running feet crunching across the snow and Magda's scream.

Méret stood in the doorway. Half a dozen men in quilted, white winter overalls, giant babies in romper suits with tiny red stars on the forehead were standing around watching as a comrade ripped Magda's rags from her body and fumbled at the zips on his whitesuit.

Magda screamed. Méret stood rooted to the spot, facing Russian troops, wrapped in the uniform of an SS Sturmbannführer.

Behind the troops, two officers approached without urgency. One short, one tall, major and lieutenant. The short major put a revolver to the rapist's right ear, and what she said needed no translation.

The man spat, cursed, and ignored her.

She shot him in the head, turned her gun on the spectators, and waited until they slowly turned away and walked back to the road.

The tall lieutenant came right up to Méret.

"At last. I was beginning to think we'd never find you," he said in flawless German.

It was as though he was talking to a wayward child lost now found in a street market.

"Don't worry. You're safe now. Both of you."

Her own helplessness appalled her. She let the man take her by the arm, hustle her past Magda. The woman major was helping Magda dress. The rapist lay sprawled on his back, blood melting the snow around his head.

She wanted to see Magda's eyes, to look her in the face, but they moved too quickly.

The lieutenant opened the rear door of an armoured half-track and gently pushed her in.

"Trust me," he said. "Your friend will be fine."

A minute later the woman major joined them and the half-track started up—a fug of smothering heat and diesel.

"Where is Magda? I want to see Magda."

The man answered.

"She's fine. No harm will come to her."

§57

The half-track had only slits to see through. Méret had stopped trying to look out. Trees in winter all looked the same. North and south looked the same, but when a line of barbed wire flashed by the slits she became alarmed—and when she caught a glimpse of the words *Arbeit Macht Frei* wrought in steel and realized where they were heading she lunged for the back door. The man blocked her way, got both arms around her, said, "It's not what you think." And it wasn't.

A few hundred yards farther on, the half-track pulled up and the rear door opened. The Russians got out first, both of them extending a hand to her. They had stopped outside the commandant's house. Two huge Soviet supply trucks stood in the road and a generator truck had backed though the hedge onto the remains of the rose garden and sat like a great, grey tomcat, purring with electricity.

"You will be warm," the Russian man said to her. "You will be clean."

They went in through the front door.

To her right was the drawing room in which she had played Bach. It had been ransacked. A Russian private was righting chairs and sweeping up broken china. The Russian major babbled in Russian and the lieutenant translated.

"We'll have things sorted soon. The prisoners took all the food and bedding. It's surprising they didn't take everything, but they didn't."

To her left was the kitchen. Every drawer and cupboard open.

"They took what was useful," Méret said. "Food tastes the same from a tin bowl as it does from Dresden china."

§58

They sat her down at the kitchen table. A cup of hot, black tea in front of her. She had no idea what they expected of her. And they seemed to be arguing: the man still somewhat deferential to rank, the woman on the verge of exploding at him. A flurry of Russian in rising volume went back and forth. Then the woman put her hands in the air, fists clenched in exasperation, and yelled, "Fuck it, you dumb fuckin' Ivan, you're doing this all wrong!"

And she had yelled it in English.

Méret put out a hand and touched her arm.

"I speak English," she said simply.

It seemed to be the one thing the major needed. She turned to the lieutenant, uttered a softly spoken instruction, and he left the room. Then she sat down opposite Méret.

"I'm Larissa Tosca, major, NKVD. And my German ain't so hot."

"And you learnt your English in America."

"How ever did you guess? Listen. If we can work without an interpreter, it'll be good. Gregor's a guy. He thinks like a guy. He sees this as an . . . an interrogation."

"Isn't it?"

"Well . . . yeah. But later. Later. What would you like . . . right now?"

Méret could not remember when anyone had last asked her a question with so much choice built into it.

"Right now?"

"Sure."

"Do you have hot water?"

"I think so."

"Then I'd like a bath, clean clothes, and a meal."

"In that order?"

§59

From somewhere, Tosca found bubbles and Méret sank to her neck in foaming hot water in a bathroom on the first floor. Eyes closed, skin tingling. A warmth beyond dreams but not beyond desire seeping into her flesh.

Tosca came in and sat on the lavatory seat, took a packet of Lucky Strikes from her breast pocket.

"You want a cigarette? I thought you might like a cigarette."

Méret just stared back.

Tosca took out a Zippo lighter and flicked a spark off the wheel.

"I don't smoke," she went on. "Most people do. Gregor does. I got him to hand 'em over, so if you . . ."

"I gave up. I gave up when they sent me here."

"They didn't have cigarettes?"

"Oh, yes, they had cigarettes."

"Then why deny yourself?"

Méret sank beneath the bubbles, surfaced, and wiped the soap from her face. Tosca still sat on the banks of Jordan.

"When you were a child, in whatever country you were a child, did your mother have a drawer, or perhaps a box or a biscuit tin? Whatever it was, it would be near her sewing or perhaps in the kitchen, in the woman's domain . . . and in this drawer, box, or tin she would save things that your father thought were useless and that he derided as eccentricity or folly or penny-pinching. She would save buttons that had come off shirts long since torn up for dusters, the elastic band with which the postman bundled the mail, the string that came off brown-paper parcels, the brown paper itself, an odd shoelace, a zipper from a skirt that no longer fitted, the stub end of a piece of sealing wax even though no one used sealing wax anymore, a blunt pair of scissors, a broken watch that someday someone might tease into ticking once more. To your father it was junk, to you a treasure trove to be tipped out, fondled, and tipped back. Was this not so? Of course it was. And your father was wrong and you were right. In Auschwitz, the contents of your mother's biscuit tin were riches, because in Auschwitz everything became a commodity. There was nothing that could not be traded. You could sell butter with green mould on it. You could sell a piece of wurst as hard as bullets. You could sell sex. When could you not sell sex? But a cigarette cost more. You could use cigarettes like money. An egg? Put a price on an egg. Imagine how many fucks would buy you a cigarette. Imagine how many cigarettes would buy you an egg. I gave up. It was one less commodity to have to think about. It was one less craving, and in the absence of desire, one more freedom."

Tosca said nothing to this, but then Méret never thought she would. She just put the whole pack on the side of the bath, flicked the lighter one last time to see it worked, and set it down next to the cigarettes.

Wrapped in a billowing white towel, she wiped at the film of steam across the mirror. She had not looked in a mirror since February the year before. She had caught sight of her own reflection in windows but had always turned away. She knew her hair was white but she'd never seen the full extent of it. She tilted her head this way and that. Her eyebrows were still black, and her eyes had that deathly sparkle that seemed to enhance the half-starved, but her skin was pale and papery. She turned away once more. Perhaps she could learn to live a life without a reflection, like a modern-day Nosferatu. There were bathroom scales on the floor but what would be the point?

Tosca had set out clean clothes for her—a new Russian infantry uniform, without insignia and only slightly too big—and before she dressed a doctor gave her a once-over in the main bedroom. A vaguely floral-patterned room—a large dressing-table with its triptych of mirrors and a scalloped valance—and a lingering odour of whatever Frau Commandant sprayed herself with to deter the grease and stench of death. A haven of clichéd femininity at the arsehole of the world.

"There will be no long-term effects," the doctor said when he was done. "You will keep your teeth. The loose ones will probably firm up in a matter of weeks, and the brittleness and ridges in your fingernails will pass in about a year if you eat well. There's nothing I can do about your hair. As far as I can tell your internal organs are fine. Again, if you eat well you may resume menstruation shortly. When was your last period?"

"August."

"Then I doubt that you are barren."

She'd never thought about this possibility. Now she did, it did not bother her.

In the kitchen, Tosca served an omelette with brown bread toast and butter. Méret had no idea whether this was lunch or breakfast.

"Where did you get them?"

"Out back. The commandant's wife seems to have kept chickens as a hobby. When your comrades looted the house they took the chickens but forgot to look for eggs."

"How many?"

"Three apiece."

"Good Lord. A three-egg omelette. I don't know whether I shall weep or choke."

"Do you think that's likely? Eat slow."

She was eating slowly. She had eaten slowly for the best part of a year. She wished she could describe the sensation on her tongue to Tosca but she couldn't. Egg was taste and texture, a plethora of taste and texture to someone who had grown used to all tastes being tainted by decay and most textures reduced to a greasy swill. Her internal organs were fine—she'd just been told that—her taste buds, too. The damage was to her vocabulary.

Tosca said, "I wish I could have got you some real coffee. But our rations don't run to that, and if the Krauts had any then the guys who tossed this place got to it first."

"They are welcome," Méret replied.

"Yeah, ain't they."

§60

That night she had a room to herself, a double bed and clean sheets. Finding that she could not sleep on a mattress, she pulled the clean sheets and bug-free blankets onto the floor and slept there.

A three-egg omelette was not served again, and after a breakfast of combat rations and ersatz coffee, Tosca was ready to talk shop.

Méret was savouring her barley roast ersatz. Despite what she had told Gregor, just to hold a china cup was a pleasure. Gregor was twitching to get on and Tosca was gently keeping him in line.

"We were looking for you."

"I gathered. But I don't know how you knew who or where I was."

"No matter—we found you."

"And I am grateful, so much so that I will risk asking what it is you want of me."

"Good. That saves a lot of time. We want you to work for us."

"Where? In Russia?"

"No—you get the cherry on the top of the cake. You work for us in the West."

"Where exactly? And where is the West?"

"The West is whatever's west of the line made when our guys meet up with their guys. The way things are going that'll be somewhere west of Berlin, sometime in June."

"And in the middle are the Germans?"

"Do you really give a gnat's ass about the Germans?"

"No."

"When it's all over, dust settled, borders redrawn, you join the refugee drift westward."

"Where? France? England? America?"

"Not gonna tell you. Wherever you go we'll keep in touch. In fact, that's what we want of you—that you keep in touch."

"Keep in touch without the police of France, England, or America knowing?"

"Glad you got the picture."

"So I would be what? A sort of conduit?"

"That about sums it up."

"I said I was grateful, but tell me . . . why would I do this for you? Why would I not simply go back to Vienna and pick up where my life left off?"

Tosca slapped a brown cardboard file on the table and slid out three photographs. Méret reached over and spread them with her fingertips, her incredulity growing with each passing second.

"You know these people?"

"Yes."

"They all work for us. We have them. And if we have them I think we have you."

Méret stared at the photographs. For a whole minute she could not take her eyes off them, then the right words came to her, not her words, but the right words.

"The rule of possession."

"I'm sorry?"

"You have me. That is all that matters. You have them . . . you have me. And if there's one thing the Germans have taught me it is that possession is everything."

§61

Jornada del Muerto, New Mexico:
July 16, 1945
Trinity

After a fortnight of sporadic dry storms, the wet one arrived, as it had threatened to do since the beginning of the month. It rained all night. Midnight came and went with no test.

He loved a good thunderstorm. He didn't know a physicist anywhere who didn't. You couldn't spend a working life with the elements and fail to appreciate the show they put on for free.

It was close to five in the morning before the wind drove the rain clouds away.

Outside the shelter at South 10,000, there were shallow trenches and a raised ridge. Szabo sloughed off his rain slicker and lay down next to Frank Oppenheimer—his brother Robert was in the hut behind them where the countdown was approaching its final, automatic phase. George Kistiakowsky, the lanky, crazy Russian who had built the explosive casing, was buzzing too much to sit or lie down, and jigged up and down around their feet.

It was close to dawn but with the floodlights behind them the night ahead, looking straight at the tower, seemed blacker than ever. Some had welder's goggles, some had sunglasses, all of them had a small sheet of toughened, tinted glass.

A figure slipped in beside him—sunglasses, a fedora, a waft of Indiscret. Zette in trousers.

"Are you trying to pass for a man?"

"Something like that."

"You might have left off the scent."

"Mea culpa."

"Aren't you supposed to be up a mountain somewhere?"

"I'm not missing this. And I'm not watching from twenty miles away. I've been imagining this moment for years."

So had Szabo.

He could project the equations involved onto a mental screen—the lines and letters and numbers of the formulae, the chemical symbols and atomic numbers of uranium and plutonium, of beryllium and polonium, U.92, Pu.94, Be.4, Po.84, and their reckless offspring, the alpha particles and neutrons that would uncork the genie from the bottle—they all appeared in the mind's eye as a sequence of connection and causality.

He had come to think of it with a simple logic as being like the old Negro spiritual he had learnt back in Tennessee. He had come across it in the cinema, an old flickering cartoon from the early days of sound. A song of the inevitability of connection and disconnection, of structure and destruction that had fixed in his mind the image of a dancing skeleton:

Your knee bone connected to your thigh bone,
Your thigh bone connected to your hip bone,

Your hip bone connected to your back bone,
Your back bone connected to your shoulder bone,
Disconnect dem bones, dem dry bones,
Now hear de word of de Lord!

Im Anfang war das Wort? Nein. Im Anfang war die Tat . . . and the deed of the Lord was a silent flash that seemed brighter than a thousand suns. Nothing he had imagined came close. Night became noon.

And although his scientific training told him that light would race ahead of sound, he had not anticipated such silence.

A gut instinct overtook his curiosity and momentarily he put his face down in the sand. When he looked again, white light had turned to colour and a giant mushroom cloud was rising, twisting leftward, corkscrewing into the sky. The skeleton danced.

He had imagined this so often—but he had thought in pale monochrome. The colours had been unimaginable so he had not imagined them. Now they rolled out, in half the colours of the painting box . . . clouds of red and pink, darting flames of orange, yellow, scarlet, and green, an arc of iridescent blue, a billowing mushroom in deep, threatening purple.

Then the shock wave hit, and the boom of the explosion, bouncing off the mountains in an endless repetitive echo that seemed to him as rhythmical as the beating of some red Indian drum.

A war dance? Why not? This was war. A mile into the sky, a three-thousand-foot mushroom danced its dance of death.

Szabo looked at Zette, grinning as stupidly as he knew he was himself. He looked the other way to Frank Oppenheimer. At some point Robert Oppenheimer had slid in next to him. They exchanged glances, then Oppy said, "It worked." And Frank finding no better summation repeated back, "It worked."

It worked.

Kistiakowsky had been standing when the shock wave hit and it had lifted him off his feet. When they all stood up, he was laughing and beating the dust off his pants. One hand moved to slap Oppenheimer on the back.

"That's ten bucks you owe me, Oppy."

Szabo had no idea they'd bet on anything. There was a pool to bet on the tonnage of the blast—he had a dollar on 20,000—and he'd heard

Fermi taking bets that the bomb would ignite the whole of New Mexico, but now it seemed that Oppenheimer had taken a bet that it would be a dud.

Oppenheimer turned out his wallet to show it was empty. Such an odd gesture at such a frantic moment.

"Kisty, you'll just have to wait."

Failing to find a one-cent coin in his pocket, Szabo flipped a buffalo nickel into the wallet just as Oppenheimer turned it upright.

"Penny for them, Oppy. Whatever you say next is history."

Oppenheimer picked out the nickel.

"For five pennies, Charlie, you only get one thought."

"For sure."

"I was thinking of a line from the Bhagavad Gita, 'I am become Death, the destroyer of worlds.'"

By the time he'd finished speaking, and he spoke so softly, he was all but drowned out by the roar of congratulation, and as it subsided Szabo heard a voice behind him say, "We're all sons of bitches now," and he wondered if the two statements did not amount to the same thing, and whether crudity bore history somewhat better than poetry.

Then Oppenheimer tugged at the brim of his fedora and walked on to shake more hands, the inherent sadness of his words offset by the Gary Cooper strut in his walk.

It worked.

Ezekiel connected dem dry bones and Oppenheimer disconnected dem.

§62

"Do you know what I'd kill for right now?"

He tried not to take her literally.

"A martini," she said. "With real gin, not pure alcohol from the lab, and a real olive. And a twirly stick to make twirls in it."

"Okay. How about we take a night out."

"Santa Fe?"

"I was thinking more of Taos."

"What's in Taos?"

"Not much. More Indians, more pottery, more blankets."

"But a bar, right? They do have a bar?"

"I'm sure they do. It's just that I don't want to be hanging around the bar at La Fonda for one more night with our own people."

"And if Taos can't make a martini?"

"Then you can show them."

Months ago the army had decided on a programme of disinformation. What this meant in practice was that the scientists should prop up bars in Santa Fe, and be indiscreet—letting any drunk they could converse with know that after a couple of drinks they were willing to spill the beans, and the beans were that they were all busy making rockets. "Rockets" was understandable as an idea and might quell speculation as to what was really going on. It was a PR disaster. No one had been the slightest bit interested in what was happening out at Los Alamos. Truth or lies. They were happier with their running gag—"they're making windshield wipers for submarines."

The conversation he wanted to have with Zette he'd rather have anywhere but in a bar in Santa Fe. So they drove fifty miles on, to the Hotel Martin in Taos.

"With a name like that I'd hope they make a damn good martini." They did.

She twirled her twirly stick and took a first sip.

"S'truth . . . Booth's gin! Wherever did they get that?"

A second sip.

"You know. I think you'll be doing all the driving on the way home."

Szabo left his Mexican beer untouched.

She gazed around the bar. It was mostly empty, and looked as though it hadn't changed much in twenty years or more.

"Does anything put this joint on the map?"

"It attracts painters. And one of your famous English writers lived here. I believe he's buried somewhere nearby."

"Well . . . it won't be Byron or Shelley . . . and as I can't guess you'd better tell me."

"Lawrence."

"Lawrence?"

"D. H. Lawrence."

"What, the chap who wrote about going down the pit in Nottingham and fucking in the woods?"

"The same, but he lived here . . . one of his novels is even set here. *St Mawr.*"

"And you've read it?"

"They had a copy in one of the camps I was in. It's all about never being able to beat the desert. You can work the land, till the soil, and still the desert will come back to beat you. A rather large metaphor for life itself I thought. You can love the desert, as Oppy surely does, and still it will defeat you."

"And this week we roasted it."

"Turned it to glass. Nothing will grow at that spot in Jornada del Muerto for years."

"You bugger . . . I knew you got me here just so you could get morbid on me."

"Not so . . . but there *are* things to be said."

She finished her martini and held out the glass for more.

"See if he's got a slice of lime this time. One more and I'm all ears."

Over her second martini, he said, "Leo has got up a petition to the president, urging him not to use the bomb we are making."

"Another one?" she said. "He's doesn't give up, does he?"

"No, he doesn't. But his concerns are our concerns. Everyone at the Chicago lab has signed it."

"All of them?"

"Sixty-nine, seventy with Leo."

"But no one here? I mean, Leo didn't circulate it at Los Alamos? We all had a meeting. Oppy saw off Leo's last attempt rather easily."

"I doubt Leo even tried to circulate it—we're an army base not a college campus—but I received a copy and so did Edward Teller."

"But you didn't sign?"

"No. Nor did Teller. We both considered it. Oppy asked us not to, but now I cannot help but wonder how little we might have had to argue to get him to sign, too."

"He's said all along that we will have to use it. He said so at the meeting."

"It was more than two weeks ago that we discussed it, but his attitude has not been the same since we tested the bomb. He knows it works now, he knows the power it has . . . and he feels . . . responsible."

She swirled her martini, fished out the olive and ate it.

"Tell me, Charlie Parker, did you and Oppy rehearse that line from the Bhagavad Gita?"

"No."

"There are times I think he rehearses everything he says. Even the one-liners."

"An academic practice, perhaps, born of standing up in front of rooms full of students."

"I am become Death, the destroyer of worlds . . . I wonder whether he might not have meant it personally. He seems to take everything so damn personally. The weight of the world on those bony shoulders. The power of life and death in those spindly fingers."

"It is an ungodly amount of power."

"Au contraire. It's godly in the extreme. A destroyer of worlds. Sounds pretty godlike to me."

"I meant—a frightening amount of power to be possessed by a single nation."

"Single nation? Well, you might be right. A step on from a single individual, I suppose. But . . . I'm English, Tuck and Chadwick are English, you're Hungarian, Teller and Leo are Hungarian, so's Wigner, Fermi's Italian, Kistiakowsky is Russian, Peierls is German, Bethe's German, Frisch is Austrian, and most of the others are German or Austrian. Oppy's American, Serber's American. There are times they seem to be the only ones. Social nights when you'd think we were all in a café in Vienna rather than stuck in a Sheetrock hut in the middle of the desert in New Mexico."

"You think they'll share it?"

"With whom?"

"With our allies."

"Our current allies? Don't be daft. An ally is simply an enemy you haven't met yet. We'll be squaring up to Joe Stalin the minute this war's over. Of course I don't think they'll share it. I don't *care* if they share it. I just want one dropped on Berlin."

"Three months after they surrendered?"

"I don't give a toss. Call it insurance. Call it a preemptive strike against the next German war. And you know better than me. Do we have another bomb up our sleeve? You know better than anyone on Earth how much plutonium we have."

"Zette, I can't tell you that."

"Of course you bloody can. We've earmarked three bombs for the Japs, right?"

"Yes, but—"

"But nothing. Once we've nuked the Nips how many more damn bombs can we make?"

He hesitated.

"Come on. Oppy's first law of the colloquia, there are no secrets. We all know what there is to know. If you don't tell me, somebody on your team will."

"Five, possibly six, by the end of the year."

"Then we've got a fucking arsenal haven't we? And you think we won't use it? We'll drop the bomb for one simple reason: because we can. Japan can surrender tonight. We'll still drop the bomb. The army won't miss the chance to see what it can do. Even Oppy refutes the idea that we can stage a demonstration. He might fear a dud but he knows damn well that the army wants to see a bomb take out an entire city. The generals must be praying Japan doesn't surrender. I don't know the target but I do know it'll be a city the air force hasn't touched yet. Pristine. Virgin. Just asking for it. Leo has wasted his breath—we're going to bomb Japan, and when that's done, as far as I'm concerned, we can drop the rest on Germany."

Talking to Zette once she'd lost her temper was close to pointless. He tacked away from Japan, back towards Russia.

"How about some sense of . . . of . . . of a balance of power?"

"When has power ever been balanced? Balanced power. That's the perfect oxymoron."

§63

As they left, she bribed the barman to part with a full bottle of Booth's gin.

On the road back to Santa Fe, he asked, "What's so special? One gin is much the same as another."

"No, it's not. You just take a sniff."

She uncorked the bottle and wafted it under his nose as he drove.

"See? It's sort of flowery and oily at the same time. Reminds me of home. God knows why. It's as though they'd mingled summer and autumn—summer scents and autumn drizzle. A bit of England in a bottle."

But he wasn't thinking of England. He wasn't thinking of Zette. On a rutted, washboard road, rolling into the New Mexico desert under a cobalt sky with the smell of juniper wafting up from the open bottle and the scent of night-blooming jasmine drifting in through the open window, he was thinking of Russia.

§64

Poland: July 1945

The Russians kept her in Poland. She wasn't sure where. No more than fifty miles from Auschwitz by the time it took to get there. It was a big, ancient country house, remarkably unscathed after five years of total war, on a vast estate far from the sound of anything. A fading dacha in dusty shades of red and green. Once it had been full of servants. Now it was full of soldiers. It didn't look like a prison. It merely felt like one.

They told her she needed to build up her strength.

She watched spring arrive.

She taught Tosca to speak better German.

She told them she needed to see Magda.

Tosca told her this was not possible. Magda was fine; that was all she needed to know.

There were books in half a dozen languages—enough to keep her occupied in French and English as well as German. She read novels by the English writer Charles Dickens for the first time. And one evening in April, Tosca turned up with a film projector and reel upon reel of prewar Hollywood and they found a common taste in Fred Astaire and Ginger Rogers dancing across a bedsheet tacked to the drawing room wall.

And in the absence of a cello she played piano at a concert-sized Bechstein very like the one Viktor Rosen had owned.

By the summer, she had regained most of the weight she had lost. She had come to terms with mirrors, telling herself they'd never figure much in her life evermore, and dyed her hair blonde.

She told them she needed to go to Vienna.

Tosca told her that this was possible.

Two days later they set off.

Across Czechoslovakia and into the ruins of Vienna from the east.

§65

Her parents' apartment was now in the French sector of the occupied city. Méret and Tosca stayed in a house in the Russian sector on the far side of the Danube Canal.

Tosca kept her commissar's uniform but had Méret kitted out in civvies—a two-piece in drab grey, but a good cut.

"We can go anywhere, it's joint occupation, but, y'know, the city is patrolled constantly . . ."

"That's okay. I wasn't planning on wearing that uniform forever."

"And the natives can be hostile."

"I'm not surprised," Méret said. "You're treating them like the enemy.

There will be many Viennese who regard themselves as among Hitler's first victims."

"Well. Maybe a little token resistance in thirty-eight might have established that fact. You should have seen the bonfire of the swastikas the day we took Vienna. There wasn't an apartment in the whole goddamn city that hadn't got a flag or a portrait of the crazy corporal to throw on the pile."

Méret let the matter drop.

"I want to go there alone."

"That's okay. How long do you need?"

"Half an hour?"

"Fine. I'll meet you there."

In the literal sense the dust had settled. The Russians had taken Vienna in May and only days ago had carved up city and country between the victorious powers.

It could be worse, she thought. Tosca had brought her newsreels while they were still in Poland, showing the centre of Berlin after the surrender. The Brandenburg Gate was still standing—little else seemed to be. Vienna had taken shelling—here and there a house was reduced to rubble, and occasionally a whole block—but it was still a recognizable city where people tried to live their lives. She wondered that anything larger than rats and mice could live in Berlin.

Devastation lent a curious intimacy. It turned the inside out. To see the interior of a house, for no other reason than that the exterior no longer existed, was a prurience, almost an espionage—the zigzag line up a bare brick wall where a staircase had once stood; a door halfway up a wall that once led to a child's bedroom and now opened onto a void; a fireplace, grate still intact, perched in space. It was a glimpse into vanished lives. Into private lives. And it felt like a violation.

The building was still standing. The ground floor apartment looked as though it was still lived in. The first floor had lost some of its windows and a lace curtain billowed out into the street as the draughts caught it, almost as though it were waving to her.

The street door was off its hinges. She stepped inside. An old woman she had never seen before was sweeping out the ground floor apartment. The door wobbled as Méret moved it.

"Russkis," said the old woman. "They kicked it in. Then they ransacked my rooms. Took my sewing machine. What would they want with a sewing machine?"

Upstairs, the door was wide open, a breeze eddying in and out of the apartment. As she'd expected, it was empty. All the traces of human habitation, but empty. The shadow line on the wallpaper in the sitting room where her piano had stood for twenty years. The four indentations on the floorboards in the dining room that marked out the position of the table. The brass hook in the wall where her grandfather's portrait had hung.

And it smelled empty—she'd no idea empty had its own smell but it had.

It didn't feel like home. It felt too big. Stripped of everything, it felt vast. As though the return of all her parents' possessions, of everything on the list, would never fill the space. She had not thought of re-creation. She had come steeled for a last look but part of her mind had always thought re-creation possible. And now she knew—you can't go back.

She walked from room to room, half hoping to find something the Germans had missed. In the bathroom, she did. Above the basin was a mirrored cabinet, and in the cabinet a small blue bottle with a conical silver cap and a gold label:

It had been her mother's. It was three-quarters full, so sparingly had it been used since an anniversary trip to Paris in 1929. She had been left with aunts and cried for a whole weekend and when her mother returned she had smelled new, different. Méret unscrewed the cap, dabbed a little of the scent on the back of her right hand and, when the alcohol cleared, smelled the new smell again, smelled her mother fresh from Paris in 1929—and with it the smell of empty vanished.

She went back downstairs.

The old woman was still sweeping up.

"And they took my Franz's bike!"

Out in the street a man in a tatty jacket and a cloth cap was wheeling a wooden cart laden with junk and rags up the street. When he drew level with Méret he stopped.

"Fraulein Voytek?"

"Herr Knobloch?"

"Your hair? You used to be so dark . . . like a gypsy . . . I thought you were dead."

"A reasonable assumption, Herr Knobloch."

"You're looking for your parents?"

"No. I know they're dead."

"They came for them. It would be March or perhaps April last year. I . . . I saw . . ."

Tosca was coming down the street towards them. Knobloch turned his cart around in a swift pivot and pushed it back the way he had come without finishing his sentence.

Tosca was next to her now.

"You know him?"

She might wonder what it was he had to say, she might not be able to stop herself. But she didn't want to know. If she ever wanted the truth of what fate had fallen to her parents' lot she could ask Tosca. She felt sure Tosca held a bag of secrets. Every so often she might open the bag and release one, fluttering like a moth to the light.

"He used to be my father's barber."

"Jack of all trades. He spies for us and I'm pretty damn certain he spies for the British, too. I guess any barber would make a natural spy. They spend their working lives listening."

"And if you were to ask him he'd tell you it's what he has to do to survive."

"His type always do. Survive, I mean. Anschluss, the Krauts, the draft, allied bombing, occupation by four armies. He's survived it all."

"His type?"

"You know what I mean."

"And me, Major Tosca? What type would you say I was?"

"I'd say you were the type that needs to shake her ass, or do you want to be standing here when some new family arrives?"

"New family?"

"Your folks' apartment may be missing a few panes of glass and some tiles but it's habitable. Much of Vienna isn't. The French have reassigned it to a homeless family, to people bombed out of their own homes by us."

"But this is *my* home."

Tosca looked straight into her eyes.

"Do you really mean that?"

Méret knew—Tosca would never tell her what type she was, and she herself would never volunteer an answer. But her last question had only one possible answer.

"No. I don't. All this happened to someone else. I don't know what home is. I've forgotten. And I lived here less than eighteen months ago."

A voice in her head telling her clearly, *You can't go back.*

"Wherever it is you mean to take me . . . take me."

"Okay," said Tosca. "How would you feel about Paris?"

In her left hand Méret still held the blue bottle of Soir de Paris. She uncurled her fingers, the bottle flat in the palm of her hand for Tosca to see.

"One of your jokes, right?"

"No," said Tosca. "No joke."

§66

Paris: Friday August 3, 1945

In August 1944, as the Allies advanced, General von Choltitz, the military commander of Paris, had ignored Hitler's order to leave the city "a smoking ruin" and had surrendered to the shotguns, billy clubs, and bread knives of the *Forces Françaises de l'Interieur* and to the Sherman tanks of the French Second Armoured Division. This had saved the city from the fate of Vienna or the far worse fate of Berlin. Rumours Méret had heard that the Germans had melted down the Eiffel Tower to make weapons turned out to be somewhat exaggerated.

On the Left Bank, the Quai Saint-Michel curved with the river pretty well opposite the middle of the Île de la Cité. One street below this the Rue de la Huchette ran between the Boulevard Saint-Michel and the Rue des Deux Ponts. Before the war, it had housed a *boulangerie,* a *bouchier chevaline,* a bookbinder, a draper, a flower shop, a laundry, two hotels, a café and a *bordel.* After the war, mostly it still did.

A German tank had blundered down this narrow street in May 1940, but managed to extricate itself with little damage—and in August 1944 some of the fiercest battles of the resistance had taken place at the western end of the street in the Place Saint-Michel and all along the boulevard . . . snipers shooting and shot at . . . tarmac torn up to discover long-lost cobblestones with which to barricade the end of the street . . . and as the Germans left they had been waved on their way to perdition with raised lavatory brushes at every window.

Two side streets led off the Rue de la Huchette—the Rue Zacharie and the short but wonderfully named Rue du Chat-qui-Pêche. On the latter corner was the gendarmerie and, opposite, on the corner of Rue Zacharie, the *bordel, le Panier Fleuri.*

She had been given an address of an apartment that turned out to be over the *bordel* and had its double, ground-floor doors next to the windows of the florist.

Tosca had left her at the Gare de l'Est.

"You'll be fine on your own, kid."

"What if I get lost?"

"It's a straight line down to the river, across the island till you hit the Boul Mich. A blind man couldn't get lost."

"What if I just disappear?"

"You think we wouldn't look? You think we wouldn't find you?"

It was her first taste of freedom. At the dacha in Poland she was never alone. Tosca had been there some of the time, perhaps most of it, but when she wasn't Gregor was. Sleep had become the approximation of freedom, the surrogate of peace and privacy.

Now she was walking down the Boulevard de Strasbourg alone. More alone than she could ever remember being in her whole life. Paris was a revelation. And what it revealed was Méret Voytek.

The concierge looked her up and down as though she were applying for a job on the ground floor establishment, and thinking little of her appeal as a whore, pointed her to the second floor.

She rang the bell and stood in front of two tall, narrow doors of dull, unbuffed cherrywood.

He took an age, looked as though she had disturbed him in the middle of something. A big, dark, Slav featured man of forty or more, wearing only a sarong knotted at his waist and trailing on the floor. Spatterings of paint across his body and his sarong, as though he had just wiped his hands on it. A mop of touselled black hair on his head, another on his chest. A bear of a man.

"You are Serge?"

He stopped scratching and snapped to.

"My dear. At last. We've been expecting you for so long. First it was Monday, and then Wednesday, and then yesterday, and here you are at last."

And a half-naked, painted bear she had never met before pulled her to him in his bear hug.

"Come in, come in. My, so little baggage. Is that all you have? Still, what does it matter? We have all of us lost so much. We have the delight of fresh beginning."

"We do?"

"Of course we do. The world stripped bare for us to fall upon like seed from the tree. And speaking of bare, excuse me a moment my dear while I fling something on."

The world stripped bare? Is that what had happened? Walking down the boulevards, across the Île de la Cité and the Pont Saint-Michel, it had been her stripped bare by the world. Perhaps this was what he meant by a seed?

He took her bag from her only to set it down a few feet inside the door.

"Permit me to dress, my dear. I shall be but a moment."

And he left her in the hall.

From whatever room he had retreated to, she heard him say, "Make yourself at home, *cherie*. Have a good poke around."

Only one of the many doors that led off the hall was open. She pushed at it and found herself in a north-facing room overlooking the street, bright with summer light, that Serge obviously used as his studio. It was all but devoid of furniture, the floor was spattered with paint, accretions of paint laid down like strata in rock over countless years, and canvases stood stacked aginst the wall in dozens.

In the middle of the floor lay a summer dress in an ivy-leaf pattern, a red hat, and a pair of roller skates. Seated on a high-backed wooden chair, sipping a glass of white wine, was a red-headed girl of about her own age, completely naked and completely without self-consciousness. Resting on the easel was a large canvas representing *Girl with Wineglass*—she was a faceless blur, her body a streak of vivid red and green.

The girl got up.

"You must be Méret. What kind of a name is that?"

It was not any question Méret had expected as a first question.

"I don't really know. Greek or something. I was never sure."

"I am Zozo. Would you like wine or tea? Do say wine, then I don't have to go and fiddle about in the kitchen with the gas stove. It has a bad habit of going *poof!*—one could lose one's eyebrows, or worse if one is naked."

"Wine, then," said Méret, devoid of choice. "Are you naked often?"

"Most of the time. He's painted me a dozen times since the liberation. He'll paint you, too. If I were you I'd volunteer now, while the weather's warm. There was hardly any fuel last winter. My arse was blue with cold."

Zozo poured her a glass of wine and the two of them stood in front of the work in progress.

"You know, part of me thinks, *Why do I bother?* They never look like me and he might just as well paint from imagination—which, of course, he won't—and part of me knows how good he is."

"Does he . . . sell?"

"Oh, yes . . . you'd be surprised how in a time of shortages people will find money for art. It is defiance, I think. Thumbing one's nose at history. It was why we threw wild parties during the war. Now we have no money for food, or worse, no food, we buy paintings, we go to concerts, we worship fashion. We go hungry just to be able to afford the price of the little red cloche hat in the milliner's window."

Serge reappeared—black, baggy denim trousers, and a black shirt merely adding to the bearness.

"Zozo, scoot. We will do no more today."

Without another word, Zozo drained her glass, picked her red cloche hat and her ivy-leaf-pattern dress from the floor, slipped both on in an instant, tucked the roller skates under her arm, and left.

"Do you paint, *cherie*?"

"No. I play."

"Play what?"

"The cello. I used to play the cello."

"Surely you haven't given up?"

"No. It's just that I don't have a cello."

He was nodding sagely, as though what she had just said required thought, which it surely didn't. Suddenly he rushed to the window, looked down into the street. Zozo was sitting on the steps of the gendarmerie, tying the laces on her skates.

"Zozo! Ten o'clock!"

"Tomorrow is Saturday!"

"So . . . are we the bourgeoisie, keeping office hours now?"

She thumbed her nose at him, stood, spun full circle, and rolled away into the Quartier Latin.

To Méret this was a moment of near-magic—a woman without underwear, dressed only in a hat and a dress so thin as to be transparent, was roller-skating across Paris in the last of the afternoon sun, dodging pedestrians, thumbing her nose at gendarmes, and showing her backside to taxi cabs. It was absurd—in a world that had seemed to be made up only of cruel rationalizations, this was delightfully absurd. The world was indeed stripped bare.

She became aware of how big the apartment was. It went two floors up and two across, over both the *bordel* and the florist. He showed her to her own room on the third floor. She set down her bag in a cream-coloured room, with woodwork in pale green and a dormer window that looked south across rooftops and peeked in through other dormers into other rooms and other lives. A plain deal chest of drawers, a half-melted candle stuck in an enamel candlestick, a narrow iron bedstead in curlicues of faded gold. A portrait on the wall—another blurred woman in strikingly unnatural colours, sprawled like an odalisque—it might be Zozo, it might be anyone

He said, "Unpack. Wash. Bathe if you like. We'll take a stroll at dusk. A stroll, a drink. Stroll some more, drink some more."

He left her alone. Twice in one day she had become mistress of her own space and time. She sat on the edge of the bed. A mattress as hard as oak. She knew at once that she could be happy here. She knew at once that it could not last.

§67

It was still light when they began their stroll, meandering along the Quai des Grand Augustins, over the Pont Neuf, onto the Île de la Cité, past the cathedral of Notre Dame, onto the Île Saint-Louis, back to the left bank to nip in and out of the bars of the Boulevard Saint-Germain—the Deux Magots and the Café de Flore—to end up, as dusk rolled down upon the city like a theatre curtain, at the restaurant Porquerolles.

He talked nonstop all the way, pausing only to acknowledge people he knew—a wave to Jean Cocteau (striking, bony, handsome); a few words in two languages and a formal introduction to Pablo Picasso (broad, woolly in a bald sort of way, looking like a Spanish peasant); a joke that set them both giggling with Samuel Beckett (bony, mysterious, far from handsome, piercing eyes behind wire-rimmed spectacles).

"Do you know *everyone* in Paris?" she asked.

He took her arm and slipped it through his. Strolling like lovers now.

"I've lived here, on the same street, in fact, since I was five or six years old. Yes, I know a lot of people, but most of them not well. Paris is a moveable feast. For example, I spent the war here. Beckett and Picasso did not. I suppose they might have been at risk. And I suppose I was not. Meanwhile, who stayed, who left, who did what has become the subject of a fiction as massive as *La Comédie humaine*. And it drives people apart. For almost a year France has been eating itself alive. I have learnt to value any friendship and not to ask too closely about who did what, with whom, when."

"I don't understand."

"Well, let me give you the obvious example. The war is scarcely over—Japan has not yet surrendered—and Marshal Pétain is on trial.

Today in fact, Pierre Laval took the stand to give evidence on behalf of the Vichy regime. It's possible they'll both hang."

"And it's possible," she said, "that that would be justice."

"Indeed, but it is not a healing process. And I fear that France will go on devouring herself for a generation."

They had reached the door of Porquerolles. He held it open, she paused on the threshold. She did not want this to be a subject that dominated their meal.

"You will understand, Serge, that I am even less likely to forgive than any French citizen."

"I do, and I would never expect you to. But we must walk away from the mess of recrimination or go on eating ourselves alive."

"And you think that can apply to an individual as well as a nation, do you?"

"Let's eat."

§68

When they left Porquerolles it was night. The street lamps ablaze. They cut like broken glass.

"What's the matter?" he said.

"Nothing," she replied, and tucking her head down walked on beside him.

Two young women, only a few years older than she was, passed them, walking side by side. One wore her mother's scent, *Soir de Paris,* the other Chanel No. 5. Two trails of perfume entwining in the night air in an invisible, delectable double helix. Wisteria and honeysuckle, wrapped the one about the other. She stopped and turned and looked. Breathed in.

"Startling, isn't it?" she heard him say.

She said nothing, watched the two women caught like flickering frames on a cinema screen by streams and pools of light as they passed the illuminated window of each café and restaurant.

"Before the war," he went on, out of sight behind her, a baritone susurrus at her shoulder, "I would have said Paris smelled of drains, castor oil and patchouli. Now every woman that passes is an olfactory delight. As though they had been saving it these last five years. Their faces are different, all but stripped of their *maquillage*. A bare simplicity. Even the way they walk is different. Watch them. There is none of the haute-couture, arse-wobbling strut of the pre-war Parisienne. They plant their feet firmly on the ground, as though stepping out into this strange new world. And it is a strange new world, is it not?"

He was by her side now, looking down as she looked up.

"Yes," she said. "Strange in that it is original. Nothing like it has ever existed. And there is none shall find it stranger than I."

Back in her room atop the studio, atop the *bordel,* in Rue de la Huchette, she took out her possession. Her sole possession. The last relic of her childhood—the small conical bottle of *Soir de Paris,* three-quarters full. She had had it for the best part of a fortnight now, had opened it and sniffed at it but not used it.

She dabbed a little on her neck, a little more on her hand, and as the alcohol cleared she smelt her mother one fleeting final moment as Paris 1929 submerged into Paris 1945, the scent became her scent, and she entwined with the honeysuckle and wisteria, spiralling out into *un soir Parisien.*

§69

In the morning she slept late. When she finally came down to the studio, the same hat and a different dress were heaped in the middle of the floor next to the roller skates, and Zozo sat naked again.

Serge was in his sarong, and she concluded it was his affectation or preference to paint bare-chested. Given his propensity to splash paint everywhere, it might even be a practical choice.

Kneeling on the floorboards was a young man who might have been Zozo's twin, skinny as he was, with a thick thatch of auburn hair. He was unpacking a suitcase and listing everything he took out.

"A kilo of butter, four jars of strawberry jam, two of honey, a kilo forty of ham, two strings of sausages, a dozen eggs . . ."

Then he noticed Méret. Stood up and played the Frenchman, taking her hand and kissing her fingers just below the knuckles.

"Zeke Dupré de Segonszac. *Enchanté*. I see you've met my sister?"

Zozo blinked and smiled but held the pose. The boy returned to his case. Last of all he retrieved a faded, battered biscuit tin, a scene in the style of Fragonard all but worn away.

"And for my last trick . . . well you'd better stand well back."

It was a brie, in a condition rapidly approaching liquid. When he popped the lid it was as though a cheeky child had lobbed a stink bomb into the room.

Zozo lost her pose, her hands held to her face.

Serge said, "What the hell is that?"

But Méret went up to the tin, knelt down, and inhaled.

"It's rather strong," the boy said, half-apologetic and understating the obvious.

"No," said Méret. "It's beautiful. It's a beautiful smell. A good smell."

"A good smell? Where *have* you been?"

"Oh, yes, a good smell."

"Ah, well . . . I'm glad someone is happy."

Serge leaned over them and stuck the lid back on.

"Enough!"

Méret asked, "Where do you find such things?"

Zeke rested on one elbow, stretched out his legs, shrugged a Gallic shrug as though the answer were obvious.

"About once a month I take the train out into Basse-Normandie and I buy directly from the farmers. Mostly relatives—uncles and cousins."

"You mean the black market?"

"*Naturellement.*"

"Isn't that . . . unpatriotic?"

She'd no idea she'd said anything funny but Zeke and Zozo began to giggle and in seconds Serge was guffawing—a bellowing laugh that left him red in the face.

He put an arm around her, lifted her bodily off the floor as though she were no lighter than a bird, hugged her to him—half-naked, sticky with paint—twirled her round and round.

"Of course, it's unpatriotic! That's the reward of victory. To know we can be unpatriotic. To be able to beat the system with a clear conscience. And it's the best game in town."

§70

Serge encouraged her to go out alone. Each day she went in a different direction. By Monday she had already visited the Champs Elysées, the Champs de Mars, and the Jardins du Luxembourg and found herself drifting off the end of the Boulevard Saint-Germain and into the Rue Mouffetard.

Early in the evening she sat in the window of Les Hérons Rouges, a small café about halfway down the Mouffetard. She would have liked coffee but they had none, so she sipped at a weak black tea. She would have sold her soul for a croissant but they had none of those, either. Instead, she found a phrase of her father's popped into her head like a warning from the dead and she deployed it—she counted her blessings. August in Paris—a Paris that might get too hot and was pitifully short of everything—but so what?

It was around half past six in the evening. There had been a human surge up and down the street for the last hour that was beginning to thin. It had been the best free entertainment she had ever seen that didn't involve music.

She had looked out fascinated, and now she was aware of someone looking back at her from the street, seemingly equally fascinated. A thin man in a shabby olive-coloured cotton suit that hung badly on him. It was Georges Pasdeloup, the roofer who had fed her dried fruit and wrinkled apples in Auschwitz.

He came into the café, stood a moment in silence before saying, "It is you isn't it? I never knew your name."

Every hair on her head bristled but there were only two things she could possibly say.

"I'm Méret Voytek. Please, won't you join me?"

He waved to the bartender, mouthed *vin rouge,* and sat down.

"You've . . . you've gained w . . . w . . . weight," he said. "Not that I would normally comment on a lady's w . . . w . . . weight. But we were all of us so thin a year ago. I . . . I . . . have not."

He tugged at his bag of a suit.

"This was still in my w . . . wardrobe where I had left it when the *boche* came for me. I used to fill it. Somehow, I cannot seem to. No m . . . m . . . matter what I eat."

Another phrase sprang to mind, not one of her father's generous helpings of homespun philosophy but one of her mother's scathing criticisms. He looked, as she would have said, "like death warmed up." And she could not recall that he had stammered.

"Georges, is it not?"

He nodded as though uttering any more might be an effort.

"When did you get back, Georges?"

"In May. The B . . . B . . . British took the camp I was in. The Germans had abandoned us already. We were starving. I thought nothing could be worse than Auschwitz. I was wrong."

She listened to Georges's tale—how he had survived the journey from Auschwitz to Belsen; how the British found so many dead they had buried them with a bulldozer; how, on their return, the French had deloused them en masse at the Gare d'Orsay not thinking that that was exactly what the Germans had done at the other end of their journey—and she had agreed that yes, they could meet again.

And all the way back to the apartment she had regretted the promise, knowing all the while that she was bound to keep it.

§71

When she got back to Rue de la Huchette, Serge and Zozo were listening to the wireless. Something had happened.

"The Americans have bombed Hiroshima."

"Where's that?"

"I don't really know, somewhere in southern Japan."

"And this is news? They bomb Japan every day."

"This was just one bomb. And there's nothing left of Hiroshima."

§72

The following morning every newspaper had the story—one or two talked of a "new age" or an "atomic age." Theirs had been the last weekend of the preatomic era, it was just that they hadn't known it.

At about half past ten, Serge in his sarong, adding finishing touches to *Girl with Wineglass,* Méret with her nose in a huge bowl of café au lait—the fruit of Zeke's encounter with two GIs the night before—and a naked Zozo roller-skating around the room in circles and daring figure eights, two men appeared at the door, wheezing from the burden of a big wooden packing case.

They set it down in the middle of the studio. Looked at Zozo as she shot past them and then tried to pretend they were not looking.

She could see from the expressions on their faces that neither Serge nor Zozo knew what was inside. She did. She'd been here before. She let Serge prise off the front and finished her coffee without a hint of curiosity.

Zozo lifted it out and opened the case.

"My God . . . it's . . . it's beautiful!"

It had caught up with her at last. Part of her always knew it would.

"And indestructible," said Méret. "Nothing will kill it."

They gazed at it, almost inhaling its smell as she had done with the cheese. Awed, as she had been, by beauty.

Serge looked more closely, his artist's eye appraising, trying to read the label.

"Who made it?"

"The Venetian, Mattio Goffriler, in 1707."

"It must be Einstein," she thought. "Sooner or later isn't everything Einstein?" And she remembered her lycée physics, the simplicity of $E=mc^2$.

"Thousands die as E is freed from m, millions died in Auschwitz . . . but my cello goes on forever?"

§73

On Wednesday, in the same café on the Mouffetard, she kept her appointment with Pasdeloup.

It was a different Pasdeloup. The same baggy suit, the same gnawed fingernails, but the stammer had gone and he spoke with a confidence that was almost brash. She made no comment on the change but it was as though he had read her mind.

"We are none of us what we seem," he said. "None of us survivors. Everything is fake. Everything is false. All a necessary deception to hide an unbelieveable truth from those who cannot begin to imagine it."

She had nothing to say to this. She wished she had, but any answer would be engagement and she did not want to engage with this. She just wanted him to stop.

"Are we alive? How do we even know we are alive? We who have lived so long with death."

From somewhere he produced a small enamel badge in the shape of the cross of Lorraine. He opened the catch to straighten the pin and stabbed himself in the ball of his left thumb. A blob of blood rounded out in the wound, trapped in its own meniscus, the size and shape of a sheep tick on a dog.

"If you prick us we bleed. But can we, any of us, be sure we are still alive?"

She handed him her handkerchief as the blob burst its bounds and trickled down into the palm of his hand.

"Please stop, Georges. I know you're still alive."

He blotted his hand. A surprising amount of blood for such a pinprick. He balled the stained handkerchief in his fist.

"How do you sleep, Vienna?"

"I sleep well, thank you."

"Do you dream?"

"Yes. I dream. I can't always remember them, but I dream."

"I do not sleep. I lie awake all night. If I did not bite my nails I would tear my own flesh apart. And I dream. I dream wide awake."

"And you dream of Auschwitz?"

"Of course, I dream of Auschwitz, don't you?"

She didn't answer. She would never answer.

"We must dream the same dreams by night. All us survivors. And by day we pretend."

"We do? What do we pretend?"

"That we are like everyone else. A survivor is someone who pretends to be just like everyone else, but isn't. And we're not, are we?"

She would not answer that, either, true though it was.

§74

She was not wholly certain why she had raised the matter of Georges Pasdeloup with Serge but she had. Of all the things Tosca had asked her to do, accepting Serge as protector and mentor had been the easiest.

"It's as though he's two different people. Who will he be next time?"

"Was he drunk?'

"No."

"Then it's possible that this is what it has all done to him. One day up, the next day down. This is how he survives."

"He said, *a survivor is someone who pretends to be just like everyone else, but isn't.*"

"Do you think he's right?"

"Of course, he's right, but I don't want to be in some club of survivors with him, I don't want to join a round table of the wretched of the Earth . . . and above all, I don't want to be in a club of just two of us with him. If I join . . . I will begin to doubt my own existence. We survived—but I don't want the tag *survivor* hung round my neck like an albatross for the rest of my life. I want . . . I want to be free."

"We can handle him."

"No, we can't. How soon can I leave Paris?"

"You can't. You know that as well as I."

"I must."

"You can't."

"I must leave sometime. You must know when!"

"I don't know. They haven't told me but you shouldn't be in any hurry. We can handle Monsieur Pasdeloup. And even in an age of deprivation and denial, Paris will be a pleasure."

§75

At dusk they took their pleasure; they sat in the window, high above the street, peering down on Parisian heads, drifters crossing from the Boul Mich, gazing and dawdling, revellers—Paris seemed not to be without them on any night of the week—and customers of the brothel below, some indistinguishable from anyone else, others so obviously nervous.

Over a bottle of Chablis she raised the Russians again.

"What are they waiting for?"

"Oh, there are a few things for you to learn. Nothing quite as difficult or as important as our masters think. Spy nonsense. Basic encoding. How to use a dead-letter box . . ."

"How do you use a dead-letter box?"

"Just like an ordinary letter box, only you look both ways as though you were entering a brothel not posting a letter, thereby seeming completely shifty and attracting the maximum attention . . ."

As he spoke a man below did exactly that. He'd said it just to make her giggle.

"And, of course, we're waiting for the war to end. France is quite convinced it ended last August but we know better, don't we?"

"Why do I get the feeling you're not taking this seriously?"

"Because one cannot take it seriously. There are things to be done; of course, there are things to be done, and things you must know before they send you on to London, but perhaps there are other things, more important things, things seemingly unconnected to the nuts and bolts of the cloaks and daggers."

"Things? Such as?"

Serge said nothing to this. Merely stretched out his arm, grabbed the bottle of Chablis, and topped her up, smiling as he did so.

"How many know?" she said.

"How many know what?"

"About you."

"None, I hope. I have appeared as fickle and woolly minded as every other Parisian, with a bit of effort. Not pro-Vichy, that would be too great an illusion and utterly unpalatable to me, but I have supported the Communists at times when everyone supported the Communists and seemed no more than the laziest of fellow travellers. Picasso actually joined the party quite recently. I could have done that, published a statement as romantic, self-centred, and innocent as his, and next winter I could leave as he will surely do with some equally self-centred, romantic denunciation."

"And your friends?"

"Such as?"

"Zozo and Zeke?"

"Not friends, lovers."

"Your lovers?"

"And each other's."

"But they're brother and sister."

"No, that's just their . . . game."

"Serge, is that all this is, a game? Is it all about just beating the system? (pause) What exactly is it you do for Mother Russia?"

Serge shrugged the way Zeke did, every inch the Frenchman while speaking as a Russian.

"As I was saying, there really are things you need to learn while you're here. Now . . . let me be the one to change the subject. You have not played your cello yet. It has been here a day and a half. You have tuned up, I heard you, but you play nothing. Why so?"

He seemed to have a way of getting to the heart of a matter. The question deserved an answer.

"I'm scared," she said. "Scared shitless."

§76

On the next day, Thursday—the ninth of August she would recall later—Serge accompanied her to her next meeting with Pasdeloup at Les Hérons Rouges.

The café was fuller than usual—a delivery of coffee to draw in the punters and a front-page topic of discussion to keep them there: a second atomic bomb dropped on Japan. Nagasaki. Yet another city no one had ever heard of that would never be forgotten.

Serge joined in, standing at the bar as everyone stated one or other variation on the obvious—"it's all over but the shouting," "the Japs have got to give in now," or the more rhetorical "whatever this new bomb is, why don't they just blow the shit out of every city in Japan and have done with it?"

When Pasdeloup appeared and sat opposite her, Serge left the bar and introduced himself in exchange for a limp handshake and she knew at once that Georges was in his alternate mode, that he would stammer through their common bond and repeat himself endlessly.

Serge caught the waiter's attention, summoned a bottle of *vin rouge*, and tried small talk.

"So, Georges. What do you do with yourself these days?"

"What?"

"I meant have you returned to your old job?"

"My old j . . . j . . . job?"

"Well, you must have had a job before . . ."

"B . . . b . . . before what?"

"Before . . . the war."

"Ah . . . the war . . . I d . . . d . . . died in the war, you know."

"You died in the war?"

"I died in Auschwitz and no one noticed."

Georges had a point. As a survivor she knew what he meant and, clearly, Serge did not. And the alarm bells that rang in her head as Georges spoke were not ringing in Serge's.

He produced the gun as quickly as he had produced the little cross with which he had stabbed himself. He tilted his face upwards, placed the tip of the barrel beneath his chin, and blew off the top of his head.

Even as Serge reached out for his hand Georges's body was toppling backwards with the chair, the head flapping loosely, showering blood like a wet dog shaking itself after being out in the rain.

She had not known that men could scream like women, until they did. In moments, the bar was empty, men and women alike running for the street.

Serge pulled her to her feet, put his lips to her ear.

"Go with the crowd. Go home. Do not look back. You cannot afford to get mixed up in this. You were never here. Remember. You were never here."

She ran all the way to the Boulevard Saint-Germain, then she slowed to a sobbing pace and sobbed all the way home.

§77

She sat in dimness. The wireless was going over Nagasaki, again and again and again. She turned it off and sat in silence. Waiting for Serge to come home.

It was dark by the time he returned.

He stood in front of her, running his fingers through his hair.

"I emptied my wallet in bribes. Shutting people up. The barman, the waiter. By the time the flics arrived it was all agreed. None of us had ever seen him before. He just walked in off the Mouffetard, sat down, and shot himself."

Perhaps it was his professional mode, the secret agent in him to the fore, doing what a secret agent had to do to remain secret, but it was the wrong thing. It was not what she wanted to hear.

She punched him in the sternum as hard as she could. It was enough to budge him a millimetre. She punched him again and before he could grab her hands had boxed both his ears with stinging little fists.

Now he had her in his bear hug and she struggled against his strength and bulk.

"Oh, so you want to fight, do you?"

He threw her across the room. Kicked off his shoes, tore off his shirt and trousers and stood naked.

"Come on, then."

Méret lay staring at him.

"Come on, then!"

Still she did not move.

"Come on—I'm hiding nothing. You can see that."

She picked herself up, stripped, and squared off to him. She had never stood naked in front of a man before. And now she had, nakedness was strangely unimportant. She charged. He grabbed her left arm, spun around, put her over his shoulder and flat on her back.

He let the advantage go, circled her as she got to her feet once more, deflected her head butt to the belly by lifting her off the ground and slamming her onto the carpet. This time he landed on top of her.

"Enough?"

"You must be kidding. Of course not!"

He leapt up, held out both hands to her, and as she took them swung her up in the air, arse over tit, to land on her back once more, pinned down under his weight.

"You must teach me this," she said. "You must teach me—does it have a name?"

"Oddly enough, it's Japanese, and they call it jujitsu."

They stood up again. She roared like a Scottish infantryman going into battle with fixed bayonet, charged, and Serge simply knocked her legs from under her.

"Lesson one," he said softly. "It's all about using your opponent's speed and weight against her."

"But . . . I weigh nothing."

"And still I use it against you. But I loved the roar. Roar some more."

For twenty minutes she roared and tumbled, and in the twentieth minute, for the first time, threw Serge on his back.

She fell to the floor drenched in sweat. Serge reached out a hand and tugged her towards him. It was not a sensual gesture, it was affection and certainly unerotic. As she lay her head on his chest, she was staring across his belly to his distinctly unaroused, limp cock.

"That was good," he said. "You learn quickly."

"No, you teach well."

The change of subject was dramatic, as though they had crossed over points.

"Do you dream of Auschwitz?" he said.

"That was what I asked Pasdeloup. But no, I dream of Vienna. I dream I am playing duets with Viktor Rosen. Not in public, alone in his apartment on the Berggasse. It's like it used to be, except that I am as I am now, twenty-one not fourteen."

"That's just as well."

"Convenient, eh?"

Serge ignored this. For a while they were silent, only the night sounds of the street wafting up to the open window, then she said, "You know, Auschwitz can kill you even after you got away. It killed Pasdeloup, didn't it?"

He sighed, a long exhalation.

"I rather think we owe a debt of gratitude to the late Monsieur Pasdeloup. I had wondered how I might ever reach into you. How I might free the wolf inside. Then Pasdeloup did it with his gun."

"Is that what you think Auschwitz did to me, created my inner wolf?"

"Perhaps, perhaps not. The point is not to let Auschwitz win."

She turned over, locked her hands across his chest so she could see his face.

"And you and I are not here for you to teach me basic code and dead-letter boxes—you may well do that, but it's all . . . nonsense . . . all part of the game—you're here to analyze me, you're here to make me into the person who can do what the Russians want. So you tame the inner wolf. You take my rage and you give it direction."

"How very perceptive of you, *cherie*."

She touched a finger to his lips.

"Ah, I knew Professor Freud when I was a kid."

"That, I envy you."

153

"But I was just a kid, and so he was just another grown-up. Viktor was the first grown-up to become a real person for me."

Another set of points crossed.

"Freud's family died in Auschwitz, you know."

"No, they left when he did! Not long after the Germans arrived. I remember my father telling me that."

"His children left. His sisters stayed. They went to the gas."

She dropped her forehead onto the wet, matted hair of his chest. "Oh, God . . . oh, God . . . oh, God . . . oh, God."

A moment passed. Serge put one hand in her hair and ruffled it.

"It's time to cry or time to fight again. You choose."

"No . . . no, I think it's time to play. What piece would you like to hear from a naked cellist?"

§78

Paris: April 1946

For eight months, they wrestled, he painted, she played.

Some mornings she would climb into bed in her nightdress with Serge and Zozo or with Serge and Zeke, occasionally with Serge, Zozo, and Zeke—bring them coffee and lie with them for a peaceful half-hour before the day began, an innocent among the dissolute.

She began to think it might never end. She had always hoped it would never end.

In April, a wet afternoon, Serge stood in the studio in front of another half-finished painting and told her it was time.

"London?"

"Yes."

"There's nothing I can say, is there?"

"No. But I have something for you."

He was holding a headscarf, some object wrapped up inside it.

"I want you to have this. Think of it as something to use in an emergency, something to get you out of trouble."

She unfolded the scarf.

"Oh, Serge. I couldn't. It must be worth a fortune!"

"It probably is. But try to think of it as portable property. In an emgerency, something you can raise money on."

"It's . . . it's . . . beautiful."

"I suppose it is. Never quite seen it that way myself."

"I couldn't . . ."

He folded her hands around the gift.

"You have. It's yours. And I hope you never need it."

She hugged him, arms around his neck, one hand clutching his gift, wanting a life with him that would never end and knowing it was now down to a matter of days and hours.

§79

London: April 1946

In the spring of 1946, Viktor Rosen finally prevailed upon Frederick Troy to come to him for piano lessons.

Troy dug around in the attic of his brother's house in Hampstead, found the music case he had not used since childhood, and one fine evening late in April caught a tram down the King's Road. He walked the couple of hundred yards to the Chelsea Embankment, where Rosen lived, directly opposite Battersea Park, with an uncluttered view over the Thames.

"Mansion block" was a term that could cover a lot of things. Referring as it did to a particular, turn-of-the-century exterior style—usually favouring glazed red tiles—and to the simple fact of purpose-built flats—it could mean anything from a poky two-roomer to a horizontal palace. Rosen had the latter.

As soon as Troy stepped through the door he wondered why any single man would want or need such space. And Rosen read his mind.

"I call this the rehearsal room," he said, gesturing across a room so wide a full-sized Bechstein seemed all but lost. "It's big enough to seat an octet and a small audience. It might seat a twelve piece—it's just that I don't know what the noun for that is."

"Duodecicet?" said Troy.

"Doubt it," said Rosen. "Sounds more like an intestinal disorder when you put it that way. However, my point is that it divides the public and the private space. See?"

He was gesturing behind him. The door through which Troy had entered had vanished. It was magic. It was trompe l'oeil. The door was there; it had just been painted to match the wall, and the dado rail that ran across the wall at hip height also ran across the door. Only the handle gave it away.

"And over here . . ."

Now Rosen was pointing at an identical door in the opposite wall.

"I think of them as frontiers. Beyond this door the public world, beyond that the private, and between them a room as private or as public as I choose to make it."

What he had chosen struck Troy as little less than amazing.

Surely that was a Van Gogh hanging on the wall? A late Van Gogh from his time at Arles, one of those near-demented, lug'ole works in which his talent peaked only weeks or days before his suicide—crows, corn, and stars. And next to it, wasn't that a Picasso sketch? A roundy, baldy, speccy sort of bloke. And next to that a Matisse—one of his blurry, sexy, bizarrely coloured women?

Troy was staring. The very thing his mother had nagged him not to do.

"You are curious about the Picasso?"

"Yes. Sort of familiar, and sort of not."

"It's the Spanish cellist, Pablo Casals. Picasso sketched us both on the same day, in Paris, in 1928. Casals has the one of me."

He had always known Viktor was rich, but not this rich.

Put through his paces, Troy played his stock in trade. A selection from the two books of Debussy *Préludes*.

Rosen listened without interruption.

Troy finished on *Des pas sur la neige*.

Rosen said, "Is there any way I can make you practice more?"

"You might persuade me to resign from Scotland Yard."

They swapped places. Rosen played the same pieces Troy had played, as Troy had from memory, imbuing every one with all that Troy had not. He felt embarrassingly incompetent, until Rosen finished and said, "With practice, you could be so very, very good. Now . . . show me something I don't know."

"Sorry, Viktor . . . I don't quite . . ."

"Rod tells me you listen to the new American music."

"Do you mean jazz?"

"I do."

"Er . . . it's not all that new . . . Debussy even used jazz rhythms in *Children's Corner*. And I rather think I can hear them in that piano sonata of Prokofiev's from about five years ago."

"The seventh? Listen carefully and you will also hear the rattling parts of an old mangle falling through the greenhouse roof and two coalmen banging shovels together. No . . . a classical pianist using jazz is hardly jazz . . . I'd be more interested in hearing a jazz pianist use classical music."

"You know, I might just be able to oblige you there."

Art Tatum's party piece had long been Massenet's *Elegy in F minor*. He played it almost as often as he played "Sweet Lorraine" or "Flying Home," and had a way of making it sound like something overheard in an Arab casbah—with a drumming left-hand and a right that played lightning arpeggios undreamt of by its composer. Years ago, Troy had regarded it as a challenge to master the sheer speed of the piece.

About three minutes later Rosen blinked and stared at him.

"Forget I spoke," he said witheringly. Then, "How about Thursdays? Seven till eight? If Londoners can refrain from killing one another for an hour a week, we might yet make something of you."

Troy stepped into the street. Looked at the sky. It might come on to rain later. Looked at his watch and realized he was already late for a meeting with his brother.

§80

She stood on the opposite side of the road, looking up at the first-floor windows, her back to the Thames, her bag at her feet, her cello case propped up against the embankment wall. She had persistently refused Viktor's suggestions that he should meet her at Victoria Station. She hated railway stations. She had hated them since the day she'd been boarded up in a train at Vienna Nordbahnhof—and the difference between arrival and departure, greeting and abandonment, had long since elided.

She stood much as she had that day twelve years ago when she had arrived early at the apartment in the Berggasse—waiting simply for the time to be right.

A young man came out of the building. Short, dark—as dark as Serge. He was clutching a music case and she felt certain he had come from Viktor. He failed to notice her, glanced at the sky, glanced at his wristwatch, and set off along the embankment towards Westminster.

She crossed over, tapping at the door of the gingerbread house once more.

§81

New York: April 1946

Szabo swapped his Charlie Parker British passport for one in his own name at the British consulate in New York. He had not been wholly certain they'd do it. But it was mailed to him with a hand-written note from the ambassador assuring him that he had been a citizen from the moment the Charlie Parker had been issued. Then he wrote to Arthur Kornfeld, as he had done regularly throughout the war.

                                    6 West 73rd St.
                                    New York

Arthur Kornfeld
Pembroke College
Cambridge
England

                                         24.4.46

Dear Arthur,
  This will be a quick note to say that I will be
returning to England next month. They made me a
citizen. Call it a reward. I won't be returning
to Cambridge. There's a new place at Harwell
(Oxfordshire somewhere?) to be devoted entirely
to finding uses for nuclear fission. I am to be
deputy director. Who knows, one day soon the
lights on your Christmas tree could be lit by
nuclear power? Or perhaps an atomic toothbrush?
  I hope to see you in May or June.
Your old friend,
Karel Szabo
P.S. "Not with a whimper but with a bang?"
  Sorry, I couldn't resist that one.
P.P.S. Eliot or Auden? I seem to have forgotten.

                         §

From Stetin in the Baltic to Trieste in the
Adriatic, an Iron Curtain has descended
across the Continent. Behind that line lie all
the capitals of the ancient states of central
and eastern Europe—Warsaw,
Berlin, Prague, Vienna . . .
—WINSTON S. CHURCHILL
FULTON, MISSOURI, 1946

II

Austerity

f

Observe in what an original world we are now living:
how many men can you find in Europe who have never killed;
or whom somebody does not wish to kill?
—TADEUSZ BOROWSKI, *This Way for the Gas, Ladies and Gentlemen*

Since Auschwitz we know what man is capable
of. And since Hiroshima we know what is at stake.
—VIKTOR FRANKL, *Man's Search for Meaning*

§82

London: March, or even February, 1948

**Battersea Park where they had sat so often or perhaps
Kensington Gardens, ah, no . . . Lincoln's Inn.
The warmest spring in who-knows-when.**

It had not been the hardest winter. That had been the previous winter
—the deluge that was 1947. London like an iceberg, the Home Coun-
ties one vast undulating eiderdown of white, snowbound villages in
Derbyshire dug out by German POWs many miles and years from home
—a bizarre reminder that we had "won the war." War. Winter. He had
thought he might not live through either. He had. The English, who
could talk the smallest of small talk about weather, had deemed 1948 to
be "not bad" or, if feeling loquacious, "nowt to write home about."
But now, as the earth cracked with the first green tips of spring, the bold
budding of crocus and daffodil that seemed to bring grey-toothed smiles
to the grey faces of the downtrodden victors of the World War among
whom he lived, he found no joy in it. It had come too late to save him.
This winter would not kill him. The last would. And all the others that
preceded it would.

He longed to sit in a rose-scented garden.

He tasted dust. In the middle of the square, sluggish workmen with
sledgehammers were knocking down the concrete air-raid shelters that
had stood squat, ugly, bestial since the winter of 1940.

He took a silver hip flask from his inside pocket and downed a little
Armagnac.

"André, I cannot do this anymore."

Skolnik had been pretending to read the *Post,* billowing pages spread
out in front of him screening his face from the drifting gaze of passersby.
He stopped, turned his head to look directly at Viktor.

"What?"

"I have to stop now."

The newspaper was folded for maximum rustle. It conveyed the emotions André pretended long ago to have disowned in favour of calm, unrufflable detachment.

"Viktor. You cannot just stop. You cannot simply quit. What was it you think you joined all those years ago? A gentleman's club? As though you can turn in your membership when brandy and billiards begin to bore you?"

Viktor took another sip of Armagnac, then passed the flask to André.

"Nineteen eighteen," he said softly, as Skolnik helped himself to a hefty swig. "Nineteen eighteen."

"What?'

"Nineteen eighteen—that's when I joined. Were you even born then?"

"Not that it matters, but I was at school."

The flask was handed back, the paper slapped down between them.

"You cannot stop just because it suits you to stop."

Viktor sighed a soft, whispery, "Really," of exasperation. "Why can I not stop?"

"Because the Communist Party of the Soviet Union simply doesn't work that way."

§83

London: July 1948

"I'd like you to meet my husband."

A killer remark if uttered by a lover, but Anna wasn't his lover. Anna was . . . Troy wasn't sure what Anna was. But her request prompted him to remember when it was they'd first met and he couldn't. She had been in pathology, working for Kolankiewicz in the forensics lab out at Hendon. Had it been '40 or '41? It seemed an age ago; it seemed like yesterday. Since the war ended she'd been a GP—a doctor to the living not the dead.

"He's having a bit of a rough patch."

"He's been having those as long as you've been talking to me about him."

"It's his leg, you see."

"His leg? The one he's got or the one he hasn't?"

"The one he hasn't. Gives him gyp something awful. I've even had him on morphine, although he prefers whiskey. He seems to feel it, and it's been gone seven years now."

Angus's leg had been lost during his time as an RAF pilot, one of the Brylcreem boys—except that far from slick: Angus's hair stood up in bright ginger spirals like a demonic halo. And he had lost said leg not in combat but leaping from the walls of Colditz Castle in a bid to escape. Anna had told Troy that the British POWs had given the leg its own funeral, in its own little plot—and on liberation and repatriation the king had given Angus a medal, which he politely and utterly seriously had accepted "posthumously, on behalf of me leg." Much to the amusement of reporters, he had left Buckingham Palace with his DFC pinned to his trousers over his tin leg.

"The stump can get very sore, you see. And when his leg aches he can't sleep, and if he can't sleep he gets sort of bonkers and picks fights with anyone who so much as looks at him and, worse, gets barred from all his favourite boozers."

The latter, viewed as Troy was trying to view it from Angus's point of view, was little short of tragic.

"And of course he loses clients. There's nothing quite like telling a client to fuck off, is there?"

Quite, thought Troy. Hardly ambiguous. And from everything Anna had ever told him, chartered accountancy was quite the oddest profession a man like Angus could possibly choose.

"I have met him, you know."

"Oh . . . but that was brief . . . a sort of nod and a handshake, wasn't it? I mean really meet him. Troy, right now my old man needs pals and . . . and . . ."

"Yes?"

"He needs clients."

"I don't think I need an accountant. I doubt very much whether Scotland Yard coppers on salaries have accountants."

"Please, Troy, do this. Do this for me. There must be some sort of dosh you could have him move around on a bit of paper for you. I mean, how many millions does your family have?"

It was because the Troys had millions that Troy never thought about money or its management. In the same way he never thought about his salary as a policeman. If it were all he had to live on, doubtless he would, but he didn't. Money matters were all left to his brother or brothers-in-law. Troy never even saw the bill from his tailor. It went off to some chap who worked for "the family" and that was that. But Anna had a point. There was something to be said for taking responsibility or at least shuffling responsibility off onto a man of one's own choosing. Troy was thirty-two. An inspector on the murder squad. A string of convictions behind him. Enough blots on his copybook to delight Professor Rorschach. A grown-up. High time.

"Okay," he said. "When?"

§84

When the telephone rang again Troy was sure it was Anna calling to nitpick over details. It wasn't. It was Charlie Walsh. Chief Inspector Charlie Walsh. The only copper in special branch who'd so much as give Troy the time of day.

"Day off, son?"

"Yes, sir. Just the one."

"All right for some. So, you're sayin' you'll be in tomorrow?"

"Yes, sir," Troy said feeling slightly exasperated at the flat, northern, plain-bloke mask that Walsh habitually wore. "A normal working day."

"How would you like it not to be a normal working day?"

Now, thought Troy, we are cookin'.

"Such as?"

"I've a nark. Name of Fish Wally. 'Appen you've heard of him?"

"Wasn't he one of Walter's?"

"He was. Recruited just before old Walter copped it in '41."

Walter was the late Chief Inspector Stilton. Murdered on the job. Troy had been part of the investigation. He had solved the crime. Not that he could tell anyone. Off the record and out of the courts the killer had paid the price. For a while he and Walter had been friends. For a while he and Walter's daughter Kitty had been lovers, and that had put paid to the friendship.

"I inherited Fish Wally. He was a godsend during the war. Mixing with all them refugees, speaking all them languages . . . but truth to tell the Branch hasn't had a lot of use for him since. I'd like to place him where he'd be more use."

"With me?"

"I reckon anyone in Crime could use him. There's not a dive nor a cove in Soho and Fitzrovia Wally doesn't know. I thought of you cos you and Walter were pals. You were with him when we rounded up all the Krauts and Wops in 1940, weren't you?"

Rather than discuss an episode he would sooner forget, an episode in which Walsh had had to vet Troy for Security—not that Walsh would mention it now—Troy said, "I think the Murder Squad can afford Fish Wally."

"Fine," said Walsh. "He's got a place in Marshall Street, round the back of Liberty's. Tek down this number . . ."

§85

There might be a fashionable part of London in which to be an accountant —in much the same way stockbrokers had Gresham Street, tailors Savile Row, publishers Bedford Square. Wherever it might be, and Troy hadn't a clue, he was certain it wasn't an alley named Jockey's Fields running along one side of Gray's Inn. He was equally certain it wasn't up three flights of stairs over a mews garage with a cardboard and crayon sign marked, "Ring twice and ask for Spike."

It was typical of the character he had learnt to know from Anna's tales that a one-legged man would have his office on the top floor. Arriving at the door Troy could just make out the syllables "Cha" and "Acc" on the frosted glass. The rest, including Angus's name, were obscured by another cardboard sign reading "War Hero, Cripple, Skinflint & Piss Artist: Knock Once and Ask For Ginger."

Troy did. A booming voice yelled, "Bugger off!"

Troy inched the door open, put his head in the line of fire. Angus was leaning back in his chair, feet up on the desk, staring into space.

"Frederick Troy," said Troy. "Your noon appointment."

Angus swung one leg off the desk, grabbed the other with both hands, grunted, and lowered it to the floor. The leg clanked faintly as he did so. It clanked faintly as he limped across the floor, hand extended to shake Troy's.

"If you just let it drop it hurts like merry hell. You ever lost a limb? Thought not. You wouldn't believe how much the damn thing hurts. Imagine wiggling toes you haven't got. Imagine the ache in a bunion you haven't set eyes on since the Krauts invaded Russia. There are moments when you wish you had it back so you can rub it or scratch it and you start to think you should be searching for it somewhere, that the whole point of the war was to enable Hitler to capture your bunion and it begins to seem like some poem Lewis Carroll never got around to writing. "The Hunting of the Bunion." Call out the cavalry, line up the Lancers. The Nazis have got me bunion!"

He paused momentarily, let go of Troy's hand, perhaps aware for the first time that Troy wasn't getting a word in.

"Sergeant Troy, right?"

"I'm an inspector now. I was a sergeant when I first met Anna."

"And you have need of an accountant?"

"'Fraid so," Troy lied.

The head pulled back, tilted slightly, sunlight in the ginger curls, a twinkle in the pale blue eyes looking down at Troy.

"You're lying," said Angus.

Troy wondered if he'd flinched or blanched at such a plainly true statement.

"What would a jobbing copper want with an accountant? The old girl put you up to this, didn't she?"

Troy said nothing.

Angus wheeled around on what Troy took to be the tin leg and railed at the ceiling.

"Why in God's name does she do this? Does she think I'm helpless? Does she think I'm broke?"

"Yes," said Troy simply.

One more spin on his axis and Angus was facing Troy again. Troy drew first.

"It's not that she thinks you're broke. It's that she doesn't know what her prospects are under the National Health Service."

"Remind me, when does that start?"

Was he the only man in England who didn't know?

"It started last week."

"And the old girl's having second thoughts?"

"Well," Troy fudged. "Not exactly . . ."

"Bollocks! She's all in favour of it. She didn't have to join."

"But she has, and after three years in private practice she thinks her income, and hence your joint income, might go down rather than up."

"And you're the best she could come up with? A copper on salary. Good God, Mr. Troy, are you on even a thousand a year?"

"As a copper, of course I'm not. But on the side, as it were . . ."

Troy paused, hoping Angus might fill in the gaps.

No such luck. He scratched his ginger halo, but said nothing.

"On the side . . . I'm filthy rich," Troy concluded reluctantly.

It was a Beano moment when the lightbulb appeared above Angus's head.

"Filthy rich?"

"Filthy, grubby, downright dirty. You couldn't scrub us poor."

"You're one of *those* Troys? She never mentioned that. Bloody hell!"

Another spin on his metal pivot and Angus lurched into the corner behind his desk.

"Let us adjourn to more convivial surroundings and count your ackers, Mr. Troy. It is past noon and the pubs are open."

Anna had warned Troy that this might happen but he couldn't think of a damn thing to do about it short of outright refusal.

Angus bent from the waist and came up with what appeared to be a length of cloth wrapped around something. Looking more closely Troy saw that it was a couple feet of gents' pinstripe trouser leg, so favoured by the professions, complete with turnup, encasing a tin leg, complete with sock and shoe. Someone had gone to the trouble of shining the shoe. Someone had gone to the trouble of pinning the Distinguished Flying Cross to the fabric just below the knee. Angus handed it to Troy.

"My spare. Just hang on to it till we get to the bottom of the stairs. I'll need two hands, but I'll be in Scotland afore ye."

Troy doubted this.

Once outside his office door, Angus took hold of the banister rails, braced himself between them, stuck his tin leg out horizontally, kicked off with his good leg, and glided down to the next landing. Troy watched him vanish from sight at the next corner, heard the *swoosh-bang-ouch* as he landed at the next floor, and the floor below, and the floor below that.

It was a turn to marvel at. Helter-skelter for a grown-up—if that term could ever be sensibly applied to Angus. Troy stood for a moment wondering that anyone like Anna would ever have married anyone like Angus.

"Well," a voice boomed up from below, "what in God's name is keeping you?"

They headed west into Holborn, Troy feeling like a fussy, precise little midget next to Angus's loose, lumbering six foot and more.

They turned right into Lamb's Conduit Street, a narrow lane leading in the direction of Brunswick Square.

"We'll start at the Leper's Loincloth," Angus said.

Troy thought he knew most London pub names. They were much of a muchness—the George, the Royal Oak, the Anchor, the So and So's Arms, the Duke of Kent, the Admiral Nelson—and doubtless they all meant something to the inquiring mind, and on this matter Troy's did not inquire, but he'd never heard of a Leper's Loincloth. In fact the only pub he knew in Lamb's Conduit Street was the Lamb. Indeed, they were standing right outside it.

"I've changed the names," said Angus, tapping the side of his nose. "That way, if the old girl hears me planning a night out she'll not know where to start looking for me. You'd better learn a few if we make a habit of this. We'll have a couple here and then push on to the Nell Gwynn's Tits."

Troy felt the seeping, damp unease of despair like rain in a leaking shoe.

It was a sight to turn heads. A lanky lunatic comes into a pub carrying a spare leg. A lanky lunatic comes into a pub carrying a spare leg to which the king has awarded the DFC and which the leg wears with seeming pride. Troy concluded the lunchtime regulars in the Lamb had seen Angus before. No one batted an eyelid. Even when Angus stood the leg on the bar, all the barman said was, "Yer usual, Mr. Pakenham?" and pulled two doubles of Dalwhinnie from the optics.

"And you, sir?" the barman turned and looked at Troy.

Troy opened his mouth to speak, pointing as he did so to the nearest glass of malt the man had just set down, but the man shook his head gently before Troy could utter a word.

Angus had downed his in a single gulp and wrapped his fist around the second.

"I'll just take Ernest to a table for his nip, Tommy. Give Inspector Troy whatever he fancies."

So saying, Angus took both leg and tot to a corner table.

"Ernest?" Troy said.

"Most men," said the barman, "have names for their todgers. Leastways they do when they're boys. The squadron leader has continued this quaint affectation and has named his leg Ernest."

"And Ernest likes single malt?"

"Oddly enough, sir, Ernest seems to like whatever the squadron leader likes at any particular moment. Now, what can I get you?"

Troy asked for half a pint of ginger beer shandy and followed Angus. Angus was nursing the second tot with an affection he had not demonstrated to the first. Ernest stood bolt upright, a chair to himself, predictably mute on the matter of his purloined nip. Angus looked once at Troy's and said, "Jesus wept. Is this why we fought a war? So grown men can drink ginger beer?"

Two blokes who had been chatting at the next table guffawed at this.

"S'right. You tell 'im," said a little bloke in a battered bowler hat. "Ginger beer. Wot a liberty, eh?"

Far from seeing the funny side of it, far from welcoming the famous Cockney bonhomie, Angus took hump.

"I wasn't aware that my remark was addressed to you."

It was a rejection guaranteed to fluster, if not humble, the recipient.

"Sorry, guv. I was only saying—"

"What were you only saying? That my friend has no right to the beverage of his choice?"

"Nah. 'Course not. I was sayin', why did we fight the war?"

Against all the odds the little bloke in the battered bowler had got the bit between his teeth and managed to find his wagging finger before Angus got back at him.

"I mean. I get up this mornin'. Wot does my missis stick in front of me? Cornflakes. I sez to 'er I sez where's me bacon an' negg? I want me bacon an' negg. You can't send a man off to do a day's work on flakes o' bleedin' cardboard. You know wot she sez? She sez kids come first. An' when every bleedin' fing's rationed growin' kids gets first divvies. An' she rattles off a wot's wot o' grub. Lard—one ounce. I ask yer, one ounce. An' I'm partial to a bit o' bread and lard I am. And bread, half a pound a day. Half a pound I sez, that's not even three slices wiv or wivout the bleedin' lard. And then she 'ammers on about sugar an' butter an' milk and when she's finally shut 'er clangin' man'ole I sez to 'er I sez 'war's been over best part o' three soddin' years an' fings is worse than wot they ever was.' We didn't have no bread rationin' during the war. We got more'n a bobsworth of meat. So I sez wot you just said, 'why did we fight the war?' So I could eat cornflakes, go to work 'ungry and stand in the bleedin' bus queue in the pourin' rain waitin' for a bus that arrives stuffed to the gills if it does arrive. It's all down to yer Labour government, I sez. Reds and Commies the lot of 'em. An' I tells 'er. 'Itler was right about 'em. And I sez maybe we'd all have been better off under 'Itler"

This was a startling and rarely uttered sentiment. However many idiots might think it, it was a stubbornly stupid man who said it in a London pub in front of anyone, let alone a six foot, half-crazed hero of the Battle of Britain.

"Tell me," Angus said with a deceptive calm. "What did you do in the war?"

"Reserved occupation," Bowler Hat replied, declining to elaborate.

Angus rose slowly from his seat, grasped Ernest firmly in both hands, and plonked him down on the table between the two Cockneys, the DFC pretty well at Bowler Hat's eye level.

"Well, you ignorant sack of faeces, while you were serving with the Polished Arse Battalion of the Kings Own Skiving Pen-Pushers, Ernest and I flew Hurricanes and, whilst I am inclined to be tolerant of the odd moron who whiles away his time in a pub spouting utter tosh, Ernest is not. And he is not because the war cost him dearly and he knows precisely why we fought it. We fought for this England. And we fought it so good men like Mr. Troy and myself did not have to sit here and listen to gobshites like you while we drink our hard-earned ginger beer. I think Ernest deserves an apology from you, little fatty—indeed he's going to stand here till he gets it."

"Yer what?" was all this elicited from Bowler Hat.

Angus let go of Ernest and as Troy lunged to catch the tin man, Angus grabbed Bowler Hat by the throat and lifted him bodily off the ground.

Bowler Hat choked out, "Leggo! I'll have the law on you."

Thus prompting Troy to remember that he was the law.

"Angus, for God's sake put him down."

"No can do, old man. He apologizes to Ernest or he dangles here till my arms drop off as surely as me leg did."

Bowler Hat's mate displayed wisdom over courage and scarpered. It was left to the barman to tackle Angus, armed with a handy cliché he doubtless kept behind the bar for just such occasions.

"Leave it out, Squadron Leader. He's not worth it! He's not worth it!"

Angus hung on. Bowler Hat's face turned to beetroot and he lost the power of speech.

"Angus," Troy said softly. "If you kill him it will be murder, and my job is nicking people for murder. How will I ever explain to Anna that meeting you for a quiet drink ended up with me slapping the cuffs on you?"

Angus shook himself like a wet dog and dropped Bowler Hat back into his chair.

"Quite right, old man. Shouldn't embarrass the missis. Woman's a saint after all."

While Bowler Hat wheezed and tried to breathe again, Troy bunged the barman a ten-bob note, whispered an apology, and steered Angus and Ernest out of the door.

"Angus, it's been a pleasure but I really must be getting back to work."

"Nonsense, the night is still young."

"Actually, Angus, it's barely the afternoon."

"Good-o. We'll find another watering hole. Pay, pack, and follow."

The next watering hole was in Bloomsbury, nominally the Three Tuns, but as Angus had forewarned, known to him as the Nell Gwynn's Tits. Seeking an antidote to the experience of the Leper's Loincloth Troy joined Angus in his tipple, telling himself it would be just the one. Angus made it two, both doubles. They stayed there until it closed. When it closed, Angus tapped the side of his nose and said he knew a private drinking club on the far side of the Tottenham Court Road, in which they repeated the recipe, and when, at about half past four, feeling much the worse for abandoning ginger beer for scotch, Troy said, "I really must be going now," Angus said, "Rubbish, we haven't done Soho yet."

"I have to work this evening."

"Felons to apprehend, eh?"

"No, just a nark to meet for dinner. And I'd prefer to be sober when I do."

"Dinner at the taxpayer's expense, eh?"

"No, the Yard doesn't run to that. I've no doubts I shall be picking up the bill myself. Now if you'll excuse . . ."

Angus clicked into pro mode.

"Bring me the receipt."

"What?"

"Dinner with nark. A professional expense and hence tax deductible."

And Troy thought that perhaps he might need an accountant after all.

§86

Troy stood in the bogs down the corridor from his office, forcing water down his throat from a far-from-clean cup, wishing that somewhere in Scotland Yard there was a place where he could get a decent cup of coffee, and swearing to the invisible gods on a pile of invisible Bibles that he would never let Angus do this to him again.

When he got back to his outer office, where Jack Wildeve usually sat, a light was flashing on the base of Jack's phone and in his own office the phone was ringing loudly. In the bogs he'd mistaken this for a ringing in his head. Whoever it was had been hanging on for an age.

Troy snatched up the receiver.

"Freddie? Where the bloody hell have you been? I've been calling for the best part of half an hour."

"Sorry, Jack, the day sort of ran away with me."

Saying this, Troy realized he had no real idea of what time it was or how long he'd let Angus carouse and torment. He checked his watch, then he checked his watch against the clock on the wall. It was six o'clock. Angus had boozed away an entire afternoon and taken a bite out of the evening.

"Can you get over to Camden right away? I've a body on my hands."

The magic words. The bolt of lightning up the spine. Troy reached for a pencil.

"Where?"

"On the Underground. Northern line, southbound platform on the Charing Cross branch. I've closed the platform and all I've got are half a dozen uniformed plods to hold back a mob of very angry commuters. As soon as you can, Freddie; as soon as you can."

"Have you closed the northbound platform?"

"Not yet. I'll do it if it's absolutely necessary but I'd rather not. I'd have a riot of bowler hats and brollies on my hands."

Good, thought Troy, good. After all, he could hardly drive through the streets pissed. And with any luck he'd be an approximation of sober by the time he got to Camden Town.

"Twenty minutes," he said to Jack.

"Make it fifteen," Jack said.

§87

Troy shook himself a dozen times. He'd boarded a tube train at Charing Cross, fallen asleep at Strand, woken up as the train pulled out of Warren Street, and only stopped panicking when he realized it had been Warren Street and that he still had two stops to go: Mornington Crescent, then Camden Town. And he knew he was at Camden Town from the size of the crowd and noise it was making. It was so unlike Londoners to talk to one another and this lot were babbling, looking pointlessly at their watches and speculating on how they might eventually get home to Streatham or Tooting or wherever, wishing they'd bought that house in Finchley or Neasden when they'd had the chance in '46 or '47 or whenever.

"Of course," he heard as he flashed his warrant card, barged his way through to the southbound line. "When you nationalize everything and build nothing, what can you expect? No bloody houses and no bloody trains."

A uniformed copper stood in the tunnel linking the platforms. He saluted Troy.

"Mr. Wildeve's just 'round the corner to your right, sir."

Jack was fifty yards or so down the platform, pacing up and down with his head low, searching. He looked up as he heard Troy approach.

"It's a waste of time," he said. "Anything you might grace with the name of *clue* has been under a thousand beetle-crushing shoes since this poor bugger copped it."

So saying, he whipped an old macintosh off the corpse. That, too, looked as though it had been trampled underfoot.

"Y'know, I think a trainload of dozy dimwits walked around him or on him without realizing he was there or without realizing he was dead."

Troy knelt down next to the body.

Jack was right. He was most certainly not lying as he'd fallen. He'd been kicked and shuffled by the homeward bound. It was even possible he'd been moved several feet from where he died—there was a streak of blood a yard long.

Troy looked at the face, one cheek flattened on the concrete, mouth forced open fish-like by the weight of flesh, pale blue eyes focussed on nothing, a thin, pencil-line moustache. A man in his early forties. A single bullethole in his back, right behind the heart.

"What do we have?" he asked simply.

Jack handed him the man's wallet.

"No attempt to rob him. There's over three quid inside."

Troy opened the buff ration book. All you could ask for in the way of identity was there—name, abode, age, even the address of his butcher.

"André Skolnik. 101 Charlotte Street. Age forty-four. Buys his shilling's worth of mince at Clays in Tottenham Street."

Troy flipped through the rest. Two pound notes, three ten-bob notes, and a worn, wartime identity card indicating that the late Mr. Skolnik was a naturalized Pole.

"When do you think it happened?"

Jack paused as a train bound for Morden crawled by. Baffled faces pressed to the glass. The silent rage of rush hour.

"About an hour ago. One concerned citizen eventually noticed he wasn't moving, she alerted the station master, he called the Yard, the Yard called me in the car. I was only in Marylebone Lane. Put my foot down. I'd say about twenty minutes between the alert and me getting here . . . so perhaps more than an hour, perhaps an hour and a half. The witness is on the surface, they're giving her a cuppa in the staff room. I've left Gutteridge to take her statement but she'll not be a lot of use. She got off a southbound train here and says the body was right by the door, which means she wasn't even in the station when he was killed."

"And everyone who was has left, either up the escalators or on a train."

"Exactly. The chap who did this could have been at Leicester Square before the alarm went up."

A noise behind them made them both turn.

The short fat form of the Yard's forensic pathologist, Ladislaw Kolankiewicz, was bustling down the platform, leather soles resounding, Gladstone bag in hand, homburg pushed to the back of his head.

"OK, flatfoots, step aside."

Troy was used to Kolankiewicz. Foul-mouthed, tender, abusive, avuncular. Jack was getting used to Kolankiewicz. Foul-mouthed, tender, abusive, avuncular . . . and sentimental about few things. Polishness, being

Polish, was one of them and it occurred to Troy as Kolankiewicz set down his bag by the body that there was a chance he knew the man.

As Kolankiewicz reached out his arm to turn the body, Troy put his own hand over Kolankiewicz's.

"There is just one thing," he said.

"There always is."

"He's Polish."

A moment's hesitation. Troy's hand still on Kolankiewicz's.

"We have a name?"

"Skolnik. André Skolnik."

A moment's thought.

"No. I don't know anyone of that name."

And the body was turned. A tide of blood spilling out from the front of the shirt.

Kolankiewicz took a limp wrist and said, "No rigor yet. He was still alive at four o'clock."

He took a clean cotton wipe from his bag, unbuttoned the shirt, mopped blood, and examined the chest.

Never one to stand the sight of blood readily, Jack looked away. Troy had, on occasion, known Jack, a sergeant of the murder squad with six years service behind him, to excuse himself and throw up. In six years Jack had learnt to throw up as quietly as possible.

Kolankiewicz turned the body back, examined the entry wound.

"I would say he died instantly. If he made a sound I'd be amazed. There is no exit wound, so I conclude the bullet is still lodged in his heart. I would also say the killer simply pressed the gun to the jacket and fired. Point blank seems scarcely adequate to describe it. There are some powder burns, but not consistent . . . and there is this . . . what you call it? . . . White mush."

"Ah," said Wildeve. "There's a fair bit of that. Mostly about six feet back but I've found bits almost everywhere."

Troy looked where Wildeve was pointing. There was a drying lump of white mush turning flaky only a foot or so from his own shoes. He bent down, stuck a finger in, and brought the finger to his lips.

"Careful, Freddie!"

Troy ignored this, tasted it, and stuck his finger under Kolankiewicz's nose.

Kolankiewicz sniffed.

Kolankiewicz tasted.

Wildeve looked appalled.

"Do you two have any sense of risk?"

"Of course," Kolankiewicz said, "mashed potato."

"What?"

"He's right," said Troy. "But I'd go with baked rather than mashed. There's still a bit of the skin on this and some of it's still raw."

Kolankiewicz smiled waggishly. "So your killer bring pack lunch. Search hard enough maybe you find gherkin and processed cheese, too. Best of British, flatfoots. Now, I take the stiff."

Troy slipped the piece of potato into an envelope and handed it to Kolankiewicz. Two forensic assistants came down the platform from the escalator lugging a stretcher and a blanket for the body.

Another southbound crept by. Just in time for the curious to see the body lifted onto the stretcher.

"This'll be in the evening papers before you can say Jack." Jack yelled.

And when the train had gone, Kolankiewicz and his men had gone, too, and against the background noise of the three other platforms this one now struck Troy, in the words of a cliché, as deathly quiet. The pounding in his head had stopped. For the first time in hours, it was quiet in the skull.

"What did he mean by that crack about packed lunch?"

Troy shrugged it off.

"Nothing. The spud is part of the crime. Why else would it be on Mr. Skolnik?"

"Perhaps he fell in it?"

"He fell face down, Jack. Kolankiewicz said the potato was around the wound on his back."

"Shot with a spud gun?"

"Not a weapon much favoured by anyone over the age of twelve. Now . . . if you'd just shot a bloke at close range, underground, in the middle of a crowd, what would you do?"

Jack didn't hesitate.

"I'd just walk away. I might turn around and pretend I'd heard a bang just like anyone else, but I'd walk away. Straight up the escalator and out. I'd be very English about it and join all the others being very English and minding their own damn business."

"Quite. And the gun?"

Now Jack did hesitate.

"It would sort of depend on how much I wanted to hang on to it . . . how much it cost . . . but we are a nation awash in guns, the war's made them cheap . . . and whether I intended to use it again."

"And if you didn't?"

More hesitation, then, "I'd just drop it. After all, the body all but got lost under the tramping feet. A gun—"

Troy cut him short.

"—would be where you and I could see it now, or it got kicked into touch by those thousands of feet."

"I searched the length of the platform while I waited for you."

"Then you'd better give me a hand down to the track."

Troy slipped one leg over the edge and stretched out a hand to Jack.

"Freddie, I closed the platform, not the service. There could be a train through any second."

"I noticed."

Taking Troy's hand brought them closer than they'd yet been.

"Good bloody grief. You stink of scotch!"

Troy dropped to track level, let go of Jack's hand, and said, "Well, nothing like death to sober you up is there?"

"Watch out for the live rail!"

"Which one is it?" Troy said, not looking.

"How the hell should I know? It could be any one of them."

"Actually, Jack, it's two, and I shall try not to step on any of them."

Troy walked on slowly from the point where the body had lain, six, nine, twelve feet. There were cigarette packets everywhere and between the rails there was black, shallow, oily water—not deep enough to cover much. At fifteen feet a fat mouse scurried across the rails, unharmed by either electricity or water, leaping from the inner rail to the middle to the outer rail. Troy saw that it had landed on something black in between the rails, a small object not much bigger than the mouse and as black as the water itself.

He heard the hum in the tracks that preceded the arrival of a train. Heard Jack swear softly to himself.

He circled the black lump with his finger. Touching only the edge until he was certain he had found the barrel of a gun.

The tracks shook now, the blast of air down the tunnel lifted his hair and set his jacket flapping. Jack was holding out his hand to him now, urging him to get out. He looked into the headlights of the train; he could see the look of panic on the driver's face. He grasped the gun between the forefinger and thumb of his left hand, grabbed Jack's hand with his right, and let himself be plucked to safety by a six-foot former rugby player.

Jack held onto Troy as the train passed. Held him dangling in the air. "You arse, you complete arse."

"Got it," Troy said simply.

§88

Wildeve handed out brown envelopes to the blokes in uniform and told them to collect every bit of mashed potato. It was not a way to make friends or influence people.

Driving back along the Hampstead Road in Jack's Wolseley, Troy took the gun out of its wrapping—a page from that evening's *Standard*—and held it between his fingertips. It was tiny, almost weightless. The bore could not be more than .20. And he'd never seen anything like it. He often examined a gun by sticking a pencil up the barrel and holding it like a lollipop, but he couldn't get a pencil up the barrel of this one. It must have been like shooting someone with a needle.

At red traffic lights, Jack glanced across.

"Looks like a toy."

"Feels like one, too."

The lights changed. Jack slipped the car into first.

"Y'know what strikes me, Freddie? The balls of it. The sheer bollocks of shooting a man in broad daylight, with people milling all round; shooting a chap with something that looks like a popgun and then just kicking it away and carrying on as though nothing had happened. Now, I know that's what I said I'd do myself but that was a hypothetical me. I think this took balls of steel."

"I'm inclined to agree. Even allowing for the innate lack of curiosity of the English, their ability to walk round a corpse and hurry home for tea, I'm still inclined to agree."

Crossing Fitzroy Square, towards the north end of Charlotte Street, Troy said, "Can you handle this alone?"

"Something urgent?"

"I'm meeting a new nark. Someone I've heard of but never actually met. He's being sold to me as a man who knows everything and everyone in Soho and Fitzrovia."

"Then," Jack said, "given the late Mr. Skolnik lived bang in the middle of Fitzrovia, perhaps your nark knew him."

"It'll be the first thing I ask him about," said Troy.

It wasn't.

§89

Troy, possessing the innate curiosity most Englishman lacked, had other priorities. He had found himself hooked by Fish Wally's accent on the telephone and, on meeting, and against his better judgement, found himself staring at his Mickey Mouse, white-gloved, crabbed hands.

Fish Wally's was a name he knew. Not from Walter Stilton—he had had so few conversations with Walter after the bust up with his daughter —but from the daughter herself, Woman Police Sergeant Katherine Stilton, known as Kitty, during his second fling with her; a fling he doubted Walter had lived long enough to hear of. Kitty was long gone—the first of the GI brides, married to an American officer even before the term had been minted. She had mentioned her father's new nark just about the time Walter had been killed. He remembered that Wally was Polish—London at times seemed to be the largest Polish city outside of Poland; refugees from the Germans who'd never returned, refugees from the Russians who'd just arrived . . . and somewhere the survivors, the Polish airmen who'd flown

Hurricanes and Spitfires in the Battle of Britain, thereby making themselves into accidental Englishmen. The surprising thing was, given Charlie Walsh's description of him as someone who knew "every dive and every cove in Soho and Fitzrovia," that they had never met before. Wally had, as it were, trodden Troy's beat.

They had arranged to meet at the Gay Hussar in Greek Street, below Soho Square, a skip and a hop from the dim lights of Shaftesbury Avenue and the grim gaiety of the Charing Cross Road. Troy understood why Wally had chosen it. The Hussar attracted the flotsam of Eastern Europe in much the same way the Polish Caff did in South Kensington. After the closure of the Russian tea rooms, his Uncle Nikolai had taken to going there, and on occasion to taking the young Troy with him. Not that Polish meant a deal to the old man—his father's youngest brother, a Russian refugee from 1910 or 1911—and not that the Poles much welcomed Russians, but the sense of otherness appealed, an otherness with a Slav tint to it was better than constant exposure to an Englishness that resounded too loosely. It struck Troy as a form of music, a rough melody without harmonies. Conflicting consonants and consolation. If nothing else . . . just to be able to order tea without getting milk and sugar sloshed into it as a matter of course.

Wally had got to the Gay Hussar first. An unseasonable black overcoat on the hook behind him, an impeccably neat double-breasted black suit, a grey silk tie with a large, loose knot at his skinny throat. No, Troy didn't have narks like this. Troy's narks looked like spivs dipped in chip fat—men who made appointments with themselves to change their socks or wash behind their ears.

Wally stood. No taller than Troy himself. A small man in a world where things seemed to get bigger every day. He did not offer to shake hands—the white gloves merely poised in front of him.

"How pleasant to see you again, Inspector."

"We've met?"

A waiter bustled in with menus. They sat down, Troy hoping he wasn't compounding being late by sounding rude as well as forgetful.

"Last year. At the House of Commons."

Troy was at the House a fair bit. His brother had been MP for South Herts since the Labour landslide of 1945. They saw a lot of one another. A handy tunnel linked Scotland Yard to the Palace of Westminster and the London Underground. It might have been designed specially to keep the Troy brothers in touch.

"When your brother was appointed undersecretary for the RAF he threw a party for Polish and Czech veterans. Briefly, he introduced us."

Troy remembered being there. He wasn't sure why he had been there. He had probably blundered into it and, typically, Rod had declined to let him leave. He remembered the prolonged glad-handing. A barrage of names he could make no effort to memorize. So many of Rod's "pals" were the survivors of friendships forged in the Battle of Britain—odds on, some of them were Poles—or in the long run-up to D-day. He even kept in touch with General Eisenhower. Wally didn't look as though he fell into either category.

"Forgive me asking, but you weren't a pilot were you?"

Wally held up the crab hands in their Disneyesque gloves.

"With these? Of course not. I was the cuckoo in the nest that day. I served 1937 to 39 in the corps of engineers in Poland. I built bridges. Then I learnt to blow up bridges. In which is both irony and tragedy. I escaped that winter to Finland, and then to England. Hence . . ."

He turned his hands in the air, then set them as near to flat as he could manage upon the tablecloth.

"Fire?" Troy asked.

"Frost," Wally said. "I could not hold a spanner or a slide rule ever again. Even now I can scarcely hold a pen. I would have done what England asked of me in 1941, but they asked nothing."

He shrugged noticeably and stared down at the menu for a moment. Troy thought better of mentioning that what England had asked of Wally was to be a nark. How would anyone ever dress it up as anything but an ignoble calling?

"The Polish veterans association tracked down a few of us who had fought our last in '39. There are not many of us. A kind gesture to men long since forgotten by history. Hence I was at your brother's reception. Hence a reminder, not unwelcome, I had hoped, that Poland was at war a whole year before we Poles took to the skies over England."

"Two days before we declared war," said Troy.

"They matter, those days," said Wally. "Two days in which the Panzers rolled halfway across Poland while we waited for RAF bombers that never came."

Troy had no reply to this and hoped he could find a neat, painless way to change the subject, but Wally clearly felt much the same.

"Tell me, Inspector . . . can we possibly sit here and not order goulash?"

§90

A more than decent meal in a more than decent restaurant always made Troy wonder how many food and rationing regulations might have been broken to bring that meal to the table. The man in him did not care, and the copper in him cared even less. It had been a good meal. Even better for the thought that Angus Pakenham would end up arguing for it as a tax deduction.

At last Troy popped the question. It had been worth waiting. He felt he had got to know Fish Wally through his narrative. Felt that Charlie Walsh was indeed doing him a favour.

"I take it you know André Skolnik?"

Wally sipped at his coffee, looked straight at Troy.

"Do you mean *know* or *knew*? Would you be asking me about him if he were not dead?"

"You've heard already?"

"No. You just told me. And yes . . . I knew him. Of course, I knew him. A regular in the Fitzroy Tavern in Charlotte Street, the one on the corner of Windmill Street. Now, tell me how he died."

"Someone shot him earlier this evening. On the Underground. At Camden."

"Isn't this where you ask me if he had any known enemies?"

"I suppose it is."

"Then your most likely suspect will be an art critic. Skolnik was a painter. A bad painter, an atrocious painter, an execrable painter . . . a man for whom Cubism was the pinnacle of culture and who couldn't even draw a decent Mr. Cube for side of a packet of sugar. The Tate would never show him. Nor would Tate and Lyle."

"He didn't live by his painting, then?"

"He tried. He'd offer to sketch punters in the pubs, but that would have meant moving around a lot of pubs and Skolnik was too lazy for that. He taught some. There was a pretty young woman up in Hampstead as I recall. If the name comes to me before the bill comes to you I shall tell you. And when broke he would model nude—or as near nude as the law allows—for artists in all probability better than he was himself. You know Crisp? Ask Quentin Crisp—he got the work for Skolnik. Crisp laughingly refers to his role as being "a naked civil servant." In a country in which every other person seems to be a civil servant it is not hard to see the joke. And . . . when utterly broke, Skolnik would scrounge. He would appeal to something like "Polishness." And once or twice during the war I saw others scrounge for him—the hat got passed in the Fitzroy or the Wheatsheaf for "the starving artist," as it did for half a dozen or so . . . for Gerald Wilde . . . for Gully Jimson . . . any one of them more deserving than Skolnik. And the penniless poets, prostitutes, arse-bandits, transvestites, and army deserters of Fitzrovia turned out their pockets and divvied up their threepenny bits for him. I never gave him a farthing."

"Why not?"

Wally beckoned for a second cup of coffee.

The waiter appeared almost instantly but the pause had been all that Wally needed to collect his thoughts.

"Your family, Mr. Troy. Russians, I believe?"

Oh fuck, thought Troy, please do not let this be an issue. Please do not let Fish Wally assume the Troys were White Russian refugees. Whatever it was that the Troys were, it was so much more complex than that.

"Yes," Troy said simply.

"Can you spot a Russian across a crowded room?"

"Sometimes. Usually I have to wait until he opens his mouth."

"Quite so. I can spot some Poles almost by the range of their facial expressions. By and large you look at the way a Pole holds himself, his shoulders mostly . . . a Polish shrug isn't quite the same as a French shrug, although both do it rather a lot. I think in the end it was why Chopin felt at home in Paris. But . . ."

A prolonged, tantalizing sip of coffee.

"But . . . I could not see that in André Skolnik. And I looked for it often."

"Are you saying you don't think he was Polish?"

"Bear with me. I do not know for certain what he was. I give you the evidence of my eyes and ears and in the end of my instincts. The Fitzroy Tavern gets an odd mixture. It is Mitteleuropa with woolly English ale and soggy pickled onions. Once, I heard Skolnik talking with Russians. Merchantmen off a recently docked ship."

Troy began to see where this was leading.

"Lots of Poles speak Russian."

"Quite. I'm not bad at it myself. But Skolnik wasn't *not bad,* he was perfect."

"Perfect?"

"A good Moscow accent to his Russian."

Even more, Troy could see where this was leading.

He spoke softly in Russian, "I speak with a Moscow accent. Simply because my parents did. And I've never even been to Moscow."

This brought a smile to Wally's lips, the beginning of a chuckle.

"You make your point very well. But as I said, after evidence comes instinct. Skolnik seemed to me to be a man whose knowledge of Poland was textbook. Too precise, and largely unfelt. As though he had been coached in being Polish. He claimed to be from Cracow, a refugee who washed up here as a very young man in 1926. Even allowing for an exile of such length, it seemed to me that his knowledge of Cracow—and I went there every summer as a boy, to stay with an aunt— had been schooled. It was less like listening to a native than reading a guidebook. He had a Polish skin to him, if you will, but no Polish heart."

"You think he really was Russian?"

"I do. And you may forget my wisecrack about an art critic with a desire to rid the world of a third-rate painter."

It was not a thought Troy wanted in his head, but Wally had crammed it in.

"You think he was hit?"

"Is that the argot of the day for assassination? No. I don't think he was "hit." I merely suggest the possibility. Equally merely, I suggest that the late André Skolnik was, in the argot of the East End, a *ringer*—a fake planted here to do . . . whatever."

"I think the term is *sleeper.*"

"Apt," said Wally.

"Tell me," Troy said, "have you merely suggested this to Charlie Walsh?"

"No. You know Charlie as well as I do, I'm sure. He is a pragmatist. A subtle and inventive pragmatist, but a pragmatist nonetheless. I could not go to him with a hunch or anything quite so intangible. I would have lost credibility."

"Yet you tell me? Am I not a pragmatist?"

Wally smiled again, and Troy knew he'd walked into a trap. A trap of his own making.

"Mr. Troy, you are a dreamer. You have stepped off Chekhov's verandah and bade farewell to the sisters Prozorova only moments ago."

§91

It was a short walk home. A network of alleys. Down one to cut into the Charing Cross Road, down a second to cross to St. Martin's Lane, and into the third, in which Troy lived—Goodwin's Court.

Where the court bent, about as neatly as a bolt of lightning on a weather map, a whore stood waiting. Not waiting for Troy, just waiting.

"'Allo, young Fred."

This took no account of the fact that he was older than she. Troy had known Ruby since she first appeared at the corner shortly before the arrival of the American forces during the war. He'd thought she was about twenty or twenty-one at that time, so she'd be no more than twenty-seven now, to his thirty-two—yet he'd aways been "young Fred" from the moment she'd got over the initial panic of finding out that she'd pitched her tent in the front yard of a policeman. Troy even thought it might be to her advantage so to do. Troy held no brief for Vice. He thought policemen should have better things to do than concern themselves with who fucked who at what cost, or who smoked reefer, but he would not put up with a pimp on his own doorstep and as a result Ruby might well be the only whore within the vicinity of Leicester Square to escape the attentions of that brutal trade—none of them thinking it smart to risk his intervention. He didn't "protect" Ruby, but it was as well if the pimps thought he might. Once Ruby had grasped this they'd got along fine. She took a little convincing that he was not up for a "free one" and there were times he wished she'd show more discretion, but they got along fine. He'd almost learnt to accept her habitual flirting.

"The lane's dead tonight, Fred. I can't give it away."

Banal chatter or a big hint? He could never tell.

"It's the light nights, Ruby. Yours is a trade of darkness."

She gazed up at the summer sky. Only days after the longest day—evening redness in the west.

"You remember, VE Day?"

Who could ever forget?

"I mean . . . not just the night itself and the parties and that. I mean sort of the rest of that year. You know what got me? It was light. It was moving around in blazin', dazzlin' light after all them years in the blackout. War was over VE Day, 'less you bother about Japs an 'at, but it din't come home to me till about October when you could walk from here to the 'Dilly in light, electric light. And then, this year, they turned all the adverts back on and lit up the 'Dilly itself. And it din't matter that all they was doin' was tellin' you Guinness was good for you and stuff. It was like . . . getting washed clean. Washed clean in light."

She could do this to him. At the most unpredictable times she could utter something approaching poetry and just miss her target.

Of course, she was right. "Now" contrasted with "then" in terms of light and darkness. Troy thought it was a world without colour—the khakis and deepening blues of the war had given way to the myriad greys and browns of the peace. The grey of Chief Superintendent Stanley Onions' suit, the grey of the national loaf, the grey of fag ash. The brown of gravy, in which the national meal swam, or drowned, on the national plate. The nation of little ships had become the nation of gravy boats. Browning less evoked the name of one of our better poets, so much as presaged an unappetizing Sunday lunch. Brown, grey, brown. It left Troy, habitually in white shirt and black suit, craving colour. He thought it left England craving colour. He glimpsed it in his brother's red tie and socialist socks, he soaked it up occasionally in the cinemas of the West End—transfixed by the Technicolor of *The Wizard of Oz* whilst simultaneously bored by its banality. And when summers came, and the summers of the Age of Austerity came long and clear, Anna would drag frocks from her prewar wardrobe and appear to be dressed in petals, to be dressed by Monet or Matisse—red, pink, and purple, yellow, orange, and green. And he took more delight in Anna's frocks—invariably dismissed with, "oh, this old thing"—than he ever could in his brother's socks. He doubted he would be washed clean in light, but he'd be dunked in colour.

§92

When Troy got into his office the next morning there was a paper bag of greying mashed potato sitting on his desk. It was soggy and it was leaking. He took a cellophane bag from his desk and dumped the mess inside. Cellophane was a "wonder product," the sort of thing the papers were full of, the sort of thing that was going to transform our lives—or if not all our lives then the life of that much-anticipated figure of advertising land, the housewife known as "Mrs. 1950." So far, this was the only use Troy had found for it. It kept evidence clean and dry and visible. He dropped the dirty, oily gun into a second bag. He'd get the morning's work out of the way and take both over to Hendon for Kolankiewicz to examine.

Jack came in carrying two mugs of tea and kicked the door to with his foot.

Troy looked into the mug. The tea was grey and greasy, almost yellow.

"Yesterday's leaves," Jack said. "I think that must be mug number eight off a single teaspoon. We're the lucky ones. I hear rumors of a chap in Vice who's learnt to make tea from sawdust."

"The last time you told me that tale it was rabbit droppings."

"Ah, but even they're rationed now. Besides, where would I get rabbit droppings in the middle of London?"

Troy set his tea down untouched. Glanced quickly at his in-tray, then settled himself behind his desk facing Jack. Jack pulled a face like a schoolboy downing a spoonful of castor oil and supped on his poverty brew.

"You first," Troy said.

"101 Charlotte Street is split into flats. Some as small as bed-sitting rooms, all with shared bogs, none bigger than kitchen, bed, and sitting room—which was what André Skolnik had. On the first floor, front. Landlord not on site—the bloke in the flat below said he'd been there since 1934 and that Skolnik was already living there when he moved in. Skolnik was a painter, not very successful but well-known among what my mother would contemptuously call 'the Bohemian set.'"

"A bit of a bum, in other words?"

"Quite. And I'd describe his standard of living, based on his flat and possessions, as austere . . . if that weren't too overworked a word. Nah, I can do better than that . . . *seedy* . . ."

"Threadbare?"

"Yep. Just like the suit he died in and the spare jacket and trousers in the wardrobe. And the socks nobody bothered to darn for him. This was a bloke who lived close to the bottom of the heap. A man who kept a small pile of rusting razor blades on the side of the wash basin just in case he could squeeze one more shave out of them, and reheated the same pool of lard in the bottom of the frying pan to infinity regardless of the debris of previous meals matted into it."

Troy didn't much feel like drinking scummy Scotland Yard tea in the first place. After that unappetizing description he'd tip it away as soon as he could. There might be another use for cellophane bags after all.

"But as far as I can gather he didn't much mind. The downstairs neighbor, Gibbs . . . left-leaning sort of bloke . . . works in Collet's bookshop . . . used an odd turn of phrase . . . not one I'd ever thought of but it's apt . . . 'André dropped out years ago, that is, if he ever bothered to drop in in the first place.' Lived hand-to-mouth quite happily as long as he'd known him."

"Did he say what Skolnik had done during the war? He was almost too old for conscription."

"Forty-four, you said yesterday. Born 1904? Then, yes, he was just too old for the call-up. Could have volunteered at that age, I suppose, but no, our Mr. Skolnik wore the tin hat of self-righteousness."

"I see. Air-raid warden."

Jack slipped into a grumpy Cockney mimicry, "'Ere, put that light out!"

"In a Polish accent, Jack."

"No can do, old man. Gibbs was no help in the immediate sense. Hadn't seen Skolnik for three or four days. Said there was no pattern to his social or working life. Friends came and went, sometimes weeks without a sound from upstairs, sometimes people tramping up and down the stairs half the night. And no, he couldn't think of anyone in particular by name."

"Women?"

"Not lately. Gibbs seemed to think Skolnik had had his flings and at forty-four wasn't much of a catch. And I can't imagine any woman putting up with the state of his kitchen or his bathroom. But what struck me, for all the mess . . . there wasn't much evidence of painting considering he was a painter, so I asked Gibbs and he said Skolnik kept a studio in Rathbone Street. Top floor. Said something about a northern aspect. Painters seem to want northern light, dunno why. I went round there with the keys I found in Skolnik's pocket but none of them fitted, so I've left it for now. If Mr. Gibbs doesn't find the key in Skolnik's flat by about 10 o'clock, I'll go round there with a locksmith. Meanwhile, I have Constable Gutteridge watching the door."

It was Troy's turn. He had wondered how much to tell Jack. He had wondered how much he might eventually have to tell his chief superintendent, Stanley Onions. Fish Wally had been right, one's credibility mattered.

"Does Onions know?"

"He must do. He'll have read the duty log, and even if he hadn't, it's in most of the morning papers. He's prowling corridors right now. That's why the door's shut. But . . . there has been a bonus to releasing Skolnik's name, to say nothing of releasing yours. I, as your dogsbody, took a call not fifteen minutes ago—"

Jack reached into his inside pocket and flipped open a small black notebook.

"—from one Laura Narayan."

"What kind of a name is that? Sounds sort of Indian."

"Dunno. When in doubt I always plump for Welsh."

"Did she sound Welsh?"

"Absolutely not. As posh as you or I, posher if that's at all possible, the epitome of a deb voice."

Class in England was never far away as an issue or a dilemma, and it bred suspicion. At last we were one nation under Socialism, the end of deference, but the suspicion lingered, the suspicion thrived on accent and emblem. Jack could on occasion be seen wearing his old Etonian tie. Troy's brother Rod habitually wore his old Harrovian tie when not wearing his Labour MP's near-obligatory red. Troy didn't. He wore plain black—as Onions had remarked more than once to him, "You look like you're going to a funeral, lad." All the same, most of Scotland Yard referred to Jack and Troy collectively, suspiciously, as "the Tearaway Toffs."

"Laura Narayan of Fitzjohn's Avenue, Hampstead. She was very upset but through the tears managed to tell me that Skolnik had been with her yesterday afternoon until about four thirty. Appears she was one of his pupils. I think this is what we call a lead."

Troy listened, scribbled down the address as Jack spoke, then described loose circles in the air with his left hand and a pencil.

"It fits," he said. "Skolnik gets on the Underground at Hampstead, city-bound train . . . first place he can change to a West End train is Camden . . . gets out at Camden . . . crosses to the other line to board a train to Goodge Street . . . and gets shot as the train pulls in."

Jack was staring at Troy across the top of his mug, quizzically.

"Why so precise?"

"If you're going to shoot someone you'd want as much noise as possible to mask the sound of the shot and, if, as you and I both surmise, you mean to walk away as cool as cucumber once you've done it, you want a rush of people heading for the exit to blend into . . . a human tide to carry you along."

"Smartarse."

The telephone on Jack's desk in the outer office rang. He left to answer it. Troy heard a, "Yes, jolly good, half an hour? Fine," and then Jack reappeared.

"Gibbs. We have a key to Rathbone Street."

"I'll take the gun and the mash to Kolankiewicz. And I'll call on Miss, or is it Missis, Narayan—?"

"Missis," Jack said.

". . . on the way back."

Ten minutes later, as Troy passed Jack's desk on his way out, Jack was on the phone again. He cupped a hand across the mouthpiece.

"Freddie? I've just realized. You haven't told me a bloody thing!"

§93

They began with the gun.

"It's filthy," Kolankiewicz said. "Where did you find it?"

"Between the tracks."

"Ach, you won't get prints off this."

"There won't be any. He'd not have thrown it away if there were."

Kolankiewicz wiped the gun clean. What appeared was a small, black-painted automatic that fitted into the palm of the hand. It was scarcely more than three inches long from butt to barrel. The paint was matte black—household paint. Kolankiewicz scraped at it with a penknife to reveal grey gunmetal.

"Odd thing to do," he said. "As though someone wanted to disguise it. A gun still looks like a gun even if you paint it sky-blue-pink."

"May I?"

Troy took the gun, turned it this way and that, took Kolankiewicz's penknife, and scraped away at a hollow point on the butt.

"There's about a dozen of these; what do they look like to you?"

"I seen some fancy guns in my time. Some even jewelled. To me they look like the settings on my mother's engagement ring, as though they once held gemstones or some such. See, just by the trigger guard, a convex point remains."

Troy scraped too clumsily at the protrusion and it came away in his hand.

"Damn!"

"No matter; let me see."

Kolankiewicz rinsed the object, held it under a spotlight, and scraped the last of the paint away with his thumbnail. It gleamed, red and radiant.

"My God. It's a ruby."

"Correct, my boy. Now, smartyarse. Tell me who would want to paint over rubies?"

This was where Troy's expertise outstripped Kolankiewicz's, if only in the field of popular culture. He doubted Kolankiewicz had been to the pictures since they added sound.

"There was a film during the early part of the war," he said. "You won't have seen it. Bogart, Peter Lorre—"

"Ah . . . him I remember. The little German with the fish eyes."

"—and Sydney Greenstreet."

The name did not register with Kolankiewicz.

"It was called *The Maltese Falcon,* and the title referred to a statue studded with precious stones that had been passed around Europe for centuries disguised in black paint."

"Save one, this has been stripped of its jewels."

"That's because, first of all, someone needed to move it around without its worth being recognized, and then they needed to cash in."

"But missed one?"

"Quite."

Kolankiewicz flipped out the magazine.

"It's empty. I would say it held only three bullets. Did you find the spent case."

"No. I was lucky to find the gun. The case may be on the tracks, too, but to get it I'll need to close down the Northern line. I'll get lynched for even asking. Can we work with what we've got?"

"What we've got is that bag of mashed potato you brought in."

Kolankiewicz tipped the bag onto a sheet of blotting paper. Pushed a rubber-gloved finger around in the mess. Then he bent down and sniffed at it.

"We been calling this mash, right?"

"My word was baked."

"Okay. Baked, mashed, shmashed . . . whatever. What do you think cooked it?"

"No idea."

"Look here, at the end of my finger."

Troy looked at black stains on white mash.

"Dirt?"

"Gunpowder residue."

"Bloody hell. You don't think—"

"Not yet, I don't. Let's examine the body before you leap to any conclusions. If you're coming in, scrub up and find an apron."

§94

"What's this green stuff under his fingernails?" Kolankiewicz asked.

Troy peered over the naked body of André Skolnik.

"Paint, I should think. He was a painter."

"As in house?"

"As in art."

"Art, shmarrt . . ."

Kolankiewicz looked to the stenographer on her stool in the corner. "Ready?"

"When you are, professor."

To Troy he said, "This is all very well, but when the Yard gets around to a new laboratory could we have a thing that records what I say?"

"Thing?"

"No matter. Just nag the bastards. I work with two classes of tool here—out of the ark and homemade."

So saying, he sliced the flesh over Skolnik's heart down to the bone. Troy handed him the rib spreader and watched as Kolankiewicz cranked the rib cage apart to see the stilled heart itself. Kolankiewicz inserted his right hand.

"It's not here. Must be lodged in one of the chambers of the heart. Scalpel again, I think."

Troy gave a couple more turns to the rib spreader. Kolankiewicz sliced the heart free of arteries and veins—a little, Troy thought, like prising another jewel from its setting—and laid it on the slab above the head.

"Entry wound is in the left ventricle."

He sliced the heart open, spread the left ventricle out like a dog's dinner, and said, "I see it now. I'll hold. You take the tweezers and remove it."

Troy held up the smallest bullet he'd ever seen. Air rifles fired bigger shot than this.

"Curiouser and curiouser," said Kolankiewicz.

"Amazing," Troy said, "that anything so small could have killed him."

Kolankiewicz took the tweezers and bullet from him and rinsed them off in the sink.

"Anywhere else and it would not have done. Puncture a lung with this and, short of drowning in your own blood, you'd live. Almost anywhere on the torso there would be limited damage, and short of hitting your man right in the eye, I doubt such a bullet would penetrate the skull. God knows, in winter it might have bounced off his overcoat."

"Can you match it to the gun?"

"With what? The magazine was empty. You think I have bullets like this in stock? The smallest I've ever seen is .17, and does this not look smaller? At that bore there'll be no rifling. Matching a bullet, impossible. Matching a cartridge case, maybe, but that you don't have. If this merely fits the gun, I think that will be all the evidence you need."

So saying he took measuring calipers and read the bullet's bore.

"Point 15 or near as damnit. 3.75mm. I do not know of anyone who makes ammunition this small."

"The gun's an antique," Troy said. "Looks donkey's years old. Perhaps they made .15 bullets once upon a time?"

"Once upon a time. How very apt, my boy. You bring me a gun that has been encrusted with jewels, that fires what I can only describe as toy bullets, and you speak to me of 'once upon a time'—a fairy tale, is it not?"

"Maybe," said Troy. "But you're not telling me it's a dead end?"

"I can do no more with the gun. I think you need to go and see Bob Churchill. But before you do, give me hand to turn the body."

They returned to the corpse.

Kolankiewicz peered into the entry wound. For all the world it looked to Troy as though Skolnik had merely been stuck with a knitting needle.

Kolankiewicz eased in his tweezers, gently slid them out again, and held up his find with a glimpse of triumph in his eyes.

"Mashed potato," he said almost gleefully, the bushy eyebrows rising up to meet the bald head in scornful pleasure. "Do you know what this means?"

"The potato was on the end of the gun."

"Like . . . ?"

"Like a silencer? But . . . but would it silence the gun?"

201

"I don't know. You had better take the gun to Churchill. But given the low load of cordite in the bullet and the hubbub of the London Underground, would it have taken much silencing? And that's why your spud is part mash, part baked, and part raw. It was cooked where it was in contact with the gun and the bullet. The firing of the gun blew the potato apart, scattered it across the platform, where, without flattery, in the hands of dimmer plod—and you know how dim some of your colleagues can be—it would have been dismissed as lunchtime litter."

"Clever, eh?"

"Perhaps. Perhaps just crude."

The hint of schadenfreude vanished. Kolankiewicz slipped back into the routine of the job, bustling around his laboratory, leaving Troy still more than a little baffled.

"I shall do all the usual things, brain, guts . . . it'll all be in the report."

Troy batted back.

"Oh, I can tell you what will be in the stomach."

"You can?"

"Five bob on Earl Grey and Battenberg."

"Suddenly you're cocky?"

"He'd just had tea in Hampstead."

"So? Is Hampstead above rationing?"

§95

It was a massive house, just south of Hampstead village. Gates and a drive—gates that hadn't been claimed in some spurious metals campaign during the war, a drive that hadn't even been tarmaced let alone built over. A house that wasn't partitioned into flats. Troy would put the house at about 1880. Perhaps of its era, not quite the Edwardian villa—only a villa in the Italian sense, as in Villa Cimbrone—but post-war, even in a borough of big houses, this one seemed absurdly grand. What new money had been pumped into this? What new money had lasted long enough to get old here? How did they run a place on this scale without servants on the Victorian scale. He'd find out. He had rung from Hendon and "was expected."

He left his tatty Bullnose Morris next to a shining black Daimler. He'd bet even money that it had spent the war up on blocks just like his father's Rolls. But they, whoever they were, were running it now. His brother Rod was looking forward to the day they could get his father's 1922 Silver Ghost, the one with the cream paintwork and burgundy uphol-stery, running again—petrol permitting, and Rod's image as a Labour MP most certainly not permitting. He'd have liked the car himself, but coppers didn't roll up in a Rolls, only the Wimseys and the Campions would ever get away with that. Whatever he had next, he'd wait until the Morris fell apart first.

The "girl" answered the bell. Black and white uniform, cap awry, tongue ababble.

"Miss Laura says to go straight up, sir, top floor, only I can't come meself as there's only been me and cook since Dunkirk when Mr. Spiggot and Stanley Moon joined up, only Spiggot never come back and Stanley Moon says he'd sooner drive a tram than work for toffs again."

Well, that was one question answered, but as Troy set off up the wide, winding staircase another arose. When had he been here before, climb-ing these stairs to an attic room? A tidal surge of memory and he could see himself aged five or six, in 1920 or 1921, warily making his way to a children's party that only the propellant force of his mother could make him attend. This house had belonged to the Gore-Neames. Now, what had been their daughter's name, the one that was about a year older than him, whose party it was. Louisa, Lorna . . . Laura?

He was at the top now. A half open door, a child of four or five dash-ing out to say, "Mummy's in here!"

Not a child such as he had been—frail, small, pale. This was a robust, clumping, coffee-colored child. Another question answered. Narayan was indeed an Indian name.

"I say, you're Frederick Troy aren't you?"

"Yes."

"I used to be Laura Neame. Surely you . . . ?"

Yes. He did. About his height, blonde, blue-eyed, beautiful, but she'd put on weight. That was the first thing that struck him, how unkind time had been to her in piling on the pounds.

"When you said 'Inspector Troy,' I didn't make the connection."

"Really? I thought I'd scandalized half London when I joined the police."

"And I thought I'd scandalized the other half when I married Indra Narayan, and you don't seem to have noticed that anymore than I noticed you'd gone for a copper."

She led him into her studio—top floor, north-facing, stuffed with clutter: canvases finished, canvases half-finished, canvases terrifyingly blank, a huge, fading red, Bakhtiar carpet spattered with paint.

He'd bet she'd scandalized London society marrying an Indian—or as society undoubtedly tagged him, "a nigger." It was the sort of thing he'd have noticed if he paid more attention to the gossip his sisters doled out but it was precisely because they were his sisters, hedonists to the point of banality, litanists of who fucks who, that he didn't pay any attention. One could get away with being a copper—if needs be it was a job that could be passed off as a "profession"—but young women, "gels," didn't get away with marrying niggers.

She plucked another child, half the size of the first, off the carpet and took a paint brush from his mouth.

"I'd say stay for lunch, but as you can see the studio is also a nursery and, given the situation downstairs, the most I could run to is a cup of tea except that I think the milk's off—summer after all—and I rather think André polished off the cake . . . but . . . of course . . . I've waffled right to the point haven't I? André. Do sit down . . . Inspector."

"Troy will do," said Troy.

She balanced on the edge of a wicker chair, the toddler still in her arms. Troy sat on a spoon-back Victorian nursing chair and, as he felt one wonky leg shift under him, he knew in an instant what the situation was. In this England of the New Socialist Era, the England of the Five-year Plan, no one in a respectable area would rent to a mixed marriage with babies doubtless referred to as half-caste, and in all probability no one would give her husband a decent job. Laura had moved into her parents' attic and was utilizing all the junk of centuries stored up there. He was sure she had made a point of using junk as a symbol of an independence she didn't have, and he was sure it half-suited her parents, not having a woodpile, to hide the niggers in the attic. Why they didn't just bankroll her was not a question he'd ask. Maybe the Daimler represented the last of the old money and no one was making the new?

She read his mind.

"Daddy died eighteen months ago. The death duties have been crippling. I'd love to have my own flat. But during the war . . . well, you know how it was . . . and since then, well, waiting for probate . . . taxes . . . I teach a little, you know, everything helps."

It was the cue he had wanted.

"And I gather André taught you?"

She looked startled.

"Taught me? Is that what he told you?"

"I never met him."

"Oh, silly me."

She set the toddler down upon the worn Persian rug to crawl and chew once more, brushed a stray lock of hair from her eyes, and Troy could see that the nearer they got to the purpose of his visit the nearer she was to tears.

"No. André didn't teach me. I'd nothing to learn from André. I taught him."

Troy was not much when it came to art. He knew enough never to say, 'I may not know much about art, but I know what I like,' and that, in part, was because he didn't know what he liked. He could see enough of Laura Narayan's work scattered about the room to see that she had a gift for portraiture, and to know that she had, mercifully, learnt more from Matisse than Picasso. She loved color. That much was obvious.

"And that was why he was here yesterday?"

"Yes. A free lesson. No money again. He arrived about 2.30 and left sharp at 4.30. I saw him to the door. The last I saw of him he was walking up the hill towards the tube station. And that's about all I can tell you. He wasn't behaving oddly at all. He didn't seem bothered by anything. Didn't mention what he was doing with the evening. I assumed he was just going home."

"How did you meet?"

"Chap name of Gibbs . . . lives in the same house as André . . . works in Collets. Now, my husband is rather left-wing . . ."

Another reason to hide him in the attic, thought Troy.

". . . he's sort of the Mr. Toad of politics . . . rowing boats, canary-colored caravans . . . poop, poop . . . you know, that sort of thing. At heart he's a complete anarchist, but he will flirt with organized politics. There was a brief spell, I suppose it would be about the time Russia came into the war, we were all feeling so patriotic, when he thought he might be a Communist. He took to spending all our money in places like Collets. That's where he met Malcolm Gibbs, and when Indra told him I was a painter somehow the two of them cooked up that André and I would get on like a house on fire if only they could contrive a meeting, which of course they did."

"At Collets?"

"I don't think wild horses or Russian tanks could have dragged André Skolnik into a communist book shop. Politics bored him. When Indra gets on his hobby horse I've known André to actually fall asleep with boredom. No, dashed if I know where we met, but we did and we clicked. He may have been a third-rate painter—Good Lord, here I am talking ill of the dead and the poor man's not been dead twenty-four hours—but he talked art rather well. He was a lovely man—a charmer."

"If I told you I'd heard he was a scrounger?"

Her head jerked up, the reverie of grief suddenly curtailed.

"Then I'd say you'd been talking to an enemy."

"Did he have enemies?"

Something in Laura's spirit sagged. She covered her eyes with her palms for a moment.

"Silly word. Double silly when talking to a policeman, I suppose. No, André didn't have enemies, and I can't think of anyone who'd want to harm him, let alone kill him. Yes, there was an André that was forever borrowing money. But he always paid me back, every last farthing. I could not afford to give it away. He has a studio near his flat—I suppose you know that—I paid the rent for the first six months. I got it all back. I divvied up for three months last year and got that back, too. André's fortunes ebbed and flowed. There were times when he was flush, and when he was flush he was generous."

"And the nude modelling? Does that not sound desperately poor to you?"

"No, it doesn't. We all do it. All us painters pose for one another. If we didn't, we'd end up paying rather than paid. I've done it myself. If he hasn't sold it, and André rarely made a sale, somewhere in his studio there's a nude of me when I was seven months gone with Raman. I'm sure I'd've been a more successful model than André, if I'd wanted. Painters like big women, you see. I should be glad somebody does. And André was always so skinny."

Troy took this away with him—that Skolnik's fortune ebbed and flowed, which prompted him to think that Wally had only seen him in the down part of the cycle . . . and to wonder why the cycle was there at all, and who was funding it . . . and that a shining, buffed black Daimler parked in front of a house the size of a Venetian palazzo, in which someone struggled to get by with just the cook and one maid while someone else counted every last farthing, was far too symbolic of the England of 1948. He'd respect Laura's privacy but he dearly wished he could explain to Rod the paradoxes of wealth and poverty, of standards still maintained, in the country he was working so hard to bring into being.

§96

Rod wasn't even a quarter of a mile away. Thinking of him had given Troy an inkling to see him. He usually worked from home in the mornings and unless there was an afternoon session in the Commons he meant to attend, set off for Westminster somewhere around three. Besides, it was lunchtime, past lunchtime. Troy drove up the hill, into Heath Street, turned into Church Row, and parked. Parked in front of him was a car of a type he'd never seen before. It was ugly as sin—brown? green? greeny-brown? mud?—resembled a frog that had been run over in the road, and, alarmingly, it was right in front of his brother's house. Rod had a thing about cars. He'd driven a nice little HRG 1100 during the war, replaced that with a longer, sleeker V8 Morgan—run with one carb shut down to eke out the petrol. This tally took no account of the Rolls, the Crossley, and the Lagonda left by their father—and Troy found himself hoping that this blob wasn't the replacement for the Morgan.

He rang the bell. Since his father's death almost five years ago Troy had always knocked. It wasn't his childhood home anymore, it was his brother's house. His sister-in-law Lucinda said plainly and often that this was "daft." It was Lucinda who answered the door.

"You're late," she said.

"Late for what?"

"Oh . . . perhaps you weren't invited . . . no matter, you know them all, you'd better join them—there's pudding if you want but the chicken's finished."

"Cid . . . join who for what?"

"Oh, you know . . . Fat Billy . . . Skinny Joe . . . the talented Mr. Rosen . . ."

"Ah," said Troy. "The Stinking Jews Reunion."

"Yep. And all my efforts to persuade Rod to come up with a better name have come to nought. Go in, I'll bring you coffee in a jiffy."

In the summer of 1940, Rod had spent several weeks banged up with Billy Jacks, Joe Hummel, and Viktor Rosen. It had been called the internment of aliens. Rod, being less alien than most, had been let out in time to win the Battle of Britain for the nation and mankind at large. Over the ensuing weeks and months, more of his "cellmates" had emerged and just before Christmas that year Rod had staged the first reunion. As the releases progressed—Oskar Siebert to dig for the Pioneer Corps, Arthur Kornfeld to work subatomic wonders with quantum physics at Cambridge—so the numbers at the dining table grew and Rod switched the reunion to summer, when he could guarantee more for the table from his mother's garden and off the ration. Troy could guess at roast chicken, the first spring greens, and new potatoes brought on under cloches—perhaps even an early pot of broad beans. Whether or not Troy got invited to the Stinking Jews Reunion always seemed, as now, to be a matter of chance.

He opened the door gently and quietly but still managed to stop the chatter of half a dozen voices. They all looked at him momentarily—there was not a face he didn't know, and the only one he hadn't mentally ticked off the list was Lou Spinetti, the pastry cook from Quaglino's—then Rod rose, rich with bonhomie, smiling, a bit pissed, fraternally fulsome in a way that both pleased and annoyed Troy by making him feel smothered.

"Freddie! Brilliant timing, absolutely ace!"

The arm around his shoulder all but made his ribs crack, and then he found himself shoved into a chair next to Rosen, clutching a glass of champagne he didn't much want.

"It's been a while, dear boy," said Rosen. "Are you practicing daily?"

"Of course," Troy lied.

"I was hoping you might be here."

Rosen reached into his breast pocket and laid two tickets in front of Troy.

"The Wigmore Hall, Saturday. Bring a friend."

Troy quite liked the Wigmore. A depressing shade of brown marble inside, like a gents' lavatory designed for the gods on Mount Olympus, but the acoustics were superb. He'd been there often with his dad in the twenties.

"What are you playing?"

"Big band stuff," said Rosen. "Schubert Trio in E-flat before the interval, then we bring out the heavy guns for the Octet after."

"And if they want an encore?"

When did audiences not want an encore?

"Four minutes of the B-flat sonata. Three if I get zippy on the ivories. It's an all-Schubert evening. If they want Mozart they can whistle, and I do mean that literally."

"Thanks," said Troy, wondering who on earth he could ask to go with him. "I'll be there."

"Do you know the Octet?"

"'Fraid not."

"Then I advise you to pee in the interval. It lasts the best part of an hour."

Hummel said something to Rosen in German, a language Troy had sort of left behind when he left school. Rod was laughing with Siebert, Kornfeld, and Spinetti at some joke or other—and, happy or grumpy, Billy Jacks always scared the bejasus out of Troy. It was timely that Cid brought coffee when she did.

"When you've got moment, young Fred, I wouldn't mind a couple of minutes of your time in the kitchen."

"I'll come now."

Troy left his champagne untouched and followed Cid downstairs.

"I can't get his nibs to pay the slightest bit of attention to this."

She had spread out a dozen or more photographs of her children on the table—Alex, who Troy thought must be about twelve; the twins who were ten; and Nicki who was seven. They ran the gamut from shots so posed it was obvious one parent or another was just off-camera yelling "do this or else" to the utterly unposed, neck-twisting pseudojollity of polyfoto.

"I don't know whether to get some of these enlarged and framed or simply to call in a photographer and have a new picture taken. I want something that captures them as kids before they're much older. Alex is an adolescent—something that seems to escape his father—and before I know it he'll be six feet tall and I'll have to strain to remember him as he was."

Troy looked at them. Rod's omissions as a father were nothing compared to his own as an uncle.

"Have you considered," he said. "Having a portrait painted?"

Cid turned the polyfoto this way and that with her fingertips.

"Hmm . . . it would mean them sitting still an awfully long time."

"Not necessarily . . ."

"Do you have someone in mind?"

"Do you remember the Neames—just down the hill?"

"I never knew the family as such. I see the daughter from time to time when I'm shopping. Lorna or Laura wasn't it? Married that Indian chap, the philosopher. Name escapes me."

"I had occasion to call on her today. She paints."

"A professional call, Inspector? Do I want a murderer painting my brattish offspring?"

"She's just a witness, Cid. You should give her a call."

"Perhaps I will. What has she witnessed, by the bye? Not the killing on the Northern line?"

Troy could see no point in secrecy.

"As a matter of fact, yes. That is the case. Looks as though Laura might have been the last person to see the victim alive."

"You know," Cid said, "you're lucky you weren't here an hour ago. Rod's expecting questions in the house about it. 'Is public transport safe for the public on the eve of the London Olympics? . . . blah blah blah' . . . He thinks this is just the sort of publicity London doesn't need, at what he calls 'an international moment' . . . 'the eyes of the world upon us' . . . blah blah blah. He read the front page of the *Post* out to them all before lunch in a 'what's-the-world-coming-to' tone of voice . . . It brought out the residual hang-'em-and-flog-'em in Billy and Lou, something I think Rod is prepared to beat out of them if he has to. Joe let go with one of his world-weary sighs and old Viktor went so pale I thought he was going to faint. If Rod had known it was your case . . ."

"Well, we won't tell him. At least you don't tell him until after I've gone."

As Troy was leaving, Rod had gathered his guests on the pavement to show off for a bit. The blob-car was indeed his.

"This," he said with a certain pride Troy took to be national, governmental even, on the part of the Undersecretary of State for Air, rather than personal, "is a Morris Minor, a 900cc, 62mph . . . 500 quid . . . people's car."

"Nah," said Billy Jacks, "it's just an 'orrible blob."

"To me," said Rosen, "it resembles nothing quite so much as a poached egg. If you want a people's car why not just go the whole hog and call it a Volkswagen."

"Because no one wants to be reminded of Hitler, that's why."

"Reminded? Who can forget him? Besides, the Germans are all ready to export the Volkswagen. For the first time since about 1910, I feel a shred of pride in my native land."

"Well," said Rod, his bonhomie beginning to evaporate, "it won't sell here. Nobody will buy a car with a Nazi name. Volkswagen sounds like troop transport for the SS. They'll buy this, the Morris Minor. Sounds as honest as the day is long."

"No, it sounds like an unfortunate, put upon, and bullied fag at a third-rate public school," said Troy. "More to the point, why have you bought the people's car? Your English Volkswagen. You own a Rolls-Royce with cream paintwork and burgundy leather upholstery, and you want to drive a car that looks like a frog?"

"No, no," said Rosen. "A poached egg, the poached egg of the damp British breakfast, floating in its own small pool of water and ruining the toast."

This set Jacks and Hummel giggling, and turned Rod a little red in the face.

211

"It's the future!" he said, to more giggles.

"Then give me the past," said Rosen.

"The past did nine miles to the gallon."

Rosen took the words out of Troy's mouth and said, "Can we expect to see that in your manifesto?"

"Bollocks to you. Bollocks to the pair of you. And Freddie, you own half of that Rolls. If you want it all . . ."

Troy replied, "You know, brer, there's no talking to you sometimes, and increasingly it's when you've got your man-of-the-people hat on."

Troy had no wish to provoke the Undersecretary of State for Air and instantly wished he hadn't. For a moment it looked as though the Undersecretary of State might shove a Rolls-Royce with cream paintwork and burgundy leather upholstery right up his arse. But the gods favoured him, Cid appeared in the doorway saying, "Freddie. Telephone for you. Jack wants a word."

Saved by the bell.

"I missed you at Mrs. Narayan's. But she said you'd driven uphill, not down, so I sort of figured you'd be at Rod's. Any chance you could come by Skolnik's studio—you know, Rathbone Street?"

"I'll leave now. Is it interesting?"

"Oh, yes, it's that all right, but whether it's also informative rather depends on you."

§97

The building in which Skolnik had his studio ran between Rathbone Street and Charlotte Street. The front was on Charlotte Street, not quite a London boulevard, but home to shops and restaurants and caffs. If it were in Paris there would be tables on the pavements. If it were Rio, dancing in the streets. But it was in London. Rathbone Street was an alley with a pub. It was much more London.

Troy yanked at a peeling, green-painted door and stepped into a building that, while it had not taken a direct hit, had clearly taken some secondary bomb damage. A shock wave that had rippled across the street from somewhere. All the way up five brown and cream flights of stairs to the top floor, wooden beams the size of telegraph poles shored it up.

The studio was desirable space, spanning the building across the top floor, a storey or more higher than the building to the north on Charlotte Place, and hence free from the southern glare of summer light. It had the constancy that painters craved.

Jack was mooching around. Troy approached slowly, sideways along a wall of hanging, unframed canvases. Wally was right. Skolnik's work was execrable. Endless Picassoesque poses, armpits, elbows, and skewed noses . . . a generation or more of cheerless demoiselles d'Avignon.

"Uplifting, eh?" said Jack.

"Hardly. And you didn't get me here to tell you Skolnik was a tenth-rate Cubist."

"Quite. I may not know much about art but I do know what I don't like, and I think André Skolnik just went to the top of that list. No, I got you here to look at his work, but not the mainstream as it were . . . this one's an oddity."

Jack led him across the room to an easel with a canvas still on it.

"It's this. It's different. And while it looks finished, it's fairly obvious that he was working on this until he died. Paint's still a little tacky."

Troy found himself gazing upon a wholly different style of painting. Just as derivative as Skolnik's faux Cubism, but owing more to the Renaissance or to pastiches of the Renaissance. It was based on Botticelli's *Birth of Venus*. He'd pared it down to the central figure—no serving wench with a necklace of laurels and a red sheet to wrap the goddess in, no brace of angels puffing from the wings. The shape of the woman's figure was identical, the off-centre posture that would topple her in anything "real," the knees touching, the feet gently splayed, one hand not quite concealing her breasts, the other wholly concealing her quim with a tress of golden hair . . . only she rose not from a clam shell but from a cello case, and on her rib cage just below her breasts were two *f*-holes, as though her body itself were a string instrument.

Troy said nothing.

Jack said, "He hasn't signed it properly so I'm not wholly sure it's a Skolnik, it's just that that does seem logical—but he has left an inscription, see? There at the bottom right. Now, you see why I sent for you?"

"Quite," said Troy, bending to look closely. "It's in Russian."

"Any chance you could translate?"

"It seems like a dedication, to a nameless waif, who—he would smudge the verb—but I think it's 'blinded,' as in deceived. 'You who blinded two countries, you deserve'—I think 'deserved,' actually—'you deserved success, your audacious fraud maintained by deep and constant secrecy.' And it's signed AP."

"Ah . . . I'd be useless at this sort of thing. I was thinking that Π might be a Russian way of writing S and hence A. Skolnik."

"It's a P, and I rather think it stands for Alexander Pushkin. I don't know the play well, but I think it's from *Boris Godunov*. It would fit. There's a character in it, known as the Pretender, who cons both the Russians and the Poles into thinking he's the heir to the Russian throne."

"Sticky end?"

"Probably. Mussorgsky made an opera out of it. Name me an opera without a sticky end."

"And does it help?"

Troy said nothing. He had put off telling Jack about Fish Wally's suspicions until any other scrap of evidence pointed the same way. Quoting Russian verse and getting the rhyme right might be that scrap.

"May be," he began. "May be. The new nark I met last night is a Pole named Fish Wally who's worked for the Branch since '41—for Stilton and then for Walsh. He knew Skolnik, didn't much like him, which makes me allow something for bias, but he was pretty adamant that Skolnik was a Russian, not a Pole, and that he was a wrong 'un. A sleeper planted here by the Russians just after the Civil War."

"Oh, shit," said Jack. "Here we go again."

"Then let us pull up packing cases and be comfortable while I drop us in it one more time."

Troy sat on the nearest, Jack sat opposite, rippling with concern.

"You've taken on an ex–Special Branch nark?"

"Yes. Charlie Walsh made me a present of him."

"What does Onions say about this?"

"He doesn't need to know."

"Freddie, can I remind you of what he said to you this time four years ago, when I plucked you off a bomb site with a bullet in your gut. He said, 'Don't ever mess with the spooks again.'"

"Jack, don't get me wrong. I'd've died without you that night. But that was a case Charlie Walsh handed me because his hands were tied."

"And you picked it up, and Onions went ballistic."

"Initially Stan was only too happy I did. I remember his words, too. 'Nobody blows coppers away on the streets of London and tells me there's not a damn thing I can do about it.' And that was about an hour before I first called Charlie. I picked up a murder no one else was willing to look into. That's what we do; that's why they call us the Murder Squad."

"Freddie, you went up against the Branch and MI5 and the OSS . . . you got shot . . . and the murderer is still at large!"

The murderer was not at large, the murderer was buried in her family plot in a small cemetery in Fermanagh. Diana Brack was dead, apart from the eternal life she seemed to have achieved in Troy's dreams. Her . . . what was the word? . . . Svengali . . . Major Wayne, was still at large. That much he'd silently concede to Jack.

"Can't win 'em all," Troy lied.

Jack sighed. "Can I take it you'll tell Onions about this?"

"I'll tell him but not just yet. I'd like to be more convinced Wally's right before I do."

"What have you got? We're pretty close to clueless at the moment."

"I talked to Laura Narayan this morning. By and large, what she said about Skolnik squares with your appraisal and with what Wally said, a scrounger living low on the food chain. But she liked him more than Wally did, and I think she knew him a lot better. She described him as generous."

"Generous with what?"

"Quite. She said he was intermittently flush with money. And at times when he was, all debts would be repaid."

"Okay, that matches something Gibbs said when I picked up the key this morning. How Skolnik threw parties at no notice or suddenly rounded up half a dozen ne'er-do-well mates and took them all to Bertorelli's for a meal. But I don't know what it means."

"It might mean he was on someone's payroll, and every so often that someone paid him in cash."

"Maybe he sold a painting?"

"Does it look like he sold anything?"

"Okay, tell me what you have in mind."

"First, I'd like to get Laura Narayan down here just to be sure this *is* a genuine Skolnik. Then I think I'll need to talk to Fish Wally one more time."

"And if it turns out that Skolnik was a Soviet agent?"

"I'll let the spooks handle it," Troy lied.

Jack mulled it over.

"Might be a godsend if he was and they did. We're at the point of going through every scrap of paperwork he left—of course that may not amount to a pile, probably not much more than a gas bill—and of going onto the Underground at 4.30 every day for a week with a photograph asking, 'have you seen this man?' and that will amount to a pile."

"Hmm," said Troy, "4.30 is not a good time. If he'd got on half an hour or three-quarters of an hour later it would have been the rush hour—regular travellers. At 4.30 you don't know who you'll get."

"Are you trying to depress me?"

§98

Troy's last call of the day was to Orange Street, which snakes its way from the Haymarket to the Charing Cross Road, hidden on the one side from Leicester Square and on the other from the National Gallery. It's one of those streets best described as "you'd never know it's there." It is so narrow that cars cannot pass one another at the eastern end. Troy left his Bullnose Morris in Whitcomb street and walked the last few yards to the premises of Robert Churchill, gunsmith.

Mr. Chewter answered his ring. Chewter had been Churchill's factotum, his everything, since time immemorial. Troy knew full well his Christian name was Jim, but had never heard anyone address him as anything but "Mister."

"Mr. Troy. What a pleasant surprise."

"Not too much of one I hope. I've no appointment."

Chewter looked at his pocket watch, dropped it back into his waistcoat pocket, and said, "I'm sure we can fit you in, sir. You go up in the lift. I'll call up and let the guv'ner know you're here."

As the coffin-sized cage wound up to the top floor, Troy was struck by an annoying thought. Angus had made him petty, because all he could think of for fifteen seconds was that this was a service for which the Yard would not pay, and that Angus would add it to his list of claims. Troy realized that accountancy, chartered or otherwise, could infect the soul.

Bob met him at the lift gate.

"Freddie! How nice to see you again. Is this what I think it is? The body on the Northern Line?"

"Am I so predictable?"

"No . . . but you'd not come to me if you hadn't found the gun."

"I have found it. It's a real oddity."

"Let's go to the desk, shall we?"

Churchill led him into the inner office. He bore a more than passing resemblance to his distant cousin Winston, the same round face, the same ready wit—and as he followed, Troy found himself pondering the common girth of the two men. A large arse in voluminous trousers preceded him.

"Are you practicing regularly?" Churchill asked.

The same question Rosen had put to him only hours before. Rosen taught him the piano, Churchill how to shoot, and so the same lie served.

"Of course," Troy lied.

Churchill flicked on a desk lamp, rolled out a clean sheet of white paper. Troy handed over the three packages Kolankiewicz had given him. The gun, the bullet, and the ruby.

"My oh my," said Churchill. "What have we here?"

"I've never seen anything like it, and nor has Kolankiewicz."

Churchill held the gun under the light, turned it this way and that.

"So light. So . . . delicate."

"There is one other thing," Troy said. "We think a potato was used as a silencer."

Churchill raised one eyebrow at this but said nothing. Lowering said eyebrow, he put a jeweller's lens to his eye and continued to examine the gun. Then he removed the eyeglass and began to strip down the gun.

He laid the pieces out in a neat line across the paper. Put the eyeglass back in.

"Well . . . ," he said after a minute or two of silence in which all Troy had heard was the ticking of the clock and the rumbling of Churchill's stomach. "All I can tell you right now is that the mechanism is Swiss. There is a maker's mark. Gebrüder Altmann. As I recall they were based in Zurich, packed up shop just after the Great War. They did make small guns, but I'd no idea they'd ever made anything as small as this."

"It's .15," said Troy.

"Amazing. They probably had to make the ammunition as well. However, the casing, and the . . . whatdeyecallit . . . ornamentation, is another thing entirely. Indeed, before somebody knocked it about it must have been beautiful. The engraving, the leaves, the ferns. So . . . I say again, delicate. Puts one in mind of a Fabergé egg."

Troy kicked himself inside. He'd seen all sorts of things in the engraving on the gun but the similarity to a Fabergé egg had not once occurred to him.

"But of course," Churchill went on, as though reading Troy's mind and trying to soften the blow, "there could be dozens of people who did that sort of thing at the time. And I've never heard that Fabergé worked on guns. But it does look very Fabergé."

"What time would that be, Bob?"

"Well, this century I think. But only just. Say 1905. 1910. Not later than 1917 . . . if my Russian hunch has anything more to it than a style of jewellery. Fabergé fled west that year. The name survives but he made nothing after the revolution. Three hands at work here. The Altmanns made the gubbins, somebody else made the body, and someone else did the decoration. Look there, I think these blips held jewels at one time."

Troy pushed the ruby across the paper to him. It looked like the packet of salt at the bottom of a bag of crisps, wrapped in a twist of blue paper.

Churchill unwrapped it.

"My," he said. "Just the one?"

"Whoever prised them out missed one. It's all I have."

Churchill put back his eyeglass.

"It's beautiful, simply beautiful. Of course, there's nothing to say they were all rubies."

"There might have been diamonds."

"Exactly. Who knows? A gun like this would be unique—a one-off. Made to order."

Troy knew what this meant.

"That doesn't help, does it?"

Churchill sighed a little.

"In a country that kept records it would be a positive advantage. In Russia, after all it's been through these last thirty years, quite the opposite. I shall do what I can do, but if you're relying solely on the gun as your lead to the killer I'll disappoint you now. This could take weeks. I can't just phone anyone up. I shall have to write letters, and I shall have to be very discreet. And when I get replies, *if* I get replies, I shall in all probability have to write more letters."

"Then I'll leave it with you."

Troy got up, pushed the last package across the paper to Churchill, and headed for the lift. Over his shoulder, he said, "It's the bullet, Bob. Many thanks."

He'd just got the lift door closed, when it was wrenched open. There stood Churchill, something between glee and astonishment lighting up his face and quivering his jowls.

"It's silver, Freddie. The bullet is made of silver!"

§99

Troy's father had thrown nothing away. The man had been an habitual hoarder. His study at Mimram, the country house in Hertfordshire where Troy's mother had lived permanently since the death of her husband, was a Chinese box of a room—strip away one layer of junk and you will find another. Rod could not abide such disorder, and Troy had taken over the study at Mimram. In London, the old man's study had become Rod's domain. Troy expected to find it somewhat more organized. Somewhere in his past, and he had lived well into his eighties, Alex Troy had been a cigar smoker, and when nagged by wife and doctors to give it up he had done so—and when most men might have put the Fabergé cigar tools up for auction or presented them to a son who smoked (none of his did), Alex had simply left them where they had stood since 1910 on his desktop. Troy hoped they were still there.

Rod had entirely forgotten his mood of only hours ago. The blob was still out front. Rod didn't so much as glance at it and Troy did not mention it.

"Back so soon? Ah, well, the sun is over the yardarm, come and have a drink."

"I need a few minutes in the old man's study."

"Fine, you know where to find me."

The study was at the back at garden level. Alex was often to be found, rain or shine, summer or winter, simply standing by the French windows staring out, or at his desk leafing through Quiller-Couch's *Oxford Book of English Verse* to find something that matched the mood of the day. If he'd still been alive, doubtless Troy would only have had to mention the quotation from Pushkin for the old man to have found it in his capacious memory of Russian verse.

The Fabergé set was still there, next to the green-bound edition of Quiller-Couch. Troy had no idea of the technical names for these devices. There was a thing that lopped one end off a cigar—as a boy Troy had thought it could as easily lop off offending fingers—a thing that pricked the other end, and a penknife—with which the ten-year-old Troy had once attempted to whittle a bow and arrow. But their function was as nothing to their form.

There were no diamonds or rubies but the golden swirls, flower-like, fern-like, tapering into infinity were all but identical to those that decorated the gun. It was, as Churchill had insisted, a delicate work of art. The eggs had always struck him as overblown and indulgent.

The gun was Russian. Wally would have it that Skolnik was Russian. Quite soon now he'd have to ask.

He found Rod in the small sitting room on the floor above—ground level at the front, one flight above the garden at the back. Shoes off, one black sock one green, tie at half-mast, a red ministerial box open on the carpet.

"Do we have a complete Pushkin?"

"Did you look downstairs?"

"It's not there."

"Must be up here, then."

Rod gestured to a column of bookshelves in the alcove of the fireplace. It was mostly texts in Russian and French, and someone, undoubtedly Rod, had alphabetized them. Troy, like his father before him, had always thought the alphabet overrated.

He found a copy of *Boris Godunov* and flicked through it. A few scenes from the end, he found the passage that Skolnik had painted beneath his *Venus*. "A dark and constant secrecy." Skolnik had quoted accurately and it meant what Troy had thought it meant—but what it meant in the context Skolnik had newly ascribed to it remained a mystery.

"I'm glad you dropped in. I wanted a chat about this Northern Line thing," Rod said.

"Am I talking to a politician or a brother? Are you talking to a brother or a copper?"

"Could we not just talk without the labels? I've got some responsibility for the games—the Olympics . . ."

"Why? It's hardly an RAF matter."

"Use your imagination, Freddie. It's the biggest thing . . . since . . . since . . . well, since the war . . ."

"Part of the healing process?"

"Exactly, part of the . . ."

"Then why aren't the Japs and the Jerries invited? Why aren't the Russians coming?"

"You're nitpicking. It might be a bit soon to have the German flag flying in London even if the new one doesn't have a swastika on it . . . and I've no idea why the Russians aren't coming. Ask Stalin, not me. But it is an international effort, and every minister has extra responsibilities."

"And yours just happens to include the Northern Line?"

"You're taking the piss. Stop it. Mine include public relations."

"And how does that involve the killing on the Northern Line?"

"Simple. We may not have a flood of visitors, God knows most of Europe can't afford the bus fare to the next town, but we *will* have visitors and the PM's worried about anything scaring them off. Foreign currency, balance of payments . . . blah blah blahdey blah. Every country is pitching in to stop this event looking any shabbier than it is. Between you and me it's a threadbare business, cobbled together, and I dearly wish the Mongolians or the Mexicans were staging the games not us. We cannot afford it. Half the countries are bringing their own food with them!"

"Decent of them."

"Decent, helpful, and bloody embarrassing. The Swedes, or is it the Norwegians? . . . Anyway, they're shipping in their own peas! Can you imagine it—shipping in their own peas?"

"Is this why bread has suddenly come off the ration? To make us all seem better off than we are, in the eyes of other countries?"

"Sort of."

"How sort of?"

"Sort of . . . yes."

"And will it go back on ration when the rest of the world departs?"

"My God, you're so cynical. No, it won't."

"I still don't see where you come in."

"Public relations . . . the PM wants to know there isn't a nutter loose on the Underground."

"What . . . Béla Lugosi? Lon Chaney? The phantom of the Northern Line?"

"Freddie, please take this seriously. Tomorrow I have to call the Yard and seek reassurance from the copper in charge."

"Then why not ask me now?"

"It's you? You total bastard! You could have told me that at lunchtime."

"You didn't ask. And no, Rod, there are no more nutters loose on the London Underground than there used to be. Your problem is that London is a city full of nutters anyway. Let's see you smooth that one over with publicity. I can tell you this much: it's an odd case, but it's not the work of a nutter or of anyone who intends to go on killing."

"Why so sure?"

"I have the gun. If you mean to make a hobby of killing it would make sense to hang onto the weapon."

Rod cooled rapidly. Anger, outrage were never his modi operandi for long.

Troy said, "If you're in the know, tell me: what are our chances of a few gold medals?"

"Don't Freddie, don't ask. We're going to get our national arse kicked."

§ IOO

Laura Narayan had very strong views on the work of André Skolnik.

"Of course, it isn't just Botticelli. That's merely his starting point. Knowing Botticelli means no more than knowing nursery rhymes. Everybody does. And he hasn't assimilated a fraction of Botticelli's technique. Botticelli is light and air, paint applied with a hummingbird's tongue. This is glossy, a bit slablike. But that he owed to someone I did wake him up to, Magritte. I don't think André had paid the slightest bit of notice to surrealism until I made him. They don't influence me, I don't copy them, but no painter can ignore them. André, as ever, has been a bit of a literalist and a bit more of a plagiarist. I mean, look in the background over her left shoulder. That's a Magritte lamppost."

Troy had missed this completely. He peered, feeling faintly foolish.

"I don't think you'll find Botticelli painted many lampposts. And there at her feet, next to the cello case . . ."

"A seashell?"

"No, Troy, it's a bowler hat. Magritte dressed like the continental bourgeoisie, and never seemed to tire of painting their icon. This is a genuine Skolnik, Troy. And I rather think it's unfinished."

"Why do you say that?"

"Those smudges around the left hand. It's not bad workmanship on André's part. He's still thinking about the painting as he works, and he means to add something. He's traced the outline with a cloth on the end of his finger. Damned if I know what it is, except it's painting by numbers and I'm afraid I gave him the numbers."

"And the portrait?"

"It's hardly that."

"It's someone. It's not just Skolnik's imagination."

"It might be, but you're right, there is something vaguely familiar about the face. But given André's talents, if he'd set out to make an accurate representation we'd be none the wiser, would we? And speaking of portraits . . . would you mind if I took mine? I mean the one he did of me. It's not as though it's evidence is it?"

"It is subject to probate."

"I doubt very much whether André has any heirs or left enough of anything to rack up death duties."

"If you can find it, take it."

She walked across to the wall of demoiselles and picked three up five across.

"Laura? How do you know it's that one? They all look alike to me."

"Simple, Troy. She's fatter than all the others."

As she was leaving, Troy asked, "Are you busy tomorrow night, Laura?"

"Busy, Troy? I've got two children. Of course I'm busy. Why do you ask?"

"Viktor Rosen gave me two tickets for his Schubert concert at the Wigmore."

"Oh, I would have loved to come. I get out so rarely. But Indra cannot be relied upon in the evenings. He's always speaking at some political gathering or another. And my mother has a silent attitude of 'bed made, in lie' that I've really no wish ever to hear gain utterance so I tend not to ask her to babysit. Still, I'm glad you had the nerve to ask. Most men look upon married women as though they were in purdah. Not like the war when I was a copper. One went down the pub, we all went down the pub."

"You were a copper?" Troy asked, slightly incredulous. "Tell me more."

"Love to, but it'll cost you a lift home to Hampstead."

In the Bullnose Morris, crawling up Haverstock Hill, Troy heard how she had quit London for Berkshire during the war and enrolled as a WPC. It sounded like the time of her life, except that she seemed to have times of her life in a distinct plural.

As she stepped out of the car in Fitzjohn's Avenue, Laura said, "I forgot to tell you. Your sister-in-law called. I have a commission. I suppose I have you to thank for that?"

Troy said, "And I forgot to ask you—what does André's painting mean, I mean, does it mean anything?"

"Mean anything?" said Laura. "Well, a painting isn't a sentence, there's no agreed syntax, but now I've said that the best I can come up with is that *Venus Meets Magritte* was André talking to himself."

Venus Meets Magritte—it sounded like the title of a third-rate horror movie from before the war. Bela Lugosi, Lon Chaney, the phantom of the Northern Line.

§ 101

Troy called Anna with the same question he had put to Laura Narayan, and she said, "oh, God, I wish I could. I've worshipped that man's fingertips since I was about twelve . . . but . . ."

"But?"

"But Angus. I've banged on to you about what a pain he can be. Pissed, remote, angry, still fighting a war in his head when the real one's been over for almost three years . . . I can't just up and say I'll be out for an evening. Now it may be he won't be home tomorrow night. He'll tell me he's nipping out for five minutes, bump into some RAF crony, go on a pub crawl, and by closing time he'll be organizing the pub regulars into squadrons and re-acting fighter skirmishes . . . with him zooming around yelling '*takka takka takka,*' and telling blokes who spent the war in the docks lifting barges and toting bales that they've pranged or pancaked or some such rot. On the other hand, it might be like tonight. Friday night— he's come straight home from the office and he's sitting on the sofa doing *The Times* crossword over a scotch and water, calling me 'old girl,' and asking me about any clues that seem to revolve around novels, as he's never actually read one. You see, Troy . . . I have to be here."

"I see," he said, and he did.

"Is there no one else you could take?"

"What? Do you think I have a little black book labelled 'totty'?"

"Of course not. Some men do, but not you. You're useless at socio-sexual preamble."

"Eh?"

"Chitchat, Troy. You've never been able to do it."

At that moment a booming voice yelled, "Piglet? Who wrote the fucking *Waverley* novels?" and Troy took that as his cue.

225

Troy needed to ask Fish Wally another question about Skolnik.

He telephoned him at his home in Marshall Street.

"I need to talk to you," he said. "Not over the phone. Although now I've said that I don't know why not."

"Troy, I understand. You may ask me any question you like, but if it's about a recently deceased Pole, I won't answer you over the phone anyway, so . . ."

"So?"

"We could meet tomorrow night."

"Ah . . . that's the one night I'm busy. I don't seem to have a social life at the moment, but tomorrow I'm at the Viktor Rosen recital at the Wigmore."

"Ah . . . lucky you . . . a more pleasing performer than Gieseking, and possessed of more political savvy."

Troy was very partial to the playing of Walter Gieseking, but Gieseking had not left Germany when anyone who was anyone in art and science did. No one had called him a Nazi, but his failure to criticize them or to abandon them told. He now played to half-empty houses and on occasion got the slow hand clap. Rosen's war was impeccable—a prisoner of both the Nazis and the British. He played to packed halls and the tickets changed hands at twice the price.

"It so happens I've a spare ticket."

"Then I shall not wait to be asked. Shall we say seven o'clock?"

§ 102

Wally dressed for the evening. Black tie. A black suit with satin lapels and the obligatory ribbon down the seam of the trousers. The suit had been made for someone bigger and fatter than him, but Wally wore it as he wore his white gloves, without self-consciousness. Before the war everyone would have dressed for a concert at the Wigmore Hall. Even now about half the audience had. Troy was not one of them. It had not even occurred to him.

"My cousin Casimir," Wally said. "Killed by a V1 whilst out walking the dog in '44. I was his only relative and hence his heir. He left me the rooming house in Marshall Street, the contents of his bank account, which were not insubstantial, and this suit. Since when, although the logic of the phrase eludes me, I have, as you say, been 'sitting pretty.' The rooming house is a gold mine, I could let every room twice over. And the pleasure I got from putting the Cockney nose out of joint when I let to West Indians last week is pure schadenfreude. If you had met me in the early years of the war you would have thought I was a penniless bum. Now, if clothes rationing ever stops, I have every intention of getting a tailor of my own."

Wally was fastidious. Troy would have to get used to that.

Rosen had given him two seats in the third row of the stalls—Wally dusted his before he sat down—slightly left of centre with a good view of the keyboard—Troy liked to see a pianist's hands while he played. They were first-rate seats.

The violinist and the cellist took the stage to a round of applause.

Troy glanced at his programme:

Piano Trio in E-flat, op. 100
by Franz Schubert

I. Allegro
II. Andante con moto
III. Scherzando
IV. Allegro moderato

Piano Viktor Rosen
Violin Rhian Davies
Cello Méret Voytek

Rhian Davies was in her early twenties, tall, dark, and Welsh. She had come to prominence as a child prodigy 'round about 1939. Troy recalled that she had played all the Bach suites for solo violin over an entire week as part of the National Gallery's lunchtime "we can take it" concerts during the Blitz. He'd managed to catch precisely one day of this.

Méret Voytek had appeared out of nowhere in the summer of 1946. She had taken London by storm, also by performing an entire Bach work, the solo suites for cello, in this very hall. Troy had caught none of it. He wished he had. The newspapers had praised her to the skies afterwards, "The Left-handed Wonder" "The Viennese Wunderkind." He'd settled for buying the records. He wasn't at all sure whether he'd met her until she took the stage. He'd met a lot of Viktor's pupils and entourage but Viktor was never one for effecting introductions—he'd find himself turning up for a lesson in Cheyne Walk just as someone else was leaving and then shaking hands with someone who's name he hadn't quite grasped and who he was damn certain he'd never meet again. But when Méret Voytek took the stage he knew her at once. It had been just before Christmas 1946. And she had indeed been simply a handshake and one of Viktor's mumbles as she left and Troy arrived in the dimness of Viktor's hallway.

She was slight, even slighter stood next to Rhian Davies, nearer thirty than twenty—striking rather than pretty or beautiful, with dyed blonde hair that served to make her dark eyebrows seem faintly sinister by making the dark eyes inescapably haunting. Despite the odd-sounding name, she was from Vienna, that much he did know, and the profiles in the newspapers said she was a survivor of Auschwitz, but Viktor had never mentioned this—but then Troy could not recall that, one brief meeting excepted, he had ever mentioned Méret Voytek.

Rosen took the stage, the volume of the applause soared. A single bow to his audience, then straight to the piano, a nod to his musicians—Rhian standing far right, Méret seated in the curve of the Bechstein—and for the next forty minutes he held a couple of hundred people in rapture.

Troy had seen plenty of cellists over the years—face-pullers, grimacers, eye-closers, dreamers who swayed, rockers who shifted their weight constantly between one foot and the other, one buttock and the other. Méret Voytek was perhaps the calmest he'd ever seen. The emotion was in the music, not in her face—it was a little like watching someone play behind a glass wall.

When they returned from the interval the piano was gone, pushed to the back of the stage.

Troy consulted his programme again:

Octet in F-major, op. 166
by Franz Schubert

I. Adagio Allegro Pi̧ allegro
II. Adagio
III. Allegro vivace Trio Allegro vivace
IV. Andante variations. Un poco pi̧ mosso Pi̧ lento
V. Menuetto. Allegretto Trio Menuetto Coda
VI. Andante molto Allegro Andante molto Allegro molto

Clarinet Daphne Wright

French Horn Gillian Cooper

Bassoon Daniel Freeman

1st Violin Rhian Davies

2nd Violin Susan Lord

Viola June Horsley

Cello Méret Voytek

Double Bass Elizabeth Stafford

Troy turned to Wally.

"I don't get it."

"What's to get? Have you never heard the Schubert *Octet* before? It's one of the oddest lineups in nineteenth century music. Two violins, viola, cello, double bass . . . coupled to woodwind—clarinet, bassoon, horn— there's no piano. Huge for chamber music, about right for a jazz band."

"No piano? But all these people have paid to hear Viktor."

"No, Troy. I think they will still hear Viktor. They will hear him through the work of his protégés, for that is surely Herr Rosen's intention. To give us a work in which he has schooled them all. He is in effect the conductor, but one conspicuously offstage. Roll with it. It is bliss. And as you are an *Octet* virgin, double bliss. You will not go home disappointed."

Wally was right. It was an introduction to something Troy wished he'd known about years ago. He'd always found string quartets a bit harsh—crudely put, they could be "scrapey." The woodwind softened the whole effect—the French horn, the dreamiest of brass, burnished, it and the addition of a double bass gave it a bottom end quartets could only dream of, but probably didn't.

Rosen joined his players for bows and when the cry of "encore" went up it required neither ego nor modesty to know they were calling for him, not the seven young women and one young man who had played the *Octet*. The piano was pushed centre stage once more.

Rosen sat down, pushed up his jacket sleeves, and turned to the audience.

"I had had it in mind to devote an entire evening to Schubert, but I find Massenet at the tips of my fingers like static electricity. So I play Massenet, an elegy composed I know not when."

He placed both hands on the keyboard, then removed them, turning to the audience once more, much in the frustrating manner of Victor Borge. "I forgot to say, Massenet elegy in F minor, in an arrangement by the American pianist Art Tatum."

Someone in the audience laughed. Rosen shot him a look, saying, "You think I'm joking? Stick with me, kid."

Then the whole audience laughed and Rosen let rip with Tatum's arpeggio-laden Massenet.

It was the version Troy had played for him a couple of years ago, only to be greeted with withering disdain. Perhaps it was how badly Troy had played it that been the problem. Clearly, Rosen had sought out the original. Troy could not imagine any pianist holding out against Tatum for long. The sheer skill of the man was all but overwhelming. Perhaps three minutes of Tatum was quite enough for anyone new to him, and three minutes twenty-eight seconds was all they got.

Afterwards Troy would have slipped away quietly but Wally wanted to meet Rosen, and as Troy could oblige, he did.

Wally bagged Rosen readily by recalling to him a recital of Chopin he had given in Warsaw in 1929 to a thunderously patriotic reception, and the two of them vanished into a Mitteleuropean world—Wally seeming as fluent in German as he was in English—that left Troy shaking hands, saying thank you to the other musicians—polite English reserve from the woodwind, not quite knowing how to take a compliment; a bone-crunching grip from Rhian Davies; a limp, unengaged one from Méret Voytek and dark dungeons of eyes that would not meet his.

Walking home to Marshall Street Wally said, "What was the question?"

"You said you hadn't ever mentioned Skolnik to Charlie Walsh. Did anyone in the Branch ever mention him to you?"

"No."

"Did you deal with the spooks only through Charlie or did you meet them personally?"

"I met them."

"And you said nothing to them, either?"

"No, and for the same reason I gave you. Troy, where is this leading?"

"I think I need to talk to someone in MI5, someone in the right department. Can you find me someone?"

"Of course . . . but you are well-enough connected, surely . . . ?"

"I'd rather it wasn't someone I know. I don't want to be seen to call in any favours and I don't want it common knowledge in Scotland Yard that I'm doing this. I want it kept well away from the Yard. Just find me a spook . . . I hesitate to say this . . . a spook I can trust."

"Consider it done," said Wally.

§103

When he got home a whore was waiting. Waiting for Troy. Sitting on his doorstep.

"You'd better come inside," he said.

"Sorry."

Scarcely audible for the handkerchief pressed to her split lip.

Troy turned the key in the lock and pushed the door open.

"You know where the bathroom is."

He watched her dash to the staircase, took off his jacket and waited till she came down. It seemed an age—listening to the running water gurgling through the pipework.

She'd cleaned up the blood, staunched the bleeding, but the lip and the flesh around one eye were swelling badly and her dress was torn and stained. Whichever punter she'd misjudged was going to cost her a couple of nights' work at least. She sat down opposite him, red-faced and tearful.

"Did you know him?"

"Nah. New to me. Just strolling down the lane he was."

"Can you describe him?"

"What's the point? Doesn't happen often but when it does . . . well, it's like an occy wostit init?"

"Occupational hazard."

"Yeah."

"And an occupational hazard in my job is wanting to catch him."

"Occy . . . thing hazard in your job, as I recall, is gettin' beat up. Some fare gave me a fat lip and a black eye, Fred. So wot? I can live with it and I can live without you comin' on copper to me. Maybe you live with gettin' beat up, too, but that time in '44 you took the kickin' of a lifetime and damn near got yourself killed."

It was a defensive move, designed to shut him up. Ruby probably hadn't saved his life but he would not deny that he'd taken the kicking of a lifetime or that she had found him, rescued him, and nursed him. Only when he had recovered enough to walk downstairs again did he realize that she'd plied her trade out of his front room in the meantime.

"There's the spare room if you want."

She stood up, smoothed down her dress, tucked the torn bit under the shoulder strap of her bra.

"Nah, I'll go home. I didn't want to walk the streets lookin' like I was, but nah . . . not as if he'll be waiting, is it? That's the thing about the violent ones, they never come back."

§ 104

It was Tuesday of the following week. About ten thirty in the morning. Troy was at his desk, the door to Jack's office wide open, the window onto the Embankment and the Thames letting in cooler air and the hum of traffic. There was a gentle tapping at the door. Troy glanced up, wanting to get on with his report without disturbance and, seeing Jack's legs, glanced down again.

A polite, fake cough followed.

Troy looked up. The legs were Jack's, the lean six-foot figure and laconic posture as he leaned one shoulder against the door frame were Jack's—the suit wasn't. Whoever this bloke was he was the dandy Jack couldn't quite be arsed to be—he spent his money, quite possibly all his money, on clothes. He looked like a million dollars while Jack rated a mere ten grand, and Troy, in his own eyes, a five-bob postal order. And while Jack was handsome in a Denham or Ealing film star sort of way— Michael Wilding sprang to mind, perhaps Robert Donat—this bloke was pure Hollywood English and looked more like Cary Grant.

He beamed his showbiz smile at an unresponsive Troy and said, "Jordan Younghusband."

"You're kidding?" Troy said.

"'Fraid not. A father who served with Allenby in Palestine—and it was a remote cousin of my grandfather who invaded Afghanistan."

"Well, we've all done that," Troy said. "And you are . . . ?"

"From another place," Jordan said in a stage whisper.

"Wally?"

"Wally."

Troy recalled clearly what he had told Wally, to keep this away from the Yard, and here he was, a six-foot spook from MI5 leaning in his office door and shooting the breeze.

"Don't worry," Jordan said in the same whisper. "I am quite literally just passing. I've booked us into the Ivy. Be there at one."

Three things were possible. Jordan Younghusband was loaded, Jordan Younghusband had an expense account with his masters that defied the spirit of the age, or Jordan Younghusband had Angus as his accountant.

Jack came in seconds after Jordan left.

"Who was that?"

"Fish Wally's spook. The flash bugger thinks lunch at the Ivy is a suitable place to talk secrets."

"Hmm," said Jack. "Ask him for the name of his tailor, would you?"

§105

Troy was first to arrive. He'd not been to the Ivy in a while. His father had favoured the Ivy, in much the same way he favoured the Garrick, the London club that was very actorish, a bit bookish, when he could have joined clubs full of other newspapermen. He had liked the Ivy for its theatrical flair, something Troy found he could take or leave. To find himself seated at the next table to Margaret Lockwood, James Mason, or Douglas Fairbanks Jr. did not thrill him, although he thought it might have thrilled his father if only the old man had known who they were. His father's idea of a film star was Douglas Fairbanks Sr.

Troy liked the Ivy because he liked Art Deco—on his one trip to the United States, long before the war, he had watched, spellbound, the work on a new skyscraper, an Art Deco masterpiece to be called the Chrysler Building.

The bloke steering customers to their seats seemed vaguely familiar to Troy, and clearly Troy was more than vaguely familiar to him, as he had greeted him by name. As ever, Troy thought, it was his father they remembered. He was merely an adjunct.

He felt as out of touch as his father. The place was doubtless stuffed with talent, and he didn't think he recognized anyone. He could be content looking at the menu. Menus at a time when almost everything required one to produce a coupon or to queue, at a time when bread was an unappetizing shade of grey, when lard was rationed to two ounces a week, cheese to one and a half ounces, butter to seven, and the water from boiled carrots passed off as soup . . . were like works of fascinating fiction. A list of ingredients constituted a good read. The menu in a place like the Ivy was worth a Balzac or a Dickens or two. A prewar menu was a journey into a foreign country: *Filet d'agneau aux fines herbes Poulardine rôtie à la broche, zabaglione*—"I nearly wept when they got to the soufflé."

For no reason he could think of, not that he was drooling, Troy felt like the convict in the opening chapters of *Great Expectations*—Abel Magwitch—so hungry the food scarcely touched the sides on the way down. And then it dawned on him why he had thought of this. On one level he had recognized a film star—Valerie Hobson, who had played Estella in the recent film of *Great Expectations,* was sitting at the next table.

Jordan swept by her table with a blown kiss and a, "hello, Valerie," to plonk himself down opposite Troy.

"Have you ordered?"

"No."

"I could eat a horse," Jordan said, picking up his menu, "but I'll settle for bangers and mash."

While Jordan's head was down in the menu, Troy said softly, "Do you really think we can discuss this in public?"

"Discuss what? Old Wally didn't tell me a thing. Just said you were investigating the killing on the Northern Line and needed to meet me . . . or someone very like me."

"And you came without knowing why?"

"Oh, no, Inspector, I came knowing exactly why. I would imagine you think your father's famous—and you'd be right—or that your brother's famous—he will be one day I'm sure—but that you aren't. Believe me, Troy, in my profession 'The Tart in the Tub' case is legend. You took on the OSS, the Branch, and MI5 . . . you are known, Troy, you are known. Of course, I wouldn't turn down the chance to meet you. Odd thing is we've never met before."

Troy did not know how to take this. The killing of Diana Brack had been four years ago. He doubted he would be allowed to forget it. It had cost him half a kidney, all his heart, delayed his promotion, and made him a bête noire with the Special Branch and certain members of military intelligence. It was why he'd asked for someone unknown to him and trustworthy. But Jordan was smiling. He might be frank, blunt even, but he was smiling.

"Shall we order?"

"Bangers and mash will be fine," said Troy.

"And listen for a moment, would you."

Jordan waved a hand in the air, drawing an arc in the space between them. Troy listened; Troy looked around.

"Now, can you honestly tell me you can hear anyone else's conversation? Can you hear anything except for the odd 'darling' above the hubbub? And we have to allow them that—they're actors."

Over bangers and mash—"I nearly wept when they got to the onion gravy"—Troy told Jordan everything he had found . . . Wally's suspicions, the Russian gun, the Russian inscription.

Jordan ate, listened, made indeterminate movements of the head that Troy could interpret as neither nodding nor shaking, and eventually said, with a mouthful of sausage, "I put two and two together. Wally asking me to meet you, the front pages of the London papers . . . Wally can be very discreet when he wants but it was obvious what was at the heart of his request. And the name of André Skolnik rang a few bells. I knew you'd be asking about him even if I didn't know what you'd be asking. There's a file on him. I read it before I left the office this morning. He was vetted, very quickly, after Dunkirk. So many people were, it's almost meaningless—there's a file on you from that time, as I'm sure you know—we were looking for a Nazi fifth column, which, mercifully, didn't exist. There are no entries between then and early 1946, when someone thought it worthwhile, in view of our changed relationship with Poland—stuck behind what we weren't yet calling the Iron Curtain—to look once again at Polish nationals who'd been granted British citizenship. Skolnik has been British since 1937. I vetted some of the Poles myself at that time. Not Skolnik, but I can assure you he was vetted again, very quietly. The second look yielded nothing. Ever since the hot war turned chilly, it's been my job to know who the Russians have got working for them over here, and I can tell you now, André Skolnik was not one of them. I could name you several who are, from trade union leaders to members of the House of Lords, but Skolnik wasn't working for the Russians."

"You're absolutely certain of that?"

"Yes."

"Do you know who vetted Skolnik?"

"Of course, and I can't tell you."

"But somebody talked to him, somebody trailed him, somebody interviewed friends and known associates?"

"'Known associates'—very Scotland Yard. Troy, I can't discuss our methods, either. Read what you like into me saying it was done 'very quietly.' Ask yourself . . . in 1940, did any of us talk to you?"

Troy said nothing.

"Quite," said Jordan.

Troy leaned in a little closer across the table. He might just annoy Jordan and if he did he wanted be sure what he said was smothered in "darlings."

"Consider that your people might have made a mistake. It hardly seems a high priority, checking out Poles who'd been here twenty-odd years. Supposing someone in your department preferred wielding a rubber stamp to wearing out his shoe leather and just stamped Skolnik's file in the interests of a quiet life?"

"Spoken like a copper. And I won't deny we have lazy buggers, drunken buggers, and that there are one or two who think I'm a flash bugger, but take it from me, Troy, it was done properly, and in the absence of any other evidence—"

"The gun."

"Coincidence. You said yourself, Swiss-made. Probably just looks Russian."

"The inscription?"

"Most Poles speak some Russian. Wally does, after all."

"So . . . more coincidence?"

"I'm afraid so. I think you're doing what the taxpayer pays you to do, Troy. You're looking for a murderer, not an assassin. Someone who knew him. Some jealous girlfriend, some bloke who'd got fed up waiting for money to be repaid . . ."

Troy knew in his bones this was not the case but said nothing. Instead, he said, "Is there a way I can reach you without going through Wally?"

Jordan handed Troy his card, called for the bill, and said, "By all means, keep in touch . . . this has been . . . shall we say . . . simpatico."

Troy had not got what he wanted. He had a dead spook on his hands and, given the brick wall any copper hits sooner or later in trying to investigate a dead spook, he wanted MI5 to pick up the case and let him move on to something he could solve.

He wondered how much thought, how much self-conscious flash buggery had gone into the choice of a word like "simpatico." But Jordan was right. He liked the man; he'd been charmed by the good looks, the easy manner, and the gentle blue eyes. It had been frustrating, but it had been simpatico.

§106

Routine took over. Routine is not the reason anyone chooses to become a Scotland Yard detective.

Jack had ordered Constables Thomson and Gutterridge to approach travellers at Hampstead and Camden Town Underground stations with a photograph of Skolnik. Troy would have liked posters but as they had found no photograph of the living Skolnik the mugshot was of the corpse and Jack had argued that this was grotesque, unproductive, and would frighten children. This yielded nothing. The next day Troy released the photograph to the papers. This yielded sightings of Skolnik at Tooting Bec, Maida Vale, and South Acton, in the latter case the day after he had died.

Troy took the paperwork as part of a bargain with Jack. He searched both flat and studio, and at the end of the searching day wished he could say, "I told you so," to anyone other than himself. He had found no paperwork of any kind in the flat, save newspaper (Skolnik had been a *Daily Mail* reader with occasional weekend forays into the *Reynold's News*) and bog roll (the shiny sort that doesn't do much), and in the studio had found seven shoe boxes full of bills—paid bills, for gas, electricity, water rates, and milk going back to 1927, all in chronological order. Skolnik did not appear to have a bank account, but, then, so few people did. So few people had need of one. Most people in Britain received cash in a small brown envelope on a Friday afternoon. It was known as wages. The salaried were few and far between. He did not find a photograph of anyone, he did not find a postcard, a letter, a memo, a jotting, a used bus ticket, a railway timetable . . . although he did find several sketchbooks in which rough versions of Skolnik's paintings were even rougher in pencil or charcoal. But from this he learned two things, that Skolnik was methodical, obsessive even, and most certainly had something to hide—the disposal of the personal was too thorough to be innocent. Everybody's life left detritus. The life that didn't was a contrivance and hence it was suspect.

Jack got to work the pubs and caffs on and off Charlotte Street.

238

"Skolnik was well-known. No denying it. Twenty-odd years on the same turf and there's scarcely anyone who wasn't on nodding terms with him. The Newman Arms pub in Rathbone Street, right opposite his studio, saw a fair bit of him at lunchtimes. There are blokes in there who say he still owes them money, but there was no one I found with any particular resentment of that, or any particular insight into the man.

"In Gennaro's caff, one chap described him to me as 'a bank clerk disguised as a bohemian,' which was pretty much echoed in the George and Dragon in Cleveland Street, where he was 'a man who would sell his soul to have a dark, deep secret, but alas no one was buying.'

"In the Marquis of Granby he was 'someone who'd show you a good time if he happened to find one stuck to the sole of his shoe.'

"I've picked up enough aphorisms on Skolnik to publish a small book. Me asking about him seems simply to have given every wag in Fitztrovia the chance to sharpen his wit on the dead. Some of it has more depth, for example, 'a master of sophistry, half-truth, and fractions thereof.'

"Against this there are plenty of blokes—you don't get a lot of women in these places, it's not like it was during the war—plenty of blokes who'd agree with Mrs. Narayan, that he could be generous when flush. That bit about whipping everyone into Bertorelli's for example. I talked to the waiters there. They say often as not when that happened, Skolnik would have no real idea who he'd brought in his wake, and frequently treated people he'd never met before who just happened to be in the pub he'd gone to for the round-up. And he never queried the bill. A waitress told me he rolled up one day with what she thought was a tramp in tow, who managed to set fire to the tablecloth. Turned out it was Augustus John. They stuck the cost of the tablecloth on the bill. Skolnik didn't query that one, either. Didn't bat an eyelid, she said.

"But the matter of women remains. No one ever mentioned a girl-friend, a mistress . . . and that brass in the tweed oufit who's always in the Wheatsheaf, the one they call Sister Ann, said 'he's one o' the lucky ones, ain't 'e? one o' them wot ain't bovvered' . . . well, it's been my experience in twenty-eight short years on this planet that everyone's 'bovvered' . . . so I had to ask someone, 'was André Skolnik queer?'

"And in the Fitzroy on the corner of Windmill Street and Charlotte Street I bumped into your old pal Quentin Crisp. Who better to ask?"

Jack read his notes out in a passable imitation of Crisp's languid baritone.

"Was Mr. Skolnik queer? Well, we none of us have it thrust upon us, and we none of us achieve it. Try as you might. Some of us are born queer. It's the hand life deals you in the great poker game of sex, and in that great poker game of sex, André didn't even bother to turn over the cards he'd been dealt. No, André and sex didn't go together in the same sentence. André and money, well there you might have something. I used to call him the Cadgepenny Count. He sounded more than a little like Dracula ought to sound and he was always cadging money. I introduced him to the art schools as a model in the hope that a regular income might reduce his importuning, but what do I have of André now he's gone? A Polish voice echoing in my ears and it's saying, 'Five bob and I will gladly repay you Friday.' I've said this before and it's worth repeating . . . Poland isn't a country, it's a state of mind."

Troy was smiling. A Crispism never failed to produce that effect. To Jack he said, "The Cadgepenny Count. Let's see that one doesn't get into the papers shall we?"

§ 107

Troy hoped the ballyhoo of what his brother had mercilessly dubbed the "Threadbare Olympics" would pass him by. It did. As Rod joined the king and half the government at Wembley for the opening ceremony at the end of July, the job wrought one of its grisly miracles in the shape of a body on the railway tracks just south of Vauxhall station, and for ten days he and Jack pieced the case together until they found out which Surrey commuter—Wicked of Weybridge or Evil of Esher—had thought so little of a fellow traveller as to shove him out of the carriage door. While the names of Fanny Blankers-Koen or Emile Zatopec filtered through to them, they were spared the spectacle. By the 11th of August they had a prisoner in the cells, booked and charged, the case of

André Skolnik on the back burner, and a fine, sunny day on which to take a cheerless lunch in the park: grey bread—the national loaf, as an idiot in the government had labeled it in an attempt to evoke pride where only guilt would suffice—and Spam. Troy was not entirely certain what was in Spam, but if he had to eat tinned meat he would probably have killed for a slice or two of good Argentine corned beef.

"Sorry, old man. Gonna have to scratch. There's this new WPC down on—"

"Jack, we have an hour for lunch. What can you possibly do in a hour?"

"Freddie, when it comes to women you have no imagination."

So Troy ate alone.

The choice of parks was limited. He could eat in the Victoria Embankment gardens, practically next door and stretching along the river all the way to the Savoy, but carrying the risk of meeting other coppers just when one wanted a half an hour without them; or there was a delightful little spot, a sort of tarmac park, on top of the Temple Underground station, but farther than he wanted to walk; or there was St James' Park—out the back, a short walk along Whitehall, cut through Downing Street, and over Horse Guards . . . St James' Park with its echoes of Lord Rochester's verse—he could never sit there for long without hearing Rochester whisper in his ear—and the lesser risk of coppers and sandwiches, leavened by civil servants and sandwiches, politicians and sandwiches, or even spooks and sandwiches.

The spook standing in front of him wasn't carrying sandwiches. Troy thought better of offering him any of his when he opened his jacket long enough for Troy to see the Tokarev TT-33 automatic in its shoulder holster.

"And just in case you have any doubts, Inspector Troy . . ."

The spook tilted his head to the right—"Jan"—he tilted his head to the left—"and Jiri."

They were thirty feet away, right at the water's edge, but they turned to make eye contact with Troy as their names were called.

He was not a handsome creature. He was about 5'9", fortyish, balding, squarely built, big in the chest and shoulders, and had old scars on his top lip and his chin as though he'd been in a knife fight twenty or so years ago.

"How can I help you?" Troy asked, not rising from the bench he had chosen, setting his sandwiches carefully to one side and wondering about the accent.

"I would like to ask you questions about André Skolnik. You answer my questions and there will be no trouble. You go your way I go mine, you finish your lunch if you like."

He wasn't Russian. Troy would have spotted that at once. After years of listening to Kolankiewicz he didn't think he was Polish, either. What kind of a name was Jan? Universally Eastern European? A name you could take anywhere? Jiri? Jiri sounded Czech or Hungarian.

"Ask away," said Troy.

"Who killed André Skolnik?"

"I don't know. If I did he'd be in custody."

"Maybe. Maybe not. Maybe you been told not to get too close?"

"Now who would tell me that?"

"Don't play clever dick with me, Mr. Troy. Were you told to drop this by MI5?"

"No, I wasn't. In fact I haven't dropped it. It's an active case. It's just that it's a case going nowhere for lack of new evidence. Unless, of course, you're the new evidence."

"I do not understand."

"I mean . . . Skolnik worked for you, and I assume you work for Russia—"

"Of course. You think I come all this way just to eat fucking Spam?"

"Well, you may congratulate yourself. Whatever it was Skolnik did for you, our boys hadn't noticed. In fact they're quite convinced Skolnik was bumped off by a jealous lover or someone he'd quarrelled with over money."

"Bumped off?"

"Killed."

"You believe that?"

"I was getting ready to believe it until you boys showed up. I'm now quite convinced Skolnik was killed by secret agents. Our secret agents, or your, as it were, no-longer-quite-so-secret agents."

Troy gestured beyond the man, in the direction of Jan and Jiri—two look-alike blonds, younger and taller than their spokesman. Jan and Jiri watched the paths, every so often they watched each other, and every so often they looked into the distance, focused somewhere behind Troy.

The gesture was more provocative than he'd ever intended or imagined. His interrogator stooped slightly to lean over Troy, lowered his voice to a snarl.

"These men can break your legs with their bare hands. These men will bite off your balls if I tell them."

Troy did not doubt it.

"I'm telling you the truth. I don't know who killed Skolnik. And if I did, I'd tell you. It might be a feather in my cap if I did. If I find the jealous lover or the aggrieved creditor, I'll be a hero. But if it's you, or worse, if it's our lot, then I'd just be pissing in the wind."

The man smiled. The phrase resonated with him.

"Peessing in the wind. Yes. Well put, Mr. Troy. You very funny man. This very funny man, boys! Peessing in the wind. Yes. You would be peessing all over yourself."

He looked over his shoulder, translated what Troy had said for his henchmen. A language Troy did not recognize. They laughed. All three laughing so vigorously a woman passing by with a poodle on a lead could not help but smile broadly at what she took to be the warmth of their bonhomie.

His chuckles subsiding but a big smile still bending his scars upwards, he said, "You know what, funny man? I think maybe you do tell me truth. Peessing in the wind. Exactly so. So, we go now. Just never forget."

Before Troy could ask what it was he should never forget, he was treated to another glimpse of the Tokarev in its leather shoulder holster. When he looked away from it, Jan and Jiri had gone, and their leader was buttoning his jacket and, still chuckling to himself, walking away in the direction of the Buckingham Palace as though he had not just engineered a diplomatic incident.

Troy, finding he had no appetite, threw his lunch to the ducks and went back to the Yard.

§ 108

He said nothing to Jack. He said nothing to Onions. For a while he thought better of saying anything to Jordan. He went to bed with the piano wedged behind the front door. About two in the morning, thinking this was childish, he got up and moved it, but after a night's thinking decided he should call Jordan.

The card Jordan had given him that day at the Ivy had a home number in Chelsea on the front and, scribbled on the back, what Troy took to be the number of the switchboard at MI5's headquarters in Curzon Street.

He wondered how they'd answer. It had been different during the war. They tended to wear uniforms and be less clandestine. They were military intelligence in a nation that had been mobilized for war. He'd heard rumours about MI6 having a shingle hanging out front that read something like "Frank's Carpentry & Joinery: No Job Too Small." Did they answer the phone with that particular fiction? Was he now about to find himself talking to the receptionist at "Joe's Plumbers" and asking for a plumber with the unlikely name of Major Younghusband? But all he got was the anonymity of "Good Morning." And, "I'll see if I can find him, dearie."

Eventually, a man picked up and said, "Smith here."

"Good morning. Inspector Troy, Scotland Yard. I was hoping to speak to Major Younghusband."

"You've just missed him. Dashed in and dashed straight out again."

"Would you ask him to call me?"

"Wilco. What's your number?"

"Whitehall 1212," said Troy, hoping that the exasperation he felt at having to repeat a number that was broadcast in the course of the six o'clock news on the Home Service most nights did not show in his tone.

It did.

"Silly me," said Smith.

It took five days for Jordan to return his call. On the following Monday he called shortly before ten, which left Troy thinking that he was top of a list that Jordan tackled after he'd tackled the important stuff.

"We need to talk," Troy said.

"When a chap uses those precise words I tend to add a silent 'not over the phone.'"

"You may be right."

"Then you'd better come over now. You know where we are?"

"Of course."

"Then I'll tell old Doris to let you in."

Troy parked opposite Leconfield House and found that Leconfield House was all MI5 had on their shingle and that Doris matched the voice he had heard on the telephone. He had heard that fag dangling from her bottom lip as surely as he'd heard the dropped aitches and stopped consonants of Bethnal Green and Stepney.

"Sign the book, dearie. Third floor. Lift's bust. Mind 'ow you go."

Jordan greeted him with a handshake. Smith excused himself almost at once and left them alone.

Jordan babbled.

"I know I was late getting back to you, Troy, but you wouldn't believe how hectic the last couple of weeks have been. The Olympics have been a security nightmare. Would you believe one of the Czech gymnasts chose last Wednesday to tell us she wasn't going home? Bunged in a formal request for asylum. And of course, we none of us expected this, so we had no contingency plan. Which, of course, meant we . . . meaning I . . . had to keep her hidden in a crappy hotel in Finsbury Park until it was all over, just in case they made any retaliatory moves against her. Russia didn't take part but most of the satellite states did, and the Soviets took the opportunity to send over the most dodgy-looking bunch of sport and cultural attachés imaginable. We've been awash in foreign agents. For a while I thought every thug from Petrograd to Prague had been turned loose in London."

"I know," Troy said calmly, hoping some of it would rub off on Jordan. "I had a visit from three of them."

"Oh, hell . . . oh, bloody hell . . . shall we . . . sit down?"

Jordan slipped his jacket off onto the chair back and loosened his tie.

"Oh, hell. This is going to be a stinker isn't it? You're going to tell me they came asking about Skolnik, aren't you?"

"Yes."

"Then you'd better tell me everything."

Troy told him.

Jordan said, "In the park? In broad bloody daylight? The cheek of it, the sheer bloody cheek of it."

Troy tried to soften what he had to say by using a plural he did not think to be true, and said, "It makes a nonsense of the conclusion *we* drew about Skolnik. It confirms the worst."

"Indeed, it does. Care to take a shot at their nationality?"

"I think they were Czech. Jiri sounds more Czech than anything else."

"Makes sense," said Jordan. "The Communist takeover in February gave the Russians a whole new set of pawns to play with, and with the added advantage that most of them would be unknown to us. We can have a crack at identifying these blokes but it's almost academic. The Czechs went home yesterday. If they hadn't, I'd still be at the Gladstone Arms, Finsbury Park, with a very bored gymnast. I can get files sent up. Won't be quick. Any chance you could come back in the morning?"

In the morning, Smith had a stack of cardboard files spread out across Jordan's desk. He had none of Jordan's flamboyance—he was dowdy rather than dandy, but he was calm and methodical.

"Don't expect too much, Inspector. I imagine you're used to mug shots. All in order, right profile, left profile, front. We have nothing so useful. Most of these—and in the case of the Czechs we only have about twenty files—are taken with hidden cameras or at a distance. They can be fuzzy."

But he, the brick shithouse of a man with the facial scars, was the third photograph Smith turned over. In a winter coat, collar turned up, half in profile, but nothing would hide the scars on the top lip.

"Milos Danko," Smith said with a touch of pride. "Snapped in Paris in March. Rumour has it he was on the other side during the war—SS *Einsatzgruppen*. The Russians thought too highly of his talents as a killer to waste him on a firing squad. Let me check him against the embassy's list."

Jordan leaned over and looked at Danko.

"Looks like a thug, doesn't he?"

"Quite," said Smith, running his finger down a column of typed names, "But the Czechs have him down as a cultural attaché. I must say he looks about as cultured as next-door's dog. He came in with a bunch of cultural attachés and sporting coaches on July twenty-seventh. That's two days before the official opening. And if you two will hang on a minute . . . well, I count two Jiris and three Jans in the Czech contingent. Not a lot of help. I suppose we could check the athletes themselves, but that will take time."

Troy had flicked through all the files and photographs. "I wouldn't bother, they're neither of them here."

He looked from Smith to Jordan as he spoke, wondering if both might answer. "I'm the innocent in all this, so tell me, is everyone working for a foreign embassy a spy?"

"Dunno," said Jordan. "But it pays to act on that assumption."

"And does that mean you have them under surveillance?"

"No. We don't have the manpower, and if we dogged their men in an obvious fashion they'd simply do the same to ours. We follow the buggers when we know they're up to something specific. Anything else just wears out shoe leather. And before you ask, no, no one was following Danko. We simply don't have the resources. If I'd known Danko had a specific mission to nobble you . . . take it as read, I'd've been on to him. He'd not have got out of St James' Park."

"But for you to know what Danko was up to, you'd have needed to know what Skolnik was up to, wouldn't you?"

Jordan said nothing, much as Troy would have done confronted by the same question.

"And, of course, we still don't know what Skolnik was up to, do we?"

Jordan told Troy that he would have to "kick this one upstairs," and that, like everything else, it would take time.

"But you're not at risk. Honestly, Troy. They went home on Sunday. I think it was a one-off attempt to find out what happened to their man. Opportunistic might be the word."

"Time, you say?"

"Couple of days. A week at the most."

"Good," said Troy, "because I have to tell my superintendent something very soon."

§109

The best part of a week passed. When Jordan phoned again he said, "Could you come over after work this evening? Say about half past six."

He was waiting in the foyer of Leconfield House when Troy arrived, leaning against Doris's desk. Doris had gone, a plastic cover over her typewriter, a brimming ashtray, and a half-finished cup of tea.

"Sign yourself in, Troy, and we'll go downstairs."

"Downstairs?" Troy asked, thinking dungeons and torture chambers, but following where Jordan led.

"We have a club. Strictly staff only . . ."

"I just signed in as Inspector Troy, Scotland Yard."

"That's okay, they'll just think you're a plod from Special Branch. As I was saying, we have a club—not sure who's idea it was but the point is to stop blokes like me from drifting into a pub at this time of night with a colleague, propping up a bar, and talking shop in public. When we were at St James's it happened all the time. Not that I think any secrets were betrayed to any eavesdropping Nazis after the third or fourth double, but you never know."

They'd reached the bottom of the staircase. Jordan yanked open the heavy door to let out a torrent of voices and reveal a wood-panelled pastiche of a London club—a shabby Garrick, an economy Athenaeum. A job lot of anonymous portraits on the wall—a few examples of Sir Alfred Munnings at his most horsey. The odd framed photograph of a man with a dead beast by his side, be it lion, tiger, or rhino—and the odd framed photograph of a rowing team from one university or the other. MI5 had gone to a lot of trouble to make its staff feel "at home"— if anyone other than a public school-educated, Oxbridge Guards officer could ever feel at home in a London club, let alone one set aside exclusively for the use of spies. It said, Troy thought, a lot about the recruiting practices of this "other place." There were no horny-handed sons of toil in here, there were no women, there was no Doris—it was chockablock with men, men like Jordan and men like Troy. It was a slice of the Britain his brother had set out, if not to destroy, then to change—and it seemed to Troy as Jordan said "What can I get you? We do a rather palatable house claret," . . . that Rod, on his quest for equality, was, to reuse a phrase that still rang in his ears, "peessing in the wind." He wondered why Jordan was showing him this place within the other place.

"We're not going to pursue the Skolnik affair. We simply don't have enough to go on. I just wanted to be able to tell you face to face."

"You could have told me that over the phone."

"I wanted to be able to look at you as I told you. I know what you're thinking; you made it pretty obvious the last time we were here."

"I'm listening," Troy said.

"Don't make me spell it out, Troy."

"When someone says they know what you're thinking, they set themselves up for that."

Jordan sighed—a sadness in his tone, a wordless appeal to Troy that seemed to want to be trusted.

"You think we did it."

"Jordan, I don't know who did it. It was why I came to you in the first place."

"I can't deny we screwed up. We didn't know what Skolnik was up to, and it's because we didn't that we'd have no motive to kill him. And if we *had* killed him do you think we'd have left the body on the London Underground for commuters to trip over? We could have made Skolnik vanish."

"Why were the Czechs here?"

"I don't know. They could have been here just to throw a spanner in the works. Someone comes over in early July —maybe even the same three someones on fake passports. Skolnik gets hit. Then a legit Czech contingent arrives for the games and someone, possibly the same three someones, decides to muddy the waters by putting pressure on you. They sow confusion and they also find out how little we know."

"When three blokes armed with Tokarevs decide to ask me questions I tend to think answering politely might be a good idea."

"I wasn't accusing you, Troy. I'd've done the same. From what I've learnt of Danko in the last few days he's capable of shooting you and just walking away. He's a pro."

"Which is how Skolnik died. A pro job?"

249

Another of Jordan's sad sighs.

"All the same. You think it was us, don't you? Troy, please trust us on this. We don't know what Skolnik was up to. We didn't kill Skolnik. We don't know *who* killed Skolnik."

"Trust *us*?"

"Okay. I can understand that. You're a natural cynic where an organization like ours is the issue. Trust *me*."

Troy echoed Jordan's sigh.

"When a spy says trust me, my copper's hackles rise."

"Troy—that's unfair, bloody unfair. And considering the company we're in, bloody tactless."

Troy looked around at the oblivious men in suits lost in the hubbub of their own importance.

"Oh, Jordan, really. I don't think they heard me above the 'darlings,' do you?"

Standing up to leave, Troy slipped his card across the table. Scotland Yard on one side, his address in Goodwin's Court on the reverse.

"Keep in touch. We might find occasion to be simpatico again. You never know."

§110

It was a Woodbine moment. And they were late for it. Troy was used to them. In seven years, Jack had not got used to them, and dreaded finding Onions as he was now, hunched over an unlit gas fire in Troy's office, puffing on a fag.

Occasionally, Troy had wondered why Onions gravitated towards the fireplace regardless of season or weather. He thought it might be a northern, working class childhood at the turn of the century—a Lawrentian scene, a large family huddled round the embers of two smoldering chimney sweeps who had perished on the job—you can never get enough of enough, so you get it while you can. "Never enough of enough," . . . it sounded like a campaign slogan for a political party far more honest than any England had to show. It was a slogan for the postwar era . . . and "get it while you can" . . . well, wasn't that the message of every spiv?

"Summat to tell me?" he said simply.

"Yes," said Troy.

Onions caught sight of Jack heading for the door.

"Park yer arse, lad. We'll all hear this and then there'll be no misunderstanding."

Jack froze midstep, then slipped quietly onto a chair on the periphery of Onions's vision. Troy sat down directly opposite Onions, and whilst careful to be vague about the dates the three Czechs had nabbed him in the park and the length of time that elapsed before he had decided to tell Onions anything, gave him a largely truthful account of what had happened since they last talked.

"And the spooks reckon they've gone back?"

"They're pretty well certain of it."

"And they reckon these blokes did the killing on the Northern Line?"

"No. They're more open-minded than that. And even if they were certain it was the Russians who ordered this hit they'd still be uncertain it was the same men who actually did the job. They have Danko recorded as entering England on July twenty-seventh, in time for the opening of the Olympics. Too late to have killed Skolnik. And, of course, whatever reasons the Russians might have for wanting Skolnik out of the way, our side had even better ones. They're not going to pick this one up."

"You're sure of that?"

"Jordan was quite clear, Stan. They're not picking up."

"You think MI5 might have done it?"

"I don't know. I do know it's a professional job. One side or the other killed Skolnik."

Onions lit a new ciggy from the end of his last, the third or fourth time he had done this while Troy talked. It was a handy ritual, like donning the black cap. It bought time and tension for all concerned. And when he spoke it was judgement and it was final.

"Then I say we drop it. If Five can't be arsed, why should we? It's spook business. It's not as though this Skolnik was a real person, is it? He was a bum and a scrounger and a spook. An adopted Englishman, someone we'd welcomed in when Eastern Europe went up in flames and how does he repay us? Works for the fuckin' Russkis. Well, fuckim. I'm not wasting any more manpower on it. Case closed."

The idea of someone not being "real" entered Troy's consciousness and vocabulary, to germinate, to grow, and to lodge there permanently.

§III

Troy was getting ready to leave for the evening. Jack had gone twenty minutes ago—relieved Onions had not called upon him to speak, boasting of the "totty" he had lined up for the evening—and the temptation to ignore the telephone's ringing wrestled with Troy's curiosity. It might be Stan, wanting to bury their confrontation in some Soho pub, anonymity coming more naturally to him than it did to Troy. Troy wasn't in the mood. It wasn't Stan. It was Churchill.

"Find a blank evening in your diary, Freddie. I think I might have got to the bottom of the mystery of the Fabergé gun, and I have a tale to tell you."

"Now is as good a time as any."

"Shall we say half an hour?"

Troy rooted around in the bottom drawer of his desk. He kept the odd bottle hidden from Jack for occasions like this. If Churchill had a tale to tell, he could hardly turn up empty-handed. He found a bottle of claret, a Duhart-Milon-Rothschild '34. He had the vaguest memory of his father saying 1934 had been a very good year, and God knows the old man had bought enough of the stuff.

Churchill answered the door in person, no Chewter, no jacket, red braces holding up the capacious pants, shirtsleeves. About as clear a statement that they were after hours and off duty as a man could make. If it were Rod he'd have kicked off his shoes and be padding around in odd socks.

"I like August evenings," said Churchill. "June and July can be too hot for me. I like August; you can feel the city begin to cool off a bit."

He rambled as they squeezed into the lift up to his office and workshop —that was fine with Troy.

"Y'know the French almost evacuate Paris in August. I wonder London doesn't do the same in June."

"Protestant work ethic," Troy replied. "And where would they all go? There are only so many boarding houses in Torquay, Ilfracombe, Bognor . . ."

"Okay, Freddie, I get the point. You can stop the list of undesirable British seaside resorts before we get to Skegness."

"Which can be so bracing."

"Nothing on the North Sea is bracing. The word is *cold*."

Seated at his desk, reading glasses on, Churchill handed Troy the corkscrew, listened to the pleasing glug of a decent claret hitting the glass, and placed the gun on another clean sheet of paper. It almost shone. He had removed every scrap of paint. The tracery of Fabergés loops and swirls stood out with a detail and a delicacy the paint had masked and rendered crude. Only the gems were missing.

"Did your parents ever mention to you the name of Astrov? Prince Yevgeni Astrov and his wife Natalia Astrova?"

"No. But there were so many tales of the old country . . ."

"And this will be another. Astrov was a favourite of the Tsarina Alexandra in the nineties and the noughts. She adopted oddities as we know—Rasputin is the best known of her odd choices. Astrov was a much more conventional courtier. A nobleman, after all. But . . . he was a pig of a man. A brute who beat his wife, consorted with whores, and squandered her fortune. It was said that he even brought whores back to the family home in full view of his wife and the servants. Princess Astrova tired of this. In 1903, she took a lover, Count Ostrog—a perfectly decent man who would have married her if she could ever have been free of Astrov. After about six months, Astrov found out about the affair, challenged Ostrog to a duel, and shot him dead.

"It was at this point that I think the princess approached a Moscow gunsmith named Verdiakoff. She commissioned from him two pistols, the guideline being that they should be as small as her own hand. Verdiakoff sent to Switzerland for the mechanism. The Altmanns were experimenting with small guns and had already produced 22s and 17s, but nothing as small as this and, as I suggested to you when you brought me this, they had to make the ammunition, too. Eventually, Verdiakoff delivered two plain, identical .15 automatic pistols to the Princess Astrova —quite possibly the only .15 guns in the world—and she took them to the court goldsmith, Peter Fabergé, who engraved the gunmetal and added the jewels. I can think of two reasons for this—it enabled her to pass them off as art, perhaps *toys* might be a better word, something designed to be decorative, never to be used, like the canteen of cutlery every pair of newlyweds gets, that spends the rest of its life set aside for 'best,' but 'best' never arrives. I think the touch of genius here was in having the bullets made of silver. If Astrov had ever found the guns, it would have reinforced the idea that it was simply a way to spend money. One can almost hear her saying they were for shooting vampires or some such beast. The second was that it made some of her personal fortune very portable. I've no idea who painted the gun black, but there was no paint in the gem settings, and I'd be prepared to bet the one stone you found was black when you found it."

Troy just nodded. This was not a time to interrupt.

"But of course, she did mean to use them. And the moment arrived at Christmas 1904. Astrov came home drunk, decided she needed a beating. The gun was up the sleeve of her dress, light enough to be held there by elastic. When Astrov hurled himself upon her, she simply pressed the gun to his heart and pulled the trigger."

Troy could not help thinking that she had indeed killed a vampire.

"Of course, it was murder. And you can imagine what rights a beaten wife had in the tsar's Russia, and, of course, Astrov had been a court favourite. There was a trial. But Moscow was divided. It became, as it were, a surrogate trial of the Romanovs themselves—she was in the dock for murder, they were in the dock of public opinion for favouring and promoting a beast like Astrov—and in the end no jury would convict her. All the same, she was a social outcast and the doors of the great houses were closed to her and her son. Later that year, the revolution of 1905 . . . you know better than I the circumstances . . . Princess Astrova took her five-year-old son and vanished."

Churchill was silent for a moment, rolling the claret around on his palate. Troy knew the circumstances of '05 very well—it was the moment his parents had fled westward, to Vienna, to Paris, to London—a child in each city, thereby Troy had a Viennese brother, Parisian twin sisters and was nicknamed "my little Englander" by his mother.

It was Troy's turn.

"And this is the gun that killed Astrov?"

"No, that's in the police museum in Moscow. This is its twin. I'd bet a fiver it had never been fired until that day on the Northern Line."

"Do you have any idea where she went?"

"No. She disappeared without trace. Nice trick if you can do it, and damned difficult. I'd say one has to go to South America these days to do a convincing vanishing trick. Everything in Europe is so knowable. There was talk she had reverted to her maiden name but I've no idea what that was. I've got as far as I can with this. What you need now is an old Russian with a good memory for the ancien régime."

"Like . . . my mother?"

"Precisely."

Troy swigged claret, mused a while.

"Y'know . . . this would fit together more neatly if this were the gun that killed Astrov, if this gun had stayed in Russia when Princess Astrova left and had become the property of the Soviet Union."

"Why's that?"

"Because André Skolnik was a Soviet agent and, during the Olympics last month, three Czech agents working for the Russians came looking for him."

"Bugger!" said Churchill.

"I don't know whether there's bluff or double bluff going on here. But Skolnik was assassinated by one side or the other."

Churchill was shaking his head. Vigorously.

"The last ingredient, Freddie. The potato."

"I'd almost forgotten."

"Quite. I paid it no mind when you first mentioned it. This gun would not have made much noise in the first place. A potato would not have silenced whatever noise it did make. All the potato did was confuse you and me. You know what this looks like to me? The improvization of an amateur. And the gun itself . . . whoever pulled the trigger was lucky it fired. The cartridge was forty years old. The Altmanns made only fifty bullets and that was in 1904. You cannot buy .15 ammunition. No assassin, and you will agree that if this was an assassination there has to be an assassin, would trust such a weapon. A handgun useless at more than a couple of feet? Freddie, I can't dispute what you say about Skolnik or the concern the Russians have shown for the fate of their man . . . but this was the work of an amateur. This was right up your street, plain old-fashioned murder."

"Oh, bum," said Troy, "I've just told Jack Wildeve, Stanley Onions, and a chap at MI5 that it was a pro job."

Churchill opened a second bottle. Let the evening fall softly upon the two of them. Troy marvelled at his capacity, but pound for pound he weighed twice what Troy did. The more flesh and blood to absorb the booze. If anyone paid the price with a hangover it would be Troy.

At the end of the evening, it was pitch dark. August leeching into September. Churchill slipped the gun, the silver bullet, and the ruby into a brown paper bag and handed it to Troy as he left. The walk home took less than five minutes. Across the Charing Cross Road, behind the National Portrait Gallery, down Cecil Court, past the Salisbury pub, and home. He arrived clear-headed but tired, opened the small drawer in the hat stand where he usually kept keys, dumped in the entire contents of the brown paper bag, and forgot about them entirely.

§112

Troy took Sunday lunch with his mother out at Mimram. After lunch, Rod had constituency matters to attend to, Cid insisted on her children getting exercise and enforced a walk upon them, leaving Troy alone with Maria Mikhailovna.

"Mother, did you ever know the Princess Astrova?"

"I met her once or twice. We did not moof in ze same circles."

If Troy had been talking to his father this would have been enough to set him off on a train of thought and chat that would, sooner or later, have answered all Troy's questions. With his mother, it paid to have a follow-up.

"But you remember her trial?"

"Who could not? It was że biggest scandal of ze time. First ze killink of poor Ostrog, and zen ze killink of Astrov himself. A dreadful man. Zey talked of little else in Moscow zat winter."

"I don't suppose you recall her maiden name?"

Maria Mikhailovna thought a while.

"I can see her face . . . she was younker than me . . . in her midseventies if she is still alive . . . but her name . . . she was . . . Nadia . . ."

"Natalia."

"Yes . . . Natalia . . . Natalia . . . Natalia Oblonskaya."

Troy wondered.

"And her son was Sergei," the old lady added as he wondered.

That clinched it. Troy might have fallen for the "Oblonskaya," but not for the "Sergei" as well. Her memory was playing tricks upon her. Perfectly logical tricks—Oblonskaya was the maiden name of Russian literature's greatest heroine and greatest adulteress, Anna Karenina . . . who had killed neither husband nor lover but, herself . . . and Sergei, Seriozha as Anna called him, was the name of her son. It was as useful as if he had asked her the name of the president of France and she had replied "Bovary."

§113

The following Wednesday, Anna phoned him at the Yard.

"Have you had a holiday this year, Troy?"

He hadn't.

"I'm in a bit of a pickle. I've booked into hotels in North Devon. The summer's been such a stinker, I fancied sea breezes and a dose of ozone. I had it in mind to walk some of the coast. You know, start at Ilfracombe, round past the headland and down to Baggy Point and Woolacombe, past Barnstaple and Bideford to points west, as it were."

Churchill's disdain for English seaside resorts flashed through his mind. He'd been pretty scathing about the pleasures of Ilfracombe himself.

"What's the problem?"

"Angus. He's gone walkabout on me. Just upped and buggered off and I've no faith in him being back by lunchtime on Friday."

Angus did this. He was capable of disappearing for weeks at a time. It was why he lost clients; it was why he lost friends. Every so often Anna would get a call from an obscure police station—Sixpenny Handley, Wyre Piddle, Frisby-on-the-Wreake—and be asked by a deferential station sergeant to collect an errant husband who might otherwise be charged as drunk and disorderly (and few men did disorder quite as well as Angus), and, "after all, ma'am, none of us wants to throw the book at a war 'ero."

"I'm puzzled," said Troy. "A walking holiday with a one-legged man?"

"Oh, he was just going to drive from one watering hole to the next. I was walking alone. Angus would have been company in the evenings, otherwise I'd be dining alone. That's sort of why I'm calling. You don't fancy this, do you, Troy? You don't have to do the walk. Just be there in the evenings."

"Do you think hotels will take to a Mr. and Mrs. Smith routine?"

"I booked separate rooms. Lately, Angus's snoring has reached danger level."

Troy had never quite known what his relationship was with Anna. Less so since he had met her husband. He found this statement oddly reassuring. It was as though she'd said, "no hanky panky."

"Okay," he said, "and I *will* do the walks with you."

"Thanks, Troy. It's four days on foot. I thought we might take my car as far as Ilfracombe, park it at the Imperial, and bus back to it on the Wednesday after. I've saved up loads of petrol coupons and I'd rather not trust to that jalopy of yours."

Troy's car was past its best. They hadn't made them since 1930, and he clung to it in part because his father had given it to him.

"I've a better idea," he said. "Let's pool our coupons and arrive in style."

He could hear the mixture of anticipation and anxiety in her voice.

"Not . . . not that Rolls you and Rod have mothballed in the garage in Hampstead?"

"No . . . my mother's Lagonda. You'll like it. It's got a V12 engine. It'll do one-ten on the flat."

"Gosh."

The word almost stopped Troy midflow. So English; too English.

"We could rip down the Thames valley, have lunch at the Rose Revived . . ."

"The what?"

"Trust me . . . it's a sweet old Elizabethan pub right on the river at Newbridge."

"And rip, Troy? Rip?"

"Rip . . . roar . . . you don't just motor in a Lagonda."

§114

Ilfracombe was fading fast. Whilst he thought the idea of the grand tour unlikely ever to be revived, something would surely come along to render the traditional English seaside holiday resort redundant. All it required was an open Continent and cheap petrol. Rod had assured him they'd not be going into the next election with petrol still rationed and who knew how long the restrictions on foreign exchange might last? Given the vagaries of the English summer—he had memories of years when summer simply failed to arrive, as though the turning planet had skipped a season—if an ordinary family could choose between the cosmopolitan delights of Paris and the sun, sand, and vino of the Amalfi Coast, why would anyone choose Blackpool, Broadstairs, or Ilfracombe? Even the names were enough to put you off. Siena, Firenze, San Gimignano?—they spun magic.

Troy thought Anna had probably been thinking prewar—a habit they would both find impossible to break, and in years to come would run a contest to see how many times each began a sentence with the phrase "before the war"—when she booked the Imperial. Perhaps the name alone had been evocative? Was there a seaside town in England without an "Imperial" any more than there was a suburban street south of the Trent without a "Dunroamin" or a "Monabri"?

During the war, the Royal Army Pay Corps had taken over this one-hundred-room anachronism—a battalion of clerks had spent four years here, all pink forms and inky fingers. It seemed to Troy that they could have left but minutes ago, the dreariness of clerkery miasmic in the air.

When he told Anna as much, she said, "You hammer the English for their class obsession and their snobbery and then you come out with lines like that. There are times, Troy, when I think it's easier to get a handle on that mad bugger I married than it is on you."

But by then they were well on their way out of town, stepping westward, the morning sun behind them, knapsacks on their backs, stout walking shoes upon their feet. Anna had chosen to walk in culottes, a chance, as the enlisted man was wont to say, and as she did, "To get me knees brown." And a chance for Troy to gaze on said knees. He hadn't seen them in a while. Anna had been an early convert to Christian Dior's "new look" the previous autumn—coupons saved and coupons blown on way-below-the-knee skirts and rustling petticoats. If it caught on, and it had been slow to dent the moral authority of short skirts in a time of clothes rationing, Troy doubted he would ever see a seductive pair of calves again.

"I've hit on a super way to cut down on the hump and carry," she said. "I've posted clean knickers and socks to each of the hotels we're booked into. Every morning I shall get up to clean knickers and dry socks and know that whatever the day holds I can be run down in the street with no embarrassments in the ambulance."

"You might have shared this plan when you knew we'd be leaving the car back there."

"Never thought men gave a toss. Angus leaves the same sock on his tin leg from one year's end to the next. He'll tell me tin doesn't sweat of course, but it's the principle of the thing. Mens sana . . . wotsit . . . wotsit. If you end up in crusty pants because you haven't planned ahead, will you actually mind?"

Troy had never seen the coast of North Devon before, a saw blade of bays, and promontories, and rock formations that left him wishing he knew the first thing about geology. Pottering about Lyme Bay as a boy he had returned home with a shoe box full of fossils, determined to identify them all and learn enough geology to place each in its eon. He never had.

They had passed Baggy Point and were not far short of their first day's destination at Croyde, when a large, flat-topped rock just within the tide caught his imagination.

"Do you remember that Peter Wimsey novel that came out just before the war? Can't remember the title but Harriet's walking and discovers a body on a rock—a rock very like that. Surely it's the same rock?"

"*Busman's Honeymoon*? Or was it *Have His Carcase*? And he turns out to be some sort of haemophiliac Russian prince, doesn't he?"

"That's the one. And of course she sends for Wimsey."

"Well," said Anna, slipping an arm affectionately through his, "I don't have to send for a detective. You're already here."

It was the most demonstrative gesture she'd made in a while. She had kissed him but once, as he lay prone and passive in a hospital bed in 1944, and in the same breath had called him a fool. But Troy's mind was already wandering from her touch—the one thing leading to the other, the flat-topped tidal rock to a Dorothy L. Sayers plot, to the Russian body, to the bleeding prince of the house of Romanov, to a missing Russian prince of the house of Astrov whose likely name his mother had unhelpfully jumbled with yet another novel. Oblonskaya, Oblonsky. He wished she'd got it right. Then the next thing he knew, Anna had kissed him again, the lightest of pecks upon the cheek, and strolled on ahead, saying as she did so, "Of course, it's not the same rock; she made it up. That's what novels are for."

Her blouse was white and the tails flapped loose and occasionally the whole blouse caught the wind and billowed out full sail. Her culottes were of a shade that might be described as army surplus, except that Troy could not imagine that the army had ever manufactured or issued culottes for there to be any surplus three years after the war. Craving colour, he wondered what colour the knickers in all those envelopes might be. He knew they'd be white, but he could imagine red. A poppy in a cornfield by Van Gogh or Monet. He could imagine that.

"Troy, you're dawdling. And you're daydreaming. Do get a move on!"

§115

They took rooms at the Goat and Periwinkle in Croyde, not far north of Barnstaple.

Much to Troy's surprise, and most certainly to the surprise of all the locals, Anna changed for dinner. A black dress that was sleeveless, backless, and almost arseless.

"Don't you have any of those gloves that go past your elbow?"

"Now you're just being silly. It's steak and kidney pud with mash, in a country pub."

"Quite. I wondered if you'd noticed."

With the arrival of dessert—stewed pears with condensed milk—small talk turned big.

"I could do with your advice," she said.

Troy doubted this but said, "Of course. What about?"

"My job. The National Health Service. I joined it because I believe in it. I believe in it as firmly as Rod."

"But?"

"But I've done two months and I find I'm exhausted. I'm twenty-eight and I feel fifty."

"You'll get used to it."

"Or perhaps I won't. Perhaps it isn't me? Perhaps it's the system?"

"Are you writing it off already?"

"No. We have to have a national health system. I just find myself wondering if we have to have this one, wondering if we got the mix right."

"Rod doesn't think we have. He told me he thinks there were too many compromises to get the consultants and the old fuddy-duddies among the general practitioners on board. He thinks it was an all-or-nothing call. The coexistence of private practice within the NHS is bonkers, according to Rod."

"He's right. We simply don't have enough troops at whatever the medical equivalent of the coal face is."

"How about 'skin level'?"

"Sounds about right. At skin level the demand is overwhelming. Perhaps I had a sheltered upbringing. My experience of rickets comes out of a text book . . . but I can scarcely believe the state of the health of the nation . . . that so many people can be quite so ill with so many ailments that ought to be readily preventable. I find myself trying to remember what it was like before the war but I can't remember because I didn't know. We *gels* knew fuck all—'scuse my French. So much of it comes down to simple matters of nutrition, and if there's one thing rationing did, it was to give everyone a much better, balanced diet. You might hate the national loaf but it's full of what those idiots in advertising call 'goodness.'"

"Then perhaps you'd better write to Mr. Strachey at the Ministry of Food and tell him we should hang on to rationing."

"We should . . . it sounds bonkers, but we should. The question is whether I can hang on to the NHS."

"Are you thinking you might not?"

"I'm thinking I'm a coward. I'm thinking right now that I'm glad it's you across the table, not your brother. I'd hate to have to tell Rod they didn't get it right. I couldn't tell Rod they didn't get it right. I'm a coward."

"I just told you: he already knows."

"If I leave . . ."

"Yes?"

"Don't judge me. Don't . . . try not to think the worse of me. I believed in it, I really did."

"But?"

"But Paddy Fitz has offered me a job in Harley Street."

"Well, that should be fun. I gather he leads a life not unlike Errol Flynn's."

"It gets exaggerated."

"He asks for it."

"Okay. He asks for it. All the same, it's a tempting offer. It would leave me time to study nutrition. As long as the government leaves an 'outside' to the NHS, I may be able to achieve more on the outside."

"If you do, I shall not utter a word of criticism."

"Thank you."

"But there's a quid pro quo."

"Oh, you . . . bastard!"

"Take me on as a patient."

"Why, haven't you got a GP?"

"I have one of the old fuddy-duddies, when what I really need is a doctor as discreet as Kolankiewicz for the times when I don't have Kolankiewicz."

She was nervous, she'd been that all evening, but now she seemed to Troy to be close to anger.

"Now why would that be? Planning on getting shot again, are you?"

In the corridor, her room to the right, his to the left; she dawdled, the nervousness of the evening wrapped like a veil around her. Dawdling led nowhere. He no more understood the next move than she did.

He asked about the book she was clutching.

A matter-of-fact question eliciting a matter-of-fact reply.

"Eustace and Hilda," she said.

He looked at the spine. L. P. Hartley. He'd heard of the author but not the book.

He jingled his keys and said, "good night."

Anna pecked him on the cheek, still beneath her invisible veil, and said, "Try not to get shot Troy."

§116

They spent the following night at the Pig & Strumpet in Instow, about halfway between Barnstaple and Bideford, just across the bay from Appledore.

At breakfast, each had a poached egg—the landlady had rustled up a third, which Anna had sliced fairly between them, the knife hovering over the yolk until she was sure it really was fair—two slices of toast—mercifully free from rationing—and a pitifully thin newspaper—newsprint still being rationed—Anna had the *Manchester Guardian*, Troy *The Times*, although the headlines were identical:

"Atomic Scientist Arrested as Spy"

"Have you ever heard of this Szabo bloke?" Anna asked.

"No. And I'm glad to be out of London when something like this breaks. Or I'd have Rod bending my ear, telling me it's a national disaster, how the Americans will never trust us again . . . and so on."

"But they won't, will they? This chap worked on the bombs that were dropped on Japan, then he seems to have been made deputy head of whatever it is they do out at Harwell, and all the time he was working for the Russians and has given them all the know-how to make their own bomb. Doesn't exactly inspire confidence in us."

Troy had abandoned the headlines for the inner pages.

"He wasn't English; he was Czech or something."

"Hungarian, and it says here we took him on in 1941 and gave him citizenship a couple of years later."

Troy did not wish to have this conversation with Anna any more than he wished to have it with Rod. Angus would have been a better choice, or even Onions—"Spooks? Fuckem." But then the waitress appeared at his side, saying, "Inspector Troy? Telephone call for you. Scotland Yard."

Anna looked at him, daggers drawn.

"I can't not give the Yard my itinerary, can I? It's probably nothing. And certainly nothing to do with this twaddle."

It was Jack.

"I'm sorry to have to do this to you, Freddie, but there's been a death. I think you should come back."

"Can't you handle it?"

"I can, of course I can. But I think you'll want to. Freddie, it's Viktor Rosen. He was found shot through the heart in his flat about forty minutes ago."

§117

The local police told Troy that the quickest way to get him back to London was for them to drive him south to Exeter, where he could board an express to Paddington.

Anna wanted to come with him but Troy kept saying no until she gave in.

"Finish your holiday," he said.

"It'll be no fun."

"It'll be *less* fun. You were planning to do the walks alone anyway—and I've done half with you. It's only a couple of days. Finish your holiday. Pick up the car and I'll see you back in London on Wednesday night."

She had been tearful. Not for the first time he wondered what it was she wasn't saying. But on the train, in a deeply sprung and ancient ex-GWR first-class compartment, hauled by a somewhat newer ex–Southern Railway Bulleid Pacific locomotive at one hundred miles per hour, he gave in to the *diddley-da, diddley-dum,* sat back, and slept. Only when he woke to find the train rattling across Salisbury Plain did a vision of Anna at the wheel of his mother's car, foot on the floor at one hundred and ten miles per hour, come to him.

§118

"We've touched nothing," Jack said. "We waited for you."

It was almost four o'clock when Troy arrived at the apartment on Chelsea Embankment. Jack had sent a car to meet him off the train at Paddington. A silent, almost rank-intimidated WPC had driven him across West London, through Hyde Park, and down to the river.

Touching nothing was a gesture of respect. Troy could not be certain whether it was respect for the dead (Rosen), or for the living (Troy). He could understand it, but it had also cost four hours. Kolankiewicz, too, had waited.

Standing in the hallway, just this side of the "magic" trompe l'oeil door, Kolankiewicz said, "You sure you want to do this?"

"Yes. I can be the formal identification, and then you can take the body away."

Head shots were messy. Almost the first thing he'd had to get used to with gun killings was the sight of the inside of the human skull, of blood and bone, which were imaginable, and brains, which were not, plastered across the walls and furniture. Heart shots were wet. Few suicides pointed a gun at their heart. Few suicides would know its precise position.

Troy stared. Viktor had dressed for death. One of the immaculate suits he'd had tailored in America during the war. A neat knot in the dark blue tie, silver cuff links in his shirt; even the shoes were shined. He lay slumped in a high-backed wing chair, head down, torso upright as though the impact of the bullet had bounced him off the back of the chair and simultaneously knocked the gun from his hand. It lay on the carpet about eighteen inches from his right foot. A wartime Beretta. Every British Tommy who'd served in Italy had brought one home as a souvenir, or so it seemed. Every street corner spiv would sell you one, or so it seemed.

"Why the heart?"

Kolankiewicz said, "I have learnt over the years that it is the romantic's way. Most of us desperate to die, most of us desperate pragmatists, blow our brains out. Romantics desperate to die still have their nature and their aesthetic to contend with. They aim for the heart."

Troy knelt and looked up into Viktor's face, pale and bloodless, eyes closed. To look for expression was meaningless—Troy thought those who pronounced the dead "peaceful" as idiotic as those who chipped "asleep" on tombstones—he did it all the same.

"Time of death?"

"Around midnight."

Troy turned to Jack. "Anyone hear anything?"

"People above are holidaying in Cornwall. Chap below is very deaf."

Troy stood up and looked around. Familiar objects rendered alien by the fact of death. The Bechstein piano, the score of Mozart's twenty-third piano concerto still open on the stand; a cello stood in the curve; the signed photographs of Toscanini and Furtwängler; the Picasso sketch of Casals, the walls lined with books in three or four different languages, the lithographs of eighteenth-century Vienna; the Matisse portrait he knew simply as "blue woman," the Van Gogh of some waving cornfield near Arles.

Jack touched him on the arm. "Freddie, there's something else you should see."

Jack steered him gently to a door in the rear wall. Troy had never been beyond this point. It had always seemed a frontier of some sort. It led to a long corridor, with what Troy took to be bedrooms and bathrooms off—and he'd no idea how many of those there were.

"All this is new to me," he said. "Viktor's public rooms were very public, and his private very private. "

"I think," said Jack, opening the first door on the left, "that this has to be Viktor's bedroom."

Troy stood in the doorway, unbelieving.

"No, surely there are other rooms . . . ?"

"There are. In fact, there are four other bedrooms. All smelling a bit airless, all obviously guest rooms. This was Viktor's room."

Troy stepped in. A rectangular room about ten feet long and seven across. A narrow window looking out onto a brick wall. Torn and fading yellow wallpaper from some era late in the last century. In an apartment like this it was a box room or a maid's room. An alarm clock showing the right time ticked softly on an upturned orange box, next to it a candle stub in a tin candlestick and a box of Bryant & May matches. The orange box stood by a camp bed, neatly made up in Spartan fashion. Coarse cotton sheets, coarser woollen blankets of the kind every army-surplus store in every town in the land had been selling off for the last couple of years. On the lower shelf formed by the box divider stood a cream-coloured enamel mug and a pair of tortoiseshell reading glasses. On the bare, carpetless boards a hardbacked German book lay splayed—*Doktor Faustus,* by Thomas Mann.

There was nothing else.

"I'd no idea," Troy said. "No idea at all."

"Does it make any sense? I mean, there's enough money hanging on the walls in the next room to offset the national debt. He spent more on his suit than he did on this room . . . and he lives like this?"

"Oh, yes, it makes sense. Of a kind. Doesn't mean I know why he chose this. It's a bit like a cell, isn't it? Viktor was one of the first to be rounded up by the Nazis—a spell in Oranienburg in 1933. And then we added insult to injury by interning him on the Isle of Man for nearly six months in 1940. And it really was an insult to a man like Viktor. And, of course, it's where he and Rod met."

Uttering the name brought home the thought of his brother. He'd have to be the one to tell him.

"Freddie, I have to ask . . . was Viktor the kind of man to take his own life."

"I haven't the faintest idea," Troy said. "But I'll ask Rod."

§119

When they emerged from the foreign country at the back of the apartment, Kolankiewicz had taken the body and his men were dusting for fingerprints. For the first time, Troy noticed the bottle of Hine Armagnac on the small, pedestal table next to the chair in which Viktor had died, and the empty glass that stood with it.

He declined to ride back to the Yard, and walked along the river in the direction of Westminster. It might give him time to gather his thoughts before he faced Rod. The House was not sitting. Troy would call at his office; there was a fifty-fifty chance he'd be there, and if he wasn't, he'd take the Underground up to Hampstead. Above all, he did not want to call him on the phone. He could imagine no worse way for Rod to find out Viktor was dead. He had to tell him himself. He had to tell him face to face.

"I thought you were in Cornwall with the gorgeous Anna."

Rod was in shirtsleeves, back to window, scribbling something at his desk, a cooling September breeze wafting across the terrace from the Thames.

Troy waited till he looked up again, stacked his papers, and shoved them to one side. Rod was about to indulge in one of his big man's sprawls of relaxation, a cat stretch, chest out, back arched, fingers locked behind his head.

Troy said, "Viktor died last night."

The fingers never met behind the head; Rod almost slumped back to the desk, but righted himself with a jerk to stand up straight. A quick turn to the window, then a turn back to Troy, his eyes already brimming with tears.

"How?"

"It looks as though he shot himself."

Rod turned away again, rummaged in his trouser pocket for his hanky, and honked loudly into it.

"Freddie, you say 'looks' . . . ?"

"A copper's caution, Rod. Jack's been looking into this for less than eight hours. We have nothing but the ostensible to go on. At the moment *looks* is everything. And, of course . . . I can't think why Viktor should want to kill himself."

"And you have to ask me if I can?"

"It can wait."

Rod sat down. Troy took the chair on the other side of the desk. Rod took a bottle and two glasses out of the bottom drawer and poured brandy for both of them. It was the same mark Viktor had used as Dutch courage.

Rod sipped his in silence for a few moments, wiped each cheek with the back of his hand.

"You know, I met him that day you saw me off at St Pancras in 1940. He was in the same compartment. Don't think I noticed him for ages. Not sure he spoke until we'd passed Derby. Inauspicious beginning. I suppose all beginnings are. Cid swears I actually asked her to dance a second time without recognizing her from the first. And that's the woman I'm spending the rest of my life with. I knew within a couple of weeks that I'd know Viktor the rest of my life . . . or his."

Rod downed the rest of his brandy, corked the bottle, and stood up.

"It's a day to get pissed, but not here. Knock that back and I'll drive us home. Sooner or later you'll feel like asking me questions and I'll feel like answering them."

The drive to Hampstead was in Rod's "blob" car.

"Viktor was scathing about this," Troy reminded him. "The poached egg."

"He was scathing about a lot of things," Rod said. "If you knew Viktor, you had to learn to take the rough with the smooth."

§120

Troy slyly declined Rod's invitation to get drunk. Rod unearthed a bottle so old the label had perished. Only the date remained: 1926. Troy occasionally sipped half an inch off the top of the glass and obediently stretched out his arm for a top up when Rod flourished the bottle, and then the second bottle. Between the two, Rod had reminisced without interruption.

"He was . . . a difficult man. Such a touchy bugger. Took a long time to get to know him."

Troy wasn't at all sure he had got to know Viktor Rosen. They had stuck to the issue—music. And while music was what Viktor Rosen was "about," it had taught Troy more about Troy than it had about Rosen.

"He had . . . nothing . . . and he had everything."

Rod was pretty pissed by now, shoes off, tie at half-mast, hunched on the edge of the armchair, all odd socks and socialist-red braces, cradling his glass as though he could read the future in the crystal.

"I don't quite catch your drift," Troy said as Rod's silence simply added to the enigmatic nature of the remark.

"He was one of the most successful performers of the century. Top of the . . . wotsit. And he was canny. Got all his stuff out of Germany when he saw Hitler coming. Made the mistake of staying too long himself and got nabbed . . . but he got out of Germany and he got out of Austria . . . and when he got here his money and his piano were waiting for him. As soon as we let him out of chokey . . . the Americans wanted him. He made a packet in the States just before the end of the war. And when it was all over, we gave him citizenship and the king offered him a knighthood . . . and we all smoothed things over when Viktor said no . . . didn't go with the job of playing the piano he said. As if it could be just a job. And . . . you saw his place on the river, the Bechstein . . . a Van Gogh on one wall . . . Chagall on the other . . ."

"I didn't see a Chagall?"

"Used to be next to the fireplace. Must have moved it. Anyway, where was I? Yes. He had . . . everything and . . ."

The sentence trailed off, Rod rocked gently on his buttocks. Troy was not at all certain that he wasn't about to topple backwards into oblivion.

". . . And he had . . . nothing."

"What nothing?"

Rod had to think about this. For a few moments the glassy eyes tried to lock onto his, but the booze won and he stared into his glass once more.

"No nothing. That's about as much nothing as you can have. None. Nada. Zero. Zilch. Fuck all. Fuck nothing . . . heh . . . heh . . . Billy taught him that . . . 'Fuck nothing' along with 'tickle the ivories,' 'the joanna' . . . Viktor loved slang . . . he loved shocking people with it."

Troy remembered the "stick with me kid" that had so amused the audience at the Wigmore but he was none the wiser. He tried a different tack.

"Did Viktor ever say there was anything . . . missing?"

"Nope . . . not in his nature . . . that would be too . . . sentimental . . . not an overtly sentimental man . . . but it was obvious. Parents long dead. Brother killed in the First War. Sister . . . sister . . . well, he looked into that afterwards . . . I helped him . . . as far as we could ever tell . . . looks as though she died in Treblinka . . . he could never persuade her to leave Berlin. No, the nothing of which Viktor had plenty was . . . family."

Another long, wobbling pause, Rod teetering on edge of seat and sentence.

"Of course. We were his family. Us 'Stinking Jews' . . . he was very fond of Joe Hummel and Arthur Kornfeld . . . and I think Billy and Oskar infuriated and amused him by turns . . . but the real family were his pupils . . . all those kids he got together . . . and he was fond of you, y'know . . . said you'd go far if you'd just concentrate on the piano and forget playing coppers . . . fond of all his pupils . . . they were his kids . . . they *were* his kids . . . do you know . . . do you know . . . ?"

This surely was it? He'd never get to the end of this sentence.

"Do you know, that young girl who plays the cello . . . Voytek . . . the Austrian girl . . . Viktor gave her the cello she plays . . . just . . . gave it to her . . . y'know what it is . . . ?"

Troy had paid no mind to the cello at the Wigmore, he'd drunk in the music and he'd drunk in some of the player, but he'd scarcely noticed the instrument.

"It's not a Stradi . . . Stradivarius. But it's some bloke like him . . . made in seventeen something or other. Now . . . whadya think that's worth? Gotta be worth a packet hasn't it . . . I mean . . . a Straddithingy . . . just *gave* it to her . . . children. Kids. His kids. They *were* his . . . his . . ."

It was a minute or more before Troy realized that Rod was no longer seeking wisdom in the bottom of his glass of claret and had fallen asleep. He gently prised the glass from his fingers and went in search of Cid.

They tumbled him into the marital bed.

Troy tugged at one trouser leg, Cid at the other.

"How long have I known you, Inspector Troy?"

"Since you became engaged to Rod, Lady Troy. The summer of 1932."

"And how old were you, Inspector?"

"I was sixteen, ma'am. A tad shy of my seventeeth."

"And how many times have us five-foot midgets tipped this six-foot drunk into bed, whipped off his socks and his trousers, and tucked him up for the night?"

"I've lost track. But this isn't like any other night. He lost friends in combat. To be expected in war, and Rod was at the sharp end. He lost our father, who took long enough in dying to bid the fondest farewell to us all. Viktor is different. Viktor's death is different."

"No anticipation, no farewells."

"Quite," said Troy.

Cid said, "I've made up the bed in your old room. Stay for breakfast. I'm sure he'll want to see you at breakfast."

§121

At breakfast, Rod was nose down in the morning paper when Troy appeared. He folded it, tapped with his forefinger on the headlines, and shoved it across the table to Troy.

Troy glanced at it and as Rod had said nothing, he didn't, either. God knows, they'd all be bored rigid by this topic over the next few weeks. More public breast beating, more revelling in our rapid decline to the second rate. What was Professor Szabo's crime? Giving our atomic secrets to the Russians, or telling us he'd done it?

Troy shoved it back without a word.

Rod whacked the top of his egg with his teaspoon and said, "I can't remember. Did you ask me your question?"

"No," Troy replied.

"Well . . . the answer is, 'I don't know whether Viktor had any reason to kill himself.' I would say, ordinarily, that he wasn't the type. He could always laugh at himself and I tend to think that's a saving grace."

"But?"

"But I haven't been through what Viktor went through. Being locked up by the British was nothing . . . a doddle . . . like being sent away to school except that the food was better and sport wasn't compulsory. But that's an Englishman speaking. I witnessed two suicides of refugees who'd been locked up by the Germans and would rather die than be locked up again by anyone. And there are plenty who chose to live who still found internment an ordeal far too reminiscent of what they'd been through at the hands of the Nazis. But . . . Viktor never seemed to be one of those . . . and for it to surface in him . . . eight years later . . . in such a dreadful way . . . well . . . it doesn't seem plausible."

Troy wondered about the wisdom of what he had to say next, but Rod seemed to have shed the worst of his grief in his reminiscences last night. He was eating a hearty breakfast and showing no signs of paying for the night before with a hangover.

"Tell me, did you ever see the back of Viktor's apartment? The rooms beyond?"

"No," said Rod. "He was very private about that. That big room with the piano—the one he always called the rehearsal room—the bog off the hallway, the dining room, the small sitting room, but I've never seen the kitchen or the bedrooms. It was like a lost domain. Sort of 'backstage.'"

"I had to go backstage yesterday—as you would expect—and I went into Viktor's bedroom. It was minimal. It seemed to me that he kept one room in his apartment to remind him of being locked up. He slept on a camp bed, read by candlelight, drank from a tin cup, and had an old orange box as his only furniture."

It stopped Rod midtoast. He was as surprised as Troy had been.

"You know," he said, after thinking for a moment. " 'Remind' doesn't seem the right word. That would suit a token of some sort . . . the memento mori . . . but what you've just described is Viktor reliving his imprisonment, *still living* his imprisonment, as though some part of him had never been set free. As though having hit rock bottom he could never live at any other level, whatever his means. It was always there, underlying everything. The money, the success . . ."

"The Van Goghs, the Picassos, the Chagalls . . . sounds like a form of masochism."

"Well . . . you wouldn't get me doing it. But I can see a sort of sense in it."

"Would you say imprisonment haunted him?"

"No. I would have said it strengthened him. You might even say that rather than being something as crude as masochism it was more like a hair shirt. Suffering was part of the making of him. To be terribly corny, what is art, what is music, without suffering? Are a camp bed and a tin cup a form of torture or merely tolerable discomforts set against a life of luxury and success? Pricks to keep you on your mettle."

Cid came in and told Troy that Jack wanted him on the telephone.

"What did Rod have to say?"

"He's telling me in convincing detail that Viktor wasn't the type, and at the same time he doesn't seem to have any doubts that it was suicide."

"Well . . . Kolankiewicz does. I think you'd better call him."

Troy called Hendon.

"Ach . . . I have things to report. First the body. Single shot to the heart. Death was instantaneous. No marks to indicate restraint or coercion. The bullet I removed matches the Beretta."

"Then why is Jack telling me you have doubts?"

"Fingerprints. The only prints on the gun are Herr Rosen's. The only prints on the brandy bottle and the glass are Herr Rosen's."

"So?"

"The only prints anywhere in that room are Herr Rosen's. Troy, someone wiped the place clean. How many suicides have you ever known to do that?"

Troy went back to Rod. There was no way he was going to mention this.

"I have to meet Kolankiewicz. Are you in a position to tell anyone who should be told before we tell the press? It's been close to twenty-four hours now."

"I know. My fault. I should have been practical last night, not maudlin. Yes. I can tell them all. Not many. Just his students and his protégés—there are about a dozen of them. If you went to that last recital at the Wigmore you'll have seen most of them on stage."

He slipped it in as an afterthought—the two of them standing on the doorstep on a fine late-summer morning—passed it off as routine.

"And . . . do you know of anyone with a reason to kill Viktor?"

"A routine question?"

"Of course."

"Then I give you a routine 'don't be daft.'"

§122

Kolankiewicz met Troy at Rosen's apartment.

"Show me," Troy said.

"My guys did everything in this room. Everything that anyone might touch in the course of a crime. Anything that would bear the weight of a hand. The place is clean of prints. Yet, the person who found the body was the cleaner. Jack talked to her. She cleans twice a week. Yesterday was her day. The room should have been covered in prints. Even if Rosen had received no vistors in the three days before his death, think how many objects he would have touched, how many leant upon. See the bookshelf at hip height? By now it would have a fine sheen of dust on it. When my guys dusted it down it was spotless. It had been wiped that day, ahead of the cleaner."

"It's too thorough, isn't it?"

The room—the rehearsal room—still had that odd feel to Troy. He'd been here dozens of times, perhaps close to a hundred over the last two years—and it was still as though he was seeing things for the first time.

"Let us suppose for a moment that Viktor was killed. We have no motive in robbery. The first thing I'd take would be the Picasso—under my jacket and away. If I'd planned well, the Van Gogh fits in a suitcase. And then we have the problem of how to make it look like a convincing suicide. And it *is* convincing isn't it?"

"It is. The prints on the gun are quite consistent with Herr Rosen having loaded it himself, and with the grip he would have on it to point it at his own heart. Not as easy as pointing it at your head."

"Did you dust beyond this room?"

"No. We had no reason to."

Troy led him backstage, into the foreign country. Kolankiewicz showed less surprise at the "cell" than he or Jack had. A Polish shrug seemed to say, "So what?"

Down the corridor three of the four other bedrooms smelled of non-use. The last, the biggest, did not. Jack's nose had deceived him. This room was in use. Troy could swear there was a trace of scent in the air but could not say what. It was a lavish room, quite the biggest bed Troy had ever seen; hand-printed, hand-trimmed wallpaper in a large Monet-inspired pattern; a large, French cherrywood wardrobe; a bergère sofa along the foot the bed; and over the bed an unframed Chagall that stretched from bed head to ceiling, and almost wall to wall—a dark painting, executed lightly, cobalt blue; navy blue; a deep, entrancing green; a bouquet of crimson . . . a girl: part girl, part what? Mermaid? Bird? Floating in midair . . . or was she borne aloft by the fiery, feathery thing above her?

Kolankiewicz sniffed the air.

"A woman," he said. "Not a man's room. It's not a bedroom, it's a boudoir."

He opened the wardrobe door, he opened the drawers in the tallboy but both were empty.

"I still say woman."

"With not a knickknack in place, no mirror, no dressing table, no dresses, no knickers?"

"Can you not smell it? Say it is an absence of smell if you like. But it *is* in the air."

"Yes," said Troy. "I can smell it. I'll be in the other room if you need me."

Troy sat at the piano. Looked at the open score. Viktor had played the Mozart twenty-third at Carnegie Hall last year. Perhaps it was the sheer quality of his performance, perhaps it was the memory of the war years and how much Viktor had raised in U.S. war bonds, but the audience, to a man, to a woman, had stood and cheered at the end. Troy held his hands over the keys poised for the opening notes of the piano, hearing in the mind's ear, rushing through, the long, two-minute string introduction. His fingers never touched the keys. He went back to Kolankiewicz.

"Do you have a spare print kit?"

Kolankiewicz pointed at his Gladstone bag on the floor and said, "In there. Somewhere."

Troy dusted outward from middle C an octave either way. And then octave by octave until he had reached the extremities of bass and treble. Keys he'd never touched on his own piano.

Kolankiewicz returned.

"The cell, as you put it, has prints in all the obvious places. On the door knob, on the tin mug, and smudged all over the reading glasses. They look like Rosen's but I will need to check that to be sure. The other room, the boudoir, is spotless."

"So's this," said Troy. "Now tell me, what murderer, what assassin, would be so foolish as to play the piano before committing his crime and then have to wipe down every key?"

§123

About three in the afternoon, Rod called him and said, "I've talked to them all, Freddie. You can give it to the papers in time for the late editions."

But by then Troy had worked out the question that mattered most. "Rod, who was Viktor hiding?"

§124

Rod said, "I'm over the way. As we're this close, why don't I come to you, or you to me?"

That was a nonchoice. Troy dashed out of his office, down the subway under Bridge Street to the iron gate that segregated the Palace of Westminster from the British public and the Circle and District Lines. A quick salute from the copper on duty, up the stairs, and into Rod's office, not quite breathless.

"I've spent half the day toying with the idea that someone might have killed Viktor. No suicide I've ever seen, and I've seen plenty, ever wiped the scene free of fingerprints. You don't reach the point of not giving a damn and then do something like that. It smacks of murder. Kolankiewicz thinks it was murder. But no murderer would scrupulously have wiped down the piano keys. Every single bloody one. And it had me baffled. But Kolankiewicz says the spare bedroom, not the one Viktor slept in, but one of the others, was also wiped down, and that doesn't fit, either. And then I put the pieces together. The piano, the bedroom, the faint scent in the air . . . someone who played the piano . . . someone he still gave a damn about at the moment of his death. Rod, Viktor had a mistress . . . and you could have told me yesterday."

Rod took the blast standing but as soon as Troy stopped he sat down, looking sad and tired. He pushed a list of names across the desk to Troy.

"He had twelve pupils—apart from you, of course—I've called them all. They're shocked, to put it mildly. And it would be good if you could leave this until tomorrow . . . but the one you want is Méret Voytek."

"How long have you known?"

"Since it began. That must be about eighteen months now."

"Would you ever have told me?"

"Probably not. I didn't think it mattered, and I can't see that it matters now. But since you asked, I won't lie to you. I don't know why you need to know, but you'll tell me you need to know everything. When you came to see me yesterday I thought about telling you, but I thought better of it, I thought about Viktor's reputation."

"He can hardly suffer for his reputation now."

"I think he can. An affair with a woman less than half his age? And what about Miss Voytek?"

Troy sat down. Rod's reasonableness would erode stone.

"Rod, it doesn't need to be public, but I do have to talk to her. For all we know she may well have been the last person to see Viktor alive."

"I think she was. She told me she was there until late Sunday night."

"Then you were an ass not to tell me about her. If I talk to her and there is nothing crucial to the case I can't see any reason why her relationship with Viktor should be known. Now, where can I find her?"

"She lives in Clover Mews."

"Doesn't ring any bells."

"It's a cul-de-sac off Dilke Street."

"What? At the back of Viktor's apartment?"

"Yes. I concluded he wanted her close."

"Close but unseen?"

"Freddie, don't try to make a moral fog out of this. He was an old man—he was sixty-six. He never married. I think Méret was all he ever had in life. The money meant nothing to him . . . and what is music if you have no one to share it with?"

"I rather thought he shared it with the world."

"Which is, word for word, what I said to him when he told me about Méret."

"Did he tell you everything?"

"Pretty well. I think everyone has someone from whom there are no secrets. You're the great exception to that. You're here, on your professional high horse, as you have every right to be, but personally, you have more secrets and lies in you than anyone I know and I've known you since the day you were born. Now, tell me you can wait until the morning and I'll phone Méret and agree a time. And if you can release the body, I'll arrange the funeral."

Troy said yes to both.

Later, back in his office, Rod called and said, "Méret Voytek is expecting you at ten a.m. tomorrow. I'm expecting you at ten a.m. on Friday, Golders Green crematorium. Be there."

§125

When Troy had bought his first, and only, house in Goodwin's Court, in 1937, he had been drawn to Mews houses. He liked the off-the-beaten-track feel of mews, the sense of hidden corners in the city . . . streets that led nowhere . . . streets down which no one strolled . . . houses that didn't look like houses. Before the war many mews still housed chauffeurs, but not as many as housed merely cars. Now, hardly anyone had a chauffeur—they had, like his father's, like Laura Narayan's father's, gone off to the armed forces, got demobbed, voted Labour, and chosen not to return to the tugged forelock and the low wage. Goodwin's Court pleased on most counts. It was a little-used alley—although since 1942, Ruby the prostitute had worked the St. Martin's Lane end as her "beat"—and the house he lived in looked less like a house than a Georgian shop.

But Clover Mews had it all. It was a cul-de-sac, tucked away only yards from the Thames Embankment, and the flats over the garages had a look of the warehouse to them, chains and derrick arms intact on one, makeshift balconies on all, precariously perched flowerpots full of geraniums and trailing nasturtiums. It had the Bohemian touch he lacked the courage to create for himself. It looked to be years since anyone had got out a pot of paint and a brush. Everything was faded, everything was peeling back to bare wood. But then he thought, that was England—a faded country sadly in need of a metaphoric, symbolic coat of paint.

That was Attlee, that was Bevan, that was Rod—a man with a giant paintbrush, sadly short of a giant pot of paint.

Above number seven, the French window onto the tiny balcony was ajar and the sound of someone playing scales on a cello drifted down to the street.

Troy rang the bell. It made no sound. He stepped back and called out hello to the upstairs window.

A blonde head appeared on the balcony and said, "I cannot abide bells. Door is open."

She met him at the top of the stairs, barefoot, a voluminous blue dress worn like a tent, billowing around her, the dungeon eyes that had avoided his backstage at the Wigmore now looking straight at him.

"Thursdays. Seven till eight. Am I right?"

"I'm sorry, I . . ."

"You came to Viktor for lessons, Thursdays seven till eight. You have not been since last Christmas. We met once as I was leaving."

Whatever the scent he had noticed in Viktor's flat was, he was smelling it now and realized he had smelled it long before Kolankiewicz had pointed it out. It was there, tucked away in his unconscious until she resurrected it.

"And sometimes," he said, "you were there in the rooms at the back, while I played, and you did not come out. You were hiding."

"Yes. Quite so. Come in, Mr. Troy. Today is not a day to hide."

She disappeared into her bedroom, saying she would be but a moment.

Troy stood alone in the large sitting-room-cum-study. It was as Mitteleurope as Viktor's, but in a completely different style. It was almost shtetl—not that Troy had ever heard that Voytek was Jewish—broad, bare, blackened boards; bare brick walls; an upright, cylindrical, wood-burning stove; a tatty, possibly Persian rug; a bursting Edwardian armchair so large she could have used it as a bed; and a litter of books and music scores, strewn everywhere, stacked on every surface, piled in every corner. Gathering dust. It would have driven Viktor mad.

And on its metal stand, just in front of the door to the balcony, her cello.

In the midst of structured chaos and benign neglect, the cello almost shone, a midbrown shade—he'd no idea of what wood cellos were made—to which the centuries had imparted a glowing sheen, a patina of use. He daren't touch. He'd never played a stringed instrument. They looked so fragile. And *f*-holes—where was Freud when you needed him?—always struck him as sexy.

She emerged, the only changes seemed to be a grip in her hair to stop it falling over her eyes and a pair of espadrilles on her feet. She reached down to the loose Italian tiles that formed a fire drop in front of the stove and picked up a roll-up machine to make a cigarette.

"You want?"

Troy shook his head. Waited while quick fingers rolled a cigarette as thin as a knitting needle—the fine, white tube in her fingertips, the darting tongue along the gummed line. Oddly, he could see the same grace and care in rolling a quick smoke as in her fingers stopping the strings on the neck of her cello. It was as though the woman didn't have a clumsy bone in her body.

The flick of a match with her thumbnail, Bogart-style; a single, deep drag, then, "Ask, Inspector. Ask whatever."

"You told my brother that you saw Viktor on the night he died?"

"Yes. That is so. I dropped in late. I had been to flicks. Viktor never cared for flicks. I go alone. I call by on my way home."

"About what time?"

"After ten. Maybe half past ten. I catch tram from West End to Chelsea Bridge and walk."

"How was he?"

"Well, he not talk like a man about to kill himself. He dressed, as you say, to the nines, but Viktor often did that. He was not a man for mufti. He was drinking Armagnac, his favourite. He offer to open wine for me but I say no, it will keep me awake. So we talk."

"About what?"

"About when we first met. Then I get ready to go home, and he say, 'Play for me, play for me, Méret.' So I play, and then I go."

"Did you go into the back of the apartment?"

"Not this time. We did not always make love, Inspector, and there was no reason to hide."

"But you have, the both of you, hidden the relationship."

"Inspector, I am twenty-four years old, Viktor was sixty-six. A gap of forty-two years. Why would we invoke the judgement of society upon us? Besides, there are things you not know. Viktor was my tutor back in Vienna before the war. He was friend of my father's, friend of many of my father's friends—I was ten years old when I first went to him for lessons. It would be very foolish to give anyone the right idea about me and Viktor, even foolisher to give them the wrong one. Not that I think there are many left alive in Vienna who knew us . . . but . . ."

"So, when you say you talked about the time you first met, you were talking about Vienna, not your arrival here?"

"Yes. Vienna. Vienna in 1934."

"Did that make Viktor sad?"

"No, Mr. Troy. It made *me* sad."

"Did you see the gun?"

"No. I had no idea Viktor owned a gun. I think he probably bought it only a few days ago, but that is just my feeling."

"Did you know how Viktor slept?"

"You mean his room? Of course I knew. I think perhaps he slept that way ever since he was released by the Germans. I never saw his private quarters in Vienna, but it would not surprise me to learn that he had a room there just like the one he had here."

"If he had, what would it tell you?"

She'd reached the end of her cigarette. She took the grip from her hair, splinted the fag end with it and drew two or three more puffs. Troy realized that that was why the grip had been there all along.

"Tell me? You mean, does this hold the key to Viktor's suicide? Is it to be explained by his time in Oranienburg or on the Isle of Man? That this is why Viktor killed himself? A little too easy perhaps? The first thing I did when I moved in here was to cut the wires on the doorbell. I cannot stand the sound of bells. Everything in the camps was governed by the sound of bells. Every aspect of life was summoned by bells. Bells to work, bells to eat, bells to shit. I don't care if I never hear a bell again. But I wouldn't kill myself if I did. Mr. Troy, I don't know why Viktor killed himself. Viktor had no reason to kill himself."

"What was it you played?"

She stood up, opened the lid on the unlit stove, and flicked the last fraction of her cigarette into it. The grip went back into her hair, tucking it out of her eyes once more, and she crossed the room to her cello, sat in the window, and played.

Troy knew the piece at once, it was a Fauré elegy. Originally written as a duet for cello and piano. Three mournful minutes, in which he learnt what it was he liked about the cello. It was an instrument that fell asleep in your arms. The piano was an instrument you assaulted—*biff, bash, bosh*—and then it kicked you back. Rockers and swayers notwithstanding, there were really only two kinds of cellist—nodders and not nodders. Voytek did not nod—the tilt of her head in contrast with the frenetic, voltaic activity of her fingers on the neck of the cello, the head lolling almost motionless against the instrument, not nodding, not bobbing. He'd never claim the piano was an extension of himself, it would be as sensible as laying claim to a weaving loom—the cello was Voytek, Voytek was the cello, nurse, baby, lover. Strings bowed and plucked for her immersive bliss and his delight.

When she had finished, she said, "Viktor and I played it together many times. He made an arrangement just for piano and another just for cello last year. I didn't see it as a separation, but now I have the power of hindsight. His last wish was that I should play the piano version, rather than the cello. I don't know why, perhaps he wanted to hear the sound of his Bechstein under fingers other than his own, to die with that sound still in his ears—but then I didn't know it was going to be his last wish."

"An elegy," Troy said. "A song for the dead."

"When you listen to Mozart's requiem, or Fauré's own for that matter, do you always think of the dead? Did you weep at Viktor's playing of Massenet's elegy as his encore? Read what you will into Viktor's choice. I read nothing."

At the door, her hand on the latch, Troy hesitating at the top of the stairs, he said, "Could I ask you . . . the scent you're wearing?"

"I not wearing scent today."

"Then, perhaps yesterday . . . and before that many times in Viktor's apartment?"

"Oh, I see. Soir de Paris, Mr. Troy. And I thought I had been sparing with it. I have only the one bottle. I found it in my parents' flat. After the war."

It seemed to Troy that she had uttered the last three words as a whole, separate sentence, and that it had the same import and inflection, the same stand-alone, conceptual quality the English gave to "before the war." It was a time, it was a place, it was an idea . . .

§126

Troy had only been to the crematorium once—for the funeral of Sigmund Freud in 1939.

He knew he'd blend in—the world of classical music would turn out en masse for Viktor Rosen. All Troy had to do was be anonymous. The place was packed; half of central Europe, half the orchestras in Britain were represented here. Rod and Cid were up front. It would be typical of Rod to want to make a speech. Sir Thomas Beecham was up front—they'd have to shove a cue ball in his mouth for him not to make a speech. And Voytek was up front. Troy had no idea whether she'd say anything or not—whether she would speak for her generation of young musicians nurtured by Viktor or whether she would, however inadvertently, cast herself as the widow.

It was a purely secular affair. Troy would not have known from anything said that day that Viktor was Jewish, and was pretty certain that he had left instructions to that effect. He wondered if Rod and Beecham had done a deal: Beecham, in a rich, almost caricature English voice that rose at the end of every sentence—a little too high-pitched, a little too ripe—paid tribute to Viktor the musician. Rod paid tribute to Viktor the man: the way they had met, which Troy had heard a hundred times, although oddly enough never from Viktor's point of view . . . how difficult it was to know Viktor . . . his combination of "tolerance and irascibility" . . . "one who did not suffer fools gladly" (which was English for "rude") . . . his "unpredictability" . . . and what was more unpredictable than the manner of his dying?

Lastly, Méret Voytek stepped up to speak, a scrap of paper in her hand. All neat in a ballerina "new look"—the page-boy, tightly nipped jacket, the long flared skirt. Effortlessly frail. She glanced down at the paper only once, and then recited from memory, word perfect if somewhat accented:

Peace, peace! he is not dead, he doth not sleep!
He hath awakened from the dream of life.

'Tis we who, lost in stormy visions, keep
With phantoms an unprofitable strife,
And in mad trance strike with our spirit's knife
Invulnerable nothings. We decay
Like corpses in a charnel; fear and grief
Convulse us and consume us day by day,
And cold hopes swarm like worms within our living clay.

He has outsoared the shadow of our night.
Envy and calumny and hate and pain,
And that unrest which men miscall delight,
Can touch him not and torture not again.
From the contagion of the world's slow stain
He is secure; and now can never mourn
A heart grown cold, a head grown grey in vain
Nor, when the spirit's self has ceased to burn,
With sparkless ashes load an unlamented urn.

He wondered how she had come across "Adonais." It would be typical of Rod to have steered her toward some classic in the English canon—their father would have relished the moment, leafing through his books of poetry to give her what she wanted—untypical of Rod to have chosen it. It wasn't his view of life, of anyone's life, let alone Viktor Rosen's. Besides, the urn, whatever became of it, wherever it lodged, would hardly be unlamented.

Throughout, Troy had stood next to Billy Jacks. On the other side of Billy stood Arthur Kornfeld. He heard Billy whisper, none too softly, "S'truth. What the bleedin' 'ell was that?"

And Arthur had replied, "Billy, I will say to you what Viktor would say were he living at this moment. Mein Gott, do you Cockneys know nothing? It was Shelley. Shelley writing on the death of Keats in eighteen and . . . whatever."

"Yeah, well, I ain't none the wiser."

Troy had always wanted to meet Beecham. Now, as they all dispersed, was not the moment. It was a musician's moment. He edged his way through the crowd. Beecham was kissing Voytek, one cheek then the other as Troy slipped past unnoticed, or so he thought.

"Mr. Troy?"

Troy looked back. Beecham was cheek to cheek with some other "gel." Voytek was looking at him.

"You are driving back into town?"

"Yes, I am."

She stepped closer, held out her hand. Thinking she meant to shake his, Troy reciprocated—instead she clutched it the way a child clutches its mother's, more holding hands than shaking. Her gloved hand wrapping itself in his gloveless.

"Please, take me home."

He apologized for the state of his car: the shot springs, the worn upholstery.

She said, "When I was girl in Vienna, all cars were like this."

But the bait of small talk had been batted back. She said nothing all the way down through Hampstead and Marylebone, across Knightsbridge and Belgravia.

He turned into Dilke Street. She'd closed her eyes miles back, and only opened them as the car stopped.

"Do you have time? Then park car. Come inside."

Inside, the little black hat with its little black veil was tossed carelessly across the room and the little black jacket followed. She sat on the overstuffed armchair, appeared to notice for the first time that she was wearing black gloves, tore them off, and threw them at the wall. Troy sat down opposite her, perched on the edge of his seat, wondering where all this was leading.

She was staring down at her hands, turning them slowly, knuckles up, palms up, as though they were not her own and had been grafted on by some mad Frankenstein—and as the tears burst in her eyes she buried her face in her hands and wept loudly and without restraint.

Troy did not move. There seemed to be nothing she wanted from him but his presence. Buried in her hands she had little need of his. When the volume of her grief diminished, Troy got up quietly, found the kitchen, found her tea ration and a kettle, and made tea. The kettle boiled so slowly on the pathetic jets of gas that idleness poked him into curiosity and he wandered out of the kitchen to open whatever door came next.

It was her bedroom. A rough palliasse upon the floor, an orange box next to the bed, a candle in a tin holder, and a battered enamel cup on the shelf beneath. Splayed upon the bare boards of the floor, a large, cream-coloured French paperback with torn, feathery edges—Editions Gallimard: *Memoires par Hector Berlioz*. Only the choice of book was different.

When he carried the tea tray back to the sitting room, the black shoes had been kicked off, the legs were tucked up beneath her and her head was resting on one outstretched arm, and she was silent.

Troy put the cup where she could reach it, and when he spoke she made no response. He knelt and looked in her face—her eyes were closed and she was asleep. As he stood, he noticed for the first time, on the outstretched left arm, just beyond the spread of her bleached hair, bold and blue upon the pale skin, a five figure tattoo ending 757 . . .

He took out a calling card, identical to the one he had given Jordan Younghusband: Scotland Yard on one side, his address in Goodwin's Court on the reverse, and lodged it in the saucer. She'd find it later, next to a cold cup of tea. He made as little noise as possible leaving. He wasn't sure why she had asked him in, she had no need of him—what she needed, he told himself, was sleep.

'Odd,' he thought, descending the stairs, 'Most odd, but there wasn't a single mirror in the whole apartment. She must put her make-up on by a sort of braille.'

§127

Jack spent more time rubbing shoulders in Scotland Yard than Troy did or could. Jack had not offended quite so many people, Special Branch still spoke to him, and at the rank of sergeant he could take tea in the canteen without reducing the other tables to silence or whispers. Troy had no idea how long this would last but as long as it did, Jack would surely drop in, as he had now, with tidbits of Yard gossip, whether Troy wanted to hear it or not.

"I just had a cuppa with two blokes from the Branch. They spent the morning at Leconfield House."

Troy had been scribbling notes, had not even bothered to look up as Jack swanned in and plonked himself down. He stopped.

"Okay. I won't pretend you don't have my attention."

"Szabo."

"The spy?"

"Is there another? Of course, the spy. Anyway, these blokes heard that Five have put Jim Skardon on the case—"

Troy had never met Skardon—he doubted Jack had either—but he was known as the Secret Service's best interrogator.

"—and he's got Szabo owning up nicely. But when Skardon referred to him as a 'spy' he protested. Told Skardon he was a British citizen and hence a traitor not a spy. Of course, the Branch think this is hilarious. Then Szabo tops it all. Skardon asks about the information Szabo passed to the Russians and he replies, 'I cannot tell you. You don't have clearance at that level.' Imagine. The sheer bloody cheek of it."

Troy went back to his notes.

"You know Jack—loyalty is a distorting mirror. Depends entirely on the angle you're at. Szabo may well be quite serious. His loyalty to Russia somehow coexisting with his loyalty, nay gratitude, to Britain. Proud to be British even as he sells us up the Swannee. Nothing would surprise me. Did you know Napoleon applied for asylum here after Waterloo?"

"You're kidding?"

§128

Out of nothing more than idleness of interest, Troy relayed Jack's gossip to Rod. Rod rattled off the standard line that Troy had predicted about the "embarrassment to the government," "the Americans will never trust us again," and "looking like complete clowns on the world stage."

And then he said, "You know, I narrowly missed meeting Szabo in nineteen forty."

"How was that?" said Troy.

"When I got to the Isle of Man, they'd just shipped out a lot of internees . . . Australia, Canada . . . Szabo was one of the ones sent to Canada. One of the lucky ones. The boat bound for Australia got torpedoed. He shared a room with Arthur Kornfeld. I think they kept in touch for ages after—then Arthur quit physics. I think they drifted a little after that. Surprising really. Those sort of bonds last forever."

There was a pause. Troy could not have said how long. Rod, hands in pockets, head down, kicking idly at a ball of paper he'd thrown down some time before.

Then he said, "Of course, I shared a room with Viktor."

There were tears welling in the corners of his eyes. And Troy realized he did not grasp the depth of his brother's grief, and that behind Rod's assertion that he knew of no reason why Viktor had killed himself was a crippling desire to know—to have a motive, any motive, rather than none at all.

He said, "Rod, you've done the public bit—it was a terrific speech at the funeral—perhaps it's time to do the private bit. Get all your old pals together. Have a wake for Viktor."

§129

Troy would have preferred it otherwise but it was inevitable. Rod invited him to the wake.

He arrived late, deliberately to let them be the group they were without Rod's absurd social inclusiveness fracturing the boundaries for them, to find, yet again, inevitably, it was an all-bloke do. Cid had retreated, somewhere, and there was a spare place at the table for him between Joe Hummel and Arthur Kornfeld.

He had not arrived late enough. Rod was on his feet, coaxing them all into paying tribute to Viktor. Troy would have raised a glass, toasted the name of Viktor Rosen, and then left them all to reminisce as they saw fit and as the memories seeped to the surface. Not Rod. Rod was the sort of arse who'd call an informal meal to crippling formal order with a teaspoon against the side of a glass making a sound like goat bells in the distance.

Nothing, it seemed, would induce Joe Hummel to speak. Joe was quite capable of it on a topic of philosophy or politics, but not once had Troy heard him utter a statement on an emotional matter. Oskar Siebert, ever the one-man awkward squad, contented himself and his listeners with a raised glass and 'a mensh'; Billy Jacks was terse but pointed with, "the bugger gimme a hard time, but I needed a kick in the pants and I needed an education—Viktor was part of that, part of me learning to look outward and not up me own jacksey"; and it was up to Lou Spinetti to say something that amounted to a paragraph.

"It was about two years ago. I'd fallen out with the boss at Quaglino's and he'd said summink like "scarcity o' sugar these days, who can be bothered with a bleedin' pastry cook?" . . . I must have told Viktor because next thing I know he's booked a table at the restaurant and brought along a dozen of his mates. You'll remember this Rod, as you was one of 'em. Waiter asks for starters, or as we posh put it *primi piatti,* and Viktor says, "Signor Spinetti's pudding for all"—and what's more he says it in Italian, *"Dolci di Signor Spinetti per tutti"* . . . so there's a bit of an argy-bargy but he gets his way. Waiter comes back for the main course— *"Dolci di Signor Spinetti per tutti."* And when it comes to dessert, *"Dolci di Signor Spinetti per tutti."* After that they didn't dare take puddings off the menu, nor me off the job, an' Rod . . . your waistline ain't been the same since."

Rod's eyes roamed the table and came to rest on Troy—but Troy was prepared for this.

"Viktor Rosen was a complex man, but I know that at the heart of him there was a bedrock of simplicity, of simple tastes and simple needs. Viktor knew how low a man could sink, and he never let the riches he acquired, the luxury in which he could live, become a mask to hide that depth and that simplicity."

Troy knew this might baffle them. It would undoubtedly set everyone but Rod thinking, but he'd said as much as he could. Viktor's room was a private matter. It died with him. Of course he had hidden it— he'd hidden the tin cup and the palliasse from everyone but himself and Méret Voytek—but that was as it should be.

He sat down to murmurs of puzzled assent. Arthur Kornfeld topped up his glass and whispered, "Me next."

"I think my abiding memory, though not my fondest, is a recent one. This spring I accompanied Viktor to the Studio One cinema in Oxford Street to see the Walt Disney film *Fantasia*. After ten minutes of this technicolor rubbish, I whispered 'why are we here?' and he said, 'because it's shit, but it is shit about which everyone will ask me for an opinion, so I have to be able to say it's shit, and to do that we have to sit through shit.' We suffered Tchaikovsky and *The Rite of Spring* as we might witness a massacre, we giggled guiltily over Mickey Mouse as *The Sorcerer's Apprentice* and at the mishmash of Schubert and Mussorgsky, and we left to sotto voce muttering from Viktor, '*Scheiss, scheiss, scheiss*.' I have always been the devil's advocate, and pleaded the cause of the film one last time as we rode the tram back to Chelsea. 'Think that it might introduce children to classical music.' And he replied, 'It will lead them to think it is easy. Nothing worthwhile in life is easy.' That was Viktor Rosen."

Rod insisted on telling them what they all knew—the tale of their rounding up by the British in 1940 . . . how most of them had met in the railway carriage whisking them to an unknown destination, how this had proved too much for some, how a man had leapt to his death under a railway train on Derby station . . . how, in the wake of this and other tragedies, they had become the ad hoc family . . . the *Stinking Jews,* a title bestowed upon them by a fascist that none, not even the very English Rod, the very Italian Spinetti, the lapsed Lutheran Kornfeld, and the cynical, atheistic Viennese Siebert had ever thought to shrug off. It occurred to Troy that it was a suicide that had these men gathered here, and a suicide that had brought them together in the first place. It was a disturbing symmetry. But he was pleased with the tale. It bore repetition. It was worth the telling. If there was one thing the war had given them it was this bond, something Troy could only imagine.

"And I think what I relished most about Viktor were the inherent contrasts in him, because they amounted to a combination of the high seriousness that one would expect in anyone who'd achieved what he had, and an ability to take the mickey out of himself. I once heard him lament that a pianist I shall not name had rushed through the wonderful first movement of Mozart's twelfth piano sonata—a piece Viktor always played with a languorous, almost lazy relish. 'Is he late for something?' he said to me. 'You would think the man had a train to catch.' The following night, with a bit too much to drink inside him, he decided to see how quickly he could play the last movement of the eleventh sonata, the "*Alla Turca*"—a piece every schoolboy knows so well it's all but corny—and he wrapped it up in well under three minutes. It became his party piece when pissed. I believe my little brother once timed him at one minute fifty-five—and when fed up with audiences who demanded encore after encore, that was what he'd give them, two minutes of rushing to catch a train—he'd even look at his watch while he did it! And he looked for all the world less like the greatest pianist of his time than an outsize Chico Marx."

Arriving late left Troy sober, while almost everyone else was half-pissed by the time the pudding was served. Lemon meringue pie was a shocking dish to serve to half a dozen palates starved into hypersensitivity by eight long years of deprivation.

"Where did you get the lemons?"

Rod said, "Chap on the Foreign Affairs Committee went on a junket to Portugal. Portugal, though I'm sure you lot haven't a clue, is our oldest ally ever, since the Treaty of Windsor in fourteen something or other . . . and being our oldest ally they showered him with gifts, including a crate of lemons."

"But . . . but . . . the eggs?"

"My mother, ever the practical one, has kept chickens as long as I can remember."

"The sugar?"

"I saved my rations, you dozy buggers!"

It was more than a little like being at a children's party, like being at one of those controlled but indulgent sugar feasts that Laura Narayan's parents had invited him to so long ago. Looking at Arthur Kornfeld, Troy thought the man might die of ecstasy. He didn't, but when he turned to converse with Troy it was death that was on his mind.

"Am I right, you are the investigating officer in the matter of Viktor's death?"

Troy just nodded.

"And, of course, it was suicide? Forgive me asking but I would not have said Viktor was the type. Indeed, is there a type?"

Troy replied, "In his roundabout way, Rod has just told us that we didn't really know Viktor. You may find echoes of that in what Lou and I both said. You're asking me, 'Is there a type to commit suicide?' I don't know. It may be that we are all capable of it. I deal in murder—all I can tell you is there is a type to murder and we are not all capable of it. We are not all capable of killing, per se."

"Well," said Kornfeld. "If, as you say, there is a type to kill, I can say without doubt that Viktor wasn't that type."

Troy had known Viktor Rosen as well as Kornfeld had. He could not say one way or the other whether Viktor could kill, it was scarcely a question that mattered. But he had one that did.

He said to Kornfeld, "Rod tells me you knew Karel Szabo?"

"Yes. I knew Karel. I knew him before he was interned by the British, I knew him as he was interned by the British, and I knew him when he returned to England to work for the British. In fact, he told me the moment he became British. And now I wonder if I knew him at all."

Without naming any sources, Troy gave him the gist of the Skardon story, of Szabo splitting hairs over "spy" and "treason."

"Ah . . . that I can understand. It is a willingness to own up to the greater of the two sins, is it not? But I can take an educated guess at why he sinned at all. I think Karel really does have loyalty to Britain, and I suspect he feels the sin of his treason acutely—but he has a greater loyalty elsewhere and that is not to the Soviet Union. No, Karel would say his loyalty was to mankind. I'm reading between the lines, the lines of more conversations than I can count, but he would say that for one power to possess the atom bomb was fatal to the species. It was fairly common around nineteen thirty-nine or nineteen forty to listen to a physicist elaborate on the science of nuclear fission, only to end with either a caveat on its use as a weapon or a touching hope that something so terrible would be the ultimate weapon and, as such, put an end to war. No one would dare use it. Otto Frisch, Leo Szilard, more colleagues than I could count . . . they all uttered or published statements like that. And I gather such arguments went on in Germany as well as in the U.S.A. and here. Karel . . . and remember I saw nothing of him between nineteen forty and nineteen forty-six, and by then we knew exactly what an atom bomb could do to a city . . . Karel came to the conclusion that any imbalance of power would sooner or later lead to the use of the damn thing. If two powers have the secret . . . then there would be, and I invent a phrase for him here, a balance of power."

"Or a balance of terror?"

"Quite, as you Troys are wont to say. But Karel was one of those physicists the Americans sent out to Japan after the surrender in forty-five. He saw the terror. He saw the bomb tested in New Mexico, and then he saw what an identical bomb had done to Nagasaki. And it left him scarred.

"He felt he knew America, though I doubt that he did—what had he seen? The inside of a couple of universities, a city in Tennessee so secret it wasn't even on the map, and the desert around Los Alamos—and he said to me only a year or so ago that a world in which the United States took on the role of world policeman was an inherently unsafe world. It is America he has betrayed far more than he has betrayed Britain. Now, tell me, Inspector Troy . . . will you people hang him for this?"

Rod summoned them to the drawing room for coffee, to more cries of, "where did you get it?" Rather than listen to any tale of an MP just back from a junket to Brazil, Troy wandered downstairs in search of his sister-in-law. He found her in the study, her three youngest children ranged on floor, cushions, and a chaise longue, posing while Laura Narayan painted them.

"How goes it?"

Troy turned to see Cid on the far side of the room. Laura turned at the sound of her voice, brush in hand, and smiled at him without speaking.

"I'm dodging awkward questions," he said.

"And Alex is dodging being painted," said Cid. "But he won't get away with it. Now, are the boys happy up there?"

"I think so. But I also think that this might be the beginning of the end. The first death is inevitably the first rift."

"Oh, bum. These do's mean so much to Rod. It's a life before parliament, a life outside parliament. He'd be devastated if they didn't meet once in a while. Most blokes his age have their battalion or their squadron reunions. So does Rod, he goes to them and sometimes they all come here. But it doesn't matter to him in the way this does. Rod has the blokes upstairs. While he has them he has the best of his war, his 'good war.' The Battle of Britain was a skirmish compared to what he thinks he went through with them."

"Look at it this way," Troy said softly to avoid the kids hearing. "Suicide is a stone dropped in a pond. The ripples are little short of infinite. There is nothing, and I have no better word than this, there is nothing *natural* about suicide . . . you don't need to be religious, you don't need to be Hamlet to recognize the canon 'gainst self-slaughter. It is a more disturbing death than murder. It can destroy a society beyond any healing."

"I sort of see what you mean and I sort of don't."

"Well, let's deal with Rod—the only mind we can read after all . . . I don't know what makes Billy or Lou tick and I doubt even the Almighty has a handle on Joe . . . but Rod is dogged by Viktor's death. Rod is asking why. And he may never get an answer."

§ 130

The telephone was ringing.

"Troy? Is Voytek."

Well . . . he had given her his card.

"Do you wish to walk out with me on Saturday night?"

It was such an old-world turn of phrase he could not be certain what she had in mind.

"Er . . . yes . . . why not?"

"I have two tickets for a music evening at Hampstead Library. They send them to Viktor ages ago, and Viktor give them to me."

"Great. What time?"

"Seven thirty. I see you there."

Hampstead Library held bad memories. In 1940 he had been a reluctant member of a team of coppers tasked with rounding up enemy aliens—people like Viktor Rosen. It left a bad taste in the mouth, doubly so since the chief inspector in charge had thumped Troy in the jaw for his disobedience that day.

He brushed the memory aside. Contemplated the banner hung above the door.

```
The Indian Music Circle
          presents
      Jaya Deva—Sitar
     Rajan Angadi—Tabla
```

He'd no idea what a sitar was. Nor a tabla. Indeed, he'd no idea Hampstead had an Indian Music Circle.

Voytek appeared at his side.

"I'm baffled," he said.

"Listen and learn," she said.

Inside, a fat woman wrapped in an Indian sari greeted them in the plummy tones of the English upper classes. It was Laura Narayan. Laura Narayan in a sari, with a red spot painted just above the bridge of her nose.

"Oh, you should have told me you were coming!" she said to Troy. "And Miss Voytek. I loved your recital at the Wigmore in '46. Simply wonderful."

They were shown to seats at the front. Troy hated seats at the front if the object of the evening was unknown—made it all the harder to sneak out.

"What's a sitar?" he whispered.

"Traditional stringed instrument. Not sure how many strings. Some fingered, some just drones. And to save you asking, a tabla is a drum."

§131

He wasn't at all sure he'd ever get used to music such as he'd just heard, and as he and Voytek walked back to his car he broke her contemplative silence and uttered an enquiring, "Well?"

"Give it time," she replied. "I've never heard a sound like it. It is . . . unique . . . it has qualities you could never get from a western stringed instrument. We have nothing that uses drones—only bagpipes do that—and it adds something, a bedrock to the music, a core of . . . of humming . . . that's not the right word . . . I cannot think of the right word in English."

"But will it ever catch on?"

"What do you want, Troy? Predictions? All right—here's a prediction. In ten or twenty years time it could be all the rage."

Troy unlocked the car.

"I'll drive you home," he said.

Seated next to him as they drove down the Finchley Road, she said, "I needed to get out. I needed to get Viktor out of my thoughts, if only for an hour. If I stay at home I think of Viktor. And if I think of Viktor I find only questions without answers."

Troy said, "I keep getting asked if Viktor was the type."

"The type of what?"

"The type to kill himself."

She was silent as far as Baker Street, as though working out the precise use of English in her head.

Then she said, "In Auschwitz I would hear of suicides, though there were fewer than you might imagine. A shot in the night usually meant someone had tried to reach the wire, and that was tantamount to suicide. I saw several women hurl themselves against the electrified wires, I saw their bodies in the distance, strung out like scarecrows until the Germans ordered them taken down. And I saw two suicides close up, in that they were women I knew, women who, against the odds, in a world without knives or razor blades had contrived to kill themselves . . . by hanging. I helped cut them down and remove the bodies from the hut in which I lived. We took suicide as a fact of life. We did not need to enquire about motives or types. However many or few of us did commit suicide, any one of us could have. That is what places like that did— they redefined what was normal."

Troy said, "But you survived. Viktor survived. He survived . . . everything."

From the tone of her voice Troy thought he might be being ignored. He wasn't. The flat constancy of her delivery belied her subject.

"In Paris, after the war, I met, quite by chance, a 'survivor.' A Frenchman. A man who had been very good to me. Georges Pasdeloup. One night he followed me to a café. I had not asked for his company. Indeed, I had grown tired of it. Tired of being another 'survivor.' I wanted people with whom the bond was other—I wanted no part of a society of survivors. In the café, he produced a gun, put the barrel to his chin, and blew off the top of his head. I have no idea whether Georges was the 'type'—given what he had been through it could not possibly have surprised me—it merely shocked me."

"Merely?"

"Yes. Death retains the power to shock long after it has lost the power to surprise. If we knew what it was Viktor had survived, rather than simply being able to say that he had survived, then we, too, might fail to be surprised . . . we would not be asking pointlessly if he was the 'type' . . . we would merely be shocked. As I was and you surely were."

Troy said, "And you weren't surprised by Viktor's suicide?"

"No, Mr. Troy, I was not."

They had reached the corner of Dilke Street and Clover Mews. Evening had cooled into night.

"Come, Troy. Make tea once more and I shall play for you. I shall blow away the sitar and tabla that clearly did so little for you."

She lit a wood fire in the iron stove while Troy boiled the kettle. As he set a cup of tea—black in the European fashion as she had requested—in front of her, she said, "You pick."

"What if I pick something you don't know?"

"Try me."

"I have two recordings of the Bach suites. Pablo Casals's . . . and yours."

"Aha . . . which of the six."

"The third I think."

"Pick a movement. Something long enough for my tea to cool, short enough for it not to go stone cold."

"This sounds like Viktor choosing an encore . . . 'how quickly can I get off the stage' . . ."

"Just pick."

"Sixth movement, the . . . er . . ."

"It's a gigue, Troy."

She took up her cello and played the piece from memory. Her touch was lighter than Casals—when he played Troy could hear darkness, could almost hear the strings bang on the neck—not that Casals was undancelike, but he felt that she gave it more the feeling of a dance, as the word "gigue" implied.

She came back to the fire, picked up her tea.

"I used to play that for the commandant of Auschwitz."

Troy must have looked surprised, as she said, "Don't be surprised. It was in my repertoire long before I met him. I first played it for Viktor when I was a child. Auschwitz killed my taste for bells. Auschwitz killed my taste for "*Kraut und Rüben.*" And I find I have no fondness left for lice or scabies either. But nothing could kill my taste for Bach."

§132

The weather turned at the end of the month. A wet Friday evening Troy was content to spend alone. Content but not happy. He had books—indeed he had started the new Graham Greene, Rod had given it to him, the one about some chap in Africa called Scobie who kills himself; and he had the new Somerset Maugham, Rod had given him that, too; and he had an oddity by some Russian bloke who wrote in English, whose name Troy had not grasped and whose book (*The Real Life of Sebastian Knight,* about which Rod was enthusing madly . . . "it's these two brothers who don't really understand one another") he had lost down the back of the sofa— but he felt like reading nothing, and certainly nothing about a suicide. It was an effort to let himself be drawn into a world of another's making. He had music aplenty. Tatum, Ellington, Goodman . . . but no record lasted much longer than four minutes and if he was feeling relaxed or lazy it was a pain in the arse to get up and turn the record over. He had heard talk of a new format that used an unbreakable plastic as its base and, as it played at 33⅓ rather than 78 rpm, could fit half a dozen songs to a side or a whole symphony over two sides. It might be real, but it smacked to him of those dire exhibitions at which improbable futuristic gadgets—the nostick frying pan, the telephone answering machine—were displayed as part of a future that seemed to be forever in retreat.

Now he was listening to Dizzy Gillespie and Charlie Christian. He had flipped three 78s and felt that at the end of this one he could just let the needle spin in the groove until the clockwork motor wound down.

He had, he had always told himself, a great capacity for being alone. Why then had he found himself contemplating his single life with a cup of tea and Dizzy on a night when he could be out roister-doistering, as he was almost certain Jack was? When they were younger, not long after they had met in the middle of the war, Jack had tried to take Troy with him on double dates but had soon recognized Troy's innate uselessness at what Anna called "sociosexual chitchat," but Jack neatly reduced to two syllables as "pulling." He had turned thirty-three at the end of August. No great age. A bit biblical in its significance—an age at which, as Dizzy might say, you "get it together, man." Thirty-three and single. Rod had been married . . . he had to think now . . . at twenty-six . . . by thirty-three he had three children. Troy had not even come close to marriage. There had been no significant relationship in his life until 1939—a trip to Monte Carlo with his father just after the outbreak of war, whisked into bed by Zette Borg. With hindsight he had merely glanced off Zette, she had flicked him away with such ease, no more than a fly upon a rhino's arse. Zette had gone to the United States in 1940 at the height of the Blitz. Years later he thought to ask Kornfeld if he had ever heard of her, as they worked in the same obscure nook of subatomic physics. "I suppose there's no way you would know," Arthur had replied. "But she worked on the Manhattan Project at Los Alamos, with Oppenheimer. She is the fairy godmother of the atom bomb." The Zette of Troy's memory would have pushed the button in person. And it now occurred to him that to the name of Oppenheimer they could add that of Karel Szabo.

Then there had been WPS Kitty Stilton, who had dumped him for two-timing her with Zette, reappeared a few months later, two-timed him with an American army officer, and gone back to the States with him as what Troy was pretty certain was the first ever GI bride. He'd read in the *Post* only the other day that her husband was running for the senate. Which fact pretty well guaranteed they'd never meet again.

In 1944, at the height of the Little Blitz, he had fallen for a Wac, Sergeant Larissa Tosca. He had two-timed Tosca with the biggest mistake of his life—an affair with a witness in a murder case, Lady Diana Brack.

The mistake being that Brack had turned out to be the culprit, not a witness, and in the unravelling mess she had shot him and he her. She had died, Troy had lived with her ghost ever since. Tosca had vanished, presumed dead—and somewhere in the deeper recesses of the unconscious mind Troy did not believe this.

The knocking at the door was too solid to be ghostly; it cut through the last blast from Dizzy and it saved him from the oppressive weight of the recognition of his own deceit.

A short, stout man in a fawn mackintosh and a homburg hat stood dripping on his doorstep. Kolankiewicz.

"Aach!"

Troy took the needle from the groove and said, "I'll put the kettle on."

"No," said Kolankiewicz. "It is a night for booze. Do you still have Polish vodka?"

Troy kept a bottle just for him under the sink—110 proof and, as far as Troy was concerned, undrinkable—along with odd bottles of claret from the wine cellar that he and Rod had inherited from their father (rationing was meaningless when you'd inherited a cellarful of booze), and the 90 proof Russian vodka he kept for his Uncle Nikolai, and the cheap, blended scotch he kept for Onions.

Kolankiewicz had hung up his mac and hat, left his shoes to drip upon the doormat, plonked himself upon the chaise longue. He looked uncomfortable. Troy stuck the bottle and a shot glass in front of him, left him to pour as much as he wanted and settled himself back down. From the look on Kolankiewicz's face this probably wasn't a purely social call.

"I fucked up," Kolankiewicz said.

Troy said nothing.

"You phoned me, when was it now? I forget. Seems like weeks."

It was weeks. Troy had not seen or talked to Kolankiewicz in more than a fortnight.

"We agreed that there was no evidence that pointed to murder in the matter of Viktor Rosen. You asked me to release the body for cremation, you told the coroner you would be presenting no evidence to contradict a verdict of suicide, and because I was rushed off my feet, I fucked up."

"Unlike you," Troy said, trying to ease him into the facts and out of self-recrimination.

303

"Then . . . Tom Henrey asked me to go up to Lincolnshire . . . the matter of the 'Lincolnshire Poacher' as the papers have dubbed him . . . One murder in the woods, a very battered body, followed by another, and after the second Tom sends for me . . ."

Tom Henrey was Troy's immediate superior on the Murder Squad—detective chief inspector. He was one of those vague, upper-crust, ineffectual Englishmen who Troy found he could tolerate without actually liking. His saving grace was that he was either too dim or too polite to notice or comment on the number of times Onions gave the tricky cases to Troy and that there existed a short circuit in the chain of command between Troy and Onions that cut him out.

"I go up to Lincoln, and I do the postmortem on the second corpse, and I tell Tom I will stay for the third. Tom says 'what third?' I say, 'he'll do it again, trust me.' And sure enough, thirty-two hours later another body turns up and I do another postmortem on a battered body, only this one was battered after death, not to death, and I upset all Tom's theories by telling him the victim was poisoned. So now Tom is looking for two killers not one and I sneak back to London and leave him to it. And when I get back I find one of my assistants—the skinny bloke with the prominent mole—has exercised his usual house-proud talents and tidied me up. Believe it or not there is now a cupboard in the corridor outside my office labelled 'Troy'—and inside it is all the evidence and all the junk that for one reason or another I have never returned to you. Cupboard? No. A mausoleum for my sins."

Kolankiewicz knocked back his first shot of vodka, poured another to stand until the need arose and opened up his Gladstone bag, from which he produced an enamel mug.

Troy did not have to think about it.

"Rosen," he said.

"Rosen. I took it away to compare prints. I was all but certain they were his and they are. But, you will recall, the bedroom, the boudoir as it struck me, had been wiped completely. And I became curious as to where he kept his personal possessions . . . his clothes . . . his shaving brush."

Kolankiewicz set a shaving brush next to the mug.

"Badger-hair from Truefitt and Hill. This was in the nearest bathroom to his bedroom. It and the matching razor were the only items with prints. Both his. Then, in the long corridor at the back, I discovered two walk-in closets, disguised in trompe l'oeil like the door from the main room to the lobby to look like part of the wall. Hats from Locks. Shoes from Lobbs. It seems that he had a smattering of everything St James' Street could offer the adoptive English gent."

"It was his favourite street. Rod tells me he could get lyrical about things English. Adored the view from Primrose Hill. Euphoric about Norman churches. I never heard it myself."

"And . . . I went through his coat pockets, and in the inside pocket of a Crombie winter overcoat I found this."

Kolankiewicz set a leather and silver hip flask next to the mug and the shaving brush.

"I had meant to dust all these items. Then the urgency evaporated from the case, then I got dragged down to Lincoln . . . so it was only this afternoon when I returned to Hendon and found this new model order awaiting me . . . a cupboard with your name upon it . . . that I tested them. It is the perfectionist in me . . . sometimes I do not understand him. I call the skinny bloke with the mole every obscenity in two languages for messing with my stuff . . . but then I cannot just let it lie. I have to dust the flask. Mappin Brothers, Regent Street, prewar. Probably pre the other war. Crocodile and silver. The crocodile is not so retentive. The silver has held fingerprints very clearly. It has Viktor Rosen's right hand upon it, and also the right hand of another individual. These are the only fingerprints I have found anywhere in that apartment that do not belong to Viktor Rosen. And they belong to André Skolnik."

It was as though a bomb had exploded in the room—a blinding light and a roaring silence, and with them possibilities that whilst not infinite folded in upon themselves with a dazzling complexity.

Kolankiewicz knocked back his second shot.

Troy went into the kitchen and returned with a glass.

"I think I'm beginning to realize why you buggers drink this."

§133

"I think we have to go over it all again," Kolankiewicz was saying. "We have to reconsider."

Troy was shaking his head at this.

"No," he said. "Viktor killed himself. I have no doubts about it."

"All that from a dusting of his piano?"

"I found the last person to play that piano. His mistress. Méret Voytek. I rather think she interrupted Viktor in his preparations for death. He had in all probability wiped down most of the apartment. She turned up unexpectedly. He saw the opportunity for one last request and she played the piano for him. As soon as she left, he wiped the keys and did the deed with the sound of her playing still ringing in his ears. Your nose for woman did not deceive you."

"And?"

"The wiping of the fingerprints was Viktor's way of protecting her, protecting her reputation."

"Why so fussy? When you have it in mind to kill yourself, why think of anything else? Who would give a shit about the living?"

It seemed to Troy to be yet another strand in a conversation half the world wanted to have with him. Why did he do it? Was he the type to do it? And it was so far off the mark.

"How many suicide notes have you and I read over the years? Think of the things they wrote about that still bothererd them, things that they still had to act upon only moments before death. The tying up of a life-time of loose ends. Neither you nor I will know what passes through the mind of a dying man until it's too late. It has its own logic, and in this case he was protecting the person he cared most about."

"And Skolnik?"

"Well, he certainly wasn't protecting Skolnik. I'd bet you a penny to a quid Skolnik never set foot in that apartment. A hip flask is the kind of thing you pass around outdoors. The fact that you found it inside Viktor's overcoat surely confirms that?"

This gave Kolankiewicz pause for thought. What he said next gave Troy pause for thought.

"And has the opposite occurred to you?"

The idea took shape even as he spoke.

"It's occurring to me now," Troy said.

"That Viktor Rosen might have killed Skolnik?"

"Yes."

"Was he the type?"

The same, unending conversation again. The type to kill. The type to die—well, we were all that. And the certainties of Arthur Kornfeld flashed through his mind, "I can say without doubt that Viktor wasn't that type."

Troy could not say that. Troy said nothing.

Kolankiewicz pressed on, "And this mistress . . . ?"

"Méret Voytek."

"Is it possible she knows about Skolnik?"

"Dunno," said Troy. "I'll ask her."

§134

He thought of it as the return bout. She had taken him to hear the sitar— for all her advocacy he thought it had pleased neither of them—he would take her to hear the jazz saxophone . . . the jazz saxophone as played by Ronnie Scott (tenor) and John Dankworth (alto) at Club 11.

He was not at all sure whether the club was a place or an idea. It was a moveable feast, but had premises quite close to Piccadilly Circus in Great Windmill Street—which now found itself home to England's only nude revue, at the Windmill Theatre, and only bebop-based jazz club, at Club 11, certainly the only jazz club to be run by the musicians themselves. He'd been once or twice to the Wednesday night sessions and found they could be sparsely attended. The Saturday he took Voytek the place was packed.

"Bebop?" she said. "Is nonsense word,"

"Possibly," said Troy.

"Is new?"

"Ish," said Troy. "I'd say it's been around in bits and pieces for close on ten years, but we couldn't hear it. Swing smothered everything. After all, people wanted to dance not just the night away, but the war away. After the war the bits and pieces seemed to come together."

"And swing is dance music? Swing is Fred and Ginger?"

He was slightly surprised that she knew this.

"Among others . . . and it tended to favor the big bands—Dorsey, Goodman . . . and their English equivalents . . . except that there is no equivalence . . . such as Roy Fox and Lew Stone. Most of whom had a singer fronting them, if only intermittently. Helen Forrest, Peggy Lee, Al Bowlly, Elsie Carlisle. Bebop is bands or groups, not orchestras. Sextets, octets, sometimes as small as quartets. And I've never heard one yet with a singer."

"And what is different about it?"

He didn't know. Well he did. Sort of. He could hear it. Anyone could hear it. What he didn't have was the technical vocabulary to explain it. How to say anything about a tune like "Salt Peanuts" without sounding ridiculous? He would be lost talking about diminished this ascending that. It was a style led by sax and trumpet, by men like Charlie Parker and Miles Davis, but the root differences were in the rhythm section, at bass and drums where bassists like Charlie Mingus and drummers like Kenny Clarke and Max Roach led from the rear.

"Why don't we just listen?" he said.

The John Dankworth Quartet took to the stage. Dankworth seeming impossibly young, impossibly slim, all but swaddled in what looked to be an army demob suit topped out with a splash of colour in the shape of a wide, florid tie.

Bebop could be frantic. Particularly in the hands of a musical anarchist like Dizzy Gillespie. Troy feared there might be no tune to recognize and that Voytek would be alienated and he would find himself forced into explanations or, worse, apologies. But Dankworth played like a mellow dream—American standards laid back to the edge of the horizon, music that rolled out to the skyline . . . "Lover Man," "Body and Soul." And it was clear to Troy, watching her out of the corner of one eye, that she was rolling with it, closing her eyes and swaying almost imperceptibly to the mellifluous line of the saxophone.

As they broke for the interval Troy just heard her say "Is beautiful," before the audience volume rose and drowned out anything more she might have uttered.

Out of nowhere a tall, stoutish bloke with a mass of wavy hair appeared and plonked himself down at their table.

"Fancy meeting you here."

"Au contraire," said Troy. "I've never known you to listen to anything but Mozart. You're the last person I'd expect to find in a jazz club."

"Yes. Me, too. I rather think I've surprised myself. The booze is expensive . . ."

He held up what seemed to be a quintuple scotch in his left hand.

"But the dope's cheap enough."

A reefer held up in his right hand, a quick pull on it and his voice vanished into the back of his throat.

"Are you going to introduce me, old man?"

"Of course," said Troy. "Méret Voytek—Guy Burgess. Guy Burgess —Méret Voytek."

Sober, good manners would have prompted Burgess to stand for a lady. Drunk, stoned, little would prise him up.

"A pleasure," he said to Voytek. "I haven't heard you play, but I live in hope. Have you heard Troy play?"

"No. And I hardly dare to hope."

Troy did not understand the look she gave him, nor the one that passed between her and Burgess.

There were three Burgesses at least: there was Guy sober, a diminishing phenomenon; Guy pissed; and, Troy had concluded, Guy hamming up being pissed for whatever reason entered his unfathomable mind. Troy often thought the key to Burgess was boredom. He bored more easily than any man he knew. His kitten's curiosity demanded to be fed, and if it wasn't he poked at things, physically, verbally, critically and to find the thing broke from being poked was simply the revelation of its true nature and hence, being pissed, sarcastic, offensive required no apology afterwards.

Jazz saved them. Ronnie Scott's Boptet took to the stage. Troy counted to see how many boppers made a boptet and concluded it was seven, but the jazz mind being what it was it might be eight next week and six the week after. Scott's appearance marked the evening growing old, letting its hair down—no jacket, baggy pants, stripped down to red braces, tie at half-mast, and his collar stud popped. The nature of the evening changed with him—his bebop was more raucous than Dankworth's and he launched into Charlie Parker's "Scrapple From the Apple" fit to lift the roof off the room.

Burgess held out the lit reefer to Troy. Troy shook his head assuming Burgess would just withdraw the offer. Instead the arm extended as he leaned over Troy and Voytek took it in her left hand, put it to her lips, inhaled, and grinned. Troy tried not to see it as a taunt by both of them, a flaunting of illegality in front of an off-duty copper.

In the next break, Troy said, "What are you doing with yourself these days, Guy?"

Whatever Guy might say would be at best an approximation of the truth. The last time they'd met he'd been a foreign-office appointed private secretary to the deputy foreign secretary—whose name escaped him—all of which merely spelt "spook" to Troy. Whatever it was was drowned out by Ronnie Scott saying, "And now the '52nd Street Theme' by Thelonious Monk," and the music beginning again.

"Who?" Troy yelled in Burgess's ear.

"Some monk. I couldn't grasp anything else. Monk, that's all I got."

Leaving, out in the dank, chilly streets of London, Burgess said, "It's hardly late. Only just past midnight. Fancy going on somewhere?"

He was the sort of bloke who'd always say that. It was a favorite phrase of Troy's old pal Charlie, another spook in sheep's clothing, "Are we going on somewhere?" It was pathetic, hollow, bored, and boring. The night was never young enough. At worst, a recipe for propping up the bar in a dismal Soho clip joint and paying over the odds for drinks—the pleasure of the company of other bored, hollow men. At best, they'd end up at the Coconut Grove or the Gargoyle Club. Either way, the night would end in the same shabby manner, with Troy picking a paralytic Burgess off the floor and being politely asked to take him home or impolitely thrown out by bouncers. He prayed she'd say no and she did.

"Thank you. But I am tired and I have to rehearse tomorrow."

Burgess went north and they went west. Troy flagged a cab in Piccadilly and was thinking he'd just put her in and bung the cabbie half a crown when she said, "Take me home, Troy. That's all. Just take me home." And he got in beside her.

It might be the last opportunity, so he asked. "I have another lead on Viktor. Or, rather, something I think might be a lead. Did you know a man by the name of André Skolnik?"

She stared ahead. No particular expression on her face.

"There's something about the name. I cannot help thinking I have heard it before."

This didn't help—Skolnik's name had been in all the London papers and most of the nationals.

"A friend of Viktor's?"

"Possibly."

"Skolnik?"

"Yes."

She thought as far as Hyde Park Corner.

"No. I am certain. I have never met anyone of that name."

At Clover Mews, she said, "Come inside. Just until I fall asleep, that's all. Until I fall asleep."

She tucked her legs up under her in the armchair once more. And from her handbag took a fat, rolled reefer. A flick of a match, Bogart style, against her thumbnail and it was lit and in her mouth.

Troy said, "If I may ask, where did you get that?"

"At the club. In the ladies. A woman was selling them."

"How much?

"Seven and sixpence each. I haggled. Three for a pound. You want?"

"No," said Troy. "I no want."

Reefer begat two types in Troy's experience. Gigglers and sleepers. Burgess was a giggler. A quarter of an hour later Voytek was fast asleep. He took the remains of the reefer from her fingers, stubbed it out on the tiles in front of the hearth, threw a blanket over her, and went home.

It was a pity. He could get to like bebop. In particular, he could get to like the music of this Monk person. But he'd have to be very careful about going to the Club 11 again. It was one thing to be around people who smoked reefer/pot/hay/hemp/maryjane/hashish/tea/weed/ whatever—quite another to be caught in a police raid when the inevitable happened and the plods from Vice stormed in. It was a pity, but it had been nice while it lasted.

He wondered about meeting Burgess. It could be coincidence. It probably *was* coincidence. If they wanted him or Voytek followed they'd have sent someone else, someone Troy would never have noticed, not someone guaranteed to blow it all in the first five minutes. On the other hand, supposing the spooks had sent Burgess . . . it would be typical of Burgess to want to fuck it up by sitting at the same table as Troy. And who was he sent for? Troy or Voytek? None of it seemed plausible. All the spooks knew was what Troy had told them. It was coincidence. It had to be coincidence.

§135

Not long afterwards.

Another night alone with books and the wireless for company.

Leafing through the *Radio Times,* he turned to the BBC's venture into high art, the Third Programme. It had been going a couple of years now. Almost since the end of the war. He doubted anyone would have found time or inclination during the war for a station devoted to classical music and talk so arch it was sleep inducing at best and bloody irritating at worst. Up against Kenneth Horne, Arthur Askey, Tommy Handley, and a bunch of catchphrases that had never struck Troy as remotely funny, it would not have stood a chance. But tonight, at seven thirty p.m., just minutes away, the BBC were doing their bit for Viktor Rosen. God knows, Troy thought, Rosen had done enough for them.

He turned on the set, watched the unfailingly pleasing glow on the Bakelite grill as the valves warmed up, and tuned to the Third.

"We come now to a recording made last winter in the Kleine Zaal of the Concertgebouw in Amsterdam. It's broadcast in memory of Viktor Rosen who died last month, and features Rosen on piano accompanied by Méret Voytek on cello, playing Debussy's Sonata for Cello and Piano in D-minor, op. 58. This piece, together with Debussy's *Suite Bergamesque* for solo piano, comprised the second half of the concert. It was recorded on February fourteenth."

The usual coughs and shufflings followed. A round of applause. The players took the stage. Silence. One recalcitrant cougher. A tweak and a scratch or two of the bow as Voytek tuned a string. Troy dashed to the piano, searched hurriedly among the sheet music littering the top and retrieved the score of the sonata just as Viktor struck the first chord. He'd no idea why he had this particular score—he didn't know any cellists he could play with—he wished he did—but he had and it would be fun to follow the score as they played.

Fun and an education. At the end of the first page, Troy found himself reaching for a pencil and trying to note the variations . . . the ways in which Viktor and Voytek deviated from the "script." It didn't ruin the piece, it was nothing if not subtle, but he could not see/hear what it added. It was as though they were overinterpreting, almost improvising . . . but to what end?

And then he realized what the relationship had been between Viktor Rosen and André Skolnik.

§136

On Monday morning he called the music publisher Boosey & Hawkes, asked for someone who knew about Debussy, and was put through to "our Mr. Mapperley."

"Do you know if there's a variorum edition of the Debussy Cello Sonata? I have your edition from 1922 and, well, . . . it differs."

Mapperley did not ask from what it differed. He said simply, "Variorum?"

"Well, take the Schubert E-flat Trio. There are two different fourth movements for that. Some trios play one, some the other, and some bung in both."

"Ah, I begin to see what you're getting at. And the answer's no. To the best of my knowledge there has only ever been one published version and one manuscript version. Hence, no room to differ. They're identical. No need to 'bung in' anything."

Troy looked up the name of the producer of Saturday's concert in the *Radio Times*—one Anthea Cridlan. He rang her at Broadcasting House.

"Do you still have the recording or has it been wiped?"

"Wiped? Mr. Troy, this is the BBC, we don't wipe recordings!"

"Then I need to hear it again. Can you fit me in at ten?"

"This morning?"

"This morning."

"Is this official Scotland Yard business, Inspector?"

"Yes."

"Then I suppose I'll have to fit you in. It wouldn't have anything to do with Viktor Rosen's death would it?"

But Troy had ten years' experience and endless ways of dodging questions like that.

§137

She was a pint-sized redhead about his own age. She was looking at him intensely through round spectacles rimmed with pink plastic.

He found himself staring.

"You're staring," she said.

"Well," he said lamely. "Pink specs . . ."

"All the better to see you with. And to be precise, Mr. Troy, National Health pink specs."

"The NHS supplies pink specs? What happened to the endless shades of grey we've been hearing about since nineteen forty-five?"

"For children, Mr. Troy, for children. But if the specs fit . . . now, are we going to discuss my false teeth and my truss, too, or are we going to listen to Debussy?"

Troy said nothing. She turned her back, led off and he followed, through corridors measureless to man, down to a sunless office a couple of storeys below ground level—an office stuffed with electrical equipment.

"You're in luck. The Concertgebouw recital was recorded on one of the new Ampexs we bought from the States. Brand spanking new. Amsterdam was its first outing. Thousands of pounds of license payers' money. Fifteen inches per second. Sixty-decibel dynamic range. Fifty-to ten-thousand-kilohertz frequency response. Synchronous motors for minimal wow and flutter."

Troy found himself looking at a large grey box with reels of tape a foot across and more knobs and levers than there were on the dashboard of his car.

"I didn't understand a word of that."

"Nor me. It's what it says in the manual. All I can say for certain is it's a damn sight better than anything else I've ever used. Now, I've set up the Debussy. We'll have to change reels after the sonata. The concert doesn't fit on one tape."

"Oh. How do you manage the broadcast?"

"By having two machines synch-locked to one another just like projectors in a cinema. Or did you think *Gone with the Wind* fitted onto one reel?"

Troy had never seen *Gone with the Wind*. He might be the only person in the country who hadn't, but he'd also never given a second's thought to how any film reached the screen, or how any music reached the airwaves.

He took out his score and his pencil and tried not to look ignorant.

She worked the myriad knobs and levers, clunks and clicks louder than any note Rosen played—Debussy overheard on the factory floor—and he asked her to stop, rewind, and play back when he was certain he'd found a variation. He'd confirmed about a dozen, when she said, "You've missed one."

"I have?"

"A mistake. You're transcribing their mistakes, aren't you?"

Troy would have had no problem lying to her but before he could, she said, "What am I saying? God, I'm such a clot. Viktor Rosen doesn't make mistakes. Walter Gieseking might, but not Viktor Rosen. You're not noting their mistakes . . . you're noting . . ."

"What did you think they were doing? Improvising on Debussy? Poetic licence? It's not jazz."

"I didn't follow the performance with a score. I had my wows and flutters to think about. But . . . I had thought the interpretation a little

315

soft. A little florid . . . and truth to tell, until you forced me to consider the absurdity of it, I had assumed a few mistakes."

"Sharps instead of naturals? A note too far? A chord instead of a single note?"

"I had noticed, yes."

"Who else would have noticed?"

"Dunno . . . I'll tell you that when the letters start arriving from the sad shires. Mr. Troy, I don't know what's going on here, but shall we do it together? I'm probably a damn sight quicker at it than you."

He spread the score out so they could both follow it. It took two and a half hours to pinpoint every change, and when they had finished the sonata, they listened twice to Viktor playing solo the four pieces that made up *Suite Bergamesque*—but found nothing more.

Anthea said, "All duets are, as it were, a dialogue, wouldn't you agree, Mr. Troy? The cello talks to the piano and the piano talks back. We, as the audience, are privy to this, we partake vicariously of the emotion of the music. Savage beast, soothe . . . and all that jazz. In this instance, they are both talking to a third party, through the score and beyond the score, and we are not privy. You think you've found a code, don't you?"

"Yes. And I don't have a clue what it means. Do you?"

She shook her head, worked her specs loose, shoved them back with one finger on the bridge.

"Not the foggiest. This isn't music anymore, this is maths."

As he was packing the score back into his music case, she said, "It's all jolly exciting, but I suppose you're now going to tell me it's a secret aren't you?"

"Yes."

"And when Tone Deaf of Tunbridge Wells writes in to complain?"

"Then, Mr. Rosen was perhaps having an off night. A little too much poetic license. A little too much Armagnac . . . whatever. He can hardly suffer for his reputation now, can he?"

She said what Rod had said, almost word for word.

"And the girl? Mademoiselle Voytek?"

"Quite," said Troy. "You see my problem."

"Is there nothing I can do? This is the most fun thing to come my way since VE night. All been a bit 'back in my box' since then."

"You could stop the BBC from broadcasting the concert again."

They said good-bye on the doorstep of Broadcasting House, beneath Eric Gill's reliefs—a rare example of what Troy always thought of as British Soviet Realism. He had got as far as Great Titchfield Street when she came hurtling after him.

"God, I'm so scatty. I should have thought of this at once. Shostakovich!"

She was hopping from one foot to the other, almost dancing with excitement. Thirty become thirteen once more.

"Shostakovich?"

"Well, you recall he was declared an enemy of the state about ten years ago?"

Loosely, Troy did. Somebody had mentioned this to him at some point. Probably his father.

"He had to scrap a ballet he was working on and come up with something that pleased the commissars."

"His Fifth Symphony."

"Quite. Hardly journeyman stuff, is it? I rather think it's his masterpiece . . . anyway . . . he sticks his tongue in his cheek, if not actually straight out at the thought police . . . he works in D, E-flat, C, B as a motif . . . and, of course, if you know the Russian alphabet . . . you could read it as . . ."

"D, D+, S, V . . . Dimitri Dimitri+yevich ShostakoVich. Although SH is a single letter in Russian. Дмитрии Дмитриевич Шостакович"

"Quite. Does this help?"

Troy told her that it did, but he knew damn well that Viktor and Voytek were far from sticking their tongues out at the thought police, or from signalling themselves quite so obviously. At most, they might have got the idea from Shostakovich's prank—but this wasn't a prank. She had been right the first time. It was mathematics—now he needed a mathematician.

§138

He called Anna.

"Ages ago, towards the end of forty-four, I'd been shot, I was recovering out at Mimram. You came to see me and you chatted about your family. Angus . . . your parents . . . and a cousin who did something very hush-hush out in Bletchley Park that's still very hush-hush."

"You mean Jimmy. Yes . . . he was a codebreaker. And if what they did out there is still hush-hush they've forgotten to tell him. I think he's physically incapable of keeping a secret."

"What became of him?"

"Oh, he's back in civvy street. Downing College, Cambridge. He has a chair in maths. Why do you ask?"

"Do you think he'd invite us to tea on Saturday?"

"If I so much as hint, he'll invite us for the whole weekend. Apart from your brother I'd say he's the most gregarious man I've ever met. The donkey's arse isn't safe once he starts nattering, let alone the hind legs. I'll call him, but take it as read he'd love to see us. And it'll kill two birds with one stone."

"Eh?"

"You've forgotten your mother's car? It's still parked outside my house. In fact, I've rather gotten used to it. It has *oomph*. You were quite right—I don't know what V12 means, but I got it up to a hundred and two on the way back from Devon."

"You're not buying petrol on the black market, are you?"

"What is this, a copper's naïveté? Troy, everybody buys dodgy petrol! The war didn't do it to us, some sort of patriotism just about sufficed, but the peace has turned us into a nation of petty fiddlers. The doorman at a hotel has hooky clothing coupons, the barrow boy down the market has condemned pork under the counter . . . I would imagine if you were to bump into Queen Mary at a palace do, she'd offer to sell you nylons!"

§139

Troy had never liked driving. He would far rather somebody else did it. An initial surge of terror as Anna behaved like Malcolm Campbell going for another world record soon subsided and as she settled into a ninety-mile-per-hour cruise up the Great North Road to Cambridge, he nodded off.

When he woke, the car had stopped and he found himself in the driveway of a Victorian rectory.

"Where are we?"

"Grantchester."

"Stands the church clock at ten to three?"

"It's just past noon."

"Forget it."

Cousin Jimmy came out to meet them. A bear of a man in capacious corduroy trousers and a tattersall shirt. A man from much the same mould as Angus. Perhaps this was why Anna had married Angus. He seemed familiar.

The bear's paw extended.

"Jimmy Coburn No relation."

"Frederick Troy. No relation to whom?"

"Forget it. Now, you chaps have half an hour to scrub up. Then it's a glass or two of Pouilly-Fumé on the verandah followed by a spot of lunch."

Much to Troy's surprise, Jimmy had put Anna and himself into one room—one room with a four-poster so capacious it would accommodate a troop of boy scouts.

"He's never married," Anna said. "It wouldn't occur to him to think. He doesn't mean anything by it. He just hasn't thought. Besides, you heard him—we're both 'chaps.' We'll just have to make the best of it."

"Fine," said Troy, wondering what the best of it might be.

After lunch, Jimmy said, "What's it to be? A bash at croquet or out to the shooting range?"

Anna and Troy looked at one another.

"Actually, Jimmy," she said. "Troy's come to you with a bit of a conundrum."

"Bingo," said Jimmy.

Troy said, "Do you by any chance read music?"

Jimmy smiled, almost giggled, "I think I can safely say that the only man on Earth more likely to be able to annoy you with a turn on the violin is Jack Benny. I love my violin, I love music. I'm just bloody awful at it."

He led the two of them into what he called his music room—a baby grand piano, a drum kit, a cabinet-sized wind-up gramophone, one of the new-fangled electric radiograms, a mountain of discs, and his violin.

"Now what's it be? "My Old Man Said Follow the Van" or a quick burst of Paganini?"

Troy handed him the annotated score of the Debussy Cello Sonata.

"Ah. Know it well, old man. Now, what's puzzling you?"

Troy sat at the piano, explained as clearly as he could about the extra notes, the flattened notes, the sharpened notes, the unwritten arpeggios . . . and as he played the piano part, Jimmy deftly picked up the cello's role on his violin. No mean feat, Troy thought, for a man who professed little talent.

It was gone four by the time they had worked through to the end, with Jimmy studying, playing, and jotting down every alteration. At the end he had a page of letters, that, to Troy, meant nothing.

Jimmy scratched his head. Troy did not find this promising.

"Any joy?"

"Need to put my thinking cap on, old man. Let's get out of here for half an hour. I say again—croquet or the shooting range?"

"I feel I could shoot something," Troy said.

A couple of hundred yards from the house was an old barn. Inside, Jimmy had lined the rear wall with sandbags and set up targets.

"Took this up during the war. I find it sharpens the mind. And I think the spook stuff out at Bletchley left me a frustrated soldier. Never got into uniform. Never fired a shot at Jerry."

"Me, neither," said Troy. "In fact, I couldn't hit the barn door until I took lessons after the war."

"Really? Well, let's see how good you are."

He handed Troy a BSA .38 and hefted one himself. A bit big, a bit clumsy.

Then he banged off six rounds into his target.

Two outers, three inners, and a bull's-eye.

It was Troy's turn.

Two inners, four bull's-eyes.

"Bloody hell!" said Jimmy. "Took lessons you say. Mind if I ask who from?"

"Bob Churchill. He seemed to think I wouldn't live long if he didn't teach me how to shoot."

"Could you teach me? I don't mean the whole damn thing. Just improve my shot."

"We could give it half an hour," Troy replied. "While you put your thinking cap on."

Troy knew Jimmy was doing two things at once, and that he had reached some conclusion when he lowered the gun with a round still in the chamber and said, "Half a mo'."

He stared at the target, but Troy knew he was seeing notes on staves not concentric circles.

Then he said, "Back to the joanna, old man."

§140

"It works like this. You could create a basic code if the piano or the cello simply gave you the material. Piano plays F-sharp instead of F, cello plays B-flat instead of B—and the listener takes them down as a sequence. But you can create a more complex code this way. Piano plays F-sharp instead of F, cello B-flat instead of B, but not as a sequence. The cello plays far fewer changes, but what it does play is the modifier for all that's preceded it on the piano."

"So it *is* a code?"

"Yep."

"Do you have any idea what it means?"

"Haven't a clue, old man. I can tell you how it works in more detail if you like, but I doubt I could crack it. What I *can* say is this: it doesn't tell the listener much, but however little it does tell might be vital.

"You may well be able to convey a mathematical formula this way, but language? It's too brief. This would never translate into syntactical language. There simply isn't enough data. The most it could be is a mathematical key to something else. The chap who takes down these changes probably has a much larger document. But it's gobbledygook without this. Until the people who play this give him the code, he might as well try and read Martian.

"You've part of the puzzle here, Troy—not the whole jigsaw. It's like a one-time pad—useless if you don't know which page you're supposed to be using—or the settings on the rotors on an Enigma machine—useless without the printed code book, the key that will tell you the positions for each day."

"The what?" said Troy. "Enigma?"

"The German encoding machine they used throughout the war. We cracked it very early on. But if the Germans switched codebooks, and the Wehrmacht, the Luftwaffe, and the Navy all had different codebooks, we'd be stuffed until we could get hold of one. We'd have no idea of the position or setting of the rotors or of any of the plug-in cables. What I think you have here is the codebook that tells you the settings you need to use to decipher the code on something much larger. I must say, if it is, then it's an advance because it does away with paper altogether. Once they've worked out what they're playing, the only place it need exist is in the head of the player."

"Why so complex?"

"Because it's near-as-dammit foolproof."

§I4I

Troy's head buzzed with notes and numbers. He could not sleep.

The church clock, as if to prove it was not stuck at ten to, struck three. Anna stirred.

"You know, Troy, Monty crossed half Europe quicker than you've made it across this mattress."

§I42

It was a Sunday. Nothing in London opened on a Sunday—nothing in England opened on a Sunday except for the churches, the chapels, and a street market in Petticoat Lane. The theatres were shut, the cinemas were shut. The bookshops would be shut. Collets bookshop in the Charing Cross Road would be shut. Mr. Gibbs, reluctant custodian of the affairs of the late André Skolnik and shop assistant at Collets, might well be at home at 101 Charlotte Street. Even good Communists get a day off.

The good Communist showed no willingness to open the door any wider. His head peeped out and he told Troy that he'd "already told the other young copper everything I could," in the accents of received pronounciation. His spectacles were held togther with Elastoplast, his clothes were frayed—the shirt shot to pieces at the collar and cuffs, the knees of the green corduroy trousers balding—but the voice and the hauteur were pure Oxbridge. Troy wondered for a moment at which point Mr. Gibbs had given up a life of privilege to fight the good fight. Had the road to Damascus been the Iffley Road or the Cherry Hinton?

"I need to get into the studio," Troy said.

"Too late. It's gone. Let."

"And the contents?"

"What do you mean, contents?"

"His paintings."

Gibbs slowly pulled back the door.

"See for yourself."

A long, exasperated gesture, one hand on the door, the other point-ing down the corridor to the foot of the stairs, past the piled up, cumu-lative works of André Skolnik.

"Be my guest. They're everywhere. I wish they weren't, but nobody's laid claim to the estate. The landlord had a willing tenant for the studio . . . so they're here because they're here."

"And his flat?" Troy asked.

"Let," said Gibbs. "Could be let twice over. After you printed the address in the papers, if we had one young couple banging on the door asking for it, we had a dozen, two dozen, I should think. That's how you get a flat nowadays. You read the death notices in the papers and you nip in between the undertaker and the furniture van."

If this was the moment at which Gibbs was going to tell him that the USSR built flats while Britain built castles in the air, Troy wasn't going to argue with him, but he didn't much want to hear it, either.

But Gibbs wound up with, "So, I cleared the flat, I cleared the studio."

"May I come in?"

Gibbs's natural suspicion of a policeman seemed to be retreating in the hope that Troy might be the solution to his problem.

In the darkness of the corridor, dimly lit by an overhead bulb in a dirty shade, the enormity of the task struck Troy. He was looking for a needle in a haystack. God knows how many of Skolnik's appalling por-traits were lodged here.

Troy looked at the twenty or so facing outwards and said, "Perhaps if I described the one I was looking for?"

"They all look the same to me."

"This one was on the easel at the time Mr. Skolnik was killed. It was different. It was . . . very green . . . and a bit red."

"Do you mean his Venus travesty?"

"I do," said Troy.

"In here," said Gibbs, leading off into his parlour, where the offend-ing work was propped in front of the fireplace.

Lately, and for that matter throughout his time as a detective, Troy had become accustomed to being the alien presence in private interiors. It had become almost a game he and Jack played—guess the room from the person, or the person from the room. When the game failed it could do so spectacularly, as in the case of both Viktor and Voytek. But he had guessed Mr. Gibbs aright. The sheer shabbiness of 101 Charlotte Street and its inhabitants was thoroughly offset by the sense of order Mr. Gibbs had created. Every wall was lined with bookshelves. Every shelf bore a letter of the alphabet and a subheading. Thousands of works of nonfiction, most with tiny paper slips sticking out as clear indication that they had been read as well as ordered. Far from escaping from the workplace, Mr. Gibbs was in his element.

"I suppose I couldn't quite believe it. I brought it in to have a good look. Then I got intrigued by the Russian inscription. I taught myself Russian during the war . . . all those long nights in the shelters . . . and it's been sitting here until I get around to finding out what it is André was quoting."

"I can save you the trouble," said Troy. "It's from Pushkin. *Boris Godunov*."

"A bit before my time," said Gibbs.

Spoken like a man for whom Russia did not exist until the revolution, thought Troy.

"Does it remind you of anyone?" he asked. "Anyone André knew? Anyone who might have modelled for him?"

"Well, we all did that. It was part of the price of knowing André. Somewhere out there there's one of me waiting to be painted over."

Gibbs tilted his head a little, as though countering the angle of Venus's head.

"No," he said.

The original was golden-haired, the eyes soft and scarcely focussed. This goddess had blonde hair, darker eyebrows, and the eyes were black and hard.

"Do you mind if I take it with me?"

"I was hoping you'd take more than one," said Gibbs. "I was hoping to sell André's clothes. Fat chance. In the end, I got threepence off the rag-and-bone man. But he wouldn't take the paintings. Said he'd call back if he ever needed a new roof for his shed."

Having no shed, nor any need of a shed, Troy politely declined the offer.

On the doorstep, Gibbs said, "Did you ever find out who shot him?"

"No," said Troy, and damned himself with a back-tracking, far-too-careless, "But I will."

Afterwards, walking down towards Oxford Street clutching his cumbersome load, wishing he'd driven over to Skolnik's, he weighed up his remark, remembered what Onions had told him and what he had told Onions, and realized that he would find out and that the commitment was to himself rather than to anyone else.

§143

Troy had little that was new in his sitting room. In that respect his room was like Laura Narayan's or Méret Voytek's or even like that of Mr. Gibbs—it was all hand-me-down, and past its best, but less from its being a matter of make do and mend than of some sense of the tatty chic of heirlooms. The only thing he'd bought was the Bösendorfer upright piano—he had bought it impulsively and without regret one day in the summer of 1940—and that was far from new. Made in 1907, it was older than he was. He had two small Constables above the mantelpiece—dummy runs for works much larger, depicting near-identical views of Dedham Vale—that his father had picked up for next to nothing in an auction nearly forty years ago. If he moved them both and stuck in a hook somewhat higher up the wall there was just enough room to hang the Venus travesty.

Stepping back, he took in the posture of the goddess, the sexiness of ƒ-holes, and for the first time he could see what it was Skolnik had meant to add on the last day of his life. In her left hand, Venus was surely meant to be holding a cellist's bow? She was the cellist. A left-handed cellist. And she herself was the cello, its neck invisible between her breasts, the bridge below her groin hidden in blonde tresses. And . . . what tune was she playing?

He called the left-handed cellist and invited her to an impromptu dinner. If she said yes, he'd go on the scrounge.

"I'm not a bad cook. I know how to spin out the ration and I'll be at my mother's this afternoon. She grows all her own vegetables."

"I don't need convincing, Troy. Just don't serve cabbage or turnips. Even if your mother has grown them and blessed them."

§144

A flying visit to his mother out at Mimram in Hertfordshire yielded off-the-ration goodies—not so much loaves and fishes as spuds and fishes—spuds and fishes, and straggly spinach, and a fulsome head of celery and leeks with a foot or more of white, blanched flesh on them, and parsley. His mother's cook's father, Bert, was one of a near-extinct species of rural silents. He could sit in the pub and spin out a pint of ale wordlessly over a whole evening. Troy could not recall a single word the man had uttered to him when he was a boy, and since he had attained manhood he had been graced with little more than "Gurr," "Wosser," and "Gertcher." Troy had no idea what any of this meant. What was worth knowing was that Bert had a way with a fishing rod and a hat full of flies that brought in a prodigious haul. It had fascinated Troy as a boy to watch Bert tie his own fly feathers. Too old for the first war, too old even for the Home Guard in the second, Bert had watched London burn from a distance, untouched, fascinated but silent. In whatever decade he was now in, the old man still fished in the river and the lakes dotted around Mimram. Today he had been out with live bait and returned with a large pike, a sleek glossy-green marauder of still waters, which Lady Troy had willingly given to her son. Her son had willingly accepted. Not his favourite fish, or anyone's favourite fish—a poacher's meal if anything—but it was a gift pike and one did not look a gift pike in the gills.

He declined the offer of turnips. He knew a recipe for stuffed pike. At some point during the war someone had stuffed a pamphlet of miserly

Minstry of Food recipes through his letter box. It had taught him how to make puddings without eggs should the need arise—it never had—and how to stuff fish with celery, leek, and parsley, and pike would stuff as well as anything.

He met his brother on the kitchen doorstep—in blue, bum-saggy ex-RAF trousers and a moth-eaten Fairisle pullover, mud, and wellies.

"Gardening?" said Troy. "You hate gardening."

"King Edwards need lifting. Somebody has to do it. Do you know how hard it is to get gardeners these days?"

In the vocabulary of the English upper and upper-middle classes, window cleaner could easily be substituted for gardener in a sentence such as Rod had just uttered. The workers no longer knew their place—the war had done for the social order . . . and Rod was just asking for it, all but begging sarcasm.

"Now you mention it, I did hear that the Duke of Devonshire was down to his last dozen," said Troy. "In a well-ordered society he'd still have forty or fifty, but of course we're all equal now and a gentleman digs his own spuds. Welcome to the new Socialist Britain."

"Fuck off," said Rod.

"When Adam delved and Eve span, who was then a gentleman?"

"Chaucer?"

"John Ball."

"Hmm . . . you only come here on the scrounge these days, don't you?"

"I have a guest for dinner. The only way to get a decent meal together *these days* is to scrounge."

"*These days.* Such a telling phrase. Is it any more precise than *now?*"

"I couldn't care less. You created these days, Minister, not me."

Rod swiftly changed the subject in an effort to wrong-foot Troy.

"Dinner guest? A woman?"

"Yes."

"Anyone I know?"

Troy thought better of the truth and said, "No."

It wasn't that Rod would draw the wrong conclusion, it was simply that any conclusion would be wrong. Where Viktor was concerned, Troy did not trust Rod's emotions—but Rod walked off muttering "high time you got yourself fixed up," and Troy knew he was far from the scent. It was the sort of elders' and betters' remark—misplaced, patronizing—he usually replied to with a youthful, "fuck off," but Rod had beaten him to that one.

He said nothing.

§145

Voytek arrived with the last of the day. Nights beginning to draw in. Just as the old boy who lit the gas lamps came around with his hooked pole. There were four lamps in Goodwin's Court: three on brackets— one on the corner where the alley bent, under which Ruby the whore stood to advertise her trade; one outside Troy's house; one at the back of Giovanni's restaurant; and one on a post that shone through the arch from Bedfordbury. At best they threw soft hoops of light down to the ground; in mist or fog they glowed like angels glimpsed at a distance— less faithful light than self-adoring aura.

As she knocked on Troy's door, the pole yanked on the chain that sparked the gas and a halo of light slowly rippled out over the short, dark figure of Voytek.

The lamp lighter doffed his cap to the lady, said "Evenin' guv'ner," to Troy, and ambled off towards the arch. Voytek watched him go, stared silently as he reached up with his pole and lit the lamp on the other side. Troy found himself mentally totting up two encounters in one day with living anachronisms—Old Bert and the lamp lighter with his prewar deference. Or was it his postwar piss-take?

"Such light," Voytek said.

Troy remembered Ruby's remarks about the postwar lights, wondered if Voytek felt the same but felt disinclined to ask.

"Paris in nineteen forty-five. I had lived so long in darkness. Paris was lit up. I felt . . . I felt . . ."

"Washed clean in light?" he ventured, in Ruby's words.

"No. The opposite. Seared. Scorched. Scarred. I burnt in such light. As though every secret should be searched out and illuminated for all the world to see."

"Do you have many secrets?"

She said nothing. Stood in front of Skolnik's atrocious portrait and stared at it.

Troy ducked into the kitchen, returned with an open bottle of Brunello di Montalcino that he'd been saving since his last trip to Italy in 1939. "The good stuff" as his dad would have said.

She turned her back on the painting without comment, without apparently recognizing herself, thanked him for the wine, and said, "I felt I belonged in darkness."

"With your secrets?"

"We all have those, Troy. You can make too much of a word. A secret may not be world shattering, it may just be a private, a very private piece of self."

He heard the unspoken touché, and decided empathy might be better than enquiry.

"I have plenty of pieces like that. A jigsaw box full. Things that are probably harmless that I'd never tell anyone, all the same."

"Exactly," she said. "Harmless but secret."

She could probably go on lying all night. So could he. The difference was he knew they were both lying.

He slowed his pace. He never thought he gobbled his food, and to gobble pike with all its small bones was nigh on impossible, but she ate so slowly he was in danger of finishing his plate while hers was three-quarters full.

She noticed. Said, eyes on her food, not on him, "I learned not to bolt my food. That had its risk. What you had not yet eaten could be stolen. And while there was nothing to be savoured in grey bread and watery soup, the more slowly I ate the more filling it seemed. I suppose it's the power of illusion. But it seemed a worthwhile trick to play on myself. And now I find I cannot stop."

"I remember when the first bananas arrived after the war. Children had no idea how to 'open' a banana, and I saw one of my nieces swallow one so fast she threw up most of it seconds later like a dog that's emptied its bowl in a single gulp."

"But we all empty our bowls. At whatever speed. And we all break the polite rules of the table and wipe our plates with bread."

"Well . . . you'll never see my mother do that, but yes, most of us do. I think we've become a generation that will always eat what is put before us. Speaking of which, there is more."

"Thank you, but sufficient is sufficient."

"I have an orange for dessert. We could split it."

When he returned with the orange, Voytek had moved to the hearth rug and curled up with her legs underneath her. Troy peeled it with his thumbnails, digging into the pocky skin and tearing. He held out a half-moon of segments to her. Instead, she picked the peel up off the rug, scratched the skin to produce a burst of mist, pressed it to her face, and inhaled.

"All smells are precious. All good smells. Not death or decay or shit. The good ones. The ones you can lose."

"I don't wish to put you off your orange, but when I was at school, there was such a thing as a good fart."

"Spoken like a dog, Troy."

She was sitting close to the gas fire, much the way Onions did—but where Onions seemed no longer to care whether it was lit or not, she was almost toasting her hands against the bars, palms up at right angles to her wrists, rotating slowly, like paddles, as she stared at them, just as she had after Viktor's funeral. Troy expanded his makeshift theory of "never enough of enough" from an attempt at understanding Onions to include anyone who'd ever been so cold they thought they'd never be warm again. It was possible she'd come close to dying of cold. It was possible she'd tell him this sooner or later.

He fetched a second bottle of Brunello '37 from under the sink, with every intention of getting her drunk and loquacious, and had the cork-screw in his hand when she said, "Viktor told me you not practice enough."

"He was right."

For a moment the corkscrew stole his attention. Odd—after all, he'd used it for years, and not for the first time tonight. It was as ornate as the Fabergé gun that had killed André Skolnik. It was as ornate as the Fabergé cigar clipper. But for the incongruency of it ever being part of the same set, Troy thought it would match the kit his father had left on his desk. He was pretty certain his father had given it to him. He just couldn't remember when. He had snapped out of the reverie, pulled the cork, flipped it neatly into the bin, and was about to pour for both when she said, "Play for me now, Troy. Play me one of your jazz songs."

Troy stuck the bottle and the corkscrew on top of the Bösendorfer and lifted the lid.

"Anything in particular?"

"No. I do not know jazz. It hardly touched my youth. After the Nazis came it was forbidden to listen to it. They called it degenerate."

Troy did degenerate. Did it in spades. It gave him a broad brief. He had always been partial to the music of Hoagy Carmichael. Just before the war there had been a forgettable Hollywood film starring the delightfully erratic John Barrymore, for which Hoagy had written one of his best songs, "The Nearness of You," and someone—Troy could never remember who—had turned in one of his best lyrics: "It's not the pale moon . . . dooby doo doo . . ." If it hadn't reached Europe that was hardly surprising, but during the war Glenn Miller had recorded it and, years after his death, was there anywhere the sound of Glenn Miller did not now reach?

It occurred to him that he could play this as she and Viktor had played Debussy—he could add notes, flatten them, sharpen them . . . but would she notice? In all likelihood she would not know the song, and if she did, in all likelihood she would take anything he might do to the song as "jazzing." He played it straight, or as straight as his jazz fingers would allow.

As he finished she appeared next to him on the piano stool, nudged him none too gently with her hip to make room for her.

"A Bösendorfer? I played one as a child. I would go home from lessons with Viktor on his concert Bechstein and practice on an 1859 Bösendorfer upright."

"This is a little newer. 1907."

"Viktor also said your forte was Debussy."

"Imbibed the *Préludes* with mother's milk. And she learned them from the man himself."

"Really?"

"He taught her in Russia for a while. Long before the revolution. Just before it, they both found themselves in Paris. He was writing the *Préludes* then."

"Russia? Ah . . . that could explain why some of them are so miserable. I always thought it was raining in Debussy's world but perhaps it was snowing instead."

Troy took this as his cue. Played the most miserable sodding prelude he could think of, *La cathédrale engloutie*—a stark, languid bog of bell-like semibreves—*dans une brume doucement sonore*—guaranteed to make you reach for the booze to *englout* your sorrows in brume, in bog . . . and he tweaked it with sharps and flats, overarpeggiated, gave it a meaningless code, and still she did not notice.

He handed her a glass of Brunello. They did not move. She sipped at her wine, moved her left hand silently across the keyboard playing invisible chords.

Suddenly she was looking at Troy, her dark eyes only inches from his dark eyes.

"Did Viktor teach you *En blanc et noir*?"

"Yep," said Troy.

"And you and he played it four-handed?"

"Dozens of times."

"Me, too."

She put her glass carefully on top of the piano. Framed the first chord with her hand. Something felt wrong but he followed suit and as the first crashing chord was sounded, he knew exactly what was wrong and she burst into giggles. Giggles that grew and grew until she was crying with laughter. Troy had never heard her laugh. It was like that moment in *Ninotchka* when Garbo laughs on-screen for the first time—it is not merely that she laughs but that she laughs so long and so loud.

As the laughter subsided she was grasping at words and not managing to get a sentence out.

"Oh, Troy . . . oh, Troy . . . this is . . . this is a farce. Don't you see? Viktor taught us each the same part."

"We're two left-handed women trying to dance backward. Neither of us knows the man's part."

She reached up her sleeve for a handkerchief to dab her tears and found none. Troy gave her his, a huge square of Irish linen with an overfancy *f* in one corner.

"We know the same part. We know Viktor. We both know Viktor. But we do not know one another, do we, Mr. Troy?"

§146

Being drunk did not make her loquacious. In that she was far too like Troy. If he'd primed Rod in this way, at two in the morning he'd just about be embarking on How to Put the World or Most of It to Rights: Drunken Thesis #7. At two in this morning, Voytek was deeply asleep in front of the fire. Troy picked her up, astonished at how little she weighed, carried her upstairs, and slid her into the spare bed. She did not wake. He went to his own bed, slept fitfully, woke, and read more about Mr. Scobie topping himself in Sierra Leone, with a voice in his head saying "for fuck's sake get on with it, man!" Of Viktor's suicide he knew far too little and of Scobie's far too much.

He slept late.

§147

Late in November and into December, London was wrapped in smog that did not lift or disperse for days. Occasionally, sunlight broke through, but often only for minutes at a time, like a searchlight beamed down from Heaven, and just as briefly a breeze might blow a hole in the fog, appearing like a shapeless window only to close up and vanish like will-o'-the-wisp. The usual metaphor struck Troy as startlingly accurate—it blanketed the city. It had the weight and texture of wool. It would creep in through an open doorway like an uninvited guest. It made public transport utterly unreliable—buses plied their routes with no real idea of where they were; trams and trolleys, being held to rails and wires, fared the better but confusion reigned and cries of, "where the bleedin' 'ell are we?" filled the air. It made going out at night a hazard. It made pub conversation a nostalgic bore as every git with a couple of drinks inside him compared it to the blackout of the war years, and the complaint soon transmogrified into relish as they realized they were back with an old certainty. Few things in postwar Britain were quite as reliable as the war itself. Troy could have sworn, passing a glow he thought was a pub in a district he thought might be Seven Dials, that he had heard a robust rendition waft out along the curling smog of "We're gonna hang out our washing on the Siegfried Line." He did not pretend to understand the English but without doubt nostalgia was essential to them. It was like oxygen.

Why, given the weather, did Angus choose this moment to resurface?

It was six-ish when he phoned; dark and miserable. Another of those nights when the street lamps glowed like glimpsed angels.

"Meet me in the Fitzroy as soon as you can, old man."

The Fitzroy was not on Angus's usual beat or he'd have renamed it by now.

"If I can find it."

"Ha bloody ha. Just be there. Ten minutes. Okay?"

It was more than a ten-minute walk, and closer to seven when Troy arrived. Walking up Charlotte Street put him in mind of André Skolnik. He supposed it always would.

Being one of the most popular pubs in London, home from home to a Bohemian bunch of writers, artists, and layabouts, the Fitzroy Tavern was full if it was open. It was odd, given how far it was from the docks, that the pub attracted as many sailors as it did, but Annie and Charles Allchild, who had run the pub since before the war, seemed to Troy to have a high tolerance of London's oddities—including its homosexuals. And perhaps there was "always something about a sailor" if you happened to be queer. Troy found Angus in deep natter with one of the oddest Fitzrovia queers, Quentin Crisp. Crisp had long since given up any pretence that he might be other than he was and, as long as Troy had known him, had dressed like a fop, dyed his hair red with henna, and worn enough makeup for Troy to have no real idea how old he was, although he'd guess that they were much the same age. During the war Crisp had been arrested for soliciting and had asked Troy to be a character witness. Fortunately for Troy the dozens of others he'd also asked took the witness box first and the case was thrown out without Troy being called. He'd have hated having to explain that one to Onions. Tonight Crisp had his hair coiffured into something resembling the prow of a sailing ship and wore a royal blue velvet jacket with a purple scarf at his throat. He seemed delighted, happy in the company of an oddity like Angus.

"Mr. Troy. How pleasant to see you again."

Crisp always called him "mister"—never a first name. It was one way of treading carefully. Always be polite, you never know when you might get thumped.

Troy reciprocated.

"Mr. Crisp. Mr. Pakenham. Can I get anyone a drink?"

Angus looked up from his very large scotch. Red-faced and miserable.

"Oh. You two know each other?"

"We do."

"Large scotch. And while you're at it I'll find us a corner table."

Angus got up awkwardly, pushing hard on the arms of the chair, but once up and balanced, standing at his full six-foot-plus, he towered over Troy and any man around. He turned to Crisp.

"'Scuse us old man. Young Troy and I have things to talk about. Wouldn't want to bore you with them."

A quick jerk on the tin leg, the necessary foward thrust, and Angus was in motion again.

"Big, isn't he?" Crisp said, managing to tint matter-of-factness with the merest touch of desire. "But so unhappy."

"Big," said Troy. "And married. And I fear that may be part, if not all, of the problem."

Troy asked the barman to send a pint of bitter over to Crisp and carried a scotch and a half of ginger beer to the privacy, if such it was, of the table to which Angus had moved.

"No Ernest tonight?" Troy asked, breaking ice, noticing the absence of Angus's spare leg.

"I have yarumworrrworra," Angus muttered.

"You've what?"

Angus leaned in close.

"I don't want the whole bloody world to hear do I? I've lodged Ernest somewhere safe for a night or two. He's tucked up nicely."

"Tucked up nicely where?"

"Victoria Station. In a bag. Left luggage office, Brighton Line."

There was something vaguely familiar about this.

"Ernest? Victoria Station? On the Brighton Line? In a left luggage office? In a bag?"

"Yes. Now . . ."

"A handbag?"

"A haaaandbaaaaaag??? Of course, he's not in a fucking handbag! He's in a cricket bag. What on earth makes you think he'd fit in a fucking handbag?"

"Nothing," said Troy, "I just wondered."

"Wonder ye not. Now," Angus relaunched the conversation on his own terms, "ever tried to kill yourself?"

"No" would have been truthful and easy, but Troy said, "Why do you ask?"

"Because I keep failing at it."

Already Troy was beginning to wish he'd asked for scotch instead of ginger beer, his resolution that there would be no repeat of their summer booze-up waning fast. The last time . . . the last time had been the day Skolnik was murdered. Odd how today kept dragging him back to Skolnik.

Of what should Troy enquire now? Method or motive?

"Tell me more," he said, confident he'd hit a catchall phrase.

"I was in Scunthorpe . . ."

"Where's that?"

"Dunno. But I was there. Seemed as good a place as any to kill meself. So I took a room. Paid my five bob in advance. Wrote a letter to the wife. Had a stiff one just to steady the nerves. Turned on the gas fire and stretched out on the bed ready to meet my maker and be reunited with my dad, most of my squadron from nineteen forty, and the fox terrier who was my best friend from age three to age twelve."

"What happened?"

"The dog died."

"I meant, what happened in Scunthorpe?"

Angus pushed his drinks aside, rested his head on folded arms, and moaned.

"Tragedy. That's what happened. Forgot to put a shilling in the fucking meter, didn't I? Woke up half an hour later to a stink of gas and the fat old biddy who ran the place giving me my marching orders."

He prised himself off the table. Knocked back the remnant of his first scotch, pushed the glass aside, and gripped the one Troy had bought fiercely in his giant's paw.

"And?" said Troy.

"Well . . . I found it took a day or two to work up the nerve to try again. Killing yourself isn't like killing anyone else. Nobody rings a bell, yells scramble, and lifts you onto another plane. All puns intended, by the bye, in case you thought I was so addled I'd lost all wit. So I drifted. Nottingham, Loughborough—have you ever noticed that written down in huge letters as you come into a railway station the word Loughborough resembles the manifestation of a trail of phlegm? Just try saying it, string it out as long as you can. Loooouuuuuughbooooooroooouuuuugh! Anyway, this led me to Burton-on-Trent. And the coward's way out hit me in the face like a stale pork pie. What is Burton famous for?"

"Beer," said Troy, meekly, in the face of such colossal nonsense, fearing that Angus might say "porridge" or anything but "beer."

"Yep. Beer. Beer by the millions of barrels. So I got pissed as a fart and decided to do the music-hall classic of walking the white line down the middle of the road as though it were a tightrope. Dead cert I'd get run over in ten minutes I thought. No such luck. Half a dozen cars swerve round me, blokes leaning out saying stuff like, 'Are you trying to get yourself killed?' and me yelling back, 'Yes, you dim fucker!' And then along comes Old Bill, and I get arrested for drunk and disorderly and bunged in the cells overnight. And what's the last thing they do before they bang you up?"

"They take away your belt and shoe laces."

"Indeed they do. So you can't hang yourself. So happens I was wearing braces, but they took them, too, as though I'd be dumb enough to try and hang meself with elastic and die like a yo-yo. No charge, doors open next morning. Usual crap I've heard all over the country about no one wanting to prosecute a one-legged war hero. Stuck me on a train to St Pancras. Even gave me half a crown for lunch. I suppose I could have thrown meself from the train, but as I said, it takes a day or two to rev up to meeting your maker and your fox terrier."

"And?"

"And so you find me here. Maudlin pissed, very much alive, chatting to a bloke on his way to a fancy-dress do. Once he gets the fruit hat on he'll be a dead ringer for Carmen Miranda."

Troy thought better of explaining that Mr. Crisp was in his everyday garb and said instead, "And you called me why, exactly?"

"Two things. First. The missis. I want news of the old girl."

"You mean you haven't been home?"

"Haven't been home since the end of August. Called her once or twice. In fact, I called her only yesterday. She tells me she's leaving the National Health Service for Harley Street."

"When?"

"Right now. She's taking a week or so off to get herself sorted."

"I see. Then I can't imagine what news you think I've got."

"She also tells me you went on the walking holiday in the West Country with her."

"Yes. Well . . . I went for some of it. Work dragged me back a day or two early."

"But you spent a couple of nights there?"

"Yes."

"Then I ask the obvious. Are you shagging my wife?"

"Angus, what does this have to do with wanting to kill yourself?"

"Just answer the fucking question."

"No. I'm not shagging Anna."

"Why not? She's a looker. You'd have to be blind not to fancy her."

"Angus . . . the . . . the circumstances did not arise."

"Ah . . . so you'd have shagged her if the timing was right?"

"Have you finished? Because I'm not answering anymore half-arsed accusations."

"There's one other thing. I gather you're a bit of a crack shot."

"I'm trained, Angus. That's all."

"No . . . no . . . no. I spent a night at her cousin Jimmy's on me way north. He says you're the dog's bollocks with a pistol."

"Angus . . . has this got any point? Is it leading anywhere?"

"Loosely. Loosely."

The hand waved in the air a moment or two, then his head came down, closer to the table, closer to Troy, and his voice dropped just above a whisper.

"Can you get me a gun?"

Troy hadn't seen this coming. His only thought was, "Oh, bloody hell."

"Go home to Anna, Angus."

Angus ignored this.

"It would solve my problem rather neatly, you know."

"I don't even know what your problem is."

Angus downed his scotch, got to his feet, muttered, "My round, don't go anywhere," and lurched off in the direction of the bar.

If the coward's way out is suicide, the coward's way out for the poor bugger stuck with listening to the frustrated self-slaughterer is to nip out the side door while he's not looking. Troy found to his dismay that he could not do this.

He watched Angus clump from the bar to Crisp's table, release a pint of bitter from his grip with a cry of, "Cheers, old man, where's the party?" and then do his one-legged charge back to Troy with two inordinately large scotches in hand.

"I'm not a roaring success, y'know. It's not the business. I'm quite good at that. Though God knows why I ever became an accountant."

Troy had wondered this, too. Gun runner, white hunter, proprietor of illegal distilleries on remote Hebridean islands . . . any one of those would make more sense than Angus being an accountant.

"It's me . . . I wish I had been born a simple man, shielded in a carapace of ignorance. It may be I am bollocks at living in the twentieth century, but I am bollocks at being me. To be precise, I am bollocks at being the me of the postwar world."

Troy ignored the Hardyesque self-pity of a soul too sensitive for our times. Angus could kid himself, but he wasn't that. There was too much paradox in the idea of a delicate bull in a cruel, unfeeling china shop. Yet it all depends, he thought, on what you think you are. Angus left an indelible impression. Once met, never forgotten . . . but to be remembered for what he himself perceived as an illusion, a brave front to the world . . . or as he would have it a coward's front?

"It's simple really. I miss the war. I felt safe. Not physically. Only a reckless idiot—and I knew quite a few—would ever think that. But it had psychological and emotional certainties that our present age, our less-than-brave new world, does not."

So the smog had conjured Angus this night, a golem wrought not from clay but from the foul mixture of swirling Thames mist and a couple of million belching coal fires. An Angus in a blackout.

340

"I thought you were a believer. I saw you bollock that old moaner in the Leper's Loincloth last summer for even daring to be unhappy with 'this England.'"

"I know, but this is the coward talking. This is the man who misses his dog."

"Go home. And in the morning, get Anna to take you to Battersea Dogs' Home."

"It's a symbolic dog, Troy. A real one won't do."

"I can't sit here all night while you decide whether or not to buy a dog or top yourself. And I don't have a gun to give you, and if I did, I wouldn't."

Troy's refusal froze Angus into a contemplative stillness. An island of solitary thought in a sea of beer-fueled pub natter. Fist tight around the glass. Eyes fixed on the wall somewhere behind Troy's head. He wasn't finished —Troy could see that. Half a dozen times his lips parted as though about to speak but he didn't. Whatever the madman said next might be more considered than his previous rubbish. Either way, Troy had heard enough.

Angus surfaced, a softer tone in his voice, an earnest desire to get through to Troy.

"I don't want the war back. In fact, I dread hearing the phrase 'Dunkirk spirit'—it's getting to be the most jaded two words in the English language. But I want a good and noble cause. The war was that. 'This England' isn't."

"I'm not the man to give you a run for your money on that one. My brother is. He'll defend the good and noble cause of 'this England' till your ears turn blue."

Troy didn't think this was news—surely Angus knew Rod was in Labour's first eleven, batting for socialism and country? A patriot for our times?

"He would?" Angus asked.

"Yes."

"I don't suppose you could jot down his phone number?"

It was the kind of request that required a lot of thought. Setting a loony like Angus onto a political zealot like Rod. As if Rod would provide the ginger nutcase with reason enough to live. Troy gave it none, scribbled Rod's number on the back of a beer mat, and said, "If Rod can't convince you, no one can. And with that, good night."

341

He left Angus to crash down next to Crisp with a bump and a nasty creak from the chair legs. The last thing he heard him say was, "Going on somewhere are we, old man?" And the distant crunch of all that china in all those shops being trampled underhoof drifted to him through black night and yellow smog like the sound of things to come.

§148

As soon as Troy had opened the door, Milos Danko punched him in the belly so hard he doubled up and passed out. Hitting the floor brought him round sharply to find Jan and Jiri yanking him to his feet.

They sat him on the piano stool. One of them ripped off his overcoat and jacket, the other his shoes. Danko was looking down at him. Troy was wondering why they wanted his shoes. When Danko stamped on his feet he found out why. It was all he could manage not to scream.

As Troy fought for breath, Danko stripped off his own jacket and handed it to Jan or Jiri, then the shoulder holster and the Tokarev TT-33 followed. Then he rolled up his sleeves, the barrel chest and knotted biceps bulging beneath the shirt.

Danko turned and snapped out something incomprehensible to his men. They sat in armchairs by the gramophone. One of them screwed a silencer into the barrel of Danko's Tokarev, the other rummaged almost idly among a pile of magazines, pulled out a *Picture Post* and began to thumb through it. The relaxed nature of it all struck Troy as ominous —a matter so routine, and their routine was violence and murder. He remembered what MI5 had told him—Danko had been SS *Einsatzgruppen*. A Jew killer. Before the Germans had gas chambers they had men like Danko.

"So, funny man . . . round two, eh?"

Troy said nothing.

Danko said, "Who killed André Skolnik?"

"I don't know," Troy lied.

"Wrong answer, Troy."

342

He stamped on Troy's toes again. Watched the pain write itself across his face.

"Every lie will hurt you more."

Danko stretched out his right hand and snapped his fingers. The one not engrossed in *Picture Post* slapped a folded document into his hand. Danko unfolded it so Troy could see. It was Kolankiewicz's report on the death of André Skolnik.

"You been playing clever dick, Troy. You see this?"

Troy thought it wise to nod.

"This says Skolnik was killed with a .15 gun."

"That's right," Troy said. "He was."

Danko shot out his left hand, almost without looking, and picked up the Fabergé pistol off the top of the piano. Troy had almost forgotten about the Fabergé pistol. He'd dumped it in the glove drawer of the hat stand by his front door the day he got it back from Churchill and had not looked at it since.

"And in your glove box, what do I find? A .15 automatic."

"I picked it up not six feet from where Skolnik was killed."

The next blow took him right off the piano stool and over the back. A punch to the sternum Troy felt sure had stopped his heart, but the pain and the nausea as Danko's boot rammed into his belly proved to him that he was very much alive.

He vomited.

Danko hauled him back up again.

When his head cleared he looked up. Danko was waving away the smell with the palm of his hand. Through the puke, Troy tasted blood, felt it dripping from his mouth and onto his shirt.

"Every time you lie to me, I hit you? *Capisce?*"

Troy nodded.

"Now, funny man . . . if you found this gun—"

Danko held it up to him as though demonstrating something to a particularly dim child.

". . . On the Underground . . . why is it not mentioned in this?"

He waved Kolankiewicz's report under Troy's nose, slammed the pistol down on the top of the piano.

"I took it to forensics. The day after. They measured the calibre of the bullet that killed Skolnik. Said they could do nothing with a gun that size. There were no tests they could perform. So I took the gun to a specialist. Because they had not logged the gun, because they made no tests, they kept no record."

This time Danko held Troy by the shoulder while he hit him, and saved himself the trouble of picking him up off the floor.

"You know, funny man, I am . . . how you say . . . a perfectioner . . . I hate loose ends. Now . . . I know you killed Skolnik. You were just too dumb to get rid of the gun. And I think you killed Rosen. Only this time you had to make it look like suicide, so you left the gun by the body. But . . . like I say . . . I am a perfectioner . . . I don't like to *think*, I like to *know*. And before you die, you will tell me what I need to hear. Believe me, Troy, you will tell me."

"Why," said Troy, "would I kill Skolnik?"

"You killed Skolnik because MI5 ask you to."

"Why wouldn't they do it themselves?"

"It's well known . . . you policemen are the foot soldiers of MI5 in England."

"And why would they want Skolnik killed?"

"Let's not be stupid."

The hand gripped his shoulder once more and Troy braced himself for the blow, then felt the life sucked out of him.

A few moments of Czech babble, then Troy managed to say, "I know this may sound just as stupid, but I do have an alibi for the time Skolnik was killed."

"Sure," said Danko. "Let's hear it."

"I was meeting my accountant."

Danko hooted with laughter. This set the other two off and neither of them had a clue what Troy had said.

"Meeting your accountant? Troy, you been a cop far too long."

Another snap of the fingers and Jan or Jiri slapped the silenced Tokarev into Danko's hand and the other one stopped looking at the pictures in *Picture Post* and fitted a silencer to his own gun.

"The truth will set you free," Danko said.

For some reason, the cliché made Troy smile, and Troy smiling made Danko mad. He hit Troy with his free hand and as his other hand held the Tokarev, Troy was knocked right off the piano stool and came to rest doubled up, one arm twisted behind his back and the other stretched out under the piano, his face towards the window.

A shadow passed across the glass.

Troy remembered the exchange of looks between Jan and Jiri the day they had bagged him in St James' Park, the way their eyes seemed to be focused on something behind him—and he realized what he had only half registered . . . that there had been a fourth man in the park. And he was outside now, on lookout, pacing the alley from one end to the other.

The pain in his neck was bad. He twisted it, looked up. The third man was now fitting a silencer. Good God, how many outsized thugs did it take to kill one small Englishman?

He looked away. Rolled onto his right side. Danko was jabbering at the other two and made no move to pick him up. Troy found himself staring into the accumulated dust and fluff of negligent housework beneath the piano. Up against the wall was something metallic. The Fabergé-style corkscrew that his Dad had given him. He'd not seen it since the night Voytek had come to dinner. He'd been looking for it, but not under the piano. It must have fallen off the top, slipped down between the wall and the piano, and come to rest here. If he lived through this he'd really have to be more houseproud or get a cleaner. The corkscrew was in two pieces—a short, sturdy metal bar, and a spiral thread ending in a large loop that took the metal bar. Troy slipped the largest finger of his right hand into the loop, rather like putting on a wedding ring, and closed his fist. It left something resembling a narwhal's tusk sticking out. Spirally and pointy and sharp. Troy could see only one disadvantage in the present opportunity. He was left-handed. If he meant to kill this bugger, he'd have to do it with his right.

Danko hauled him to his feet again.

The Tokarev hung loosely at his side in his right hand.

Troy kept his right just out of sight behind his backside.

Danko had him by the shirtfront with his left hand and drew him closer. Troy was at eye level with the face full of scars.

"I'm going to kill you, Troy. If you tell me what I want to know, I'll shoot you quick and clean. If you don't, I can make this last all night. Now, why not spare yourself the pain and die with a clear conscience?"

So saying, he let go of Troy, gave him a little push that seemed to Troy to be just the elbow room he needed.

"I ask you one more time . . ."

Troy punched him in the left eye with the corkscrew, felt the bone at the back of the eye socket shatter.

Jan and Jiri jerked as though he'd stung them and reached for their guns, but Troy had wrapped his left hand around Danko's right, turned the Tokarev horizontal and squeezed the trigger. Two apiece—back and forth in a split second—one to the heart—one to the head.

Danko sank to his knees. His face was twitching and his hands had gone limp. Troy pulled the gun free and aimed across the room—but they were dead, sprawled in their chairs, pooled in blood, still clutching their guns, a mess of bone and brain on the wall behind them.

Danko moaned, Danko twitched.

Troy pulled back but could not work the corkscrew free from Danko, nor could he work his hand free from the corkscrew.

He put the tip of the silencer to Danko's eye, the barrel parallel to the corkscrew, tilted his own head back as far as he could, and fired. The back of Danko's skull flew apart and the corkscrew came away. Troy shook the bloody, grey mess off the end and worked his finger out.

He looked for the shadow on the window.

None passed.

He opened the door.

It was in the nature of the gas lamps lighting Goodwin's Court that only half of them could be guaranteed to work at any given time. To-night the one outside his door was out, as was the one at the western end of the court—the one outside Giovanni's restaurant cast its halo in the yellow smog, and the one beyond the eastern archway, atop its post in Bedfordbury, was no more than a distant glow.

At the western end there were noises.

He put the gun in his right hand to feel his way along the wall with his left. Shoeless and silent, damp seeping into his socks.

At the kink in the alley, where it bent to exit into St. Martin's Lane, a hunched figure seemed to have his back to him.

The man would speak no English, and the gun would speak more clearly than Esperanto. Troy put the muzzle of the gun to the back of his neck.

"What the fuck? Who the bleedin' hell . . ."

He turned around, saw the gun. Ruby unwrapped her legs from around his waist and opened her mouth to scream. Troy clapped his free hand across her mouth and the man legged it, cock out, flies flapping.

Troy eased his hand down.

She was whispering now. Her eyes looking straight into his.

"I was givin' him a knee-trembler. You just cost me a fare, you stupid . . ."

Troy put his hand across her mouth again, his mouth to her ear.

"There's a bloke patrolling the alley. Where is he?"

He took his hand away. She whispered in his ear.

"He's up the other end, in Bedfordbury. Troy, what the hell is going on?"

He shut her up again. Whispered, "Don't move," and flipped the magazine out of the Tokarev. One shot left. He should have picked up one of the other guns. Now he couldn't afford to miss.

He reached a point between the two lamps without seeing anything. With the lamp at Giovanni's behind him, the best he could be to the other bloke was an outline. He stopped at the archway, praying for the swirls of smog to open up and give him a pocket of light.

A cigarette lighter flashed in the street. The smog parted a second later, opening up like the iris on a camera, and the head of a man lighting up appeared disembodied. He drew on the fag, exhaled once, and turned. The pocket of light grew, the smog in the archway snaked away as though blown by the gods, and before the Czech could take in the shoeless, bloody man pointing the gun, Troy had shot him through the forehead.

He was as big as Danko and a dead weight. Pulling on one leg hardly moved him.

Troy heard breathing behind him.

Ruby stood, a torrent of tears streaming down her face, her fingers stuffed into her mouth to stifle her sobs.

"Don't just stand there. Give me a hand."

Together they dragged the body as far as Troy's house, across the threshold, and into the sitting room.

As Ruby stood, Troy got between her and the bodies.

She muttered "Jesus Christ," and slumped against him, her head buried in his shirt.

"Don't look."

"I wasn't gonna."

She sobbed for what seemed to Troy like minutes, then she pulled herself up, kept her eyes on his, and said, "I suppose you're going to tell me this is your job, right?"

"Ruby, they came here to kill me."

"Oh, Jesus Christ."

Troy fished in his trouser pocket, found a couple of pound notes, stuck them in her hand, wrapped her fingers around them into a fist.

"Find a cab. Go home. Tell no one."

And for once she did as she was told.

§149

Everything cost him. Getting upstairs winded him. Getting out of his bloody clothes drained him to the point where he had to lie on the floor for five minutes and get his strength back. Pissing felt as though it should only be done under anaesthetic.

Washing revived him. He dressed with his breathing and pulse hammering down towards normal. He looked in the mirror. He'd a sizeable bruise coming up on one cheek. They'd none of them hit him in the face. Perhaps it was impossible to own up with a broken jaw? He must have hit the floor harder than he thought.

He phoned Jordan at home.

"Do you remember during the war you chaps had what Walter Stilton used to call the bin men?"

"You mean cleaners? We still have them."

"Get a team over to my house as soon as you can. I've a bit of a mess needs cleaning up."

"A bit of a mess?"

"Well . . . a hell of a mess really."

"I don't suppose you could . . ."

"The Czechs bounced."

"Oh, bugger. Troy, give me half an hour. Okay? Half an hour. Now, how many Czechs bounced."

"Four."

"Jesus Christ."

Twenty-five minutes later, the telephone rang and Troy picked it up and said simply, "Jordan?"

"No. Is Voytek. Is you Troy?"

Troy fumbled, could think of nothing to say even as obvious as "yes."

"Troy. Help me. I cannot go home. I have walked streets for hours . . . I . . ."

Suddenly, Troy knew why she had walked the streets. Four of the reasons lay splattered across his sitting room floor. They'd called on her first.

"Méret, where are you?"

"Phone box. Sloane Square. Outside Royal Court Theatre."

"Then just walk up Sloane Street to the Cadogan Hotel. It's on your left. You can't miss it."

"I not check into hotel. Cannot leave trail."

"Then don't. Just order a drink and sit tight until I get there."

"Okay. When?"

"Half an hour. Three quarters at the most."

Jordan arrived with two young men in brown warehouse coats. He turned on his heel and breathed deep as soon as he saw why they were there.

Then he said, "It's okay. Really. We can handle this. These chaps are trained for it. They get rid of everything."

Not quite everything. Troy had put the Fabergé gun and Kolankiewicz's report back in the hall stand, and the gun that killed Danko was inside his overcoat, tucked into Danko's shoulder holster.

"Jordan. I have to go out now."

"That's okay. I understand. Check into a hotel. Just let me know where."

"Could I borrow your hat?"

"Eh?"

Troy pointed to the swelling on his cheek.

"Oh, I see."

And Jordan took off his black trilby, put it on Troy's head, and tilted the brim to obscure the bruise.

"Call me. Right? As soon as you check in."

§150

Getting to the Cadogan took far too long. Piccadilly was fine, it was merely a matter of going with the flow, and only a fool could get lost going down Grosvenor Place—but the cabbie acted like a fool and decided there were shortcuts across Belgravia that would, "bring us out bang on the nail guv'nor, Sloane Street," but didn't. The cabbie swore. Troy wondered why they didn't just stick to main roads, keep their gobs shut, and charge twice the fare for their trouble—call it a smog rate.

It was gone eleven by the time he walked into the bar at the Cadogan, to find a barman anxious to close and Voytek sitting in black winter traveling clothes—very like her funeral outfit, a pillbox hat and a half-veil over her eyes—in front of an untouched martini.

"I thought perhaps you not come. We have so little time."

"We do?"

Then he noticed the carpet bag and the music case.

"Where are *we* going?"

"Boat train. Victoria Station at midnight."

Troy looked at his watch. "That's okay. We'll make it. If need be we could walk there but the Underground's still running and it is just the one stop. But let's not dawdle."

Oscar Wilde had dawdled and dithered in this very hotel some fifty years ago, torn between catching the boat train and waiting to meet his fate at the hands of a bunch of London coppers. The price of his indecision had been four years hard labour. Voytek showed no indecision. She picked up the music case. Troy hefted the carpet bag with one hand, downed the martini with the other. It was just what he needed to wash away the taste of blood and ease the ache in his guts.

He saw himself turning up the collar on his overcoat and pulling the hat brim down as low as it would go, making himself into the caricature of a spy, but inside Victoria Station the smog was, if anything, worse than it was outside, thickened and curdled by an evening of steam trains belching in and out under the glass roof. When he leant down to the slit in the small glass window of the ticket office to ask for two, first-class, on the Black Arrow, the woman on the other side could have been his sister. She would not have known him nor him her.

They found an empty compartment. Troy turned the heat up and the lights down. The inspector clipped their tickets. And as the train pulled out across the Thames, the violence and the martini and the nursery rhythm of steel wheels on steel rails lulled him into a delicious and unwelcome sleep.

He jerked into waking.

"Where are we?"

"I don't know; I cannot see a thing."

"How long have I . . . ?" He looked at his watch. He'd been out for three-quarters of an hour. It had suited her not to wake him.

"We haven't long," he said.

"For what?" she said.

"For you to tell me how you and Viktor came to spy for the Russians."

She stared at him and said nothing. Black eyes behind the black veil.

Then she said, "I don't know where to start."

"Why not start with meeting a Russian. You must have encountered one at some point. You can hardly have answered a small ad on the front page of *The Times*."

She sighed.

"Auschwitz," she said. "It begins in Auschwitz."

She sighed again, but the narrative was already in motion. She was reluctant to tell him what he wanted to know but he knew she'd do it all the same. It had its own momentum.

"In January nineteen forty-five, the Russians took Auschwitz. I wasn't there. I was on what is now referred to as the death march. I do not know how long I had been walking . . . how many miles . . . how many days . . . but they overtook us. They undoubtedly saved my life . . . and they took me back to Auschwitz. In the commandant's house they fed me and gave me fresh clothes and let me sleep. When I awoke they told me what I had worked out for myself, that they had not stumbled across me, they had been looking for me. You may imagine the odds against them finding me alive. They asked me to become a spy. They set in front of me photographs of three people, all of whom they said spied for them, all of whom mattered to me—indeed, after the death of my family, possibly the only people who mattered to me: Magda Ewald, whom I had known since childhood, who played with me in the Vienna Youth Orchestra and the Auschwitz orchestra; Viktor, whom I had known since I was ten; and Karel Szabo, whom I had known practically since I was born. Obviously, I said yes. They had me and they knew it. I never found out how they knew I knew Szabo, so I conclude he told them himself —if so, then he set me up for all that happened—the miracle is that they kept track of me while the Germans had me.

"In January nineteen forty-five, they knew Szabo was at Los Alamos and what he was working on. In the summer of forty-five, after the German surrender, they sent me to Paris, assigned me to a mentor to learn the trade of the spy while Viktor arranged the permits and visas to get me into Britain. The English were willing to give Viktor a knighthood, instead they gave him a partner. It was really very easy. They fell over themselves to please him. I arrived in the spring of nineteen forty-six, clutching my cello, a fully-fledged but untried spy.

"By then, Szabo was at Harwell. I was the one who met with him. Viktor never met him, and I never met Skolnik. Szabo would turn what he wanted to tell the Russians into a code—he loved that, it appealed to the mathematician in him—and he gave the master key to me. The basic went out via Skolnik to whoever his conduit was, and Viktor and I turned the master key into music. Then we could play it anywhere: London, Paris, Berlin. It was never written down. We never went near Russia, we never met with any Russians. It was foolproof. For nearly two years we played out the secrets of the atom bomb, worked into Schubert, Fauré, Beethoven . . ."

"Debussy?"

"Yes, Debussy. Do you know, you may well be the only person on Earth who noticed?

"This spring, Viktor met with Skolnik and told him he wanted to stop. Skolnik said no. Viktor met with him again, three or four times. Viktor had been a party member for thirty years but the truth was, he wanted to free me, not himself, to free me from being a Russian 'hostage.' Viktor did not care about himself. Each time, Skolnik said no. And then, in July . . ."

Her hand waved away the sentence into nothingness. Troy caught it midair.

"And in July, you killed Skolnik."

Voytek's hand froze in the gesture. Then touched her heart with fingertips pressed against the fabric of her coat.

Troy said, "Do you really think I thought Viktor had done it? Viktor Rosen wasn't capable of killing anyone. You killed Skolnik."

For a few seconds Voytek said nothing. The *diddley da* of the moving train loud beneath their silence. Troy filled it.

"And you told me you'd never met him."

It sounded peevish but that was not what he meant. He'd no doubt she'd told him a hundred lies. One more or less did not matter.

She answered all the same.

"I did not lie; I never met Skolnik. I shot him in the back. Do you call that meeting him? We weren't even face to face . . . I shot him in the back."

"With a gun that used to belong to Princess Astrova."

"Yes . . . with Astrova's gun."

"Where did you get it?"

"I told you, not five minutes ago, that the Russians assigned me to a mentor in Paris . . . Troy, I have to trust you now . . . this can go no further . . . if you tell me you are listening with copper's ears I stop now."

"If I were listening with copper's ears, I'd've slapped the cuffs on you five minutes ago."

"My mentor was Astrova's son. Prince Sergei Oblonsky. I knew him as Serge. He is very much the Frenchman now. The gun was his parting gift to me. I'm sure he meant the jewels to be of value, not the gun itself —who knows, that may yet come to be."

"You prized them out?"

"I have them here."

She patted the handbag on her lap.

"My own private piggy bank. Much as my two gold fillings served me for a year in Auschwitz. I prized those out, too. Portable property, I think your Charles Dickens called it. It doesn't come any more portable than teeth."

"You missed one. A ruby."

"I don't mind. I got diamonds. You keep it."

"July," said Troy, picking up the thread. "And in August, three Czech agents called on Viktor in Chelsea to ask about the death of Skolnik. Were you there when they came?"

"Yes."

"Hiding in the back of the apartment?"

"Yes. How do you know this?"

"They came to see me, too."

"Ah . . . I see . . . and this afternoon they came back. They came to me in Clover Mews. I was out, but one of the neighbours described a man with scars. Him, I remember. I saw him through the crack in the door as I hid at Viktor's. So I run. They will be back. So I run."

They'd reached the point where their stories met. Full circle. There was so much Troy did not want to tell her. There was so little he would tell her.

"No," said Troy. "No, they won't."

She looked baffled by this but pressed on with her story.

"It was August. After these men left, Viktor said that he knew we would never be free. I think it was then that he began to plan his suicide. Again thinking if he cut one more link I would be free. Without Viktor the system was useless. We had no way to communicate with them. Whereas I had thought that without Skolnik it was useless. But without Szabo it had to be useless. We would have nothing to communicate to them. So I denounced him. I hoped that if I denounced Szabo he might, in turn, denounce all of us. And we would be free."

"Free to go to prison."

"Free to go to a prison that one day would let us out. And I would have taken the blame for Viktor . . . I would have said it was me all along. They might have believed me. An old man, a famous man, a man with no apparent Russian or Communist connection. Viktor had been a party member since the Great War, but no one knew. But I timed it wrong. I gave them Szabo by an anonymous letter. And Szabo did not denounce me. Perhaps he wanted to be caught. Perhaps, as you English say, blood is thicker than water. I imagine Szabo told them nothing, and by the time MI5 decided to tell the press, Viktor had killed himself. It was only a matter of hours. If he had waited . . . oh, God, if he had just waited twelve hours."

Troy waited. She was breathing so heavily he thought she might cry, but she didn't.

"And now?" he said.

She reached into her handbag, drew out an envelope, and handed it to him.

"Now . . . I denounce myself. Anonymously. There is no one left to do it. If it works, then I shall be free. If it works the Russians will never know that I denounced myself. I cannot turn myself in—unless the English hanged me, sooner or later I would be released, sooner or later the Russians would come for me. But if I am betrayed, no matter by whom, and if upon betrayal I am lucky enough, clever enough, to escape the English, and to defect, then I shall arrive in Russia as . . . as a hero. A hero so well known that I will be useless to them. Completely useless . . . and I shall be free."

"You're going to Russia? Joe Stalin's Russia? A totalitarian state which doesn't begin to understand the word freedom? And you think you'll be free?"

"Yes."

"After all you've been through?"

"After all I've been through? Troy, what is it you think I've been through? Some mix of physical torture and moral re-education? What do you think Auschwitz did to me?

"I went into Auschwitz a girl with a stick up her arse. I came out a woman with a stick up her arse. That's the only thing a year in Auschwitz changed. Why? Because the greatest lie of all is the ennoblement of suffering . . . that suffering ennobles. It does not. Szabo summed it up very neatly to me after the war. He said he'd been in camps from Oranienburg to Los Alamos—he could not count the months he had spent behind barbed wire, German barbed wire, British barbed wire, American barbed wire—and he had learnt what I had learnt and not put into words . . . that you can come to accept almost anything as normal.

"I'll accept Russia, Troy. Russia will be a new normality to me, and after the normality of Auschwitz quite possibly a pleasant one. Auschwitz taught me that everything is a commodity. Russia knows this par excellence. It is the one country that knows the price of every commodity. It has priced and numbered them all, for all to see. I shall not find such a system strange in any way. I shall not be a victim, I shall be free, for freedom does not abide in an ideology. I shall not be a pariah, I shall be free, for freedom does not abide in a moral code. I shall not be a prisoner, I shall be free, because freedom thrives in the absence of desire. I shall be . . . a lily of the field—I shall not toil, I shall not spin, I shall play . . . because that is what Russia will want me to do—after all, I shall be useless to them as a spy—and I shall be like a star of the Bolshoi or a champion chess player . . . or a lily of the field, a beautiful but useless adornment to their culture."

Troy did not know how much of this he believed. He remembered Jack telling him that whoever killed Skolnik had balls of steel. This—throwing the Russians off the scent by defecting to Russia—this took balls of tungsten.

"A lily of the field?" he said without, he hoped, any trace of incredulity.

"Yes," she said. "Better that than some Venus rising from her cello case, wouldn't you say?"

So, she'd noticed after all.

Troy took the letter from her. Stuffed it unread into his coat pocket.

The train had pulled into Dover station. So engrossed had each been in the other, neither realized for the best part of a minute. They walked to within twenty yards of the barrier at the top of the ramp that led down to the ships and the sea, the customs and the passport control. They had missed what rush there might have been and found themselves alone by gaslight, wrapped in half-darkness. She stood with her back to the barrier. He stood with his back to England.

"If you would send one copy to MI5 and one to a newspaper—you pick, I never grasped what was what with English papers. Wait until Friday. I have things to do in Paris. Things to be, I think you would say, 'wound up.' On Friday, I play a Bach concert in Paris. On Saturday, I will be en route to Vienna. I play piano, Fauré's first Piano Quintet, on the Wednesday after. A guest of the Vronsky Quartet. With any luck the story will break between the two concerts. And while the concert hall is in the British sector, I shall, of course, be staying in the Russian sector with the Vronskys. All of whom are Russian. All of whom are at the mercy of the state. And, of course, all military patrols in Vienna are international. Four strangers in a jeep. The British would not be able to make a move against me without the Russians knowing. The concert will be cancelled—I will disappoint my public, I will disappoint myself—

it's not often I get to play the piano in public—they had asked Viktor, almost needless to say—and I was surprised when they accepted my offer to stand in, but it was as though they had thrown me a lifeline. If I needed a way out, a way east, this was it. I didn't have to take it, but it was inevitable that I would. I shall rehearse a piece I will never get to play—no matter . . ."

The backward shake of the head, the irritated tick under her left eye told him it did matter. It all mattered.

"I cannot see the Russians letting me keep that date. And . . . and a few days later I'm sure I will turn up Moscow. Maybe I read a statement they have made up for me, maybe not. Maybe they deny everything. And then, sooner or later, I start to play in public again. Not Paris, not Amsterdam . . . but perhaps Berlin, Warsaw . . . God knows, maybe Yakutsk . . . Magneto-Gorsk? Whatever."

Troy felt as though he should have a speech ready about the insignificance of two little people and a hill of beans somewhere.

Instead, he said, "I can't come any further. You know, passport control, customs. All increases the chances of being noticed."

"I understand."

"There's something you must do for me."

"Name it."

Troy opened his coat, and said, "Open yours."

As she did so, making a loose tent with his, he took Danko's gun and shoved it under her arm.

"Drop that over the side about halfway to Calais."

"I see," she said. "Is this why the Czechs will not be back?"

"Yes."

"You shot them?"

"Yes."

"All of them?"

"Yes."

"Did you have to kill them all?"

Troy said nothing.

She said, "No matter. Why do I ask? It's not as if they were real, is it?"

Troy said nothing to this. He'd known all along insignificance would figure somewhere. Instead, he said, "Did Viktor know you killed Skolnik?"

"I don't know. I can't be sure. Certainly, I never told him."
She kissed him, her head brushing the brim of his hat.
"Good-bye, Troy."
Troy pulled the brim of Jordan Younghusband's hat back down and watched her leave England. Then he went in search of a local train back to London. He was puzzled at a phrase she'd used and had not found the opportunity to ask her about it—"blood is thicker than water"— but then English was far from being her first language.

§151

He'd no idea how long Jordan would need. Even if the house was spotless by now, he didn't feel like going home to it yet. Checking into a hotel was good advice. It might be as well if he did. It was gone four a.m. when he got back into London. He walked away from Victoria Station, into night and fog, picked up a cab in Buckingham Palace Road, suffered more cabbie wisecracks about being lost, and checked into the Ritz.

Just before nine he called room service, ordered breakfast, and then he called Anna.

"I hear you have a day off."

"Oh. It's you. Yes. Ten of them, a sort of loose transition between the NHS and Harley Street. Angus calls it my demob leave. As though I'd done National Service without the capital H. Thanks, by the bye, thanks for sending him home."

"I need you."

"I'm sorry?"

"I need your professional services."

"Oh, my God, what's wrong? You've been shot!"

"No, I haven't. I just need a little TLC and I'd rather it were you than Kolankiewicz. Bring your bag of tricks. I'm at the Ritz. Room 323. Don't be long, I've ordered breakfast for two."

Over bacon and eggs she told him he had two cracked ribs and a broken toe on his left foot. The ribs would heal naturally as long as he did nothing strenuous for a week or two. The toe would be fine, it just wouldn't bend where it was meant to bend.

"Your TLC was understatement, wasn't it. You've had the shit kicked out of you. It's your internal organs that worry me. The bruising on your chest and abdomen is awful. I've never seen so many shades of black. Are you peeing okay?"

"So far."

"No blood?"

"No."

"And nothing when you cough?"

He didn't think he'd coughed lately, but that, too, she took as a good sign.

"Well, perhaps you'll live. How many of them were there?"

"Three or four."

"Bloody hell! You're lucky they didn't kill you. Will I be reading about this one in the papers?"

"No. No, you won't. Nobody will ever know about this."

Her hands paused on the open bag. It seemed to Troy that she might have worked out why no one would ever know. That if they had not killed Troy, perhaps it was because Troy had . . .

He watched the invisible veil wrap itself around her, with its gift of silence. He told her he needed sleep.

She closed her bag, ruffled his hair, kissed him lightly on the forehead, and said exactly what she'd said in nineteen forty-four when she'd visited him in the London hospital, "I always knew you were a fool."

What was it Fish Wally had called him, not a fool . . . a dreamer?

He was woken from the dream—a host of cellos as mad and malevolent as Mickey Mouse's barmy broomsticks—by the sound of the telephone. He looked at his watch. Four p.m. He'd been asleep for about five hours.

Jordan's voice saying, "Troy?"

And then his own saying, "How did you find me?"

"What? Did you think Intelligence was somehow an arbitrary name for the service?"

"I'm rather tired right now . . ."

"We need to talk and there are things I can't say on the phone."

Troy shrugged this off, "I'm sure the Ritz has learnt to keep its secrets."

By which he meant he was damn sure any spooks on the Ritz switchboard were British spooks.

"Jordan, I'll be home this evening. Come 'round after six."

Jordan was silent for a moment. Troy listened to him breathe, thought it a sad sound, and silently berated himself for imagining too much, then Jordan said, "It's thanks to me you can go home this evening, you mad bugger. It's all clean, although if I were you I'd consider redecorating that room. And if your neighbours mention a gas leak, just nod and look as though you know what they're talking about. We had to explain our presence and get them out of the way somehow. Four body bags and a wheelbarrow take some disguising."

He hung up.

§152

Troy checked out at five—he'd have fun getting Angus to rack up a night at the Ritz as a legitimate expense—and was home in less than fifteen minutes.

It was clean, Jordan was right about that. He'd never seen the place so free from dust. But they'd thrown out the Kelim rug that his mother had given him when he moved in, the back wall was stained and streaked where Jordan's cleaners had scrubbed the wallpaper bald, and the room smelled— mostly chemical bleach, a bit lavatorial with a hint of town gas—Jordan must have turned the gas stove on unlit to back up his invention—but a distinct, at least distinct to Troy, underscent of blood. And fainter still, almost beyond the nose's imagining . . . a hint of cordite.

He was glad he'd moved the Constables. Adhering to the sea, just below the cello case on Skolnik's masterpiece was a piece of brain the cleaners had missed. A wee speck of Jan or Jiri. Troy tore the corner off a page of newsprint and wiped him away. They'd missed nothing else. Even the corkscrew had been stripped of Danko's sticky mortal remains and placed neatly on the draining board. Troy didn't much feel like touching it again, but self-knowledge told him he'd change his mind the next time he wanted to open a bottle. The moment came sooner than he had thought.

On the dot of six, Jordan was knocking on his door.

"I said too much over the phone . . . and there were things I simply could not say."

He paused.

Troy sensed a difficult subject. Resisted the temptation to fill the silence and say, "spit it out."

Jordan almost whispered, as though he feared being overheard in an empty house.

"Did you have to kill them all?"

Troy said nothing.

"Well, did you?"

"Jordan, let me ask you this. What were you going to do with four live rogue Soviet agents? Four live rogue Soviet agents in all probability denied by both the Russians and the Czechs? Put them on trial and listen to protestations of innocence, put up with tit for tat measures? Try and swap them for one of ours, even after the Russians disown them? Because you know as well as I they will disown them. Jordan, four live Czechs were nothing but an embarrassment for you. Better, by far, that they simply vanish."

"It was you or them, right?"

"Of course, it was me or them."

Troy lowered his voice, took out the anger he didn't much feel in the first place. Whispered the near-whisper Jordan had used.

"Besides, it's not as if they were real, is it?"

Now Jordan said nothing.

The concept—one that had struck root, grown, curled, and convoluted in Troy's mind like bindweed since the day Onions had first uttered it—could hardly be new to Jordan, but it seemed it was. Troy could hear that same sad silence once more. Jordan looked stunned at the remark, and then passed over it without comment. An almost visible stiffening of the lip.

"I think you may be right about 'rogue' agents. We've been able to follow their trail. They came in from Dunkirk on fake Belgian passports. They probably had no contact with the Russians from the moment they assumed new identities. They certainly had no contact with anyone at the embassy here or in Paris or in Brussels. Danko's always been a maverick. I'm pretty certain he set out to solve this one on his own. If he did, there's a very good chance the Russians have no idea who he intended to see while he was here. Which means there's a very good chance they don't know a damn thing about you."

"And if your hunch is wrong?"

"Then they'll come looking for you, won't they?"

Jordan accepted a glass of wine. It was how men of their class and upbringing coped with deprivation. They uncorked a piece of history, hoping austerity would spend itself before history did. Saying it would be just the one, he was looking oddly at Troy over it. Troy did not ask. He knew the look. He'd seen it a thousand times in the job—it was saying, "I thought I knew you"—a presumption given the brevity of their acquaintance—and adding, "But I didn't." It was something akin to shock in Jordan. In its odd way—odd since it was Troy with whom or at whom he was shocked—in its odd way it was pleasing, it made Troy faintly hopeful that there was more to human insignificance than the hill of beans. He liked Jordan. Jordan was not "one of us." Onions was, Jack wasn't, Rod most certainly wasn't. Onions would not blanch at what Troy had done. He might arrest him for it, but he would not blanch, flinch, or doubt. Rod would weep, Anna would weep in torrents. Kolankiewicz would debate life's fatal necessities with him. Méret Voytek would understand. Méret Voytek was "one of us" as surely as Troy himself. And suddenly Troy knew what it was Kolankiewicz would debate with him. He had half an idea why Voytek was as she was. He had no idea why he was.

Jordan left without any word that this had been simpatico. They might never be simpatico again. Troy took down the Skolnik and rehung the Constables. The Skolnik he consigned to the cupboard under the stairs. It was too awful, and too revealing to anyone who could put two and two together and realize it was the square root of sixteen. He could give it back, but thought better of it. One day he might own a lawnmower and have to buy a shed to house the lawnmower, and one day in the unimagined future, the sunny uplands of the 1950s and beyond, he might have to patch the roof on that shed.

About half an hour later the telephone rang. Kolankiewicz.

"I can't be sure but I think my office might have been burgled. A day or two back. I cannot be certain. If so, a neat job, and the file on Skolnik is missing."

"I know," Troy said. "I found it. Nothing to worry about."

"Found it? How?"

"As I was saying . . . it's nothing to worry about."

§153

Troy sat at his desk in Scotland Yard and opened Voytek's letter. It was direct and to the point—it did not mention Skolnik—it ought to do the trick, and whilst MI5 might be permanently baffled as to who sent it, they'd be bound to act upon it.

He fed two sheets and a carbon into the roller of his typewriter, thinking that while he was at it he'd scrub up her grammar and make the author of this anonymous denunciation sound less like a foreigner. Before his fingers had touched qwerty he realized that he did not want this done on his typewriter, he wanted it done on a typewriter no one would ever think to check. He was not above suspicion but he knew a man who was.

He phoned Rod's office. It was five-thirty in the afternoon. Rod ought to be on the floor of the House.

"He is," said Megan the secretary. "It's the armed forces funding debate. Rod's the principal speaker for the government. He told me not to wait. Said it would take until at least six o'clock and then there'd be the vote. I was just packing up when you called."

Perfect.

Troy strolled out onto the embankment, ducked down the tunnel to the Palace of Westminster, accepted an unquestioning salute from the duty copper, and dashed up the stairs to Rod's office.

Megan was the epitome of neatness—the sort of woman who remembered to empty the ashtray and put the plastic cover on the typewriter before she went home in the evening. Troy tore it off and typed out the two copies he needed.

When he'd finished he read it through, concluded it did not sound like the work of someone ratting themselves out, and folded the original to put it back in the envelope.

He realized the envelope was not empty. He shook it and a small piece of yellow cardboard fell out onto the desk. A pawn ticket, the number bold and black, the edges of the card worn and woolly—an address in the unfashionable World's End stretch of the King's Road, down by the Fulham gas works.

Had she meant to give this to him, or was it merely in the envelope when she reused it? No matter, she wasn't coming back for it, whatever it was.

Rod breezed in, brimful of bonhomie. Whatever it was he'd been saying on the floor of the House, it had gone down well. Troy tore the "confession" from the roller and folded it before Rod could sneak a look.

"Don't they have typewriters at Scotland Yard?" Rod asked without a hint of resentment and scarcely any of real curiosity.

"Bust," Troy said simply.

"Well, be my guest."

Rod dropped into an armchair. Put his feet up on the edge of the desk.

"I am knackered. I have fought the good fight and I am royally and righteously knackered. There's nothing like giving the Tories a metaphorical arse kicking to cure insomnia. I could sleep the sleep of the brave, I could sleep for a week."

"Do you have a couple of envelopes you could spare?" Troy said.

"With or without House of Commons crest?"

Troy was tempted. It was all but irresistible, but resist he did.

"I think plain will do," he said, and watched a good gag vanish in the face of common sense and caution.

"Do you fancy getting pissed tonight?" Rod said. "I think it's time we showed the Age of Austerity some decidedly unaustere excess, don't you? Time to open the good stuff."

"Your place or mine?"

"Mine, I think."

"Okay. I've letters to post and a call to make at World's End, but I could be there not long after eight."

"You could drop the letters in the out tray. I'm sure the government can spare the price of a stamp or two."

Troy posted them on the other side of the road. The first envelope read simply "MI5." He'd thought hard about to whom the second should be sent. It would be a scoop for the *Post,* edited by his brother-in-law, Lawrence, but there was just a chance Lawrence would recognize the type . . . and above all he wanted it to go to a newspaper so hostile to the government that there'd be no easy deals done to delay or suppress printing. He wanted it in black and white and all over the hoardings before anyone at MI5 could even think about a D-Notice. Voytek's bunking off in Vienna depended on the story breaking before MI5 could find her. It had to be a Beaverbrook paper—he could almost imagine the relish, the schoolboy glee with which the Beaver would receive this, so he scribbled *Daily Express,* Fleet Street, on the envelope in his most schoolboy scrawl and dropped it in the box. Rod would never know the service he had rendered. If they lived to be eighty, then he might tell him . . . sometime around . . . 1995 . . . just in time to coincide with the invention of the no-stick frying pan and the telephone answering machine. Rod could hit him with one and record his confession with the other.

§154

Were it not that Rod's mood was too good for Troy to want to ruin it, it occurred to him that a way to smash through the irritating smugness of his good-feeling might be to show him, in his professional capacity as a member of his majesty's government, the interior of a London pawn-shop. It was one way to read the economic health of the nation. After all, he thought, one might readily understand the circumstances that might lead a man to pawn his best winter overcoat (display three: two black, one blue) or the wife's fox fur stole (display five: all a bit the worse for wear) or the sailor to pawn his concertina (display nine), but what in the economic downturn that seemed to be the permanent condition of the nation could be quite so bad as to compel a man to pawn his winter underwear (display: eleven pairs of long johns, condition variable)—and at that, to do so and not to have acquired the wherewithal to redeem them by November?

Gazing at the motley, Troy saw high on the shelf above the door to the back room a dusty viola without strings and he knew at last why she had given him the ticket and what it was for.

An unshaven grump in a grubby shirt and grubbier waistcoat took the ticket from him, peered at it, and said, "Good job I'm not a betting man. I 'ad 'er down as a no-show. Didn't think I'd see 'er again. But . . . I suppose I 'aven't cos you're here instead, ain't you? I told her last week there weren't no call for 'em any more. But I took it all the same. Do you know, she wanted fifty quid for it? Fifty quid! Would you Adam an' Eve it? But I told 'er straight, there ain't no call for 'em and she could count herself lucky I was offerin' a tenner for it."

"A tenner?" said Troy, incredulous.

"Well, I know it's an old un but the case is new. Gotta be worth summink init?"

Troy put down two five-pound notes and counted out the interest in silver.

"I'll take it now," he said.

"In the back. Such a big bugger I couldn't leave it lyin' around the shop."

In the back, surrounded by a cornucopia of filth, Troy opened the case and took one of the tools of his trade from his inside pocket—a small Ever Ready torch in the shape of a fountain pen. He shone the narrow beam though an f-hole onto the label:

Mattio Goffriller
Fece
in Venezia
~
Anno 1707

"Wossat?"

"The maker's label. Mattio Goffriler made cellos in the eighteenth century, in Italy."

"Worth summink, is it?"

And while tact and courtesy were clearly options, they were on a hiding to nothing when up against the sheer pleasure in annoyance that the truth would cause. Troy did not feel like sparing the feelings or the wallet of a grumpy old man who gave out coppers for long johns and who had given Voytek ten pounds for the most precious object in her life.

"Well," he said, "the last time a Mattio Goffriler cello came up at Sotheby's it fetched almost five thousand pounds."

§155

It fitted fairly well into the back of Troy's Bullnose Morris but he knew it would fit less well into his parlour. He would be forever tripping over it. And whilst part of him yearned to have a cellist to play alongside—but that Voytek was now a fugitive and had always been in a different musical league, he would have loved her company—no part of him yearned to learn the instrument himself.

Still, he had been invited to spend the evening at his brother's house—and that had possibilities. Risks, too, but principally possibilities.

His sister-in-law answered the door.

"Er . . . Freddie, what's that?"

"A cello."

"You weren't planning on abandoning it here, were you?"

"As a matter of fact, I was."

"Oh, God, not more sodding junk. This house is full of junk; these islands are full of junk. You'd think if there were one thing the Luftwaffe could have done for us, it was to blow away all the sodding junk!"

"Are you going to let me in?"

"I suppose so. Stick it in the study, perhaps no one will notice it among all that tat of your dad's that I am not allowed to throw away."

Downstairs, he took the cello out of its case and propped it up against the bookshelves. He'd have to buy a proper stand or the neck would warp, but for now it looked pretty good.

Rod came in—full postparliamentary rigging, wind in his sails, three sheets to the wind, no shoes, odd socks, red braces, tie at half-mast, a gin-and-it in hand, and not his first of the evening.

"Wossat you got there?"

Troy stated the obvious.

"Good one, is it?"

"Not bad," said Troy. "I'll take it out to Mother's when I get the chance. It can go in the study there."

"Mmm . . . where d'ya get it?"

Troy said nothing. Wondered if a half-truth might suffice along the lines of, "I found it in a pawnshop."

Rod played the violin—not that you would have known it from the idle way he plucked at a string of the cello. Then he was peering down at it, trying to see through the *f*-holes.

"I say, there's a label in here."

If Rod could read the label, read the words "Mattio Goffriler," there'd be no way Troy could ever pretend he'd picked it up cheap in a junk shop. There'd be questions.

"You don't say?" said Troy, sounding to his own ears like Bertie Wooster, midfib, but trying to sound a better liar than Bertie Wooster ever made.

But the booze already had Rod in thrall. He straightened up with no apparent further interest in the cello.

"Got a decanter breathing nicely," he said. "An 1870 Cos d'Estournel."

This really was the good stuff. Troy doubted he'd open two bottles at that vintage but if he did, Troy would let him get stewed and try not to join him—God knows that was easy enough once Rod hit drink-and-natter mode. It seemed to him now that he had spent a summer steeped in booze, since the day Angus first took him on a pub crawl. His hand forever wrappped around a corkscrew . . .

"Fine," he said. "I'll be up in a jiffy. Just one or two things to do down here."

Rod bumbled off.

Troy took a small package from his inside pocket, unwrapped the Fabergé gun with its sole remaining ruby, wiped it clean with his handkerchief, and laid it on his father's desk next to the three-piece cigar kit. It wasn't a perfect match but it was close. With any luck, Rod would never notice and if he did, Troy was prepared to swear blind it had been there all along, that he'd played with it as a boy . . . or something. And if Rod ever looked inside the cello again, well . . . he'd eat his hat . . . or something.

§156

By the middle of the following week, Troy was back at his desk, and Jack at his. He could see Jack through the door wrestling with the pages of the *Daily Express*. Then he was in front of Troy, slinging the folded paper down on the desk.

"Have you seen this, Freddie?"

Troy looked, feigning half-heartedness.

"Russian Spy Flees Across Channel: Scotland Yard Seek Mystery Man"

There was a photograph of Voytek. And next to it a police artist's sketch of a man described as, "having escorted the spy as far as Dover on the Black Arrow. Police are urgently seeking this man. Anyone who recognizes him or has any information that might lead to his apprehension is urged to call Whitehall 1212."

"Hmm," seemed to Troy to be the sort of noncommittal thing he should say at this point.

"I mean," said Jack, "How is anyone supposed to recognize this bloke from that? His own mother wouldn't know him."

Indeed, she did not—Lady Troy never mentioned the messy sketch to him. Privately, Troy thought it looked about as much like him as if it had been drawn by André Skolnik.

§157

Jack was mutterering something about elevenses—and on a slack day his sense of eleven o'clock seemed to jump forward in time—when the telephone cut him off midsentence and he put a call through to Troy from his sister-in-law, Cid, at Mimram.

"Freddie, you've seen today's *Express*? Rod's gone into a tailspin. Canceled all his engagements, called parliament, and told them he's ill. I've never seen him like this before—not when Viktor died, not when your father died. He is grief stricken."

"I'll take the day off—there's bugger all on my desk. I'll shuffle it off onto Jack and be at Mimram by lunchtime."

It was high time he retrieved his mother's Lagonda. He went round to Bassington Street, stuck a note through Anna's letter-box, opened up the car with the spare keys and set off north. He'd not been to Mimram since the day he had scrounged loaves and fishes to feed Voytek—and that had been in his tatty, slow Bullnose Morris.

He let the Lagonda rip. For once to drive suited his mood and to drive at 100 mph suited his mood even better.

§158

Rod was in their father's study—Troy's study since the old man died in 1943, but hardly worth the quibble. He was in bum mode, unshaven and only half dressed, and Cid said he had abandoned breakfast the minute he picked up the *Daily Express*.

He sought release in anger.

"Did you set a fucking lunatic on to me?"

"What?"

"Some arse calling himself Angus—said he was a mate of yours. Rang me up this morning wanting to discuss God knows what . . . the meaning of life . . . cabbages and fucking kings . . . wanting to come over for a bit of a chat . . . wanting to bring his pal Ernest . . . who the fuck is Ernest? . . . Is this man completely mad?"

"I think he probably is," said Troy. "Send him away with a flea in his ear. He'll be back, most likely at a better time. And if he does, you might find him interesting. He has a war record only slightly less spectacular than yours."

"Spits or Hurricanes?"

"Can't remember. I tend to turn off to 'good war' stories when old soldiers get going."

Rod blinked at this.

"Have I bored you that often with my war?"

"No. And by the way, Ernest is his tin leg."

"Oh," Rod mused, anger fizzling away. "He's that Angus, is he? The bugger who pinned the DFC to his tin leg in front of the king. My God, we all laughed at that one."

Anger fizzled, Rod seemed to have nothing left in him.

Troy watched as tears formed in the corners of his eyes, until he turned away, feigned looking out of the window, and said, "Oh, bugger."

Cid bought Rod another respite. Came in, hugged Troy, and told them both that lunch would be another twenty minutes. Then Troy said, "Rod, we're both standing here because of Viktor. Why don't we sit down with Viktor."

They sat in the battered armchairs, either side of the fireplace. It was set but not lit. Troy put a match to it and for a quarter of an hour they sat in silence. Only when a piece of cherrywood split and spat a spark onto the rug did Rod revive. Stamped the flame out with his slipper and in so doing seemed to kick himself into life.

"The home secretary phoned me this morning. Told me this was a barrowload of shit the government could do without. Talked about the scandal of it all. How we'd never live it down with the Americans. Asked me how well I knew Viktor. Had I ever met Miss Voytek? I told him to fuck off. Right now, I don't give a toss about the government. I want to know how this happened, how this came to be, how this happened to Viktor. I want to know why. I want reasons. I want something redeeming in all this. I want Viktor back."

They staggered through lunch. Troy thought Cid would pull a muscle straining to keep the small talk going.

After lunch Troy persuaded Rod to wrap up well and got him outside for a walk around the garden: an inspection of the state of the veg patch at the onset of winter.

In the middle of the afternoon, Rod fell asleep in his armchair. Troy stoked the fire, read the paper, and waited. When Rod awoke, he was still on the same note.

"I want something redeeming in this. I want Viktor back. I want back the Viktor I knew."

Troy had abandoned the newspaper on the floor between them.

Rod picked it up, spread the front page out.

"And shit like this destroys the Viktor I had more surely than the bullet that killed him."

He screwed up the paper, thrust it into the fire and began to weep once more.

"It's not as if I can just turn a blind eye to it—put it behind me. Viktor's will turned up. Silly bugger hadn't changed it since he got here in nineteen thirty-seven. All he did was write a separate letter naming me and Arthur as his executors. Anything he had—and it's not inconsiderable—was left to cousins and nephews and so forth. All of whom were alive in nineteen thirty-seven, all of whom went to the gas chamber by nineteen forty-three. Arthur and I now find ourselves seeking probate for an estate with no heirs. When we obtain it . . . the exchequer gets the lot."

"You know," Troy said, "that's not entirely without irony."

"Isn't it just? Positively drips with it. And it makes me want to spit."

For a while Rod said nothing, staring into the fire.

Then he said, "Why?" with all the grief of the morning rippling through his voice once more.

"Why?"

Troy knew the answers to all his questions, and more. But he could not tell Rod what he wanted to hear.

§159

It was gone midnight when Troy got home. An unstamped letter was on the doormat as he let himself in.

"Fred," in a kid-scrawl, in pencil.

And suddely the telephone was ringing. He picked up the receiver, heard Jordan say "Troy?" and knew he had been ringing all evening. That Jordan had probably chased him at the Yard most of the day, got something akin to the brush-off from Jack, and had rung and rung and rung at Goodwin's Court.

"Where the hell have you been? I've been ringing you all bloody day."

"With my brother. He and Viktor Rosen were old friends, from the war. He's taken all this very hard."

It gave Jordan pause for thought, but thinking of Rod did not deflect him from the question burning on his lips.

"Troy, how long have you known about Rosen and Voytek?"

Troy said nothing.

"Dammit, Troy! I can still remember what Fish Wally said to me six months ago when he asked me to get in touch with you. He said you'd asked for someone you could trust. And you flung it in my face that night we were in the club room in Curzon Street. But you trusting me wasn't the issue, was it? That was a total red herring. Because the issue was really could I trust you?"

Troy had stopped listening and was turning the letter over in his hands. It was no handwriting he recognized.

Dear Fred,
    I thought I should write rather than just dis-
appear, as you been good to me. You never asked
why I was a prozzie, and once I got over you
being a rozzer I realized you never would. My
bloke never come back from France in 1940. We
was going to get married. And after that I went
to work in a munitions factory in East Ham until

that blew up and took twenty-seven of my mates
with it and then I thought I'd be better off
dodging Jerry bombs up West than I would be dodging
ours in East Ham. So I took that corner by your
house. And then the Yanks came. And that set me
up nice for the duration. And you never said
nothink, and like I said I was grateful on account I gotta earn a living somehow. Anyways,
I'm movin on. One of my regular fares, Dennis,
has asked me to marry him and go to live in
Leamington Spa with him. He's been a regular since
the end of the war. Couple of times a month he's
come down from Leamington. Now, I don't love him,
wish I did, and I'm not sure where Leamington
is, but I'm getting too old to be on the game
much longer—price will start to fall won't it
and I'll be sucking cocks for tuppence ha'penny—
and after what happened in '44 I was a bit upset
but this time I realized that if I stick around
either you're going to get me killed or get
yourself killed, and if it's that last then I
don't want to be around to see it happen. The
war was bad enough, but I ain't seen nothink
like the other night and I never want to again
as long as I live. And it's like I've got this
secret, this really deep, dark secret I can't
never tell no one. And I'll find it easier to
keep that secret if I'm not around you. If I can
still have kids after two abortions I will, and
if I can't well Dennis won't let me work so I
can just be a bleedin' housewife, useless and
beautiful, you know like what they used to tell
us in Sunday school, like one of them lilies in
a field what Jesus used to talk about.

You been good to me. Take care of yourself.
Lotsa love,
  your ole pal
  Ruby

Postscript

Arthur Kornfeld
Clothmakers' Fields
London
Dear Arthur,

I am so sorry. Can you ever find it in your heart to forgive me?

Please believe me when I say that I acted for the best and I still believe that good will come of my actions.
Your Friend,
Karel Szabo
convict no. 1119757

Méret Voytek
Moscow
USSR
Dearest Méret,

I hope this finds you. 'Méret Voytek, Moscow' is a curt address, but I have no other and I cannot believe your name is unknown to the Russian post office. Nor will I believe the British will censor me by refusing to send this.

Trust me. One day we shall be free. And blood is thicker than water.

Trust me.
Your Loving Cousin
Karel Szabo
convict no. 1119757

Notes, Anachronisms, Explanations . . . and stuff

Shostakovich: I first heard it suggested that Shostakovich had encoded a musical signature into his work on the BBC Third Programme a few years ago. I checked this on a website run by Norman Lebrecht, and Norman himself subsequently confirmed to me that Shostakovich did indeed do this. Alas, I didn't know in what piece or pieces he did this— I ascribed it to the 5th Symphony because it was written at the right time and because it suited my plot. Of course, it was the 10th and that wasn't written until 1953. Tant pis.

Penn Station: was pulled down long before I ever set foot in New York. The description I give is closely based on that of Nathan Silver in his wonderful book, *Lost New York* (Houghton Mifflin 1967).

Chagall: The work I describe wasn't created until 1949, when Chagall painted it as a backdrop for the New York revival of Stravinsky's *The Fire Bird*.

Morris Minor: didn't make it's debut until the autumn of 1948. I pinched about four months.

Black Arrow: Well, I made that up. I had to. The Golden Arrow used to leave at 11 o'clock in the morning. Where's the mystery in that? If there's one hour in the twenty-four that lacks all mystery it's got to be 11 in the morning. Who trysts with anyone at 11 in the sodding morning? Even Celia Johnson and Trevor Howard left it till teatime. I am frequently not even awake at 11 in the morning . . . (shome mishtake, shurely? shut up. ed.)

Indian Music Circle: That's made up but only partly. The *Asian* Music Circle was founded in 1953—the year Ravi Shankar first performed in the West—by the Hampstead painter Patricia Angadi and her Indian husband Ayana. Twelve years later they introduced Shankar to George Harrison, and subsequently the rest of the Beatles. I have half a dozen of Patricia's portraits and sketches—pride of place goes to a sketch of Lennon made while he recorded *Norwegian Wood*.

Club 11: It had more than one home in its lifetime. In 1948 it was in its first at 44 Great Windmill St—alas it didn't open until December, so I pinched a few more weeks. That said, the club *was* based around the music of John Dankworth (quartet) and Ronnie Scott (boptet—yes, boptet) and the tunes I mention were most certainly played there. In 1949 both bands recorded for the LP (it may not even have been that . . . 78s?) 'Bop at Club 11,' and while the record purports to be from the Club, it was recorded in King George Hall, which was in Great Russell St and vanished under the wrecking ball years ago. It does, however, feature what must be the earliest English recording of a tune by Monk—52nd St Theme—even though it took thirty-seven years to get released. In 1950 the club moved to Carnaby Sreet, long before the street of tailors bacame the street of Mods—and that's why anyone who reads *A Little White Death* (set in 1963) will find Troy remembering visits to the club in that location. After a police raid in April 1953—the floor littered with ditched drugs, according the memoirs of Superintendent Fabian—Club 11 closed its doors for the last time. Ronnie and Sir John went on to bigger, probably better things.

Trinity: There are differing, perhaps conflicting accounts of where Robert Oppenheimer was at the time of the explosion. His brother Frank recalled the two of them lying down outside the shelter at South 10,000. Oppenheimer himself said at one point that he remained in the shelter until the blast had passed. Others recall him holding onto a post as the shock wave hit. I put him where I needed him for the purposes of fiction, and used Frank's version. The line from the Bhagavad Gita, Oppenheimer recalled in an interview many years later. He did not utter it at the time. Again, it served my fiction that he should, and I contrived a way. 'We're all sons of bitches now' was said by Kenneth Bainbridge, the Test Director.

There is colour film, and at least one colour photograph, of the explosion—that said any colour I ascribe to it is based on what someone, at some point, recalled seeing, not what I see in grainy footage some sixty years old.

To anyone who wants to know more about Los Alamos and the invention of the atom bomb, I would recommend *The Making of the Atom Bomb* by Richard Rhodes (1986). To anyone looking into the politics, the dropping, and the aftermath of the bomb I would suggest Murray Sayle's essay *Did the Bomb End the War?* (*New Yorker* 31st July 1995).

Paris: The description of Rue de la Huchette is taken from *A Narrow Street* (1942) by the American novelist/screenwriter/journalist Elliot Paul. I think the book is also known as *The Last Time I Saw Paris,* but has no connection with the Elizabeth Taylor film of the same name. Most of chapter 68 is closely based on a dispatch written by the photographer Lee Miller for *Vogue* in 1944, to accompany her photographs of Paris at the liberation.

Auschwitz Ladies' Orchestra: I can't remember when I first heard of this, but it was years ago. I thought up the plot of this book based around a cellist and a physicist, and then I started researching. Almost at once I found that two survivors of the orchestra had written memoirs— *Playing for Time* by Fania Fenelon (published in Paris as *Sursi pour L'orchestre* in 1976) and *Inherit the Truth* by Anita Lasker-Wallfisch, published in 1996. They are very contrasting works. Fania Fenelon was a singer and pianist. Mrs Wallfisch is a cellist (my cellist is entirely fictional and is in no way modelled on Mrs. Wallfisch) and is also the mother of cellist Raphael Wallfisch; I listened to his recording of the Kreutzer Sonata endlessly while I wrote this novel. I am grateful to Cosima Dannoritzer for translating several interviews with Mrs. Wallfisch from the German.

The most influential memoirs were *If This Is A Man* (published in Italy as *Si Questo è un Uomo* in 1958) by Primo Levi; *Auschwitz and After* (published in Paris between 1965 and 1970 in three volumes—*Aucun de nous ne Reviendra, Une Connaissance Inutile, Mesure de nos Jours*—but not translated into English until 1995) by Charlotte Delbo; and the Diaries and Letters of Etty Hillesum (published in Holland as *Het verstoorde leven,*

Dagboek van Etty Hillesum, 1981, and *Het Denkende Hart van de Barak,* 1982). They were, respectively, an Italian Jew, a French Catholic and a Dutch Jew. Primo Levi was still in Auschwitz when the Russians arrived. Charlotte Delbo was freed at Ravensbrück. Etty Hillesum survived slightly more than two months in Auschwitz and was murdered there on November 30th 1943.

Primo Levi's work is world-famous, and was the obvious place to begin, but there is the element of chance in looking into any subject and in second-hand bookshops I stumbled across the work of Etty Hillesum (Oxfam Bookshop, Matlock, Derbyshire) and of Charlotte Delbo (Housing Works, Crosby St., New York).

I am aware of only one point at which I have 'altered' the history of Auschwitz—the arrivals ramp, which enabled trains to run straight into Birkenau, was not completed until about six weeks after my character arrives there. The camp commandant is fictional—as is Von Schönbeck—to 'toggle' between the two commandants the camp had in 1944 was too complicated so I invented one fictional figure to replace them both.

Vienna: It seems likely there was a Vienna Youth Orchestra, but mine is made up—and I attached it to the Symphony Orchestra rather than the Philharmonic simply because the Philharmonic did not admit women until the 1990s.

The Artemis Theatre, whilst obviously ripped off from Max Reinhardt's theatre, is also made up. The exterior I give it is to be found on a building at 38 Linke Wienzalle.

Acknowledgements . . .

Gordon Chaplin
Sarah Teale
Zette Emmons
Amelia Wood
Sarah Burkinshaw
Elizabeth Donnelly
Sue Kennington
Ryan Law
Adam Dunn
Linda Shockley
Andrew Robinton
Morgan Entrekin
Deb Seager
Cosima Dannoritzer
Nick Lockett
Lewis Hancock
Gillian Goodman
Roger Katz
Clare Alexander
Tom Williams
Joaquim Fernandez
Sue Freathy
&
Ion Trewin